ANCIENT CHINESE FABLES
中国古代寓言

LULU ZHANG

张蓼蓼 著

 AMERICAN ACADEMIC PRESS

AMERICAN ACADEMIC PRESS

Published in the United States of America
By AMERICAN ACADEMIC PRESS
201 Main Street
Salt Lake City
UT 84111 USA
Email manu@AcademicPress.us
Visit us at http://www.AcademicPress.us

Copyright © 2024 by AMERICAN ACADEMIC PRESS

All rights reserved, including those of translation into foreign languages.

No part of this publication may be reproduced, stored in a retrieval system, or transmitted in any form or by any means, electronic, mechanical, photocopying, recording, or otherwise, now known or hereafter invented, without the prior written permission of the AMERICAN ACADEMIC PRESS, or as expressly permitted by law, or under terms agreed with the appropriate reprographics rights organization. Enquiries concerning reproduction outside the scope of the above should be sent to the Rights Department, American Academic Press, at the address above.

The scanning, uploading, and distribution of this book via the Internet or via any other means without the permission of the publisher is illegal and punishable by law. Please purchase only authorized editions and do not participate in or encourage electronic piracy of copyrighted materials. Your support of the publisher's right is appreciated.

ISBN: 979-8-3370-8905-8

Distributed to the trade by National Book Network Suite 200, 4501 Forbes Boulevard, Lanham, MD 20706

10 9 8 7 6 5 4 3 2 1

朱	引	身	香	朱
失	鏡	蒦	下	出
	后	隻	珽	雖
		桑	珽	庶
		大	錬	牆
		地	禺	士

来者 虽死犹生
留下铮铮铁骨
守护中华大地
引领后来者

The Wisdom of Ancient Sages had achieved immortality,
remaining alive in spirit.
Leaving behind a precious legacy in the land of China,
and serving as a beacon for future generations.

序 言

寓言一词，最早出自庄子之言。

《庄子·寓言》："寓字十九（十之有九）；重言（成玄英疏："重言，长老乡闾尊重者也。"意指：语重心长的言辞）十七（十之有七）；卮（zhī 古代盛酒器，不灌酒就空仰着，灌满酒就倾斜，没有固定的常态。卮言，形容没有主见的言辞。常用作对自己著作的谦辞。如《诸子卮卮》。）言日出（自己不着边际的言辞每天都有），和从天倪（犹言：随着时光流失，自然分晓是非对错）。

寓言十九，藉（假借）外议之。亲父不为其子媒（méi 父亲不为自己的儿子说媒）。亲父誉之，不若（如）非其父者也。非吾（亲父）罪也，人（世人）之罪也。与己同，则应；不与己同，则反（反对）。同于己，为是之；异于己，为非之。"

陆德明释文："寓，寄也。以人不信己，故托于他人，十言而九见信也。"

司马迁《史记·老子韩非列传》："庄子者，蒙人也。名周。周尝（曾经）为蒙漆园吏，与梁惠王、齐宣王同时。其学无所不窥，然其要本归于《老子》之言。故其著书十余万言，大抵率寓言也。"

身处战火纷飞时代的庄子，深刻感受到：能做的事，未必能说；能说的事，未必能做。不敢冒然从仕，也不甘从俗丧志。于是，借寓言故事当媒介，以此寄托心中的忧伤与期盼。

现代称寓言是文学作品的一种载体，多以简练的文词讲述通俗易懂的寓意以及为人处事的基本原则与哲理，使人从中反思并在潜移默化中修炼人的德行。

《庄子·齐物论》："是非之彰也，道之所以亏也。道之所以亏，爱之所以成。"

《易经》："元气未分，浑沌为一。"由最初浑沌未分，进化为太极，也是"是非之彰显之时。"宇宙万物有"亏损"，才能成就"双赢。"犹言：谦让、包容是宇宙万物"爱"的基础，也是万物进化繁衍的基础。

管仲的治国理念强调：国民的品德修养皆出自君王的以身作则。"非其所欲，勿施于人"（自己做不到的事情，不强迫他人去做）。"从其四欲，则远者自来。"（一欲：男女双方有追求爱情的权力；二欲：民众有追求生活美好的权力；三欲：人生有追求吃穿不愁的权力；四欲：民众对未来生活充满美好之向往。君王制定国策时，能够充分考虑民众和欲求，再远的民众也会自动前来投靠。）

道家学派创始人老子说，人生有两大灾难，一是天灾，二是人祸。最大的灾难，则是天灾加人祸。《道经·五》："天地不仁，以万物为刍狗；圣人不仁，以百姓为刍狗。"面对战乱对民众的伤害，老子无奈地提名：人生贵在精神追求，不贵物质追求。

孔子《论语·子路》："子曰：其身正，不令而行；其身不正，虽令不行。"《论语·里仁》："子曰：君子喻于义，小人喻于利。"都是对君主而言。对众生而言："子曰：君子求诸己，小人求诸人。"鼓励众生自强不息。孔子西行周王室所在地，收集史书、传记，回到鲁国著《春秋》。然则："为有所刺讥（犹言：挖苦）、褒（褒奖）、讳（忌讳）、挹损（贬损）之文辞（词），不可以书见也（不可以文书示天下）。"孔子遵从老子所言："为人之子，勿以己为高；为人之臣，勿以己为上。望汝切记。"孔子谨记在心，应用于著书论说之中。

晏婴参政的处事原则：君有问，小心谨慎对答；无问，小心翼翼做事。国策正，听令行事；不正，权衡利弊行事。由此，晏婴侍奉齐国朝政长达五十余年，使齐国常强于其它诸侯国。

列子其学本于黄帝与老子。倡导清静无为的处世方式。提出：道德标准的确立对人生、对社会健康发展很重要。对君主而言：治国在于知贤任贤，而不在于自贤。对人生而言：慎尔言，将有和之；慎尔行，将有随之（豁达、包容，赢得众人信服和追随）。对时局而言：得时者昌，失时者亡。对理想而言：吞舟大鱼，不游支流；鸿鹄高飞，不集污池。列子的思想对中华民族的信仰、政治、美学、文学、以及养生之道影响深远。

韩非著书论述《说难》："凡说之难（大凡游说的难处），非吾知（智）之，有以说之难也（不是我的智力不足，难以用语言清晰地表达出来）；又非吾辩之，难能明吾意之难也（也不是我的言辞，不足以精准地阐述我的观点）；又非吾敢横失（yì "失"古通"佚"。放纵。犹言：无所顾忌），能尽之难也（也不是我不敢毫无顾虑地把真实心态直截了当地呈现出来）。虽说之难，在知听说之心（难就难在如何感悟游说时对方当时的心态），可以吾说当之（并且以恰当言辞讲出对方心里正想听的话语）。

韩非深知游说之难，详细地著书阐明游说的难处，然而还是因"言说"屈死在秦狱中。

司马迁《史记·书·乐书第二》："人生而静，天之性也。感于物而动，性之欲也。物至（到）知知（智），然后好恶（wù 喜好与嫌弃）形焉。好恶无节于内，知诱（为物欲所诱导）于外，不能反己（不能自我克制），天理灭矣。夫，物之感人无穷（无尽），而人之好恶无节，则是物至，而人化物也（人被外物同化），灭天理，而穷尽人欲者也。于是，有悖逆诈伪之心，有淫佚作乱之事。是故（因此），强者胁弱；众者暴寡；知（智）者诈愚；勇者若怯（强悍者困苦怯懦者）；疾病不养；老幼孤寡不得其所，此大乱之道也。"

春秋战国时期，连续五百多年的战乱，侧面推动了社会思潮如磅礴江河般涌现，开创了诸子百家、百花齐放的文化盛世，为中华民族传统信仰奠定了不可磨灭的理论基础。

儒家倡导：孝、悌、忠、信、礼、义、廉、耻，以建立礼仪有序的社会。法家认为：人人都有好利恶害的天性，依法实施"定分止争"明确法权，民众为了自己的合法权益不受侵害，会主动维护法律，实现社会公平竞争，国家才能强盛。道家提倡："无为而治，不言之教。"又言："道常无为，而无不为。"后世融合儒、法、道三家之言的精粹，总结出：做人，践行儒家之礼，以致行不逾矩，举止于方寸之间。做事，行法家之术，万法归宗，有法可循。而内心平和，深藏道家之魂，则可包罗万象，以清晰的思维分析事态发展趋势，登高望远，不苟求一时之得失。儒家，律己宽人，规范言行；法家，以身立法，有言在先，违者必究，实现社会公平；道家，行德养善，有可为，有不为，用道亦有道的哲学的角度评判人生得与失。

笔者怀着对中华先祖的敬仰之情编辑此书，希望通过继承与发扬中华古文明的智慧、民族精神，为文明之延续尽一些绵薄之力。

Preface

The term 'fable' first appeared in the words of Zhuangzi.

"Zhuangzi: Fables": Nine out of ten fables, sincere and profound words are unintentional. Unintentional words are endless and emerge day by day. As time passes, the truth and falsehood will naturally be revealed.

"Implication in fables" means the art of conveying meaning. Because people are often prone to suspicion, they will agree with views that align with their own and oppose those that differ; they will affirm views that align with their own and deny those that don't. So, by expressing one's own opinions through stories and conversations that are attributed to others, it becomes easier for nine out of ten sentences to be accepted and believed by others.

In the era of war, Zhuangzi profoundly realized that what can be done may not be said, and what can be said may not be done. He did not dare to take up a position rashly, nor was he willing to follow the crowd and lose his ambition. Therefore, he used fables as a medium to express his sorrow and hope.

Modern fables are a form of literary expression, often using concise language to convey easily understood moral lessons and basic principles and philosophies of human behavior. They encourage reflection and subtly cultivate one's moral character.

In "Zhuangzi: On the Equality of Things," it is written: "The manifestation of right and wrong is the reason why the Tao is diminished; the reason why the Tao is diminished is the reason why love is formed."

The Book of Changes states, "Before the primordial qi was divided, all was in a state of chaos and unity." From this initial state of undifferentiated chaos, it evolved into Tai Chi, which is also the "manifestation of right and wrong." All things in the universe have "losses" in order to achieve a "win-win" situation. In other words, humility and tolerance are the foundation of love for all things in the universe, as well as the basis for their evolution and reproduction.

Guan Zhong's governance philosophy emphasizes that the moral cultivation of the people all stem from the monarch's example. "Do not impose on others what you yourself cannot do."

Laozi, the founder of the Taoist school, said that there are two major disasters in life: natural disasters and man-made disasters. The greatest disaster is a combination of natural and man-made disasters. "Tao Te Ching · Chapter 5": "If heaven and earth are ruthless, they treat the myriad creatures as **straw dogs** *(In ancient times, " straw dogs " referred to a dog made of straw, which was highly valued as a sacrifice before rituals but discarded afterwards. Later, the term came* *to be used metaphorically to describe trivial or useless things or remarks.)*; if the sage is ruthless, he treats the people as straw dogs. " Faced with the harm caused by war and chaos to the people, Laozi helplessly proposed that the essence of life lies in the pursuit of spirit, not material possessions.

Confucius' Analects: "If one is upright, people will obey without giving orders; if one is not upright, even if he gives orders, no one will listen." The Analects of Confucius: "A gentleman values morality, while a petty person values interests." Both are for rulers. For all beings: "A gentleman, when faced with problems, first seeks the reasons within himself; an ungentlemanly person, when faced with problems, always tries to shirk responsibility and never reflects on himself." Confucius traveled westward to the location of the Zhou royal family, collected historical books and biographies, and returned to the state of Lu to write the "Spring and Autumn Annals." However, it is said that "words of ridicule, praise, taboo, and derogation should not be expressed in writing to the world." Confucius followed Laozi's advice: "Maintain humility and respect for elders and superiors. I hope you remember this." Confucius kept it in mind and applied it to his writings and discussions.

The principle of Yan Ying's participation in politics: When national policies are correct, follow orders; when not, weigh the pros and cons before acting. As a result, Yan Ying served the state of Qi for more than fifty years, making Qi stronger than other vassal states.

Liezi's learning originated from Huangdi and Laozi. He advocated a peaceful way of life. He proposed that the establishment of moral standards is crucial for the healthy development of life and society. The philosophy of Liezi has exerted a profound influence on the beliefs, politics, aesthetics, literature, and health practices of the Chinese nation.

Han Fei wrote a book discussing "Difficulties in Persuasion": "The general difficulty in persuasive communication is not due to my lack of intelligence, which is difficult to articulate my thoughts clearly through words; nor is it because my words are not precise enough to convey my points; nor is it that I am afraid to directly reveal my true intentions without reservation. The challenge lies in understanding the other party's mindset during the persuasion process, and to use the right words to convey what the other party is actually thinking." Han Fei was well aware of the difficulty of persuasion and wrote detailed books to explain the difficulties of persuasion. However, he still met a tragic end in the Qin prison because of his 'speech'.

Sima Qian's "Records of the Grand Historian, Book of Music II": "Human nature is peaceful, but when exposed to external things, it can trigger various desires and emotions. If human preferences and aversions are not restrained, then people will be swayed by external things as soon as they appear, this will lead to bad behaviors such as rebellion and fraud that violate natural laws and moral norms. For example, bullying the weak with the strong, bullying the small with the masses, deceiving the foolish with the wise, and besieging the cowardly with strength. The sick will not receive treatment, and the elderly and young will have no one to rely on, ultimately leading to social chaos."

During the Spring and Autumn and Warring States periods, over five hundred years of continuous warfare indirectly spurred the emergence of social ideologies like surging rivers, ushering in a cultural flourishing era of diverse schools of thought and a hundred flowers blooming, laying an indelible theoretical foundation for the traditional beliefs of the Chinese nation.

Confucianism advocates for filial piety, fraternity, loyalty, trustworthiness, propriety, righteousness, integrity, and shame, aiming to establish a society with orderly etiquette. The Legalists believe that everyone has a natural inclination towards good and avoids harm, and implementing the principle of "settling disputes and clarifying rights" in accordance with the law to clarify legal rights. In order to protect their legitimate rights and interests from infringement, the people will actively uphold the law, achieve fair competition in society, and make the country strong. Taoism advocates for "governing by non-action and teaching by non-verbal means." It also states, "The Tao always acts without doing anything, yet accomplishes everything without exception."

Later generations integrated the essence of Confucianism, Legalism, and Taoism, summarizing that in life, one should practice the etiquette of Confucianism to ensure that one's actions do not exceed the bounds and one's behavior is within limits. In work, one should apply the techniques of Legalism, where all laws converge and there are laws to follow. And with a peaceful mind and a deep Taoist soul, one can embrace all things, analyze the development trend of events with clear thinking, look far ahead, and not be overly concerned with temporary gains and losses. Confucianism emphasizes self-discipline and leniency towards others, regulating words and deeds; Legalism advocates setting an example with one's own actions, having words in advance, and those who violate will be held accountable, then achieving social fairness; Taoism emphasizes cultivating virtue and goodness, knowing what to do and what not to do, and judging life's gains and losses from the philosophical perspective of following the Way.

The author compiled this book with admiration for Chinese ancestors, hoping to inherit and promote the wisdom and national spirit of ancient Chinese civilization, and contribute humble efforts to the continuation of civilization.

目录 Contents

	序 言 Preface	I
《管仲》 *Guan Zhong*	头像铭文 Head Portrait of Guan Zhong	1
	墙有耳伏寇在侧 Walls Have Ears	3
	傅马栈最难 Hard to Build Horse Stakes	5
	驳象虎疑 Puzzled Tiger	7
	富之涯 Boundary of Abundance	9
	任人唯贤 Appoint men on merit	9
	老马识途 Old Horses know the Way	10
	先见之明 Prescient Person	13
《老子》 *Laozi*	头像铭文 Head Portrait of Laozi	15
	老子出关 Laozi Leaves Hangu Pass	19
	欲不欲 Desire or Not	21
	学不学 Learn or Not	22
《孔子》 *Confucius*	头像铭文 Head Portrait of Confucius	24
	苛政猛于虎 More Threatening than Tigers	27
	直于行者曲于欲 The Desires	28
	举鲁国尽化为一 One kind of voice	29
	天道释然 Obey the Rules of Nature	31
	公德之道 The Way of Public Morality	32
	鲁人烧积泽 Burn the Marsh	33
	孔子相卫 Confucius in the State of Wei	35
	夔一足 One Foot	37
《晏婴》 *Yan Ying*	头像铭文 Head Portrait of Yan Ying	39
	社鼠 The Rats in the Shrine	40
	人有酤酒者 Liquor Seller	43
	自满的马夫 A Complacent Driver	45
《孙武》 *Sun Wu*	头像铭文 Head Portrait of Sun Wu	48
	率 然 Shuai Ran Snake	49
	同舟共济 Unity in Crisis: Crossing Together	50
《墨子》 *Mozi*	头像铭文 Head Portrait of Mozi	52
	盗其无自出 Door in the Wall	54

	楚王好细腰 Preference for Slim Waists	55
	击邻家之子 Hit the neighbor's son	57
《列子》 Liezi	头像铭文 Head Portrait of Liezi	58
	杞人忧天 The Worrier of Qi	59
	为盗之道 The Art of Stealing	64
	商丘开 Sincerity from Heart	68
	有好沤鸟者 Seagulls	74
	狙公赋茅 Three at Dawn and Four at Dusk	76
	悲心更微 Return of the Native	79
	愚公移山 To Move Mountains	80
	夸父逐日 In Pursuit of the Sun	85
	两小儿辩斗 An Argument about the Sun	87
	扁鹊换心 Heart Exchange	88
	薛潭学讴 A Subtle Hint	90
	韩娥善歌 Han E's Proficient Singing	93
	造父习御 Zaofu Learned to Drive	96
	治大者不治细 Govern the Big, Not the Small	98
	列子学射 How and Why	100
	施氏与孟氏 Two Sons	101
	道见桑妇 Served with the Same Sauce	105
	晋国苦盗 Struggling with Theft	106
	九方皋相马 True Discernment	108
	牛缺遇盗之戒 Niu Que and the Robbers	110
	不食盗食 Refusing the Food from Robbers	112
	歧路亡羊 The Lost Sheep	115
	杨布打狗 A Change of Colour	120
	献 鸠 Offering Turtledoves	122
	岂辱马医 Shame for begging	123
	枯梧不祥 Wilted Tree	124
	亡 鈇 In the Eyes of the Beholder	125
	白公胜虑乱 Dedication and Concentration	128
	攫 金 To Seize Gold	129
《秦孝公招贤令》	Qin Xiaogong's Call for Talents	131

- VIII -

《商鞅》Shang Yang	头像铭文 Head Portrait of Shang Yang	133
	东郭敞 Dongguo Chang	136
	《商君书·定分》 The Book of Shang Jun: Laws	139
《慎子》Shen Zi	头像铭文 Head Portrait of Shen Zi	141
	飞龙失乘 Flying Dragon	142
	离 朱 Li Zhu	143
	西施至姣 Xi Shi's beauty	144
《申不害》Shen Buhai	头像铭文 Head Portrait of Shen Buhai	145
	叶公好龙 The Real Thing	146
《孟子》Mencius	头像铭文 Head Portrait of Mencius	148
	五十步笑百步 The Pot Calling the Kettle Black	149
	以羊易牛 Exchange sheep for cattle	152
	揠苗助长 Giving the Seedlings a Hand	154
	王良与嬖奚 Wang Liang and Bi Xi	155
	一傅众咻 How to learn Foreign Languages	156
	攘 鸡 Once a Month	157
	齐人有一妻一妾 Sense of Shame and Honour	158
	校人烹鱼 Cook the Fish	161
	学弈 Learning the Game of Go	164
	冯妇搏虎 Feng Fu Fight Tigers	166
《庄子》Zhuangzi	头像铭文 Head Portrait of Zhuangzi	167
	不龟手之药 Uselessness and Usefulness	168
	庖丁解牛 The Skills	170
	神社里的栎社 Oak in the Shrine	173
	不若相忘于江湖 Mutual Assistance in Hard Times	176
	浑沌之死 Mean Well but Do Wrong	177
	臧谷亡羊 The Reason for Losing Sheep	178
	历人生子 The Reason for Unease	179
	轮扁斫轮 The Art of Crafting Wheel	180
	丑女效颦 Aping a Beauty	182
	望洋兴叹 Sighing Over the Vast Ocean	183
	埳井之蛙 The Frog in the Shallow Well	186
	鹓雏与鸱 The Phoenix and the Owl	188

鱼之乐 Pleasure of Fish	189
髑髅 Skull	190
鲁侯养鸟 Follow nature	193
佝偻者承蜩 Catching Cicadas	195
心有沉浮 The Heart Has Ups and Downs	197
祝宗人说猪 Talks About Pigs	198
心病还须心药医 To Cure Mental Disorder	201
纪渻子养斗鸡 The Fighter	203
吕梁丈夫 Habits Turn into Nature	204
梓庆为鐻 Devoted and Concentrated	206
林回弃璧 Lin Hui Abandoning the Jade	208
贫穷与疲惫 Poverty and Exhaustion	209
庄周逐异鹊 Forget about Dangers	211
恶贵美贱 Beauty and Plainness	213
鲁少儒 True Confucian scholars are rare	214
匠石运斤 The Carpenter and His Axe	216
一狙搏矢 The arrogant monkey	217
触蛮战争 The War between Chu and Man	218
盗之祸 Misery	219
辙中有鲋 A Fish in Straits	221
任公子钓大鱼 A Big Fish	223
儒以诗礼发冢 Inconsistency in Appearance vs Reality	224
老莱子 Lao Laizi	225
神龟 Divine Turtle	227
心服与口服 Sincerely Convinced	229
曾子心悲 Two States of Mind	231
杨朱与老子 Yang Zhu and Laozi	232
大王亶父 King Danfu	234
王子搜之惧 Prince Sou's Fear	236
子华子谏言 Zi Huazi's advice	237
颜阖守陋闾 The Simple Virtue of the Sage	238
客之言 Words of the Guest	240
屠羊说 Noble Character of Self-Awareness	242

	商汤伐夏桀 Shang Tang Overthrew Xia Jie	244
	伯夷与叔齐 Bo Yi and Shu Qi	247
	舐痔得车 Shameless Behavior of Flattering	250
	说剑 The Sword	252
	蝴蝶梦 Butterfly Dream	259
《尹文子》 *Yinwenzi*	头像铭文 Head Portrait of Yinwenzi	290
	晋国苦奢 Luxury Problem in the State of Jin	292
	宣王好射 King Xuan's Love for Archery	292
	献山雉为凤凰 Offering the Phoenix	294
	盗与欧 Theft and Assault	295
《公孙龙》 *Gongsun Long*	头像铭文 Head Portrait of Gongsun Long	297
	白马非马 White Horse is Not a Horse	298
	先教而后师之 Teach First	305
	楚人得弓 Chu People Found a Bow	306
《荀子》 *Xunzi*	头像铭文 Head Portrait of Xunzi	308
	蒙鸠为巢 The Fragility of a Nest	309
	处女遇盗 The Maiden Encountering Robbers	310
	欹 器 An Admonitory Vessel	311
	东野毕之马失 Horses Lost	312
《韩非子》 *Hanfeizi*	头像铭文 Head Portrait of Hanfeizi	315
	侵官之害甚于寒 Exceeding Authority: Worse than the Cold	317
	宋有富人 Prejudice and Rationality	319
	和氏之璧 The Jade of He	320
	春申君之妾 The Disaster of Treasonous Ministers	321
	黑牛白角 Black Cow with White Horns	324
	扁鹊说病 Bian Que's Analysis of Diseases	325
	纣为象箸 Ivory Chopsticks for a Start	328
	涸泽之蛇 Snake in a Dried-Up Lake	329
	不死之药 Elixir of Life	330
	失日之危 Danger of Forgetting the Time	331
	卫人嫁其子 Narrow Self-Interest	332
	鸟有翢翢者 Origin of "Party Cronies"	334
	与悍者邻 Unwise to Wait	334

- XI -

中行文子出亡 Friend or Foe?	335
荆王伐吴 The Eloquent Envoy of Wu	336
知伯铸大钟 Zhi Bo Casts a Huge Bell	338
韩赵相难 Conflict between two States	340
韩咎为君 Winners Rule, Losers Pay	341
海大鱼 The Giant Sea Fish	342
急与慢 Urgency vs. Slackness	343
人之本性 The Nature of Human Beings	345
法规之重 The Importance of Laws and Regulations	346
梦 灶 A Dream Come True	348
王亡其半者 Speaks with One Voice	349
宠信之祸 The Calamity of Favoritism	351
董阏于之治 Good Governance	354
魏惠王之慈 The Kindness of King Hui of Wei	355
滥竽充数 Safety in Numbers	356
吏 势 Power	357
夫妻祷者 Earnest Prayers	358
买椟还珠 The Casket and the Pearl	359
燕王学道 King Yan Learns the Way	360
说 画 Ghost Drawing	361
尘饭涂羹 Dusty Rice and Mud Soup	362
病疽者 Dilemma	363
郢书燕说 Chance Events	364
农夫惰于田 Laziness in Farming	365
裹十日粮 Honest Monarch	367
曾子杀彘 An Example to Follow	368
私仇不入公门 Recruiting Talents Without Bias	370
赵简主说税 Talking about Taxes	371
矛 与 盾 His Spear Against His Shield	372
守株待兔 The Vigil by the Tree Stump	373

《姜子牙》 *Jiang Ziya*

| Character Introduction | 376 |
| 太公望封于齐 To Set an Example | 376 |

管仲头像铭文注解 Head Portrait of Guan Zhong & Annotation of the Inscriptions

《管仲》：

管仲，姬姓，名夷吾，字仲，谥号：敬。约生于公元前723年。卒于公元前645年。后世尊称"管子"。颖（yǐng）上人。今，安徽颖上县。公元前685年，经鲍叔牙推荐，管仲任相，辅佐之齐桓公成就五霸之首。竖刁、易牙、卫开方，饿死齐桓公。

管仲是春秋时期著名政治家、军事家、哲学家、经济学家，法家代表。他倡导：为君者，要给国民留下恩惠，顺从民众期盼生活美好的愿望。颁布政令不可延误农时，要充分尊重农耕文明形成的习俗，使国民拥有归属感，才能实现民心所向国土永固的目标。

《管仲·心术》：虚无无形，谓之道。化育万物，谓之德。君、臣、父、子，人间之事谓之义。登降揖让、贵贱有等、亲疏之体谓之礼。简（辨别）物小未一道（没有符合道德原则），杀戮禁诛，谓之法。

《管仲·小问》：信也者，民信之。仁也者，民怀之。严也者，民畏之。礼也者，民美之。语曰："泽命（发令）不渝（不改变），信也。非其所欲，勿施于人，仁也。坚中外正，严也。质信（质朴而诚信）以让，礼也。

《管仲·牧民》：错（措）国于不倾之地。积于不涸之仓。下令于流水之原（源），使民于不争之官。明必死之路，开必得之门。不为，不可成。不求，不可得。不处，不可久。不行，不可复。

Guan Zhong:

Guan Zhong, whose surname was Ji, courtesy name was Yi Wu, and posthumous name was Jing, was born around 723 BCE and died in 645 BCE. He was revered as "Guanzi" by later generations. He was from Yingshang, present-day Yingshang County, Anhui Province. In 685 BCE, upon the recommendation of Bao Shuya, Guan Zhong became the prime minister and assisted Duke Huan of Qi in achieving the first place among the Five Hegemons. Shu Diao, Yi Ya, and Wei Kaifang starved Duke Huan to death.

Guan Zhong was a renowned statesman, military strategist, philosopher, and economist during the Spring and Autumn period, and a representative of the Legalist school. He advocated that rulers should leave benefits for their subjects and follow the people's aspirations for a better life. When issuing political decrees, it is essential not to delay the agricultural season, and to fully respect the customs formed by the agricultural civilization, so that the people can have a sense of belonging, which is the way to achieve the goal of consolidating the country with the support of the people.

墙有耳伏寇在侧《管仲·君臣下》

古者,有二言:"墙有耳,伏寇在侧。"墙有耳者,微谋(密谋)外泄之谓也;伏寇在侧者,沈疑(欺诈)得民之道也。微谋之泄也,绞妇袭主之请(情)而资游慝(tè 奸邪)也。沈疑之得民者也,前贵而后贱者,为之驱也。明君在上,便僻(逢迎的小人)不能食其意,刑罚亟近(近侍)也,大臣不能侵其势,比党者诛,明也。

为人君者,能远谗谄、废比党、淫悖(邪恶违道)行食之徒,无爵列于朝者,此止诈拘奸、厚国、存身之道也。

译文:古代流传下一句谚语:"墙有耳,伏寇在侧。"墙有耳,是说墙外有人听到室内密谋的内容;伏寇在侧,则是说身边隐匿着邪恶的小人,以欺诈收买人心。密谋遭到泄露,是狡猾的妃妾窃取君意去帮助四处活动的奸人。依靠欺诈收买守规矩的人士,为奸邪的小人效力。英明的君主在上,善于逢迎的小人就不能窥测国君之意,近臣中的奸诈者都被惩治了,大臣也不能侵夺君主的权势,因为结党营私的奸臣被诛杀了。君主在这样的朝政环境里,才能使政令畅明。

身为一国之君,如果做到远离谗言,铲除结党营私,并且禁止邪恶之人、游食之徒,不得在朝为官,这就是遏制欺诈、拘捕奸邪、巩固国家,保全自身的最佳良策。

寓意:家贼难防。

Walls Have Ears

There is a proverb circulated in ancient times: "The wall has ears, and the bandits are on the side." The wall has ears, which means that there are people outside the wall who hear the content of the conspiracy inside; The bandits are on the side, which means that there are evil villains hiding around them, to win over people's hearts by fraud. The plot was leaked, and it was the cunning concubine who stole the king's will to help the traitors who were running around. Relying on deception to bribe people who abide by the rules, they work for the evil villain. A wise monarch, not subject to flatterers' intrigues, punishes the traitors among his ministers, and keeps the officials from usurping the power by executing the traitors who form cliques. Only in such a political environment can the monarch make his policies clear and explicit.

As a monarch, if you stay away from slander, eradicate cliquism, and prohibit evil people and idle people from serving as officials in the government, this is the best way to curb fraud, arrest evildoers, consolidate the country, and protect yourself.

Meaning: It is difficult to guard against domestic villains.

隔墙有耳 Walls Have Ears

傅马栈最难《管仲·小问篇》

桓公观于厩（jiù 马棚），问厩吏曰："厩，何事最难？"

厩吏未对，管仲对曰："夷吾（管仲的表字）尝为圉人（yǔ rén 养马人）矣。傅马栈最难：先傅曲木，曲木又求曲木；曲木已傅，直木无所施矣。先傅直木，直木又求直木；直木已傅，曲木亦无所拖矣。"

译文：齐桓公与管仲一同来到马棚视察。桓公问管理马棚的官吏："在马棚工作，什么工作比较难办？"

掌管马棚的官吏还没有来得及回答，管仲接过话说："我曾经担任过养马的官吏，在马棚最难的就是编排拴马桩：先竖起弯曲的木桩，第二根木桩也需弯曲使用，弯曲的木桩都用上了，笔直的木桩就用不上了。如若先竖起笔直的木桩，向后排列的也需要笔直的木桩，笔直的木桩都用上了，弯曲的木桩就用不上了。"

寓意：人以群分，物以类聚。贤者引荐贤者，不肖者引荐不肖者。所以，用人之道贵在慎始。

Hard to Build Horse Stakes

Duke Huan of Qi and Guan Zhong came to the stable to inspect. Duke Huan asked the official in charge of the stable, "What job is more difficult to do when working in the stable?"

Before the official in charge of the stable could answer, Guan Zhong said, "I once served as an official raising horses, and the most difficult job in the stable is arranging the horse tethering stakes: Erect the curved wooden stake first, and the second wooden stake also needs to be bent. After all the curved wooden stakes are used, the straight wooden stakes will no longer be used. If you choose to erect the straight piles first, you will still need straight wooden piles for those that are to be arranged behind. The straight wooden piles are used, and the curved wooden piles cannot be used."

Meaning: People are divided into groups, and birds of a feather flock together. The wise recommend the wise, and the unworthy recommend the unworthy. Therefore, the most important thing in employing people is to be cautious from the beginning.

傅马栈最难 Hard to Build Horse Stakes

驳象虎疑《管仲·小问》

桓公乘马，虎望见之而伏。

桓公问管仲曰："今者，寡人乘马，虎望见寡人而不敢行，其故何也？"

管仲对曰："意者（我猜想），君乘驳马而洀桓（pán huán 盘旋），迎日而驰乎？"

公曰："然。"

管仲对曰："此驳象也，驳食虎豹，故（因此）虎疑焉。"

译文：齐桓公骑马出外郊游，一只老虎在远处望见齐桓公，连忙趴在地上一动不动。

齐桓公返回之后遇见管仲问："今天，我骑马出外郊游，有一只老虎远远望见我，连忙趴在地上一动不动，这是什么缘故呢？"

管仲回答："我猜想君主骑的是一匹驳马，而且，还是迎着太阳盘旋而驰？"

齐桓公说："正是如此。"

管仲回答："驳马在阳光的反射下很像驳，驳是吃老虎和豹子的猛兽，因此，老虎疑惑了。"

寓意：英明的君主，也容易被假象所迷惑。

Puzzled Tiger

Duke Huan of Qi went out on horseback for an outing. A tiger saw Duke Huan in the distance and quickly lay down on the ground without moving.

When Duke Huan returned, he met Guan Zhong and asked, "Today, when I went out on a horse outing, a tiger saw me from a distance and quickly lay down on the ground without moving. What is the reason?"

Guan Zhong replied, "I suppose you are riding a spotted horse and still circling toward the sun?"

Duke Huan of Qi said, "That is exactly so."

Guan Zhong replied, "A spotted horse looks like a fierce beast that eats tigers and leopards when it is reflected by the sun. Therefore, the tiger is confused."

Meaning: A wise monarch is also easily confused by false appearances.

驳象虎疑 Puzzled Tiger

富之涯《韩非子·说林下》

桓公问管仲："富有涯乎？"

答曰："水之涯，其无水者也；富之以涯，其富已足者也。人不能自止于足，而亡其富之涯乎！"

译文：齐桓公问管仲："人的一生享受富足有没有边际？"

管仲回答："水的边际，就是水到不了的边缘地带。富足的边缘，就是自己感到富足的时候。人若不能自我停留在感到富足的境域，将会失去感受富足带来的惬意。"

寓意：知足者常乐。

Boundary of Abundance

Duke Huan of Qi asked Guan Zhong, "Is there a limit to the enjoyment of abundance in one's life?"

Guan Zhong replied, "The edge of water is the edge that water cannot reach. The edge of abundance is when you feel rich. If people can't stay in the realm of feeling abundance, they will lose the comfort of feeling abundance."

Meaning: Contented people are always happy.

任人唯贤《韩非子·外储说右上》

桓公谓仲曰："官少，而索者众，寡人忧之。"管仲曰："君，无听左右之请，因能而受禄，录功而为官。则莫敢索官。君何患焉？"

译文：齐恒公问管仲："官职少，而求官者却很多，我为此很忧虑。"

管仲回答："您不必听任左右侍臣的口头请求，您根据各自的能力授于俸禄，并且以他们各自的业绩评定升迁或者罢免，那些不能胜任的官吏，就不敢轻意索要升迁。您还担心什么呢？"

寓意：健全的官吏任免制度，是根除索官的良策。

Appoint men on merit

Duke Huan of Qi asked Guan Zhong, "There are few official posts, but there are many people seeking them. I am very worried about this."

Guan Zhong replied, "You don't have to listen to the verbal requests of your ministers. You should award salaries based on their abilities and promote or dismiss them based on their performances. Those who are not competent officials, they won't dare to ask for promotion easily. What are you worried about?"

Meaning: A sound system of appointment and removal of officials is a good way to eradicate such behavior of soliciting official positions.

老马识途《韩非子·说林上》

管仲、隰朋，从于桓公而伐孤竹（商周时期的国名。今，河北省卢龙县至辽西一带）。春往冬反（返），迷惑失道。

管仲曰："老马之智可用也。"

乃放老马而随之，遂得道。

译文：齐桓公应孤竹国的请求，出兵攻打入侵的山戎（古称北方民族，或称北戎、山戎、匈奴的一支）。齐军由齐桓公亲自率领，管仲为相，隰朋为左相随军出发。齐国在春暖花开时出征，凯旋时已是草木萧疏的冬季。齐军在崇山峻岭的峡谷中迷失方向，齐桓公非常焦虑。

管仲进言："老马天生具有记忆来时路径的本能，放出军中老马任其奔走，便可走出迷途。"

齐桓公许可。于是，放出军中老马，大军尾随其后，果真找到回家的路途。

寓意：恰当地利用动物的本能，也是不可缺少的人生智慧。

Old Horses know the Way

At the request of Gu-zhu State, Duke Huan of Qi sent troops to attack the invading Shan-rong Tribe (*anciently known as a Northern ethnic group, or alternatively referred to as the Northern Barbarians, Shan-rong, or a branch of the Huns*). The Qi army was led by Duke Huan of Qi, Guan Zhong as prime minister and Xipeng as the left minister. The State of Qi went out in the spring when the flowers were in full bloom, and returned in winter when the trees were sparse. The Qi army was lost in the mountains and valleys, and King Huan of Qi was very anxious.

Guan Zhong said, "The old horse is born with the instinct to remember the path when it came, and let the old horse in the army run, you can get out of the lost way."

Duke Huan of Qi gave permission. So, the army released the old horse, followed by the army, they really found the way home.

Meaning: The proper use of animal instincts is also indispensable wisdom in life.

老马识途 Old Horses know the Way

先见之明《韩非子·难一》

管仲有病。桓公往问之，曰："仲父病，不幸卒于大命（犹言：天命），将奚（何）以告寡人？"

管仲曰："微君言，臣故将谒（yè 拜见）之。愿（希望）君去竖刁，除易牙，远卫公子开方。易牙为君主味（烹饪饭食），君惟人肉未尝，易牙蒸其子首而进之。夫，人情莫不爱其子，今弗爱其子，安能爱君？君妒而好内（管理内宫），竖刁自宫（自己割去睾丸）以治内（掌管内宫）。人情莫不爱其身，身且不爱，安能爱君？开方事君十五年，齐、卫之间不容数日行，弃其母，久宦不归。其母不爱，安能爱君？臣闻之：'矜伪（jīn wěi 炫耀的假象）不长，盖虚不久。'愿君去此三子者也。"

管仲卒死，桓公弗行。

及桓公死，虫出户不葬。

译文：管仲患病在床，齐桓公亲自前来看望，问："仲父患病在床，如果天命不可违，你将对我说些什么？"

管仲说："国君不问我，我也打算禀告国君。我希望您离开竖刁，除去易牙，远离卫开方。易牙为君主掌管饮食，君主惟独没有吃过人肉，易牙为了达成你的心愿杀了自己的儿子，把孩子的头砍下来蒸给您吃。天地间，人情莫过于父子之情。当下，他连自己亲生的儿子都不爱，怎么可能真心爱君主？君主的妒忌心很强，对后宫妻妾成群不放心，竖刁对自己实施了宫刑，就是为了迎合您的心态治理后宫。人情莫过于爱惜自己的身体，自己的身体都不爱惜，怎么可能真心爱君主？开方侍奉君主十五年，齐国到卫国之间的距离不过几天的路程，开方长期在外未曾回国看望过自己的亲生母亲，连自己的母亲都不放在心里，岂能真心爱君主？我听说：'炫耀的假象不会长久，掩盖的虚伪不能持续。'希望国君远离这三个人。"

管仲死后，齐桓公没有听从管仲的嘱咐。

后来，因竖刁、易牙、卫开方三人作乱朝纲，把齐桓公饿死在后宫，三月不入葬（一说：五十六天不发葬）。尸体因腐烂长出蛆虫，满地蛆虫爬到了室外。连"死者为大"的尊严都没有得到。

寓意：人生之悲，莫过于'尸虫出于户'。品行不端又心狠毒辣之臣往往事有端倪，为迎合君上不惜违背人伦，以伪善尽忠的假象获得君王之信任；为君者起心动念为先，若不能明察秋毫又不听忠言，终引来恶果殃及自身。

Prescient Person

When Master Guan Zhong was sick in bed, Duke Huan of Qi came to visit him and asked, "Father Zhong is sick in bed. If the will of Heaven cannot be resisted, what will you say to me?"

Guan Zhong said, "If you do not ask me, I still intend to report to you. I hope you will dismiss Shu Diao, remove Yi Ya, and keep away from Wei Kaifang. Yi Ya in charge of food for you, and the only thing you had not tasted was human flesh. In order to fulfill your desire, Yi Ya sacrificed his own son, having his son's head chopped off and steamed for you to eat. In the world, there is no stronger bond than the affection between a father and his son. Given that he does not cherish this love even for his own son, how can he possibly truly reverence the monarch? You have a strong jealousy, and you are uneasy with the large number of concubines in your harem. Shu Diao submitted himself to palace punishment in order to cater to your mindset in governing the harem. Human affection values the care of one's own body above all. If one does not even cherish his own body, how can he possibly genuinely serve the monarch with loyalty? Kaifang served the monarch for fifteen years, the distance between Qi and Wei is only a few days' journey, Kaifang has not returned to visit his own mother for a long time, not even showing concern for her, how can he truly reverence the monarch? I have heard that the illusion of showiness does not last long, and the hypocrisy of concealment cannot persist. I hope our monarch will stay away from these three people."

After Guan Zhong's death, Duke Huan of Qi did not follow Guan Zhong's advice.

Later, because Shu Diao, Yi Ya, and Wei Kaifang had disrupt the order of the government, Duke Huan of Qi was starved to death in the Imperial palace, and his corpse remained unburied for three months (*or fifty-six days*). Maggots grew from the rotting body and crawled outside. Even the dignity of death has not been respected.

Meaning: The sorrow of life is nothing more than 'Worms emerging from a decaying corpse outside the house.' Misbehaving and ruthless minister's tricks often can be seen through, in order to satisfy the king ignoring the violation of morality, with the illusion of hypocrisy and loyalty to obtain the trust of the king; For the king to reflect on himself first, if he couldn't discover the minutest detail in everything and do not listen to the honest advice, eventually lead to the evil consequences of his own.

老子头像铭文注解 Head Portrait of Laozi & Annotation of the Inscriptions

《老子》：

老子，约生于公元前 571 年，卒于公元前 471 年。司马迁《史记》："老子者楚苦县历乡曲仁里人也，姓李氏，名耳，字聃。周守藏室之吏也。周敬王四年周室内乱，因失典籍老子辞官归隐。出函谷关，书《道德经》，以道佐人间。

老子是中国古代著名思想家、哲学家、文学家、史学家，也是道家学派创始人。在政治上老子主张无为而治，不言之教；在权术上阐明物极必反的客观规律；在为人处事上，提倡宽以待人；在精神追求上，遵循有可为，有可不为的准则，顺其自然而然对待人生。

Laozi:

Laozi was born around 571 BCE and died in 471 BCE. Sima Qian's "Historical Records" states: "Laozi was from Qurenli, Lixiang, Kuxian County, Chu. He was surnamed Li, with the given name Er and courtesy name Duan. He was an official in charge of the royal archives during the Zhou Dynasty. In the fourth year of King Jingwang's reign, there was internal turmoil in the royal court, and Laozi resigned and went into seclusion due to the loss of ancient texts. He left the Hangu Pass and wrote the 'Tao Te Ching,' using Tao to assist humanity.".

Laozi was a renowned ancient Chinese thinker, philosopher, writer, historian, and founder of the Taoist school. Politically, Laozi advocated governing by doing nothing and teaching by non-verbal means; in terms of power tactics, he expounded the objective law that extremes meet; in terms of interpersonal relations, he advocated leniency towards others; in terms of spiritual pursuit, he followed the principle of doing what can be done and not doing what cannot be done, and letting nature take its course in dealing with life.

老子出关 Laozi Leaves Hangu Pass

老子成仙 Laozi becomes immortal

老子出关

公元前516年，王子朝率兵攻下刘公之邑。周敬王受到逼迫。当时晋国强盛，率兵攻伐王子朝。王子朝势力不及，与旧僚携带周王室典籍逃亡楚国。老子当时身为周王室"柱下史"，因丢失宫中典籍，周敬王怪罪老子有失职之责，因此，老子辞官归隐。

老子骑着青牛，欲出函谷关。出洛邑（洛阳）不远，见四野一片凄凉，阡陌错断、四野荒芜，处处残垣断壁，遍地枯草死骨。田野里不见耕耘之马，大道上战马不息，怀孕的母马艰难地尾随其后。老子目睹此景心如刀绞，仰天长叹："以道佐人主者，不以兵强于天下，其事好还（环）。师之所处（到），荆棘生焉。大军之后，必有凶年。""夫佳（唯）兵者不祥之器。物或恶之，故有道者不处。君子居则贵左（备），用兵则贵右。兵者不祥之器非君子之器，不得已而用之。恬淡（适可而止）为上，胜而不美。而美之者是乐杀人。夫，乐杀人者，则不可以得志于天下矣。""天下有道，却走马以粪。天下无道，戎马生于郊。罪莫大于可欲；祸莫大于不知足；咎莫大于欲得。故，知足之足，常足矣。"

老子游走到函谷关，守关之将关尹请求老子留下书籍，说："圣人者，不以一己之智，窃为己有，必以天下人智为己任也。今，汝（您）将隐居而不仁，求教者必难寻矣！何不将汝之圣知（智）著为书？关伊虽浅陋，愿代先生传于后世，流芳千古造福万代。"

老子在关伊再三请求之下，许诺：以天道，论述人间正道。

天道：损有余，补不足。有可为，有不为。无张无显，自然而然。以天道言人间正道：除妄欲，消妄为。君民同心同德，民心顺，则国安。国安、民富，则江山永固。

以王朝兴衰、百姓祸福为鉴，溯其源，著上、下篇。上篇为《道经》：言宇宙本源，含天地阴阳之变。下篇为《德经》：言人间处世之方，长生之策。

老子以《道德经》规劝天下大众，期盼天下太平，民众安康。然则，老子的肺腑之言，无法应和群雄逐鹿的战乱年代，无奈地消失于荒野之中。

Laozi Leaves Hangu Pass

In 516 B.C., Prince Zhao led his troops to attack the territory of Duke Liu. King Jing of Zhou was forced to flee. At that time, the powerful state of Jin led its troops to attack Prince Zhao. Prince Zhao and his old officials were unable to resist and fled to the state of Chu with the royal archives of the Zhou dynasty. Laozi, who was the "Zhuxia Shi" of the Zhou royal court at the time, was blamed by King Jing of Zhou for his dereliction of duty for losing the palace archives. Therefore, Laozi resigned and went into seclusion.

Laozi rode a green cow and wanted to leave the Hangu Pass. Not far from Luoyi *(now known as Luoyang)*, he saw a desolate landscape with broken paths, desolate fields, and ruins everywhere. There were no horses in the fields, and war horses were constantly on the road. The pregnant mares followed behind with difficulty.

Laozi witnessed this scene and felt a knife twisting in his heart. He sighed and said, "Those who use Tao to assist the ruler should not rely on military power to dominate the world. The reckless pursuit of military power will inevitably lead to retribution. Wherever the army is, thorns will grow. After the army, there will be a year of famine."

"Therefore, sharp weapons are ominous objects that are disliked by the great Tao and unwanted by those with virtue. The noble man values the left, while those who use weapons value the right. Weapons are ominous instruments that are not needed by the noble man. They should only be used when there is no other choice, and tranquility and detachment are the best state. Victory through force is not worthy of praise even if it is achieved; praising those who achieve victory through force is like liking those who kill people. Those who like to kill people cannot earn the praise and sincere respect of all the world."

"When the governance of the world conforms to the Tao, horses used for transporting war materials are retired and used for farming. When the governance of the world does not conform to the Tao, pregnant mares cannot leave the battlefield and give birth to foals on the battlefield. The greatest sin is the things that can arouse people's desires, the greatest disaster is not knowing how to satisfy, and the greatest sin is insatiable greed. Therefore, learning to be content can bring long-term satisfaction."

Laozi traveled to the Hangu Pass, where the general guarding the pass, Guan Yin, requested that Laozi leave behind his books, saying, "Sages do not regard personal wisdom as private property, but as a tool to serve the public and benefit society. Today, you are going to isolate yourself from the world and live in seclusion. It will be very difficult for me to seek your advice! Why not write your wisdom down in books? Although I am not very talented or knowledgeable, I am willing to spread your knowledge for the benefit of future generations."

Under the repeated requests of Guan Yi, Laozi promised to discuss the righteous path of the world based on the principles of the universe. "The principles of the universe are to reduce excess and supplement deficiency, to do what is possible and not to do what is impossible, to be neither ostentatious nor conspicuous, and to let things take their natural course. Based on the principles of the universe, the righteous path of the world is to eliminate desires and actions that are not in accordance with the truth. If the monarch and the people are of one heart and one mind, and the people are obedient, then the country will be peaceful. If the country is peaceful and the people are prosperous, then the country will be forever stable."

Laozi used the "Tao Te Ching" to persuade the world and hope for peace and well-being for all. However, his sincere words could not resonate with the chaotic era of war among various factions, and the words had helplessly vanished into the wilderness.

欲不欲《韩非子·喻老》

宋之鄙人（指居住在郊野之人），得璞玉（pú yù 未雕刻的玉石），而献之子罕（宋国大夫），子罕不受（不接受）。

鄙人曰："此宝也，宜为君子器，不宜为细人（地位卑微之人）用。"

子罕曰："尔以玉为宝，我以不受子玉为宝。"

是鄙人欲玉，而子罕不欲玉。故曰："欲不欲，而不贵难得之货。"

译文：宋国有位乡民，在野外得到一块未雕刻的玉石，拿来献给宋国大夫子罕。子罕不接受他的馈送。

乡民说："这是一块宝物，应该由君子如您一般的人享用，不是我这样的乡民应该享用的物品。"

子罕说："你把这块玉石当做宝物，我却把不接受你的馈送当做宝物。"

这就是：乡民看重美玉珍贵，而子罕不以美玉为重。由此而言："欲不欲，君子不看重难得之物。"

(韩非子以此解释《老子·六十四章》："是以圣人欲不欲，不贵难得之货。")

寓意：圣人追求精神，俗人追求物质。

Desire or Not

A villager in the state of Song got a piece of uncarved jade in the field and presented it to the great master 'Zihan' of the State of Song. Zihan did not accept his offer.

The villager said, "This is a treasure that should be enjoyed by a gentleman like you, not by a villager like me."

Zihan said, "You regard this jade as a treasure, but I regard not accepting your gift as a treasure."

This is: the villager value the precious jade, but the Zihan does not value the jade. Thus: "Desire or not, the gentleman does not value rare things."

Meaning: Saints pursue spirituality, while mortals pursue material things.

学不学《韩非子·喻老》

王寿（当时一位贤者）负书而行。见徐冯于周涂（路旁）。

冯曰："事者，为也。为，生于时。知（智）者无常事。书者，言也。言出于知（智慧）。知者不藏书。今，子何独负之而行？"

于是，王寿因焚其书，而舞之。

故，知者不以言谈教，而慧者不以藏书箧（书箱）。此，世之所过也。而王寿复之，是学不学也。

故曰："学不学，复归众人之所过也。"

译文：王寿背着书箱在大道上赶路，在道旁遇见徐冯。

徐冯对他说："事在人为。人们的行为是在具体的时势下产生的，所以智者做事不会一味遵循书中教条，而是随机应变，根据不同的情境采取对应措施。书籍所记载的都是往日智者的言行，言行源于内化于心的智慧。有智慧的人无需时刻收藏着古人的书籍。今日，你为何背负昔日圣贤的言论，辛苦地赶路呢？"

于是，王寿听从了徐冯的话，焚烧了自己背负的书籍，随之而欢快地跳起舞来。

因此，智者不以古人刻板言说为教条；慧者也不以藏书的多寡而自傲。这都是世人造成的过失，而王寿重复这样的过失，这正是学了不该学的。

所以，学了不该学的，就是重复众人所犯过的错误。

（韩非子借《老子·六十四章》："学不学，复众人之所过，以辅万物之自然，而不敢为。"论述：学，古文中的精华；不学古文中的糟粕。何为精华：顺应时代发展又遵循自然法则的道理和规律为精华；何为糟粕：阻碍时代发展的腐朽言谈与思想为糟粕。）

寓意：不要刻板读书。

Learn or Not

Wang Shou, carrying a bookcase, was walking on the road and met Xu Feng by the roadside.

Xu Feng said to him, "It all depends on man. People's behavior is produced under specific circumstances, so a wise man will not blindly follow the dogma in the book, but adapt to circumstances and take corresponding measures according to different situations. What is recorded in books is the words and deeds of wise men in the past, and words and deeds come from the wisdom internalized in the heart. A wise person does not need to collect the books of the ancients all the time. Today, why do you carry the words of the sages of the past and travel hard?"

So Wang Shou followed Xu Feng's advice, burned the books he was carrying, and began to dance happily.

Therefore, the wise do not regard the rigid words of the ancients as dogma; A wise man does not take pride in the number of books he collects. It's all man's fault, and Wang Shou repeats such mistakes, which is what he should not have learned.

Therefore, to learn what should not be learned is to repeat the mistakes made by others.

Meaning: Don't study in a rigid manner.

孔子头像铭文注解 Head Portrait of Confucius & Annotation of the Inscription

《孔子》：

孔子，姓孔，名丘，字仲尼。约生于公元前551年，卒于公元前479年。春秋时期鲁国陬（zōu）邑（今山东曲阜）人。孔子问礼于老子，期盼天下太平。然则，身处战火纷飞民不聊生的时代，难以实现礼制天下的愿望。教书育人，寄托未来。

司马迁《史记·孔子世家》：鲁南宫敬叔言鲁君曰："请与孔子适（往）周。"鲁君与之一乘车，两马，一竖子俱（一起），适周问礼，盖（大概）见老子云。辞去，而老子送之曰："吾闻富贵者送人以财，仁人者送人以言。吾不能富贵，窃（自谦之词，冒充）仁人之号，送子以言，曰：'聪明深察而近于死者，好议人者也。博辩广大危其身者，发（揭发）人之恶者也。为人子者毋以有己，为人臣者毋以有己。'"

司马迁《史记·老子韩非列传》："孔子适周，将问礼于老子。老子曰："子所言者，其人与骨皆已朽矣，独其言在耳。且君子得其时，则驾（参于其中），不得其时，则蓬累（离开）而行。吾闻之，良贾深藏若虚；君子盛德，容貌若愚。去子之骄气与多欲，态色与淫（过分）志，是皆无益于子之身。吾所以告子，若是而已。"

Confucius:

Confucius, whose surname was Kong and whose given name was Qiu, was also known by the courtesy name of Zhongni. He was born around 551 BCE and passed away in 479 BCE. He hailed from the state of Lu during the Spring and Autumn period, specifically from the town of Zhou (now Qufu, Shandong). Confucius sought knowledge from Laozi and hoped for a peaceful world. However, living in a time of war and poverty, it was difficult to realize his aspiration of establishing a world governed by propriety. He devoted himself to teaching and nurturing the future.

老子送别孔子 Farewell of Laozi to Confucius

苛政猛于虎 《礼记·檀弓下》

孔子过泰山侧，有妇人哭于墓者而哀。夫子式而听之，使子路问之。

曰："子之哭也，壹似重有忧者。"

而曰："然，昔者吾舅（古代称丈夫的父亲为'舅'）死于虎，吾夫又死焉，今吾子又死焉。"

夫子曰："何为不去也？"

曰："无苛政"。

夫子曰："小子识之：苛政猛于虎也。"

译文：孔子一行路过泰山时，看到路旁一位妇人哭于墓前，形态悲痛欲绝。孔子扶着车前把手听了听，让子路前去问一问是何缘故。

子路问她："你哭地这么伤心，好似有多重伤心之处？"

妇人回答："昔日我的舅父死于老虎，后来我的丈夫也死于老虎，今日，我的儿子也死于老虎。"

孔子不解地问："为什么你们不离开这个地方？"

妇人回答："这里没有残酷的苛政。"

孔子回头对弟子们说："子路要记住：残酷的苛政比老虎还要可怕。"

寓意：横征暴敛的苛政比凶猛的老虎还要使人忌惮和恐惧，黎民能否安居乐业是执政理念的一种体现，"民生"乃国昌之本。

More Threatening than Tigers

As Confucius was passing near Tai Mountain, he saw a woman weeping bitterly in front of a grave. He leaned forward to listen, resting his hand on the wooden bar of his carriage. Zilu, his pupil, was sent to ask the woman what the matter was.

"From your weeping it seems that you have many sorrows."

"That is true. In the past my father-in-law was killed by a tiger. My husband was also killed by a tiger. Now my son too is killed."

"Then why don't you leave this place?" asked Confucius.

"There is no tyrannical government here," came the reply.

"Take note, all of you," said Confucius," a tyrannical government is more threatening than tigers."

Liji (The Book of Rites)

Meaning: The harsh government of excessive taxation is more fearful and frightening than ferocious tigers. Whether the people can live and work in peace and contentment is a manifestation of the governing philosophy, and "people's livelihood" is the foundation of national prosperity.

直于行者曲于欲《韩非子·说林下》

孔子谓弟子曰，孰能导子西之钓名也？"（子西：春秋时楚平王的庶弟，楚昭王，楚惠王时任令尹。）

子贡曰："赐也能。"乃导之，不复疑也。

孔子曰："宽哉，不被于利！洁哉，民性有恒！曲为曲，直为直。"

孔子曰："子西不免"。

白公之难，子西死焉。

故曰："直于行者，曲于欲。"

译文：孔子对弟子们说："谁能劝阻子西，不再以不正当的手法博取名誉？"

子贡说："我可以。"于是，子贡便去劝导子西，并且不再怀疑子西重蹈沽名钓誉的覆辙。

孔子对子贡说："胸怀宽广的人，不被利益所诱惑！品行纯洁的人，本性往往恒定不变！委曲求全的人，容易妥协；刚直不阿的人，从不迎合。"

孔子惋惜地接着说："子西免不了会遭灾祸。"

白公之难：白公，指楚平王的太子建之子。他在太子建死后，逃入吴国。不久被子西召回，安邑在白置，号为"白公"。公元前479年，白公胜发动政变后被杀，子西因与白公胜有牵连也被杀。

因此，"行为刚直的人，如若屈从于自己的欲望，就会被欲望所累。"

寓意：为人处世须知世间变化无常，追根溯源以正品行，则少生事端。万事由心起，内因与外因相互关联。

品行端正、修身养性可以减免因自身欲望而引发的祸事。

The Desires

Confucius said to his disciples, "Who can dissuade Zi Xi from using unfair means to gain reputation?"

Zigong said: "I can." So Zigong went to persuade Zi Xi and no longer doubt that Zixi will repeat the mistake of seeking fame and prestige in the wrong way.

Confucius said to Zigong, "A broad-minded person will not be tempted by interests! A person with pure character will always have an unchanging nature! A person who is willing to compromise is easy to compromise; An upright person will never cater."

Confucius went on to say regretfully, "Zixi will inevitably suffer disaster."

Bai Gong's trouble: Bai Gong refers to the son of Prince Jian of King Chu Ping of Chu. After the death of Prince Jian, he fled to Wu. Soon after he was recalled by Zixi. In 479 BC, Bai Gongsheng was killed after launching a coup, and Zixi was also killed because of the involvement with Bai Gongsheng.

Therefore, "If a person who behaves uprightly succumbs to his own desires, he will be burdened by his desires."

Meaning: In dealing with people and navigating life, one must be aware that the world is constantly changing. By tracing back to the root cause and conduct behaviour with integrity, which can avoid unnecessary conflicts and problems. Many things start from the heart, internal and external factors are interrelated. Good conduct and self-cultivation can reduce the disasters caused by their own desires.

举鲁国尽化为一 《韩非子·内储说上》

鲁哀公（春秋末鲁国君主，名将。约与孔子同时代）问于孔子曰："鄙谚（俗语）曰：莫众而迷。今，寡人举事，与群臣虑之，而国愈乱，其故何也？"

孔子对曰："明主之问臣，一人知之，一人不知也，如是者，明主在上，群臣直议于下。今群臣，无不一辞同轨乎季孙者，举鲁国尽化为一，君虽问境内之人，犹不免于乱也。"

一曰：晏子聘鲁，哀公问曰："语曰：'莫三人而迷。'今，寡人与一国虑之，鲁不免于乱，何也？"

晏子曰："古之所谓"莫三人而迷'者，一人失之，二人得之，三人足以为众矣，故曰：'莫三人而迷。'今，鲁国之群臣以千百数，一言于季氏之私，人数非不众，所言者一人也，安得三哉？"

译文：鲁哀公问孔子："俗话说：办事不与众人商议，一定会迷惑。现在，我所有事情都和群臣商议，但是国家反而更乱了，这是什么缘故？"

孔子回答，说："贤明的君主在朝问事，有知道的也有不知道的。如此这样，明君在上，群臣争议，明君在群臣的争议中能够领悟其中的是非曲直，君主拿出初步见解，再经群臣争辩形成的决策，才是比较正确的。如今，群臣所发表的建议，都是出自季孙氏的一家之言。举国上下都是一个声音，君主您问遍全国，答案皆同。由此以来，国政怎能不乱呢？"

还有一种说法：晏婴出访鲁国，鲁哀公问他："俗语常说：'没有与三人商议就会迷惑。'今者，我与国人共谋国策，鲁国还是难免伤乱，这是什么原因？"

晏婴说："古人所讲的'没有三人参与商议就会迷惑'，是说一人失算，余下两个人有可能是清醒的。经过三个人的争辩，足以了解众人之见，所以说'没有三个人参于争论，就会迷惑。'现在鲁国群臣虽然多，都统一于季氏的私利。人数并不是不多，但是所言却是一家之言，怎能是众人之言呢？"

寓意：国策出自一家之言，容易削弱国力。

One kind of voice

Duke Ai of Lu asked Confucius, "As the saying goes: If you don't consult with everyone, you will be confused. Now, I discuss everything with the ministers, but the country has become more chaotic. What is the reason?"

Confucius answered, "When a wise monarch asks questions at imperial court, some people know the answer and some people don't. In this way, when a wise monarch is in the imperial court, the ministers discuss with each other, and the wise ministers can identify the right and wrong in the disputes among the ministers. The monarch can come up with preliminary opinions, and then Decisions made after debate among the ministers are more correct. Today, the suggestions issued by the ministers are all from the words of the Jisun family. The whole country has one voice. If you ask all over the country, the answer is the same. Since then, how can the government of the country not be in chaos?"

There is another saying: Yan Ying went to visit the state of Lu, and Duke Ai of Lu asked him, "As the saying goes: If you don't consult with three people, you will be confused." "Now, when the people and I work together to plan the national policy, the Lu State is still inevitably in trouble. What's the reason?"

Yan Ying said, "The ancients said: 'There will be confusion if there are no three people involved in the discussion.' It means that one person's miscalculation will lead to confusion. It is possible for two people to be sober. After three people argued, it is enough to understand everyone's opinions. Therefore, if there are no three people involved in the argument, there will be confusion. Now, although there are many ministers in the state of Lu, they are all unified under the Ji family for Self-interest. The number of people is not small, but what is said is the opinion of one family, how can it be the opinion of everyone?"

Meaning: National policies come from the opinions of one family, which can easily weaken the national power.

天道释然《韩非子·内储说上》

鲁哀公问于仲尼（孔子）曰："《春秋》之记曰：'冬十二月，霣（yǔn）霜不杀菽（shū 豆类总称）。'何为记此？"

仲尼对曰："此言可以杀，而不杀也。夫，宜杀而不杀，桃李冬实。天失道，草木犹犯干之，而况于君乎！"

译文：鲁哀公问孔子："《春秋》记载：'冬天十二月降霜时，并不会摧残豆类作物。'为什么要记载这件事呢？"

孔子回答："这是大自然的选择，有可杀，有可不杀。如果，可杀而不杀者，就会造成桃李冬季也结果。桃李冬季结果，称谓天地失道。天地失道，草木尚且互相侵犯，何况人间的君主呢？"

寓意：自然界遵守天道，应时令而开花结果；人世间，顺应天道而生人道，乃人间正道。天地若失道则自然失衡，人间愦乱。

Obey the Rules of Nature

Duke Ai of Lu asked Confucius, "*The Spring and Autumn Annals* record: When frost falls in December in winter, it will not destroy the bean crops. Why is this recorded?"

Confucius replied, "This is the selection of nature. Some things are killable, while some are not. If the killable ones are not killed, it will lead to plums and peaches bearing fruits in winter. Plums and peaches bearing fruits in winter are a sign of a violation of the natural order. If the order of nature is disrupted, even plants will encroach on each other, so how about the monarchs of the world?"

Meaning: Nature obeys the orders of universe and brings forth flowers and fruits according to the seasons. In the human world, adhering to the order of nature leads to the establishment of human morality, which is the right path for humanity. If the laws of universe lose their way, nature will become unbalanced, and the human world will be thrown into chaos.

公德之道《韩非子·内储说上》

殷之法，刑弃灰于街者。子贡以为重，问之仲尼。

仲尼曰："知治之道也。夫，弃灰于街，必掩人（迷眼）。掩人，人必怒，怒则斗，斗必三族相残也。此残三族之道也，虽刑之可也。且（况且），夫重罚者，人之所恶也。而无亦灰，人之所易也。使人行之所易，而无离（lí 通"罹"，遭遇）所恶，此治之道。"

译文：商代的法律明文规定：把草木灰倒在人行道上要受到重刑。子贡认为这样的刑法太重了，于是向孔子请教。

孔子感叹地说："商代就已经懂得依法治国的道理。在人行道上抛弃草木灰，人走在灰尘上，容易扬起尘埃迷了行人眼睛。被尘埃迷了眼睛的人，很容易发怒，发怒就容易引发争斗，争斗就容易引发家族与家族相互伤残。由此造成家族之间结下仇恨的根源，所以必然以重刑治理。况且，过重的刑罚人人厌恶，不在大道上弃灰，人人都容易做到。因此，促使民众做容易的事，不遭受人人厌恶的刑罚，这就是治理天下最好的法律。

寓意：设立法律的本意是除害避祸，建立良序，也为了警戒和阻止民众犯法，并非只是为了惩治而设立。

The Way of Public Morality

The laws of the Shang Dynasty clearly stipulated that pouring plant ashes on the sidewalk would be punished severely. Zigong thought that such a punishment was too severe, so he asked Confucius for advice.

Confucius sighed and said: "The Shang Dynasty already understood the principles of governing the country according to law. Leaving plant ashes on the sidewalk can easily raise dust when people walk on it, which may blind pedestrians. People who are blinded by dust are prone to getting angry easily. Getting angry easily leads to fights, and fights easily lead to mutual injuries between families. This can lead to the root of hatred among families, so it is necessary to govern with severe punishment. Moreover, everyone hates excessive punishment, and it is easy for everyone to avoid leaving ashes on the road. Therefore, encouraging people to do what is easy and avoiding the punishment that everyone hates is the best law for governing the nation.

Meaning: The original intention of establishing laws is to eliminate harm, avoid disasters, establish good order, and also to warn and prevent the people from breaking the law. It is not solely established for punishment purposes.

鲁人烧积泽《韩非子·内储说上》

鲁人烧积泽（草木丛生的沼泽）。天北风，火南倚（偎依），恐烧国（都邑）。

哀公惧，自将众趣（古通：促）救火。左右无人，尽逐兽，而火不救，乃召问仲尼。

仲尼曰："夫，逐兽者乐，而无罪；救水者苦，而无赏。此火之所以无救也。"

哀公曰："善。"

仲尼曰："事急，不及以赏。救火者尽赏之，则国不足以赏于人。请徒（tú 仅）行罚。"

哀公曰："善。"

于是，仲尼乃下令曰："不救火者，比（等同）降北（降敌叛逃）之罪；逐兽者，比入禁之罪。"

令下未遍，而火已救矣。

译文：鲁国焚烧草木丛生的沼泽。忽然，天空刮起北风，火势向南倾斜，恐怕烧到都邑曲阜城。

鲁哀公很害怕，希望召集众臣救火，却发现身边没有一个臣子，都去追逐从火中逃出来的野兽，而不去救火。哀公立刻召来孔子询问良策。

孔子面对当时的情况，对鲁哀公说："群臣追逐火中逃出来的野兽，使人感到愉悦，况且这样做也不会受惩罚。野外救火，不但很辛苦，而且还有被火烧伤的风险，并且再辛苦也换不来任何奖赏，这就是没有人主动救火的原因。"

鲁哀公说："讲的好。"

孔子紧接着说："此事紧急，顾不上行赏，况且救火者都赏，举国之财也不足以赐赏。我请求只用刑罚。"

鲁哀公连忙说："好吧。"

于是，孔子下令："不救火者，等同于投敌叛逃；追逐野兽者，等同于闯入禁宫之罪。"

命令还没有传遍，而大火已被扑灭。

寓意：国事必先有法令，令必行，行必果。

Burn the Marsh

The state of Lu burned the overgrown swamps. Suddenly, a north wind blew up, tilting the fire southward, threatening to burn the capital city of Qufu.

Duke Ai of Lu was very frightened and wanted to summon his courtiers to put out the fire, but he found that there was no one around him. They all chased the wild beasts that escaped from the fire instead of putting out the fire. Duke Ai immediately summoned Confucius to ask for advice.

Faced with the situation at that time, Confucius said to Duke Ai, "The courtiers chased the beasts that escaped from the fire, which made them feel delighted. Besides, they would not be punished for that; Saving the fire in the wild was not only very hard, but also risky to be burned. And no matter how hard they worked, they could not get any reward. That was why no one took the initiative to save the fire."

Duke Ai of Lu said, " Well said."

Confucius continued, "This matter is urgent, and there is no time for rewards. Besides, if we reward everyone who helped put out the fire, even the wealth of the entire nation won't be enough. I suggest we use punishment instead."

Duke Ai quickly agreed, "Alright."

So Confucius ordered, "Those who fail to help put out the fire will be treated as traitors; those who chase after wild animals will be punished as if they had broken into the forbidden palace."

Before the order could be fully communicated, the fire had already been extinguished.

Meaning: The governance of a country must begin with laws and regulations. These laws must be enforced, and their enforcement must yield definite results.

孔子相卫《韩非子·外储说左下》

孔子相卫。弟子子皋为狱吏，刖（yuè 古代一种酷刑：砍脚）人足。所跀（同"刖"）者守门。

人有恶（wù 中伤）孔子于卫君者，曰："尼（仲尼）欲作乱。"

卫君欲执孔子。

孔子走。弟子皆逃。

子皋从出门，跀危（受砍脚者）引之，而逃之门下室中，吏追不得。

夜半，子皋问跀危，曰："吾，不能亏主之法令，而亲跀子之足，是子报仇之时也，而子何故乃肯逃我？我何以得此于子？"

跀危曰："吾断足也，固（固然）吾罪当之，不可奈何。然，方公之狱治臣也，公倾侧法令，先后臣以言，欲臣之免也甚，而臣知之。及狱决罪定，公憱（cù 通"蹙"。忧伤）然不悦，形于颜色，臣见又知之。非私臣（犹：无私心）而然也。夫，天性仁心固然也。此臣之所悦而德公也。"

孔子曰："善为吏者，树德；不能为吏者，树怨。概（gài 古代称量粮食时，刮平斗、斛用的小木板）者，平量者也；吏者，平法者也。治国者，不可失平也。"

译文：孔子担任卫国宰相时，弟子子皋担任卫国的刑狱吏，曾经对犯罪的人实施过砍脚的酷刑。后来，这个受过酷刑的罪人，出狱后成了一个守门人。

有人向卫国君主中伤孔子，说："孔子要谋反。"

卫国君主准备捉拿孔子。

孔子得知后连忙出逃，弟子们也紧跟着逃走。

子皋刚从大门经过，受过砍脚酷刑的那个人，急忙引领子皋逃进大门旁边自己的居室里，追捕的官吏没有捉到子皋。

夜半时分，子皋不解地问他说："我不能违背君主法令，并且亲自砍了你的脚。现在正是你报仇的时候，然则，为何你还帮助我逃走？我何以接受你的善意？"

刖危者说："我被砍脚，固然是我的罪该如此，这是没有办法的事。然而，当您给我依法定罪时，您反复推敲法令，先后向我询问其中的细节。您很想减免我的罪过，这些我心中都知道。等到最终判决下来，您忧愁的神色显现在脸上，这些我也看在眼里记在心里。您的所作所为，都是对我所犯的罪秉公办理，并不是对我个人有仇恨。您所做的一切，是您天性仁慈的体现。因此我敬佩您，并对您感恩在心。"

孔子深情地说："善为官者，树立恩德；不善为官者，树立仇恨。概，是用来刮平量斗、斛的器具；官吏用法律实现社会和谐。治理国家的君主，不能失去公平公正的治国理念。

寓意：法无情，人有情；守法度，尽人情，欲求心服口服，不可失公平。

Confucius in the State of Wei

When Confucius was the prime minister of the Wei State, his disciple Zi Gao was the jailer of the Wei State and once committed the torture of chopping off the feet of a criminal. Later, the tortured criminal became a gatekeeper after being released from prison.

Someone slandered Confucius to the monarch of Wei State, saying: "Confucius wants to rebel."

The monarch of Wei State prepared to arrest Confucius.

Confucius fled immediately after learning about it, and his disciples followed him.

As soon as Zigao passed by the gate, the man who had been tortured by having his feet chopped off hurriedly led Zigao to escape into his own room next to the gate. The chasing officials did not catch Zigao. In the middle of the night, Zigao asked him puzzledly: "I can't disobey the king's decree, and I personally cut off your feet. Now is the time for you to take revenge, but why do you still help me escape? Why should I accept your offer?"

The person said: "My feet were chopped off, and it was certainly my fault. There was nothing I could do about it. However, when you convicted me according to law, you repeatedly reviewed the law and asked me about the details. You really want to reduce my guilt, and I know this in my heart. When the final verdict is handed down, a sad look appears on your face, and I also see it in my eyes and remember it in my heart. The crime you committed was dealt with fairly, not because of any personal hatred against me. Everything you did was a reflection of your natural kindness. Therefore, I admire you and feel grateful to you."

Confucius said affectionately: "Those who are good at serving as officials will build up kindness; those who are not good at serving as officials will build up hatred. The monarch who governs the country must not lose the concept of fairness and justice in governing the country.

Meaning: The law is relentless, but people have emotions. Following the law and fulfilling humanity, we desire to earn others' heartfelt convictions, and fairness must be necessary.

夔一足《韩非子·外储说左上》

哀公问于孔子曰："吾闻夔（kuí 古代传说中的龙形异兽，商周时期青铜器，多有夔形纹饰。又，相传尧时的乐官）一足，信乎？"

曰："夔，人也。何故一足？彼其无他异，而独通于声。尧曰：'夔一而足矣。'使为乐正。故，君子曰：'夔有一，足。'非一足也。"

译文：鲁哀公问孔子："我听说夔只有一只脚，你相信吗？"

孔子回答："夔是一个人，怎能只有一只脚？这人没有别的特长，唯独精通声律。尧王说：'夔有这一个特长就足了。'于是，指派夔为主管声律的官吏。由此而言，君子说：'夔有这一个特长就足了。'而不是夔只有一只脚。"

寓意：人若有一技之长，足以赢得世人尊重。

One Foot

Duke Ai of Lu asked Confucius: "I heard that Kui has only one foot. Do you believe it?"

Confucius replied, "Kui is a human being, how can he only have one foot? This man has no other specialties but is proficient in rhythm. king Yao said: 'Kui has this one specialty, it is enough.' So he appointed Kui as the official in charge of music and rhythm. From this point of view, the gentleman said: 'Kui has this one specialty, it is enough.' Instead of Kui having only one Feet."

Meaning: If a person has one skill, he can win the respect of the world.

晏婴头像铭文注解 Head Portrait of Yan Ying & Annotation of the Inscriptions

《宴婴》：

晏婴，字，平仲。约生于？，卒于公元前500年。夷维（今，山东高密）人。历任齐灵公、齐庄公、齐景公为卿。辅佐齐国朝政达五十余年。后世尊称"晏子"。司马迁《史记》："管仲卒，齐国遵其政，常强于诸侯，后百余年而有晏子焉。"

Yan Ying:

Yan Ying, courtesy name Pingzhong, he was born around [?] and died in 500 BCE. He was from Yiwei (present-day Gaomi, Shandong). He served as a minister under Duke Ling, Duke Zhuang, and Duke Jing of Qi, assisting in the governance of the State of Qi for over fifty years. He was revered by later generations as "Yanzi". In Sima Qian's "Historical Records", it is written: "After Guan Zhong's death, the State of Qi followed his policies, remaining stronger than the other states for over a hundred years, until Yanzi came along."

社鼠《晏子春秋·内篇·问上》

夫社（古代祭祀神灵的地方统称"社"，或"神社"），束木而涂（泥涂在木上当墙）之。鼠，因往托焉。熏之，则恐烧其木；灌之，则恐败其涂。此鼠所以不可得杀者，以社故也。

译文：古代建造神社的方法是用捆成排的木材竖起主体墙，然后再用泥巴涂在木材的外表。老鼠依托墙体上的干泥巴做窝。用火熏烧老鼠窝，害怕烧坏支撑墙体的木材；用水浇灌老鼠窝，又怕墙上的干泥巴浸落。因此，神社里的老鼠难以消灭，这都是因为神社构造的缺陷。

晏婴以"社鼠"论述治国理念。并进一步阐述："夫，国亦有焉（社鼠），人主左右是也。内则，蔽善恶于君上；外则，卖权重于百姓。不诛之，则乱（扰乱朝纲）；诛之，则为人主所案据（庇护）。腹（内）而有之，此，亦国之社鼠也。"

寓意：朝中藏匿奸臣难以根除的原因，都是进官制度有空可钻造成的结果。

The Rats in the Shrine

The ancient method of constructing a shrine involved erecting the main wall using logs stacked in rows, and then covering the exterior of the logs with mud. Mice made their nests in the dry mud clinging to the wall. Using fire to fumigate the rat's nest risks burning the wood supporting the wall, while using water to flush out the nest might result in the dry mud on the wall coming loose. Therefore, it is difficult to eliminate rats in the shrine, all because of the flaws in the shrine's structure.

Meaning: The reason why it is difficult to eradicate corrupt officials hidden in the court is the result of the official system providing opportunities for corrupt officials.

社鼠 The Rats in the Shrine

人有酤酒者《晏子春秋·内篇·问上》

人有酤（gū 卖）酒者，为器甚洁清，置表（招牌）甚长，而酒酸不售。

问之里人（同乡人。或里中主事者）其故？

里人云："公之狗猛，人挈（qiè 提）器而入，且酤公酒，狗迎而噬（shì 咬）之。此酒所以酸而不售也。"

译文：有一位卖酒的人，他店铺里的器具收拾地非常干净，招牌挂得也很高很长。但是他家的酒直到发酸也卖不出去。

他请教同乡邻里主事的人，问其中的缘故为何？

邻里主事的人告诉他，说："你家门前的那条狗太凶猛，别人提壶前来买你家的酒，你家的狗扑上去就咬，这就是你家的酒直到发酸，也卖不出去的原因。"

（齐景公问晏婴治理国家最大的隐患是什么？晏婴以这篇寓言故事论述：朝中不可有"猛狗当道"，阻碍贤良之士求职，其结果造成朝政如同"死水一潭"，丧失政事清明的大好局面。）

寓意：圣贤之士不愿入朝为官的原因，都是因为奸诈的小人把持着入朝做官的门槛。

Liquor Seller

There was a liquor seller. The utensils in his shop were kept very clean, and the signboard was hung very high and long. However, his liquors could not be sold until it goes sour.

He asked the person in charge of the neighborhood about the reason. The person told him, "The dog in front of your house is too ferocious. When someone comes to buy your liquors with a pot, your dog pounces on it and bites it. This is the reason why your liquors couldn't be sold out."

(*Duke Jing of Qi asked Yan Ying what was the biggest hidden danger in governing the country? Yan Ying used this fable to explain: There should be no "fierce dogs" in the government, which would hinder virtuous people from finding jobs. As a result, the political environment would be like a "stagnant pool" and the government would miss its flourishing age.*）

Meaning: The reason why sages are unwilling to become officials in the imperial court is because treacherous officials control the threshold of becoming officials.

人有酤酒者 Liquor Seller

自满的马夫《史记·列传·管晏列传第二》

晏子为齐相。出其御之妻从门间而窥其夫,其夫为相御,拥(撑起)大盖,策马四马,意气扬扬,甚自得也。

既而归,其妻请去(离婚回娘家)。

夫问其故。

妻曰:"晏子长不满六尺,身相齐国,名显诸侯。今者,妾观其出,志念深矣。常有以自下者。今,子长八尺,乃为人仆御。然,子之意自以为足,妾是以求去也。"

其后,夫自抑损(贬损)。

晏子怪,而问之。御以实对。

晏子荐以为大夫。

译文:晏婴做齐国宰相时,有一次乘车出门办事,路过马夫家门时,被马夫的妻子看见自己的丈夫坐在大伞之下,挥舞着长鞭显露出得意忘形的神态。

马夫回到家中,妻子立刻向他提出离婚要求。

马夫连忙问妻子为何要离婚?

妻子回答:"晏婴的身高不过六尺,官居宰相之位,显赫的声誉在各诸侯之间传颂。今日,我看到他乘车出行,神态谦卑,克己自下。而你身高八尺,为人当奴仆,挥舞着长鞭显露出得意忘形的神态,自以为很了不起样子,所以我请求离开你。"

从此以后,马夫改变了自己往日的神态,变的十分谦卑有礼。

晏婴看到马夫的行为与往日不同,感到很奇怪,便询问马夫是何故?马夫不好意思地讲出事情原由。

晏婴听了马夫所言,觉得马夫能够虚心接受他人的告诫,定有所作为。于是,便推荐他担任齐国的一名大夫。

寓意:人纵然有言行不当之处,但若能谦和地听取他人的告诫,承认并及时改正自己不足之处,反而是一种高尚的品德,也使他人由衷地钦佩。

A Complacent Driver

Yanzi became the Prime Minister of the state of Qi. As he was going out, the wife of his carriage driver peeped out behind the door which was opened just a crack. She saw her husband drive the Prime Minister's carriage, sitting beneath the big canopy, cracking his whip at the team of four horses in front of him. He had a cocksure expression on his face and seemed very pleased with himself.

When the driver returned, his wife wanted a divorce. He asked for an explanation.

"Yanzi is not even six *chi*[1] tall," she pointed out. "He is the Prime Minister of Qi and enjoys a high reputation among the rulers of the different states. Today I watched him go out. He is a man of great depth but his bearing is so modest and unassuming. Now you are over eight chi tall and you are only a carriage driver. But you looked so cocky and puffed-up. That is why I want to leave you."

From then onwards the driver restrained himself and learned to be more modest. This surprised Yanzi. He questioned the driver who told him the truth. As a result Yanzi recommended him to the post of a senior officer of the state.

Meaning: Even if a person has inappropriate words and deeds, if he can humbly listen to the warnings of others, admit and correct his own shortcomings in a timely manner, it will be a noble character and will make others sincerely admire him.

---

[1] Chi: a Chinese unit of length, approximately equal to one third of a metre.

自满的马夫 A Complacent Driver

孙武头像铭文注解 Head Portrait of Sun Wu & Annotation of the Inscriptions

《孙武》：

孙武，字长卿。约生于公元前545年，卒于公元前470年。经伍子胥举荐，向吴王阖闾进呈兵法十三篇，战胜楚军。后世尊称"孙子"。或称"兵圣"。孙武曰："国之大事，死生之地，存兴之道，不可不察也。荐五事，校以计，固国本。"

Sun Wu:

Sun Wu, also known as Changqing *(courtesy name)*, was born around 545 BCE and died in 470 BCE. Recommended by Wu Zixu, he presented the thirteen chapters of the Art of War to King Helu of Wu and defeated the Chu army. Later generations respectfully called him "Sun Tzu" or "The Sage of War".

率 然《孙子兵法·九地》

率然者，常山（恒山）之蛇也。击其首，则尾至；击其尾，则首至；击其中，则首尾俱（皆）至。

译文：率然者（古代传说中的一种蛇），常山之蛇。打击这种蛇的头部，蛇尾就来相救；打击它的尾部，蛇头就来相救；打击它的中部，首尾皆相救。

寓意：全军攻伐的良策，莫过于首尾相应攻守有方，百战不殆。

Shuai Ran Snake

Shuai Ran, an ancient mythical snake, is also known as the Snake of Changshan Mountain. When you strike its head, its tail comes to its rescue; when you strike its tail, its head comes to its rescue; and when you strike its middle, both its head and tail come to its rescue.

Meaning: The best strategy for attacking an enemy army is to maintain coordination and unity, just like the Snake of Changshan Mountain. By doing so, one can fight hundreds of battles without danger of defeat.

同舟共济《孙子兵法·九地》

夫，吴人与越人相恶也。

当其同舟而济，遇风，其相救也，如左右手。

译文：春秋战国时期，吴国与越国经常发生战争。因此两国的百姓也是互相仇视。

当他们同船渡河遭遇风浪时，他们双方都会摒弃前嫌，同心协力共渡难关，好似一个人的左右手，配合地如此默契。

寓意：当矛盾的对象转移时，互相仇视的双方居然也能同心协力，共渡同一难关。

Unity in Crisis: Crossing Together

During the Spring and Autumn and Warring States periods, there were frequent wars between the states of Wu and Yue, resulting in mutual animosity among their citizens.

However, when they found themselves in the same boat crossing a river during a storm, they would set aside their past grudges and work together to overcome the difficulties, just like a person's left and right hands cooperating with each other seamlessly.

Meaning: When the focus of conflict shifts, even mutually hostile enemies can unite and work together to overcome a common challenge.

同舟共济 Unity in Crisis: Crossing Together

墨子头像古文注解 Head Portrait of Mozi & Annotation of the Inscriptions

墨子布衣之士 The Scholar in Simple Attire of Mozi

《墨子》：

墨翟，名翟，后世尊称"墨子"。约生于公元前 468 年，卒于 376 年。相传原为宋国人。后，常居鲁国。主张兼爱、非攻、尚贤、尚同、天志、明鬼、非命、非乐、节葬、节用。与儒家并称"显学。"

Mozi:

Mo Di, was revered as 'Mozi' by later generations. He was born around 468 BCE and died in 376. According to legend, he was originally from the State of Song. Later, he often resided in the State of Lu. He advocated universal love, non-aggression, respect for the virtuous, unity, the will of heaven, the manifestation of ghosts, non-fatality, non-pleasure, economical burial, and frugality. Along with Confucianism, they are collectively referred to as 'prominent schools'.

盗其无自出《墨子·尚贤上》

富者，有高墙深宫。墙立既，谨上为凿一门。

有盗人入。阖其自入而求之。盗其无自出。

译文：有一户富人家，盖了一座深宅大院。砌好高墙之后，只留下一扇院门。

有一次，小偷溜进来行窃，主人先把院门锁上再去搜寻窃贼，这样一来小偷无处可逃。

寓意：为政者，首先要建立起可行的法律法规，只留一道义门："不义不富，不义不贵，不义不亲，不义不近。"即使奸诈之人钻法律的空子，也很容易败露。

Door in the Wall

There was a rich family who built a deep and large compound. After the high wall was built, only a courtyard door remained. Once, a thief sneaked in to steal. The owner locked the courtyard door before searching for the thief, so that the thief had nowhere to escape.

Meaning: Politicians must first establish feasible laws and regulations, leaving only one door of righteousness: "Do not seek wealth through injustice, do not seek status through wrongdoing, do not seek closeness through dishonesty, and do not approach others through immoral means." Doing so, even if a treacherous person takes advantage of the law loopholes can also be easily exposed.

楚王好细腰《墨子·兼爱中》

昔者，楚灵王好士细要（腰）。故，灵王之臣，皆以一饭为节。胁息然后带，扶墙然后起。此期年（等到一周年），朝有黧（li)黑之色。

译文：昔日，楚灵王喜欢身材苗条的官吏，因此宫内所有官吏每天只敢吃一顿饭，并且吸气屏息扎上腰带，有气无力地扶着墙壁才能站起来。一年后，朝内官吏都饿得面色黑瘦。

寓意：上有所好，下必甚焉。

Preference for Slim Waists

In the past, King Ling of Chu preferred officials with slender bodies. Consequently, all the officials in the palace dared to eat only one meal a day. They inhaled deeply, held their breath, tied their belts tightly, and struggled to stand up, supported by the walls. After a year, the officials in the court were so hungry that their faces turned dark and gaunt.

Meaning: When a king has a hobby or preference, the inferiors will intend to excessively indulge in pandering to that hobby or preference.

楚王好细腰 Preference for Slim Waists

击邻家之子《墨子·鲁问》

譬（pì 比如）有人于此，其子强梁不材，故其父笞（chī 鞭笞）之。其邻家之父，举木而击之，曰："吾击之也，顺于其父之志。"则岂不悖哉！

译文：如果有个人，因其子强横残暴欺凌弱小，于是他举鞭教训儿子。邻居家的大人看见了，也举起木棍前来参于责打，并且说："我来打你，是顺应你父亲的心意。"这样的做法岂不是很荒谬吗？

寓意：墨子以"天"比作"父"。借指：以"替天行道"之名，攻伐他国的行为是荒谬的。

Hit the neighbor's son

If there was someone whose son had bullied the weak for being tough and violent, he raised his whip to teach his son a lesson. The neighbor seeing this also raised a stick to join in the punishment, saying, "I came to beat you to comply with your father's wishes." Isn't this ridiculous?

Meaning: Mozi compares "Heaven" to "Father". To borrow a reference: It is absurd to attack other countries in the name of "doing justice for heaven".

列子头像铭文注解 Head Portrait of Liezi & Annotation of the Inscriptions

《列子》：

列御寇，字云。后世尊称"列子"。古帝王列山氏之后。约生于公主前 450 年，卒于公元前 375 年。郑国圃田（今，河南郑州）人。其学本于黄帝、老子，主张清静无为。对后世哲学、美学、文学、音乐、科技、养生、宗教影响深远。

Liezi:

Lie Yukou, was revered as "Liezi" in later generations. He was a descendant of the ancient emperor Lie Shan. He was born around 450 BCE and died in 375 BCE. He was from Putian in the State of Zheng *(now Zhengzhou, Henan Province)*. His learning was based on the teachings of Huangdi and Laozi, advocating a philosophy of quietude and non-action. He had a profound influence on philosophy, aesthetics, literature, music, science and technology, health preservation, and religion in later generations.

杞人忧天《列子·天瑞》

杞国有人忧天地崩坠（倒塌坠落），身亡所寄，废寝食者。又有忧彼之所忧者，因往晓之，曰："天，积气耳，亡（无）处亡气。若（如）屈伸呼吸，终日在天中行止，奈何忧崩坠乎？"

其人曰："天果积气，日月星宿，不当坠耶？"

晓之者曰："日月星宿，亦积气中之有光耀者，只使坠，亦不能有所中伤。"

其人曰："奈（怎奈）地坏何？"

晓者曰："地积块耳，充塞四虚，亡处亡块。若躇步跐蹈（chú bù cǐ dǎo 张湛注：四字皆践踏之貌），终日在地上行止，奈何忧其坏？"

其人舍然大喜，晓之者舍然大喜。

长庐子（楚国人，属道家学派，著书九篇）闻而笑之曰："虹蜺（hóng ní）也，云雾也，风雨也，四时（四季）也，此积气之成乎天者也。山岳也，河海也，金石也，火木也，此积形之成乎地者也。知积气也，知积块也,奚谓不坏?夫天地,空中之一细物,有中之最巨者。难终难穷,此固然矣。难测难识,此固然矣。忧其坏者,诚为大远;言其不坏者,亦为未是。天地不得不坏,则会归于坏。遇其坏时,奚为不忧哉?"

子列子闻而笑曰:"言天地坏者,亦谬;言天地不坏者,亦谬。坏与不坏,吾所不能知也。虽然,彼一也,此一也。故,生不知死,死不知生;来不知去,去不知来。坏与不坏,吾何容心哉?"

译文:杞国有一人,整日担扰天塌地陷,深怕自己的身体无处躲藏,因此废寝忘食不得安宁。又有一人却为这人的忧虑而担忧,便亲自前去开导他,说:"上天,不过是积聚成云的气体,天空中处处充满着空气。你俯仰呼吸,整日在天地间行走,为什么还要担心天会塌下来呢?"

这人说:"天果真是积聚的空气,那么日月星辰不就很容易掉下来吗?"

开导他的人说:"日月星辰只是气体中有光耀的物体,即使真掉下来也不会伤到人。(此处:远古时代的人类,还无法了解日、月、星辰都是地球之外独立的星球。古希腊欧多克斯提出:地心说,日月星辰每天绕地球一周,尼古拉·哥白尼1543年提出:太阳是宇宙的中心,而不是地球。)

这人又问:"那么,地陷下去怎么得了。"

开导他的人说:"地,由成片的土石所积聚,它的四面八方都已经填满了,你整日在大地上行走,为什么还会陷下去呢?"

这人听说以后,便放心地高兴起来。开导他的人也为这人的高兴而高兴。

长庐子听说了这件事,不以为然地笑着对人说:"天空中的彩虹、云雾、风雨、四季的气候变化,与大地上的水分子的游荡有关,水分子在空中积聚成云团,它们的整体称之谓"天";承载着山川河海,金木水火土,以及生息繁衍万物的称之谓大地。明知天是积聚的气体,也知道大地是由金木水火土积聚而成,为什么还要说它不会被毁坏呢?虽然地球在宇宙中是很细小的物质,但是对于地球本身而言,地球上具体存在的事物却是很巨大。它们难以终结,难以穷尽,这是必然的;对于人类如果真的想要了解地球运转奥秘,也是难以实现的。不过,担忧它的毁灭,实在是担忧的太遥远了。说它不会毁灭,也未必就是正确的。天地在日月交替运转中,时有天塌地陷的自然灾害发生,万一遭遇天塌地陷,怎能不使人担忧呢?"

列子听说长庐子的话后表示不敢苟同,笑着说,"说天地将会毁灭是荒唐的言辞;说天地不会毁灭也是荒唐之辞。天地毁不毁灭不是人类能够操控的。因此,彼一时,此一时,由于时间不同,所形成和结果也不相同。所以,人生在世不知道死后将会遭遇什么样的境域;死亡后,也会忘却尘世间的恩恩怨怨。犹如:来者,不知要向何处去;去者,也不清楚从何而来。天地的毁不毁灭,我何必放在心头空担忧呢?"

寓意：人生在世不为不应该担忧的事而担忧，否则就成了：庸人自扰之。

The Worrier of Qi

A man of the state of Qi was afraid that the sky will fall down and the earth will cave in. The thought that he would not be able to find shelter when that happened worried him so much that he had no appetite for food and slept very badly.

Another man was very concerned about his worried frame of mind so he went to see him with the intention of straightening him out.

"The sky is merely a mass of vapour. No place is without vapour. When you breathe, walk or rest, you are moving about in this air all day long. Why are you afraid that the sky will fall down?"

"If the sky is really a mass of vapour. Won't the sun, moon and stars fall down?"

"The sun, moon, stars and planets are just luminous objects in the sky, The only difference is that they shine. Even if they fall down, they will not hurt anyone." (In ancient times, humans were unaware that the sun, the moon, and the stars were independent celestial bodies beyond Earth.)

"Then what about the earth caving in?"

"The earth is a big mass of soil and rocks. There are rocks and soil everywhere; no place is without them. When you walk or jump, you are moving about on them all day long. Why are you worried that it will cave in?"

The poor worried man, immensely relieved, was delighted and so was the one who enlightened him.

When Changluzi heard about this, "The formation of the rainbow, clouds, and rain in the sky, as well as some aspects of climate changes in the four seasons, are all related to water molecules on the earth wandering in the air and accumulating into clouds. Bearing mountains, rivers, seas, the elements of gold, wood, water, fire, and earth, as well as nurturing and multiplying all life, is what we call the earth. Knowing that the sky is composed primarily of air, and the earth is made up of the elements of metal, wood, water, fire, and soil, why do we still say that they cannot be destroyed? Although the earth is a very small substance in the universe, as far as the earth itself is concerned, the specific things that exist on the earth are very huge. It is inevitable that they are difficult to end and exhaust; For humans, truly understanding the mysteries of the earth's operation is also difficult to achieve. However, worrying about its destruction is indeed a far-fetched concern. Saying that it will not be destroyed is not necessarily correct. As the sky and the earth rotate alternately between the sun and the moon, natural disasters such as the sky collapsing and the earth sinking occur occasionally. How can one not worry about it if such disasters were to strike?"

After hearing Changluzi's words, Liezi disagreed and laughed, saying, "It is absurd to say that the sky and earth will be destroyed, and it is also absurd to say that they will not be destroyed. Whether the sky and earth will be destroyed or not is beyond human control. Therefore, due to the passage of time, the formation and consequences of events can vary greatly." Therefore, while living in the world, we do not know what kind of realm we will encounter after death; after death, we will also forget the enmity and kindness of the mortal world. It is like: those who come do not know where they are going; those who go do not know where they came from. Whether the sky and earth will be destroyed or not, why should I worry about it in vain?

Meaning: One should not worry about things that are not worth worrying about in life, otherwise it will become: a mediocre person disturbing himself.

杞人忧天 The Worrier of Qi

为盗之道 《列子·天瑞》

齐之国氏大富，宋之向氏大贫。自宋之齐，请其术。

国氏告之曰："吾善为盗。始吾为盗也，一年而给（jǐ 衣食丰足），二年而足，三年大壤（rǎng 丰收）。自此以往，施及州闾（州县乡里）。

向氏大喜。喻其为盗之言，而不喻其为盗之道。遂逾垣（翻墙）凿室，手目所及，亡不探（取）也。未及时，以脏获罪，没其先居之财。

向氏以国氏之谬（miù 欺骗）己也，往而怨之。

国氏曰："若为盗若何？"向氏言其状。

国氏曰："嘻，若失为盗之道至此乎？今将告若矣。吾闻天有时，地有利。吾盗天地之时利，云雨之滂润，山泽之产育，以生吾禾，殖吾稼，筑吾垣，建吾舍。陆盗禽兽，水盗鱼鳖，亡非盗也。夫，禾稼、土木、禽兽、鱼鳖、皆天之所生，岂吾之所有？然，吾盗天而亡殃。夫，金玉珍宝，谷帛财货，人之所聚，岂天之所与？若盗之而获罪，孰怨哉？"

向氏大惑，以为国氏之重罔（欺罔）己也，过东郭先生问焉。

东郭先生曰："若一身庸非盗乎？盗阴阳之和以成若生，载若形，况，外物非盗哉！诚然，天地万物不相离也；仞（认）而有之，皆惑也。国氏之盗，公道也，故亡殃；若之盗，私心也，故得罪。有公私者，亦盗也；亡公私者，亦盗也。公公私私，天地之德。知天地之德者，孰为盗耶？孰为不盗耶？"

译文：齐国有位姓国的人很富有，宋国有位姓向的人很贫穷。向氏从宋国来到齐国请教国氏致富方法。

姓国的人对他说："我很会偷，开始偷盗时，一年可以自足，第二年就比较富裕，等到了第三年就阔气起来。从此以后，我的致富方法，很快普及到州县乡里。"

姓向的人听了很高兴。不过，他只听进耳朵里的"偷"字，却没有明白"偷"的道理。姓向的一回到宋国就开始跳墙凿洞，凡是手能触及到的，眼能看到的都据为己有。没有多久他的行迹败露因赃获罪，连同他原有的财产也被充公。

姓向的人获罪之后，以为姓国的人欺骗他，便气愤地上门抱怨他。

姓国的人问他："你是怎么偷的？"他讲述了获罪的过程。

姓国的人吃惊地说："咳，你违背"偷"的道理竟然到了如此地步。现在，我认真地告诉你：我知道上有天

- 64 -

时，下有地利，我偷天时地利，云雨的滋润，山林湖泽的产物，培植禾苗，种植庄稼，筑我院墙，建我房屋。从陆地偷取飞禽走兽，从水中偷取鱼虾龟鳖。庄稼、土木、禽兽、鱼鳖，都是大自然的产物，并不是属于我的。我用辛勤劳作换得苍天赐予的生活富足，并不为过。然而，别人家的金银珠宝、粮食货物是通过他们的劳动一点一滴地积累起来的，并不是天地所赐，你偷取他人的劳动所得而获罪，这能怨谁呢？"

姓向的人还是不明白姓国的人讲述的道理，以为姓国的人再次欺骗他。于是，他来到东郭先生那里问个明白。

东郭先生对他说："你整个人都是偷来的。偷天地阴阳之气成就你的生命，构成你的身躯。更何况，你的一切身外之物哪一件不是偷来的？的确，天地间的万物都是相生相克不离不弃，任凭私自占有自然资源的行为都是糊涂的做法。姓国的人通过勤劳致富，这样的做法是公道合理，所以不受惩罚。你的行为是窃取他人的劳动成果，当然应该受惩罚。虽然，有公私之别，称为盗窃，无公私之别，也称为盗窃。然而天地间的自然产物允许人间用勤劳换取生活富足，这是天地对人间的恩惠，明白了这都是天地对人间赐予的大德，还有必要区分谁是偷盗，谁不是偷盗吗？"

寓意：依靠勤劳致富，这是天道酬勤；攫取他人财富，则是罪过。

The Art of Stealing

The Guo family in the state of Qi was very rich while the Xiang family in the state of Song was very poor. Mr. Xiang went to Qi from Song to learn from Mr. Guo how to become wealthy."

"I am very good at stealing," said Mr. Guo. "After I became a thief, I managed to support myself after one year. In two years' time I was comfortably off. After three years I owned lots of land and my barns were all full. From then on, my way to achieve prosperity soon spread to prefectures, counties, and villages."

Mr. Xiang was delighted. He took in Mr. Guo's remark about stealing without understanding how one should go about it. Therefore, he scaled walls and bore holes to get into houses. He took everything his eyes could see or his hands could reach. After a little while, he was convicted of theft and the in-heritance left by his ancestors was confiscated.

Mr. Xiang was of the opinion that Mr. Guo had deceived him so he went to see Mr. Guo in order to put the blame on him.

"How did you steal?" asked Mr. Guo.

Mr. Xiang gave him an account of what he did.

"Oh dear!" said Mr. Guo, "You have totally missed the point of what I meant by stealing. I'll explain, what I mean. I heard that Nature has seasonal changes and Earth produce, fair crops. I steal from Nature's seasons and Earth's produce: clouds and rain give abundant moisture while hills and ponds supply other rich yields. With these I nurture my grain, plant my crops, put up my walls and build my houses. On land I steal birds and animals and at sea I steal fish and turtles. Everything is stolen, for grain, crops, earth, trees, birds, animals, fish and turtles are all products of Nature. Which of these belong to me? But when I steal from Nature, I do not get into trouble. Now precious stones, treasures, provisions, silks, money and goods are things that are amassed by men. They are not the gifts of Nature. If you steal such things and get convicted who can you blame?"

Mr. Xiang still didn't understand the reasoning explained by Mr. Guo, believing that Mr. Guo was deceiving him once again. Therefore, he went to Mr. Dongguo's place to seek clarification.

Mr. Dongguo said to him, "You have stolen your entire being. You have stolen the Yin-Yang energy from heaven and earth to sustain your life and form your body. Moreover, which of your external possessions is not 'stolen'? Indeed, all things in heaven and earth are interdependent and inseparable, and any act of privately and arbitrarily possessing natural resources is a foolish practice. People surnamed Guo, who have become wealthy through hard work, are justly and reasonably rewarded, thus avoiding punishment. Your behavior is tantamount to stealing the fruits of others' labor, thus you should be punished. Although there is a distinction between public and private interests, those who engage in theft for personal gain are referred to as 'theft', while those who engage in theft without considering public or private interests are also referred to as 'theft'. Then, the natural resources of heaven and earth permit people to achieve prosperity through diligent work. This is a benevolent act from heaven and earth towards humanity. Once you understand that these are all great virtues bestowed by heaven and earth upon humanity, is it still necessary to distinguish who is stealing and who is not?"

Meaning: Relying on hard work to achieve prosperity is rewarded by the universe, while seizing others' wealth is a sin.

为盗之道 The Art of Stealing

商丘开《列子·黄帝》

范氏有子，曰：子华，善养私名，举国服之；有宠于晋君，不仕而居三卿之右（上）。目所偏视（看重），晋国爵之；口所偏肥（鄙薄），晋国黜（chù 贬）之。游其庭者侔（móu 等同）于朝。子华使其侠客以智鄙（聪明者与愚蠢者）相攻，强弱相凌（相侵）。虽伤破于前，不用介意。终日夜以此为戏乐（娱乐），国殆（几乎）成俗。

禾生、子伯，范氏之上客。出行，经坰（jiōng 郊野）外，宿于田更（老农夫）商丘开之舍。中夜，禾生、子伯二人相与言子华之名势，能使存者亡，亡者存；富者贫，贫者富。商丘开先窘（jiǒng 穷困）于饥寒，潜于牖（yǒu 窗户）北听之。因假（借）粮荷畚（běn 筐子）之（去）子华之门。

子华之门徒皆世族也，缟衣乘轩，缓步阔视。顾见商丘开年老力弱，面目黎黑（lí hēi 黝黑），衣冠不检，莫不眲（nè 轻视）之。既而狎侮（xiá wǔ 侮弄）欺诒（qī dài 欺骗），㧙拟挨抌（㧙tǎng：棰打。拟bì：推击。挨āi：推搡。抌dǎn：击背），亡（无）所不为。商丘开常无愠容（愤怒的神色），而诸客之技单（戏弄的手法用尽），惫（疲）于戏笑。

遂与商丘开俱（一起）乘高台，于众中漫言曰："有能自投下者，赏百金。"众皆竞应。商丘开以为信然，遂先投下，形若飞鸟，扬于地，肌骨无毁。范氏之党以为偶然，未讵（jù 曾）怪也。

因复指河曲之淫隈（yín wēi 水深处）曰："彼中有宝珠，泳可得也。"商丘开复从而泳之。既出，果得珠焉。众昉（fǎng 开始）同疑。子华昉令豫（参与）内食衣帛之次（地位）。

俄而，范氏之藏大火（失火）。子华曰："若能入火取锦者，从所得多少赏若。"商丘开往无难色，入火往还，埃不漫，身不焦。

范氏之党以为有道，乃共谢之曰："吾不知子之有道而诞（dàn 欺骗）子，吾不知子之神人而辱子。子其愚我也，子其聋我也，子其盲我也。敢问其道。"

商丘开曰："吾亡道。虽吾之心，亦不知所以。虽然，有一于此，试与子言之。曩（nǎng 往日）二客之宿吾舍也，闻誉范氏之势，能使存者亡，亡者存；富者贫，贫者富。吾诚之无二心，故不远而来。及来，以子党之言皆实也，唯恐诚之不至，行之不及，不知形体之所措（cuò 置），利害之所存也。心一而已。物亡迕（wǔ 违）者，如斯而已（如此而已）。今昉知子党之诞我，我内藏猜虑，外矜（jīn 拘谨）观听，追幸昔日之不焦溺也，怛然内热，惕然震悸（zhèn jì 震惊恐惧）。水火岂复可近哉？"

自此之后，范氏门徒路遇乞儿马医，弗敢辱也，必下车而揖之。

牢我（人名：牢予，字子我。孔子的学生）闻之，以告仲尼。仲尼曰："汝弗知乎？夫，至信之人，可以感物也。动天地，感鬼神，横六合（成玄英疏："六合，天地四方。"）而无逆者，岂但（不仅）履危险，入水火而已哉？商丘开信伪物（欺瞒）犹不逆，况彼我皆诚哉？小子识之！"

译文：晋国六大贵族之一的范氏家族有个儿子叫子华，他很会树立自己的声誉，举国上下都屈从他。他受到晋国君主的宠爱，虽然没有官爵，势力却在三卿大夫之上。他眼中瞧得起的人，晋国就会赏赐这个人。他若讨厌谁，晋国便贬斥谁。和子华来往的人，声势如同在朝官吏一样显赫。子华指使他的门客：聪明者与愚蠢者互相攻击，强壮者与软弱者互相侵犯。即使在他眼前争斗得皮破肉绽，子华也无动于衷。成天用这种方法取乐的行为，已经在全国形成风气。

禾生和子伯，是范家门徒中的上等客。有一次，他们出远门到郊野，借住在农夫商丘开的茅草屋里。半夜里，禾生与子伯谈论子华的名声与势力，说他能让活人死去，死去的人能再复活；能使富有的人变穷，让贫穷的人变得富有。商丘开当时正陷入饥寒窘迫中，他在窗外偷听到他们的言论。于是第二天，商丘开借了些干粮装入草袋，前往投奔子华门下。

子华的门客都是贵族子弟，身着丝绸素衣，乘坐辇马拉车，高视阔步，目空一切。看见商丘开年老体弱，面色黑瘦，衣冠不整洁，没有一个不轻视地的。于是众门客鄙视、侮弄、欺瞒、推操、捶打他，无所不为。商丘开面对众门客的羞辱无动于衷。日子久了众门客的花招用尽之后，也懒得再戏弄他。

有一次，商丘开跟着众门客登上一处高台，众人中有人随口说："谁能从高台上跳下去，赏金一百。"众人呼应着要跳下高台，商丘开信以为真，纵身一跃跳了下去。只见他身轻如燕，翩然落地，身骨无损，毫发无伤。范家的众门客以为这只是偶然之事，不曾觉得奇怪。

有人指着一处水湾说："那里有珍珠，潜到水底便可获得。"商丘开二话无说，跃身一跳潜入水底。等到他浮出水面时，果真得到珍珠。这时众门客开始疑惑起来。子华也因此让商丘开同其它门客一样娱乐、吃肉，穿绸缎。

不久，范家储藏锦缎的仓房燃起大火，子华十分焦急地喊到："谁能钻入火中取出锦缎，以取出的多寡行赏。"商丘开面无难色，神色不慌，立即冲进火海，来来去去多次，尘埃不沾身，体无烧伤痕。

范家门客都认为商丘开有神道法术，共同向他请罪说："我们不知道您如此神通而欺辱您，也不知道您是神人而羞辱您，您就把我们这些俗人当做蠢人、当做聋子、当做瞎子吧。请问：您修炼的是什么神道法术？"

商丘开不知所措地说："我没有修炼神道法术。其实我也不明白为什么会这样。虽然如此，我还是有件事尝试着与你们说一说，先前你们中的两位门客借宿在我家，我听到他们赞誉范家的权势。他们说：范家的权势能使活人死去，也能让死亡之人复活；能让富贵人家变成穷人，也能让穷人变为富贵之人。我诚然相信了他们所讲的一切。于是，不辞远道前来投靠。来到这里，我把你们所说的每句话都当真，只怕自己的心意不够真诚，行动上不够积极，从来没有考虑自己的身体如何，也没有计较利益得失，只想达到你们提出的要求，一切风险都无法阻挡我向你们表达真情实意。现在才明白你们只是拿我寻开心。如此以后，我内心充满猜疑，对外在环境瞻前顾后。回想起前几日没有被火烧焦，没有被水淹死，惊得我胸中阵阵发热，心都要吓出来了。想想看，从今以后水与火我怎么还敢靠近呢？"

从那时起，范家的门客在路上遇见乞丐或马医，再也不敢侮辱，都会主动下车行礼作揖。

孔子的学生宰我听说此事后告诉了老师。孔子说："你难道不明白吗？最诚信的人，能够感化万物。他们的行为能够撼动天地，感动神灵，纵横天地四方无阻挡。岂能只限于踏履危险之地，或闯入水火之中吗？商丘开听从欺瞒他的话语，心中充满必胜的信念，所以能够做出他人不敢做的事情，何况你我都是以诚实立身的人呢？学生们要记住其中的道理。"

寓意：诚心发愿，心无旁骛地去实现愿景，在忘我之境中纵使入火海、潜水底亦无所畏惧。事成之后诸多感慨：原来诚心可感动天地，犹如神助而不自知。

Sincerity from Heart

The Fan family, one of the six great aristocracies in the State of Jin, had a son named Zihua. He excelled at building his own reputation and was respected throughout the country. Favored by the Jin monarch, despite not holding any official rank, his influence surpassed the three ministers of the State. If he took a liking to someone, the State of Jin would reward that person; if he disliked someone, the State of Jin would condemn that person. Those who associated with Zihua enjoyed the same prestige as officials in the court. Zihua ordered his retainers to attack each other, with the wise fighting against the foolish and the strong attacking the weak. Even if they fought violently, tearing flesh and skin, Zihua remained indifferent. The habit of amusing himself throughout the day with those methods had developed into a nationwide trend.

He Sheng and Zi Bo were distinguished guests among the disciples of the Fan family. Once, they traveled to the countryside and borrowed lodging from a farmer named Shangqiu Kai, who lived in a hut made of reeds. At midnight,

Hesheng and Zibo discussed Zihua's reputation and influence, saying that he had the power to make the living dead and the dead come back to life; he could turn the rich into the poor and the poor into the rich. Shangqiu Kai, who was struggling with hunger and cold at that time, overheard their conversation through the window. So the next day, Shangqiu Kai borrowed some dry provisions and packed them into a grass bag, heading to seek refuge under Zihua.

Zihua's guests were all wealthy and powerful nobles, dressed in silk robes and traveling in fancy carriages pulled by fine horses. They walked with haughty strides, ignoring everyone and everything. When they saw Shangqiu Kai, an old and frail man with a dark, lean face and shabbily dressed, none of them failed to look down on him. So they treated him with contempt, mocked him, cheated him, pushed him, and even beat him up, doing whatever they pleased. Shangqiu Kai remained indifferent to the humiliation and mockery from the guests. As time went by, when they had exhausted all their tricks, they no longer bothered to tease him.

One time, Shangqiu Kai followed the other guests to a high platform. Someone among them casually said, "Whoever jumps down from this high platform will receive a reward of a hundred gold coins." Everyone echoed the idea of jumping down, and Shangqiu Kai, taking it seriously, jumped off without hesitation. He looked as light as a swallow, and landed gracefully without any injury to his bones or skin. The guests of the Fan family thought it was just a coincidence and did not find it strange.

Someone pointed to a bay and said, "There are pearls there. You can get them by diving to the bottom of the water." Without hesitation, Shangqiu Kai jumped into the water. When he came up to the surface, he had indeed obtained the pearls. At this point, the guests began to become confused. Zi Hua therefore allowed Shangqiu Kai to enjoy the same entertainments, eat meat, and wear silk as the other guests.

Soon after, a large fire broke out in the warehouse where the Fan family stored their silk fabrics and brocades. Zi Hua called out anxiously, "Whoever can go into the fire and retrieve the silk fabrics will be rewarded based on the quantity they take out." Shangqiu Kai showed no signs of concern or panic. Immediately, he rushed into the inferno, making multiple trips back and forth without any dust adhering to him or any burns on his body.

The guests of the Fan family all believed that Shangqiu Kai possessed supernatural powers, and they apologized to him collectively, saying, "We didn't know that you were so powerful and mistreated you, nor did we realize that you were a deity and disrespected you. Please regard us as foolish mortals, as deaf and blind. May we ask: What supernatural powers have you cultivated?"

Shangqiu Kai was at a loss for words and said, "I have not practiced any supernatural powers. Actually, I don't understand why this happened either. Nevertheless, there is something I would like to try and tell you. Earlier, two of your guests stayed over at my house, and I heard them praising the power and influence of the Fan family. They said, "The power of the Fan family can make the living dead and the dead come back to life; They could turn the rich into the poor and the poor into the rich." I sincerely believed everything they said. Therefore, without hesitation, I traveled a long distance to seek refuge. Upon arriving here, I took every word you said seriously, afraid only that my intentions were not sincere enough and my actions not proactive enough. I never gave any thought to my own health or worried about gain or loss, only hoping to meet your expectations. Nothing could stop me from expressing my sincere feelings to you. Now I realize that you were just mocking me. Since then, my heart is full of suspicion and I hesitate before taking any actions. Thinking back to the past few days, when I narrowly escaped from being burned to a crisp by fire or drowned in water, it scared me to the point where my chest felt hot and my heart seemed ready to leap out. How could I dare to approach fire or water ever again?"

From then on, the guests of the Fan family no longer dared to insult beggars or horse doctors they met on the road. Instead, they would proactively get off their carriages and greet them with bows and courtesies.

Confucius' student Zhai Wo heard about this and told his teacher. Confucius said, "Don't you understand? The most honest person can influence everything. Their sincere actions are capable of touching the hearts of the gods. Unhindered in all directions, across the vast expanse of heaven and earth. Can their influence be limited to merely walking on perilous paths or venturing into fire and water? Shangqiu Kai listened to the words of cheating and deception, filled with the belief of winning, so he could do what others dare not to do. Moreover, you and I are both honest people. Students should bear the lesson in mind."

Meaning: With sincere wishes and undivided attention, one can achieve their vision fearlessly, even if it means walking through fire or diving into the depths of the sea. After accomplishing the task, one will feel a sense of awe as they realize that sincerity can move heaven and earth, like the help of a deity without even realizing it.

商丘开 Sincerity from Heart

有好沤鸟者《列子·黄帝》

海上之人有好沤（ōu 通"鸥"海鸥）鸟者，每旦（每天）之海上，从沤鸟游，沤鸟之至（到）者百住而不止。其父曰："吾闻沤鸟皆从汝游，汝取来，吾玩之。"明日之海上，沤鸟舞而不下也。

故曰：至言去言，至为无为。齐智之所知，则浅矣。

译文：海边有一位渔民很喜欢海鸥。每天划船去海上，都有百只以上的海鸥在他的船边盘旋嬉戏。他的父亲知道后对他说："我听说，你每天去海上都会有许多海鸥在你的船边嬉戏，你何不捉几只回来，让我也玩玩。"第二天他划船来到海上，海鸥盘旋在半空再也不靠近他的船边。

因此而言：高深的言论是大言无言，高明的行为是无所作为。只局限于个人的认知，那就太浅薄了。

寓意：心存算计的言行，天知地知，就连动物都会有所预知。

Seagulls

A man who lived by the sea loved seagulls. Every day, when he goes to sea in a boat, there are more than a hundred seagulls circling and playing beside his boat.

His father said," I heard that seagulls like to play with you. Catch a few for me so that I can play with them too."

The next day, when he went to sea in a boat, the seagulls swooped about in the skies but none came down to him.

Therefore, profound words are words without saying, and wise actions are actions without doing. If one is limited to personal cognition, it is too shallow.

Meaning: When one's words and actions are motivated by schemes and calculations, they are known to Heaven and Earth, and even animals can somehow sense it.

有好沤鸟者 Seagulls

狙公赋茅 《列子·黄帝》

宋有狙（jū 古书中的一种猴。另说：猕猴）公者，爱狙，养之成群。能解狙之意，狙亦得公之心。损其家口，充狙之欲。

俄而（不久）匮（kuì 缺乏）焉，将限其食。恐众狙之不驯于己也，先诳之曰："与若茅，朝三而暮四，足乎？"众狙皆起而怒。

俄而（顷刻）曰："与若茅，朝四而暮三，足乎？"众狙皆伏而喜。

物之以能鄙（néng bǐ 能者与无能者）相笼，皆犹此也。圣人以智笼群愚，亦犹狙公之以智笼众狙也。名实不亏，使其喜怒哉！

译文：宋国有位猕猴公，他很爱猕猴，在家中养了许多猕猴。他能理解猕猴的意愿，猕猴也能理解猕猴公的心意。猕猴公甘愿节省家用，也要尽力满足猕猴的需求。

不久，猕猴公家道中落，无奈之下希望减少猕猴的食量。又怕众猕猴不乐意，于是诓骗群猴说："今后，给你们的橡子早上三颗晚上四颗，够吗？"众猴听了都跳起来表示反对。

顷刻，猕猴公改口说："从现在起给你们橡子，早上四颗，晚上三颗，可以吗？"众猴都趴在地上表示满意。

世间万物之所以用智巧或庸俗的手法进行笼络，都是相似的。圣人以智慧笼络群愚，犹如猕猴公用智慧笼络众猴一样，名义与实际都不亏损，却能使他们欢喜或愤怒。

寓意：同样的事情和数目，换一种说辞，结局竟天差地别。巧妙变通的思维和言辞是智者笼络庸者之手段。

Three at Dawn and Four at Dusk

In the state of Song there was a man who kept monkeys. He was very fond of monkeys and kept a large number of them. He could understand the monkeys and they could also understand him. He reduced the amount of food for his own family in order to satisfy the monkeys' demands.

After a while his family did not have enough to eat, so he wanted to limit the food for the monkeys. But he was afraid that the monkeys would not submit to him. Before doing that he first played a trick on them.

"If I give you three chestnuts in the morning and four in the evening, would that be enough?" he asked the monkeys.

All the monkeys rose up in a fury.

After a short time he said," If I give you four chestnuts in the morning and three in the evening, would that be enough?"

All the monkeys lay on the floor, very happy with this proposal.

People use clever techniques to woo or manipulate others, and these methods are all similar. The wise person employs wisdom to win over the foolish, just as this person uses cunning to charm the monkeys. Neither the nominal nor the actual value is lost in this process, yet it can evoke joy or anger among them.

Meaning: When the same matter and numbers are phrased differently, the outcomes can be vastly different. The ability to think and speak cleverly and flexibly is a means for the wise to win over the mediocre.

狙公赋茅 Three at Dawn and Four at Dusk

悲心更微《列子·周穆王》

燕人生于燕，长于楚，及老而还本国。

过晋国，同行者诳（kuáng 瞒哄）之，指城曰："此燕国之城。"其人愀然（忧愁）变容。指社（土地庙）曰："此若里之社。"乃喟然而叹。指舍曰："此若先人之庐。"乃涓然而泣。指垄（坟头）曰："此若先人之冢。"其人哭不自禁。同行者哑然大笑，曰："予昔绐若（我先前欺骗你），此晋国耳。"其人大惭。

及至燕，真见燕国之城社，真见先人之庐冢，悲心更微。

译文：燕国有一人生在燕国，在楚国长大。等到年老时，他要回到自己出生地燕国养老。

路过晋国时，与他一起同行的人故意诳骗他，指着晋国的城邑说："这就是你们燕国的城邑。"那人听了立刻面有悲容。同行人又指着一座土地庙说："这就是你家乡的土地庙。"那人听了唉声叹气。同行人又指着一处房屋说："这就是你先辈的住所。"那人听罢淌下眼泪。同行人又指着一处坟头说："这就是你家的祖坟。"那人听罢泣不成声。同行人不由地笑了起来说："我先前是在欺骗你的，这里是晋国，现在还没有到达燕国的地界。"那人听罢非常羞愧。

等当真到达了燕国地界后，看到燕国的城邑与神庙，看到先祖们的房屋与坟头，那人的悲痛之情反而减少了许多。

寓意：过度悲伤之后是平静。晋·张湛注："此章明，情有一至，哀乐既过，则向（以前）之所感，皆无欣戚（喜乐与悲伤）者也。"

Return of the Native

A man who was born in the state of Yan grew up in the state of Chu. In his old age he returned to Yan.

On his way he passed the state of Jin. His fellow travellers played a trick on him. They pointed at a city of Jin.

"This is a city of Yan," they said. His face saddened.

They pointed at a tiny temple housing a village god.

"This is the temple of your native village," said they. He heaved a big sigh.

They pointed at a house.

"This is the house of your ancestors," they said. Tears flowed down his cheeks.

They pointed at a mound of earth.

"This is your ancestor's grave," said they. He could not restrain his sobs.

His fellow travellers burst into laughter.

"We were just putting you on. This is still the territory of Jin." He was mortified.

As it turned out, when he reached Yan and really saw the city and village temple as well as his ancester's house and grave, he was even less sentimental than before.

Meaning: After excessive sorrow comes tranquility.

愚公移山《列子·汤问》

太形、王屋（即：太行山、王屋山）二山，方七百里，高万仞（一仞为周尺八尺）。本在冀州之南，河阳之北。（冀州：九州之一。今河北、山西、河南的黄河以北，辽河以西。河阳：今河南省孟县西。）

北山愚公者，年且九十，面山而居。惩（苦于）山北之塞，出入之迂也。聚室而谋，曰："吾与汝毕力平险，指通豫南（黄河以南），达于汉阴（汉水南岸），可乎？"杂然相许（纷纷表示赞同）。

其妻献疑曰："以君之力，曾不能损魁父（小山名）之丘，如太形、王屋何？且焉置土石？"

杂曰："投诸渤海之尾，隐土之北。"

遂率子孙荷担者三夫，叩石垦壤，，箕畚运于渤海之尾。邻人京城氏之孀妻有遗男，始龀（chèn 刚换乳齿。指年幼），跳往助之。寒暑易节，始一反焉。

河曲智叟笑而止之曰："甚矣汝之不惠！以残年余力，曾不能毁山之一毛，其如土石何？

北山愚公长息曰："汝心之固，固不可彻，曾不若孀妻弱子。虽我之死，有子存焉；子又生孙，孙又生子；子又有子，子又有孙；子子孙孙无穷匮也，而山不加增，何苦而不平？"

河曲智叟亡以应。

操蛇之神闻之，惧其不已也，告之于帝。帝感其诚，命夸娥氏二子负二山，一厝（cuò 安置）朔东，一厝雍南。自此，冀之南，汉之阴，无陇断焉。

译文：太行和王屋这两座山，方圆七百里，山高万尺。山体原本在冀州的南面，河阳的北边。

山北住着一位老者名叫愚公，年纪将近九十岁，他的家面对着大山。苦于山北的阻隔，出入都要绕很远的路。于是他召集全家商议，说："我同你们聚合全家的力量搬掉门前的险阻，打通去豫南的路，直达汉阴，你们说可以吗？"大家都异口同声地表示赞同。

唯有他的妻子提出疑问，"凭着咱家的力量，恐怕连魁父这样的小山丘也难以铲平，怎能把太行山、王屋山搬走呢？况且，挖出的土石又该放到哪里去？"

大伙信心十足地说："把它们投到渤海边，隐土以北。"

于是，愚公率领能挑担的子孙三人，开始凿山挖土，挑起簸箕把土石运到渤海边上。他家的邻居京城氏是个寡妇，身边有一个遗腹子刚换过乳牙，也蹦蹦跳跳地前来帮忙。一年的时光，才能走一个来回。

黄河边上有一位名叫智叟的人劝说："你也太不聪惠了，以你的残年余力，恐怕连山的一角也没办法搬走，更何况如此多的土石又该放到何处呢？"

北山愚公长叹一口气，说："你的心太死了，死得一窍不通，你还不如那位寡妇和遗腹子。虽然我会死，但是我的儿子还活着；儿子又生孙子，孙子又生孩子，孩子再生孩子，孩子又有孙子；子子孙孙，无穷无尽也。然而，山不会再增高，怎么能平不了呢？"

河曲智叟无言以对。

山神听到愚公这番话，只怕他干起来没有尽头，连忙禀告上帝。上帝感念愚公的诚意，特意指派夸娥氏的两个儿子背走这两座大山。一座放在朔东，一座放到雍南。从此，冀州的南面、汉水的北面，再也没有山岭阻碍了。

寓意：精诚所至，金石为开，中国传统信仰天人合一，认为人意与"天意"相互感应，锲而不舍又坚忍不拔的意志可感天动地。又言：人诚天助。

To Move Mountains

Taixing and Wangwu are two mountains with an area of seven hundred li square and rise to a great height of thousands of ren. They were originally situated south of Jizhou and north of Heyang.

North of the mountains lived an old man called Yugong (*literally" foolish old man"*) who was nearly ninety years old. Since his home faced the two mountains, he was troubled by the fact that they blocked the way of the inhabitants who had to take a roundabout route whenever they went out. He gathered his family together to discuss the matter.

"Let us do everything in our power to flatten these forbidding mountains so that there is a direct route to the south of Yuzhou reaching the southern bank of the Han River. What do you say?"

Everyone applauded his suggestion. His wife voiced her doubts.

"You are not strong enough even to remove a small hillock like Kuifu. How can you tackle Taixing and Wangwu? And where would you dump the earth and rocks?"

"We can dump it into the edge of the Bo Sea and north of Yintu," said everyone.

Therefore Yugong took with him three sons and grandsons who could carry a load on their shoulders. They broke up rocks and dug up mounds of earth which were transported to the edge of the Bo Sea in baskets. His neighbour, a widow by the name of Jingcheng, had a posthumous son who was just at the age of discarding his silk teeth. This vivacious boy jumped at the chance of giving them a hand. From winter through summer the workers only returned home once.

An old man called Zhisou (*literally "wise old man"*) who lived in Hequ, near a bend of the Yellow River, was amused and dissuaded Yugong.

"How can you be so foolish? With your advanced years and the little strength that you have left, you cannot even destroy a blade of grass on the mountain, not to speak of its earth and stone."

Yugong from north of the mountains heaved a long sigh. "You are so obstinate that you do not use your reason. Even the widow and her little son do better than you. Though I die, my son lives on. My son produces a grandson and in turn the grandson has a son of his own. Sons follow sons and grandsons follow sons. My sons and grandsons go on and on without end but the mountains will not grow in size. Then why worry about not being able to flatten them?"

Zhisou of Hequ was bereft of speech.

The god of the mountains who held a snake in his hand heard about this and was afraid that Yugong would not stop digging at the mountains. He reported the matter to the king of the gods who was moved by Yugong's sincerity. The king commanded the two sons of Kua'eshi, a god with great strength, to carry away the two mountains on their backs: one was put east of Shuozhou and the other south of Yongzhou. From that time onwards no mountain stood between the south of Jizhou and the southern bank of the Han River.

Meaning: Sincerity can move mountains. It is a traditional Chinese belief that man is an integral part of nature. It believes that man's will corresponds with "the will of Heaven", and that the unyielding and persevering will can move heaven and earth. It is also said that Heaven helps those who are sincere.

愚公移山 To Move Mountains

夸父逐日 《列子·汤问》

夸父不量力，欲追日影，逐之于隅谷（yú gǔ 即虞渊。古代神话传说中日落的地方）之际，渴欲得饮。赴饮河、渭（河：黄河。渭：渭河）。河渭不足，将走北饮大泽（大湖）。未至，道渴而死。弃其杖，尸膏肉所浸，生邓林（华沅《山海经校注》："邓林即桃林"。）

邓林弥广数千里焉。

译文：夸父自不量力，想要追逐太阳的影子，一直追到太阳落山之处的隅谷，感到口渴难忍想喝水。他跑到黄河、渭河边，喝干了黄河与渭河还不够，又要去北方的大湖喝水。还没有来得及到达大湖泽，就渴死在半道上。他遗弃的手杖经过尸骨血肉的浸泡，生长出一大片桃林。

桃树林绵延不断，弥漫方圆数千里。

寓意：追逐理想有时在旁人看来好似捕风捉影、不自量力。但不论路途多么遥远，只要身体力行，纵然未至，却依然可以留下曾经奋斗过的痕迹，为后世带来继续前行的便利，正如前人载树，后人乘凉。

In Pursuit of the Sun

A legendary giant Kua Fu, overrating his own abilities, wanted to catch up with the sun. He followed the sun to its setting place at a valley far away and became very thirsty. Badly needing a drink of water, he went to the Yellow River and the River Wei to quench his thirst, but the waters from these two rivers were not sufficient to satisfy him. He decided to go to the great lake in the north to drink its waters. Before he got there he died of thirst on the way.

After being soaked in the blood and flesh of corpses, the abandoned walking stick of Kua Fu grew into a vast peach orchard, which stretched for thousands of miles around.

Meaning: Pursuing ideals may sometimes appear to others as a futile effort or an act of overestimating one's abilities. But no matter how far the journey is, by taking action and putting in the effort, even if the goal is not fully achieved, one can still leave behind traces of their struggles and dedications. This not only provides a testament to their perseverance but also paves the way for future generations to build upon and continue moving forward, just as previous generations planted trees for the shade of those who would come after them.

夸父逐日 In Pursuit of the Sun

两小儿辩斗 《列子·汤问》

孔子东游，见两小儿辩斗。问其故。

一儿曰："我以日始出时去（离）人近，而日中时远也。"

一儿以日初出远，而日中时近也。

一儿曰："日初出大如车盖（古时车上蓬盖），及日中，则如盘盂（盘与盂），此不为远者小，而近者大乎？"

一儿曰："日初出沧沧凉凉，及其日中如探汤（探试沸水），此不为近者热，而远者凉乎？"

孔子不能决也。

两小儿笑曰："孰为汝多知乎？"

译文：孔子去东方旅行，看见路旁两个小孩在争辩，孔子好奇地问他们在争辩什么。

一个小孩说："我认为太阳刚升起时离人近，到了中午时分离人远。"

另一个小孩不同意他的观点，说太阳刚升起时候距离远，而中午时分的太阳离人近。

一个小孩自信地说："太阳刚来升起时，大如车篷，然而到了中午却像个小盘盂。难道这不正是远看显小，近看显大的道理吗？"

另一个小孩不认可，说："为什么太阳刚升起的时候，人身体感到凉飕飕，到了中午就像开水锅那样炎热，难道这不是太阳近了感到炎热，远了感到清凉吗？"

孔子听了各自的理由，也没法决断。

两个小孩看着孔子无奈的表情笑着说："谁说你的知识博大精深呢？"

（太阳的体积，从早上到晚上并没有改变，只是人们眼中所看到的感觉在变。日出时，大地上弥漫着晨雾，晨雾的水分子反射出太阳的光芒，增大了太阳的轮廓，营造出"红日"很大的假相。中午时分，大地上的晨雾已经消散，人们在太阳光的直射下感到炎热。由于早晚的阳光弱，所以早晚时分人们的身体会感到凉意。也可以说：早晚的太阳离地球远，中午时分的太阳离地球近。）

寓意：世间之事有许多看似互相矛盾又难以解释的客观存在，人们习惯从主观意识出发下定结论，但实际上并非是对客观存在的准确解读。如何更全面和相对客观地接近真相？如若从多方面考虑其中的科学道理，用逻辑化的思维方式去辨别、分析与总结，进而拨云见日、不至于言论上互相矛盾。

An Argument about the Sun

When Confucius was travelling in the eastern part of the country, he came upon two children hot in argument, so he asked them to tell him what it was all about.

"I think," said one child," that the sun is near to us at day-break and far away from us at noon."

The other contended that the sun was far away at dawn and nearby at midday.

"When the sun first appears," said one child, "it is as big as the canopy of a carriage, but at noon it is only the size of a plate or a bowl. Well, isn't it true that objects far away seem smaller while those nearby seem bigger?"

"When the sun comes out," pointed out the other, "it is very cool, but at midday it is as hot as putting your hand in boiling water. Well, isn't it true that what is nearer to us is hotter and what is farther off is cooler?"

Confucius was unable to settle the matter for them.

The two children laughed at him, "Who says you are a learned man?"

Meaning: There are many seemingly contradictory and inexplicable objective existences in the world. People are accustomed to drawing conclusions from their subjective consciousness, but in fact, it is not an accurate interpretation of the objective existence. How to approach the truth more comprehensively and relatively objectively? If we consider the scientific principles from multiple perspectives, use logical thinking to identify, analyze, and summarize, we can see through the fog and avoid contradictions in our arguments.

扁鹊换心《列子·汤问》

鲁（鲁国）公扈（hù）、赵（赵国）齐婴，二人有疾，同请扁鹊（战国时名医）求治，扁鹊治之。既同愈。

谓公扈、齐婴曰："汝曩（nǎng 以往）之所疾，自外而干（触犯）府藏者，固药石之所已。今有偕（xié）生之疾（先天性的疾病），与体偕长。今为汝攻之，何如？

二人曰："愿先闻其验。"

扁鹊谓（对）公扈曰："汝志强而气弱，故足于谋而寡于断。齐婴志弱而气强，故少于虑而伤于专。若换汝之心，则均于善矣。"

扁鹊遂饮二人毒酒，迷死三日，剖胸探心，易而置之；投以神药，既悟如初。二人辞归。

于是公扈反齐婴之室（家），而有其妻子，妻子弗识。齐婴亦反公扈之室，有其妻子，妻子亦弗识。二室因相与讼，求辨于扁鹊。扁鹊辨其所由，讼乃已。

译文：鲁国有位名叫公扈的人，和赵国人齐婴同时患病，请扁鹊为他们治病。他们都已被治愈。

扁鹊对公扈、齐婴说："你们二人先前所患的病，都是从外表侵入五脏六腑所造成的，用药物便可治愈。当下你们还有一种先天性的疾病，与你们的身体同生长。今日我再为二位治疗一下，如何？"

二人说："我们愿意听一听造成这种病的根源是什么？"

扁鹊先对公扈说："你的心志强盛，而气质柔弱，所以你善于谋划却缺乏果断的行动；齐婴则是心志柔弱，而气质刚硬，所以欠缺谋虑，而过于专断行事。假若把你俩的心互换一下，你们的缺陷就改善了。"

扁鹊征得他俩同意后，随即给二人服下麻醉的药酒，昏睡三日不醒。扁鹊即刻开胸换心，敷上神奇妙药，两人便醒了过来，伤痕也完好如初。两人谢过扁鹊各自回家。

于是，公扈来到齐婴的家里，高兴地与齐婴妻子说话，妻子却不认识他。齐婴来到公扈的家中，公扈之妻也不认识他。两家人因此争讼至官吏那里，官吏无奈只好请扁鹊前来讲明前因后果。扁鹊将两人为了治病而换心的经过告诉了官吏，他们两家的争讼才算停止。

（古时的先祖认为心是人体的主宰，身体服从心志。虽然他二人的外观没有改变，但心志的改变，就像是换了一个人。）

寓意：每个人的心智决定着他的言行，同时也影响着他的人生轨迹。

Heart Exchange

There was a man named Gong Hu from the state of Lu who fell ill at the same time as Qi Ying from the state of Zhao. He asked Bian Que to treat them. All have been cured.

Bian Que said to Gonghu and Qi Ying, "The illness you both suffered earlier was caused by external factors invading your internal organs, which could be cured with medication. However, there is also a congenital condition that has grown alongside your bodies since birth. Today, I offer to treat you both again. How about that?"

The two men said, "We would like to hear what is the root cause of this illness."

Bian Que first spoke to Gonghu, "Your willpower is strong, but your temperament is tender, so you excel at planning but lack decisive action. On the other hand, Qi Ying has a tender willpower but a rigid temperament, lacking in foresight and being overly abrupt in decision-making. If you could swap hearts, your flaws would be improved."

After obtaining their consent, Bian Que immediately gave them an anesthetic potion, causing them to fall asleep for three days. While they were unconscious, Bian Que performed a surgery to swap their hearts and applied a miraculous medicine. When they woke up, the wounds were healed as if they never existed. They thanked Bian Que and returned to their respective homes.

So, Gonghu went to Qi Ying's house and happily conversed with Qi Ying's wife, who didn't recognize him. When Qi Ying came to Gonghu's house, Gonghu's wife also didn't recognize him. Because of this, both families disputed and ended up taking the matter to court. The officials, at their wits' end, had to invite Bian Que to explain the situation. Bian Que told the officials about how the two men had swapped hearts to cure their illness, and the dispute between the two families ended.

(*Ancestors in ancient times believed that the heart is the master of the human body, and the body is subordinate to the mind. Although the appearance of the two of them has not changed, the change of the mind is like a different person.*)

Meaning: Everyone's mind determines their words and actions, and also affects the trajectory of their life.

薛谭学讴《列子·汤问》

薛谭学讴（ōu 讴歌）于秦青（传说中秦国善于唱歌的人），未穷青之技，自谓尽之，遂辞归。

秦青弗止，饯行于郊衢（jiāo qú 城外大道），抚节（击节）悲歌，声振林木，响遏（è）行云。

薛谭乃谢求反，终身不敢言归。

译文：薛谭向秦青学习唱歌，还没有完全掌握秦青唱歌的技巧，自以为学业有成，便向老师提出请辞回家。

秦青并没有挽留他，送他到城外大道旁，并为薛谭备设践行酒。席间秦青击节高唱悲壮之歌，激昂的歌声撼动道旁的树林，清亮的回声使空中的浮云停驻。

薛谭听了，连忙道歉谢罪，请求继续在门下学徒，终身都不敢再提回家的话。

寓意：拜师学艺以虚心求教为本，如若妄自尊大、半途而废，不仅学艺不精，也失去了提升和修为自身的机会与可能。

A Subtle Hint

Xue Tan took singing lessons from Qin Qing, a famous singer in the state of Qin. Before learning all that Qin had to teach him Xue claimed that he had mastered all of Qin's skills and asked to leave.

Qin did not try to stop him but gave a farewell dinner for him by a main road in the suburbs. There Qin sang a moving song, beating time all the while. The song seemed to stir the trees of the forest and halt the drifting clouds in their tracks.

Xue Tan immediately apologised to his teacher and asked that he be taken back as a pupil. After this, Xue dared not mention going home again throughout his life.

Meaning: Learning from a master should be based on humility. If one is arrogant and gives up halfway, he will not only fail to master the skill, but also miss the opportunity and possibility to improve and cultivate himself.

薛谭学讴 A Subtle Hint

韩娥善歌《列子·汤问》

昔，韩娥东之齐，匮粮，过雍门（春秋时期齐国城门），鬻（yù 卖）歌假食（求食）。既去而余音绕梁欐（lì 屋梁），三日不绝，左右以其人弗去。

过逆旅（旅舍），逆旅人辱之。韩娥因曼声哀哭，一里老幼悲愁，垂涕相对，三日不食。遂而追之。娥还，复为曼声长歌，一里老幼喜跃抃舞（biàn wǔ 拍手而舞），弗能自禁，忘向之悲也。乃厚赂发之。

故雍门之人至今善歌哭，放娥之遗声。

译文：昔日，韩国善于唱歌的韩娥向东去齐国，走到半路干粮不足，经过齐国雍门时，就开始以卖唱求食。离开后，韩娥的歌声依然余音绕梁，三天还在空中回响，附近的人还以为韩娥没有离去。

韩娥路过一处旅馆，旅馆的主人侮辱她无钱住宿。韩娥因悲痛长声哀哭，整个乡里的老幼听到韩娥的哭声，不由地泪流哭泣，三天吃不下饭。韩娥走了，他们急忙追赶。韩娥返回来，为他们唱起欢乐的长歌，乡里的老幼听着欢乐的歌声，情不自禁地拍手而舞，忘却了往日的悲伤。于是大家赠送给韩娥丰厚的财物，送她上路。

从此以后，雍门人一直到现在都善于以歌声、哭声述说心中的喜怒哀乐，这都是韩娥的歌声遗留下的痕迹。

寓意：孟子说："人皆有不忍人之心。"又言："无恻隐之心，非人也。"人大可不必嘲弄和贬低一个身处窘境之人，因为善歌者以情动人，言语的伤害可使歌者痛楚的哭声绕梁三日，并使周遭的人们产生悲痛之情。而反之欢快之声也可绕梁三日，给周遭的人带来手舞足蹈的欢乐。由此可见，人的言行可引发情绪的触动，情绪的触动通过歌声的抒发影响到更多的人。所以，注意言行，乃修行之始。

Han E's Proficient Singing

In the past, Han E, a singer from the state of Han went east to Qi State, but she ran out of food halfway. When she passed the Yongmen of Qi State, she began to sing for food. After leaving, Han E's singing voice lingered in the air for three days, still echoing in the vicinity, making people around believe that she had not left yet.

Han E passed by an inn where the innkeeper insulted her for not having enough money to stay. Han E wept loudly out of her sorrow, and the elderly and the young in the entire village could not help but shed tears and wept for three days, they are unable to eat. When Han E left, they quickly chased after her. When Han E returned, she sang a joyful song, and the elderly and the young in the village couldn't help but clap and dance to the upbeat melody, forgetting their past sorrows. As a result, they presented Han E with generous gifts and saw her off on her journey.

Ever since then, the people of Yongmen have been skilled at expressing their joys and sorrows through singing and weeping, which are all traces left by Han E's singing.

Meaning: Mencius stated, "All men have a heart that cannot bear to see others suffer." He further emphasized, "One who lacks compassion is not truly human." It is unnecessary for one to mock or belittle those who are in difficult situations. Skilled singers are able to move people deeply with their emotions. Hurtful words can cause a singer's sorrowful crying to echo for days, filling the surrounding area with sadness. Conversely, joyful sounds can also resonate for days, bringing happiness and excitement to those around. This demonstrates that one's words and actions have the power to evoke emotional responses, and these responses can be further amplified through the expression of singing. Therefore, it is crucial to be mindful of one's words and actions, as it is the starting point of personal cultivation.

韩娥善歌 Han E's Proficient Singing

造父习御《列子·汤问》

造父之师曰泰豆氏。造父之始从习御也，执礼甚卑，泰豆三年不告。造父执礼愈谨，乃告之曰："古诗言：'良弓之子，必先为箕（编织簸箕）；良冶（liáng yě 精于冶炼铸造的工匠）之子，必先为裘（qiú 皮衣）。'汝先观吾趣。趣如吾，然后六辔（辔：pèi 缰绳 六辔：一车四马）可持，六马可御。"

造父曰："唯命所从。"

泰豆乃立木为涂（途），仅可容足；计步而置，履之而行。趣步往还，无跌失也。

造父学之，三日尽其巧。

泰豆叹曰："子何其敏也！得之捷乎！凡所御者，亦如此也。曩（nǎng 先时）汝之行，得之于足，应之于心。推于御也，齐辑（qí jí 协调驾车的众马，使整齐均一）乎，辔衔（pèi xián 御马的缰绳和嚼子）之际，而急缓乎，唇吻之和，正度（正当的法度）乎，胸臆（心中的想法）之中，而执节（快慢）乎，掌握之间。内得于中心（心意），而外合于马志（意愿），是故能进退履绳（进退中绳：前进后退均合规矩），而旋曲（盘旋曲折）中规矩，取道致远而气力有余。诚得其术也，得之于衔（马嚼子），应之于辔（缰绳）；得之于辔，应之于手；得之于手，应之于心。则不以目视，不以策驱（鞭打），心闲体正，六辔不乱，而二十四蹄所投无差（步调一致）；回旋进退，莫不中节（合乎节拍）。然后舆轮（车轮）之外可使无余辙，马蹄之外可使无余地。未尝（不曾）觉山谷之崄（古同"险"），原隰（平原与低湿之地）之夷，视之一也。吾术穷矣，汝其识之。"

译文：驾驭马车的造父，他的师傅名叫泰豆氏。造父向师傅学习驾驭技术时，非常谦卑有礼。师傅在三年内并没有教他什么。师傅看到造父越发谨言慎行，才对他说："古诗中有句格言：'制造良弓的儿子，要跟随父亲学习制弓，必先学会编织簸箕；铁匠的儿子，要跟随父亲学手艺，必先学会缝制皮衣。'你先观察我驾车的动作，从我的动作中领悟其中的道理，当你感悟出其中的要领之后，你就明白如何驾驭四匹马，进而学会驾驭六匹马的要点。"

造父恭敬地对师傅说："听从师傅教诲。"

于是，泰豆氏竖起一排木桩当作行走途径。木桩的顶端只能容下一只脚，并且以脚步距离安置木桩。师傅脚踏木桩行走。只见他来回往返行动自如，没有跌落也没有闪失。

造父照着师傅的样子，在木桩上来回练习，三天就掌握了其中的要领。

泰豆氏看到徒弟如此灵巧，感叹地说："你怎么这么敏锐？反应如此快捷，驾驭马车也是这个道理。先时，你在木桩上行走得力于脚下，反应出你的心志，你把其中的道理应用在驾驶马车的技巧上。协调马匹的是僵绳与口嚼，缰绳的松紧要与吆喝声相吻合，轻重缓急做到心中有数。然而手中的长鞭只是为了掌握马匹之间的协调，当你感到得心应手，又能合乎马匹的意愿，因此能够达到进退合乎规矩，而且盘旋曲折也能循规蹈矩。所走的路途不论多么遥远，马匹的力气还是绰绰有余。诚然，这就是驾驭车辆的基本要领。你要明白，操控马匹的是马口中的嚼子；操控马嚼子的是缰绳；操控缰绳的是你的双手；操控双手的是你的心境。这样驾驭马车，不用眼睛看，也不用马鞭驱赶，心中悠闲，身态轻松，六条缰绳不乱，而且二十四个马蹄起落有序，盘旋进退无不合乎节拍。然后，车辙之外无余痕，马踏征途无多余。你这样驾驭马车，不觉山高路险，平原湿地皆同如一。我驾驭马车的技能只有这些，你要好好记住它的要点。"

寓意：所谓得心应手，即为心手合一。操纵马匹、驾驭马车的技巧与为人处世的道理都是相通为一。

Zaofu Learned to Drive

Zao Fu, the master of horse driving, had a teacher named Tai Doushi. When learning horse driving skills from his teacher, Zao Fu showed great humility and politeness. For three years, his teacher did not teach him anything. When his teacher saw that Zao Fu was becoming increasingly cautious in his words and actions, he said to him, "There is an ancient saying in poetry: 'The son of a skilled bowmaker must learn to weave baskets before learning to make bows from his father; the son of an ironsmith must learn to sew leather clothes before learning his father's craft.' First, observe my actions when driving a chariot, and understand the principles behind them. When you have grasped the essentials, you will understand how to control four horses, and then you will be able to master the skills of controlling six horses."

Zao Fu respectfully said to his teacher, "I will follow your teachings."

So Tai Doushi set up a row of wooden stakes as a walking path. The tops of the stakes were barely wide enough to accommodate one foot, and they were placed at intervals corresponding to the length of a stride. The teacher walked on the stakes, moving freely back and forth without falling or stumbling.

Following his teacher's example, Zao Fu practiced walking on the wooden stakes for three days and mastered the essentials of it.

Upon seeing his apprentice's dexterity, Tai Doushi exclaimed with admiration, "How agile are you? Your responsiveness is so quick, and it's the same principle when driving a chariot. Earlier, when you walked on the stakes, your feet were the key, reflecting your determination. Apply this principle to the skill of driving a chariot. The reins and the bit are used to coordinate the horses, and the tightness of the reins should match the commands. You should have a clear understanding of the weights and measures. However, the long whip in your hand is only to maintain coordination among the horses. When you feel comfortable and confident, and can also satisfy the horses' wishes, you can achieve a balance between advance and retreat, and the turns and twists can also follow the rules. No matter how distant the road is, the horses' strength will still be sufficient. Indeed, this is the basic essence of driving a chariot. You must understand that it is the bit in the horse's mouth that controls the horse; it is the reins that control the bit; it is your hands that control the reins; and it is your mindset that controls your hands. When driving a chariot like this, you don't need to look with your eyes or whip the horses. Your mind is at ease, your posture is relaxed, the six reins are not tangled, and the twenty-four hoofbeats are orderly. The turns, advances, and retreats are all in rhythm. Then, there is no extra trace outside the wheel tracks, and the horses' steps are not wasted. When you drive the chariot like this, you don't feel the dangers of the mountain paths or the differences between the plains and wetlands. These are the only skills I have in driving a chariot, and you must remember the essentials well."

Meaning: The phrase "doing things with ease and confidence" means achieving a unity of mind and hand. The skills of controlling horses and driving a chariot are interchangeable with the principles of conducting oneself in life.

治大者不治细《列子·杨朱》

杨朱见梁王，言治天下如运诸常。

梁王（魏国国君·梁惠王）曰："先生有一妻一妾而不能治，三亩之园而不能芸（耘）；而言治天下如运诸掌，何也？"

对曰："君见其牧羊者乎？百羊而群，使五尺童子荷棰（chuí 棰杖）而随之，欲东而东，欲西而西。使尧牵一羊，舜荷棰而随之，则不能前矣。且臣闻之：吞舟之鱼，不游支流；鸿鹄高飞，不集洿（不流动的浊水）池。何则？其极远也。黄钟大吕不可从烦奏（欢快的节奏）之舞，何则？其音疏也。将治大者不治细，成大功者不成小，此之谓矣。"

译文：杨朱觐见梁惠王，自己夸口说治理天下如同反掌那么容易。

梁惠王说："听说先生有一妻一妾，尚不能和睦相处，也不能耕耘自己的三亩田园，却夸口说治理天下易如反掌，这是从何说起？"

杨朱面无难色地说："君主您见过牧童吗？成百只的羊群，指派一个五尺高的男童扛着一根棰杖尾随着，指挥羊群往东就往东，向西就向西。即使尧王在世，手牵着一只羊，舜帝手拿棰杖在后面赶羊，羊也不会温顺地朝前走。况且，我还听说，一口能够吞下船只的大鱼，从来不会游到水浅的支流中；鸿鹄飞得又高又远，从来不会翔集在死水湖池，为什么会这样呢？这都是因为它们有远大的目标。黄钟的音色称谓"阳"；大吕的音色称谓"阴"，阳声为首，阴声为和，只能奏出庄严的祭祀神曲，不能伴奏欢快的舞曲，为什么会这样呢？因为黄钟大吕所发出的声音疏远辽阔。所以说，管理国家大事的重臣，不会顾及生活琐事，讲的就是这个道理。"

寓意：胸怀大志者往往不纠结于生活细碎琐事。

Govern the Big, Not the Small

Yang Zhu visited King Hui of Liang and boasted that governing the country was as easy as turning over one's palm.

King Hui of Liang said, "I heard that you, sir, have a wife and a concubine, but you cannot live harmoniously with them, nor can you cultivate your own three *mu*[1] of farmland. Yet you boast that governing the world is as easy as turning over one's palm. Where does this come from?"

Yang Zhu replied without any hint of embarrassment, "Have you ever seen a shepherd boy, my king? With hundreds of sheep, a five-foot-tall boy is appointed to follow them while carrying a cudgel, directing the sheep to go east or west as he commands. Even if Emperor Yao were alive, leading a sheep by the hand, and Emperor Shun chasing it with a cudgel, the sheep would not meekly move forward. Besides, I have also heard that a big fish that can swallow a boat will never swim in shallow tributaries; a swan flies high and far, and will never hover over stagnant lakes. Why is that? It's because they have lofty goals. The tone of the Huangzhong bell is called "Yang," and the tone of the Dalv bell is called "Yin." Yang is the dominant sound, and Yin is the harmonious one, capable only of playing solemn sacrificial hymns, not

---

[1] Mu: The unit of measurement for land area in the municipal system.

lively dance music. Why is that? Because the sound of Huangzhong and Dalv is distant and vast. So, ministers who are in charge of important state affairs will not concern themselves with trivial matters. That's the reason."

Meaning: Those who have lofty aspirations often do not get bogged down in trivial matters of life.

列子学射《列子·说符》

列子学射，中（中了靶心）矣，请于关伊子。

尹子曰："子知子之所以（怎么）中者乎？"

对曰："弗知也。"

关尹子曰："未可。"

退而习之。三年，又以报关尹子。

尹子曰："子知子之所以中乎？"

列子曰："知之矣。"

关伊子曰："可矣，守而勿失也。非独射也，为国与身亦皆如之。故，圣人不察存亡（结果），而察其所以然。"

译文：列子学习射箭，射中了靶心，很满意地告诉关尹子。关尹子问他："你知道是怎么射中靶心的吗？"

列子回答说："不知道。"

关于说："你不知道怎样射中的，那你的手法还不成熟。"

列子返回家中继续苦练射箭。三年之后，他再次拜见关尹子。

关尹子问他："你知道怎么射中靶心了吗？"

列子回答："我已知道是怎么射中的。"

关尹子说："这回可以了，保持这样的认知，不要迷失了。你要清晰地认识到凡事都有一定的规律，在规律中思考形成的原因，才能提升自己。这不仅仅只是射箭，这样的认知也可以用于治国以及修身养性。因此，圣人不看重事物得出的结果，而看重造成这样结果的原因是什么。"

寓意：圣人论断事物并不以单纯的结果为准则，而是追根溯源，找到事物的成因。提升认知、为人处世乃至治国之道皆从事物的本源思考，进而逐渐发现其中的客观规律，从偶然与必然中找到切实可行、行之有效的方法。

How and Why

Liezi often managed to hit the bull's eye when shooting with his bow and arrows. Once he asked the advice of Guan Yinzi.

"Do you know why you could hit the bull's eye?" asked Guan Yinzi.

"No, I don't," replied Liezi.

"Then you still have much to learn."

Liezi returned home and practised his archery for three years before going once more to ask the advice of Guan Yinzi.

"Do you know why you could hit the bull's eye?" asked Guan Yinzi.

"Yes, I do," replied Liezi.

"Then you have succeeded. Make sure you do not forget what you have learned."

This does not only apply to archery. The rise and fall of nations, the virtues and vices of men all have reasons behind them.

Meaning: The sage judges things not just by the simple outcome, but traces back to the origin and finds the cause of things. Improving cognition, dealing with people, and even governing the country all start from thinking about the origin of things, and gradually discovering the objective laws among them, and finding practical and effective methods from chance and necessity.

施氏与孟氏《列子·说符》

鲁（鲁国）施氏有二子，其一好学，其一好兵。好学者以术干齐侯，齐侯纳之，以为诸公子之傅（老师）。好兵者之楚，以法（兵法）干楚王，王悦之，以为军正。禄富其家，爵荣其亲。

施化之邻人孟氏同有二子，所业亦同，而窘于贫。羡施氏之有，因从请进趋之方。二子以实告孟氏。

孟氏之一子之秦，以术干秦王。秦王曰："当今诸侯力争，所务兵食而已。若用仁义治吾国，是灭亡之道。"遂宫（古代宫刑。约始于商周时期）而放之。

其一子之卫，以法干卫侯。卫侯曰："吾弱国也，而摄（shè 迫近）乎大国之间。大国吾事之，小国吾抚之，是求安之道。若赖兵权，灭亡可待矣。若全而归之，适于他国，为吾之患不轻矣。"遂刖（yuè 砍掉脚的酷刑）之，而还诸鲁。

既反（返回），孟氏之父子叩胸而让（责怪）施氏。施氏曰："凡得时者昌，失时者亡。子道与吾同，而功与吾异，失时者也，非行之谬也。且，天下理无常是，事无常非。先日所用，今或弃之；今之所弃，后或用之。此用与不用，无定是非也。投隙（伺机）抵时，应事无方，属乎智。智苟（如果）不足，使若（如）博如孔丘，术如吕尚（姜太公），焉往而不穷哉？"

孟氏父子舍然无愠容（愤怒的神色），曰："吾知之矣，子勿重言（多言）！"

译文：鲁国姓施的家中有两个儿子，一个爱好儒家学说，一个喜好兵法。前者以儒术之长去齐侯那里求职，齐侯接纳了他，让他做公子们的老师。后者去了楚国，以兵法之长觐见楚王，楚王很赏识他，任命他为军中执法官。他俩人的爵位与俸禄让所有的亲戚都感到荣耀。

施家的邻居孟氏也有两个儿子，所学的与施家子弟相同，却陷入贫困的窘迫之中。他们很羡慕施家富足，便去施家请教谋求功名的方法。施家的两个儿子如实地告诉了他们。

于是，孟家的一个儿子去了秦国，以儒学之术向秦王求职，秦王对他说："如今的各国诸侯都是以武力争夺天下霸主，当务之急是预备兵马粮草。如果用仁义道德治理国事，必然是一条亡国之路。"随后，对他施予宫刑，驱逐出秦国。

孟家的另一个儿子来到卫国，以兵法之策向卫侯求职。卫侯说："我国是一个弱小的周家，夹在几个大国之间勉强生存。我们面对强国只能顺从，面对弱国则尽力安抚，这才是我们求平安的国策。如果依赖军事强国的策略，那么离亡国就指日可待了。如果，让你全身而退，再去别的国家去游说，必然会为我国留下后患。"于是，对他实施砍脚的酷刑，送还给鲁国。

回家后，孟家父子捶胸顿脚地前去指责施家。施家说："俗话常说：'凡是得到时机的就能昌盛，失去时机的就会灭亡。'你们所学的虽然同我们一样，取得的结果却不相同。这是因为你们选择的对象与时机不当。并不是你们的行为有什么差错。况且，天下之理没有常对常错的区别。以前所用的法则，今日可能否定或抛弃；当

— 102 —

下所抛弃的原则，后世可能又要遵照执行。用与不用，并不是永恒不变，都是伺机而动。因为世间所有的事物都在不断变化中，所以应对事态变化，并没有固定的良方，事事处处都需要清醒的头脑与智慧，才能化险为夷转危为安。自己的智慧不足以应对事态变化，即使你有孔子的博学、姜太公的兵法，也无法应对千变万化的时局。"

孟家父子此时才明白其中的端倪，收起脸上的恼怒神色，连忙说："我们明白了其中的道理，请不必再多言了。"

寓意："识时务者为俊杰。"时局因"时"与"势"而变，局势千变万化。懂得技法、知识、兵法等等，并不代表拥有智慧。所谓智慧，则是：在不同的环境条件下，能够敏锐地察觉到事态的发展趋势，恰逢时机地施展才干。

Two Sons

There were two sons in the family surnamed Shi of the state of Lu, one of whom loved Confucianism, and the other preferred military strategy. The former went to the Marquis of Qi apply for a job with his expertise in Confucianism and was accepted, making him the teacher of the princes. The latter went to the King of Chu with his expertise in military strategy, and the king appreciated him very much, appointing him as the law enforcement officer in the army. Their ranks and salaries made all their relatives feel proud.

The Meng family, neighbors of the Shi family, also had two sons who studied the same subjects as the Shi family, but they were trapped in poverty and desperation. They envied the Shi family's affluence and went to them for advice on how to seek fame and fortune. The two sons of Shi family told them honestly.

So, one of the Meng family's sons went to the State of Qin and sought employment with the King of Qin, offering his expertise in Confucianism. The King of Qin replied to him, "Nowadays, all the vassal states are competing for supremacy with military might. Our priority is to prepare our troops, horses, and provisions. If we govern the country with morality and righteousness, it will undoubtedly lead to our nation's ruin." Subsequently, he sentenced him to palace punishment and expelled him from Qin.

The other son of the Meng family went to the State of Wei and applied for a position with the Marquis of Wei, offering his military strategy. The Marquis of Wei replied, "Our country is a small state of the Zhou dynasty, struggling to survive amidst several powerful states. When faced with stronger countries, we have no choice but to submit; when dealing with weaker ones, we do our best to appease them. This is our national policy for seeking peace. If we rely on military might as our strategy, our doom will be imminent. If I let you go unharmed and you continue to lobby other countries, it will undoubtedly pose a future threat to our country." So, as a punishment, his feet were chopped off and he was sent back to the State of Lu.

After returning home, the father and son of the Meng family went to accuse the Shi family, pounding their chests and stamping their feet in anger. The Shi family replied, "As the saying goes, 'Those who seize the opportunity will prosper, and those who miss it will perish.' Although you have learned the same things as us, you have achieved different results. This is because you have chosen the wrong targets and timings. It is not that you have done anything wrong. Moreover, there is no permanent distinction between right and wrong in the principles of the world. Principles that were once followed may be denied or discarded today, while those that are currently discarded may be followed again in the future. Whether to use or discard them is not eternal, but rather depends on the opportunities available. Because all things in the world are constantly changing, there is no fixed formula for dealing with changing situations. We need a clear mind and wisdom everywhere to turn danger into safety. If one's wisdom is not enough to deal with changing situations, even if he has Confucius's erudition and Jiang Tai Gong's military strategy, he will not be able to cope with the ever-changing situation."

The Meng family understood the clues behind it at this moment. They put away the angry expressions on their faces, and quickly said, "We understand the principle behind it. Please don't say more."

Meaning: "He who knows the times is a wise man." The situation changes due to the "times" and "trends," and the situation is constantly changing. Knowing techniques, knowledge, military strategy, etc., does not necessarily mean having wisdom. The so-called wisdom is the ability to keenly perceive the development trend of the situation under different environmental conditions and express talents at the opportune time.

道见桑妇《列子·说符》

晋文公出会（晋国国君，名重耳。出会：与诸侯会师），欲伐卫，公子锄仰天而笑。公问何笑。

曰："臣笑邻之人，有送其妻适（往）私家者，道见桑妇，悦而与言。然，顾视其妻，亦有招之者矣。臣窃笑此也。"

公寤（wù 古同"悟"）其言，乃止。引师而还，未至，而有伐其北鄙者矣。

译文：晋国君主重耳出行与诸侯会师，在返回晋国的半道上，想顺路攻伐卫国，公子锄听到他说的话后仰天大笑。重耳不解地问他为何而笑？

公子锄说："我笑一位邻居家的主人，他送妻子回娘家的半路上，看见路旁一位采桑叶的妇人，就微笑着前去搭讪。然而他回头看见妻子，也有人正朝他妻子招手示意。我正是为此而感到可笑啊！"

重耳领悟到他话中的含义，放弃了攻伐卫国的念头。他带领的大军还没有回到晋国，就有快马禀告：他国正在攻伐晋国的北部边城。

寓意：算计他人之时竟忽略了自身难保，制定决策不应临时起意。

Served with the Same Sauce

Duke Wen of the state of Jin led his army out of Jin with the intention of attacking the state of Wei. On seeing this, his son Prince Chu threw back his head and laughed.

"Why are you laughing?" asked the duke.

"I am laughing at my neighbour," replied his son. "He was escorting his wife to her father's house. On the way, he saw a woman picking mulberry leaves and he boldly struck up a friendly conversation with her. But when he turned to look for his wife, he saw that someone was trying to flirt with her too. I just find this incident very diverting."

The duke understood his son's meaning. He gave up the idea of attacking Wei and brought his troops home. Before he got there the northern border of his state came under attack.

Meaning: When scheming against others, one often forgets one's own precarious situation. Decision-making should not be done on the spur of the moment.

晋国苦盗《列子·说符》

晋国苦盗。有郄（xì 同隙）雍者，能视盗之貌，察其眉睫之间，而得其情。晋侯使视盗，千百无遗一焉。

晋侯大喜，告赵文子（文子：人名，姓辛，名钘 xíng 为老子弟子，赵国人）曰："吾得一人，而一国盗为尽矣，奚（何）用多为？"

文子曰："吾君恃（shì 依赖）伺察而得盗，盗不尽矣，且郄雍必不得其死焉。"

俄而群盗谋曰："吾所穷者，郄雍也。"遂共盗而残之。

晋侯闻而大骇（hài 惊惧），立召文子而告之曰："果如子言，郄雍死矣！然取盗何方？"

文子曰："周谚有言：察见渊鱼者不祥，智料隐匿者有殃。且，君欲无盗，莫若（不如）举贤而任之；使教明于上，化行于下，民有耻心，则何盗之为？"

于是，用随会（人名）知政（主持政务），而群盗奔秦焉。

译文：晋国苦于盗贼为患。有个叫郄雍人，自荐能够审视盗贼的面相，只要观察眉目神态，就能分辨是不是盗贼。晋侯派他识别盗贼，千百个当中无一差错。

晋侯十分高兴，把此事告诉给文子说："我得到一人，全国的盗贼就捉得差不多了，还要那么多捕快干什么呢？"

文子说："您依靠察看面相捉拿盗贼，这样的作法，盗贼是捉不完的。而且郄雍一定不会好死。"

过了不久，盗贼们聚在一齐商讨说："我们已经走投无路了，这都是郄雍造成的。"于是，盗贼们共谋杀了郄雍。

晋侯听说之后大为震惊，立刻召见文子对他说："果真应了你的话，现在郄雍已经死了，然而取缔盗贼还有什么更好的妙招吗？"

文子说："周代谚语说：眼力能察看到深渊里游鱼的人不吉祥；有智慧能够预料隐匿之事的人有祸殃。况且，君主只是希望天下无盗贼而已，并不希望因制止偷盗而演变成杀人。如果真想根除偷盗之风，不如举荐贤才，使政教昌明于上，感化民风于下，民众有了羞耻之心，哪里还会去做盗贼呢？"

于是，晋侯任用随会主持朝政，在他的感召之下，民众渐渐树立起以盗为耻的社会风气，只有死不悔改的少数盗贼悄悄投奔到秦国去了。

寓意：所谓察渊者不祥，意即：识别到人性之恶，但却用粗略的手法摒除恶果，不仅无法根治，反而容易引火烧身。若要根治某种不良民风，不如使政令清明，优化民风，从根源解决问题。

Struggling with Theft

The State of Jin was plagued by thieves. There was a man named Xi Yong, who volunteered to able to discern the facial features of thieves and claimed that he could distinguish whether a person was a thief or not just by observing his facial expressions. The Duke of Jin sent him to identify the thieves, and he never made a mistake among hundreds of people.

The Duke of Jin was very pleased and told Wenzi, "I have found a person who can capture almost all the thieves in the country. Why do we still need so many constables?"

Wenzi said, "Your method of capturing thieves by observing their facial features will never eliminate all of them. Moreover, Xi Yong is destined to have an untimely death."

Not long after, the thieves gathered together and discussed, "We have nowhere to turn, and it's all because of Xi Yong." So, they conspired to kill Xi Yong.

After hearing the news, the Duke of Jin was deeply shocked and immediately summoned Wenzi to say to him, "You were right. Now Xi Yong is dead, but is there any better strategy to eliminate thieves?"

Wenzi said, "There is a saying in the Zhou Dynasty: Those who have the eyes to see the fish swimming in the abyss are not auspicious; those who have wisdom to predict hidden matters will suffer misfortune. Besides, you only hope that there will be no thieves in the world, not that stopping theft will turn into murder. If we really want to eliminate the culture of stealing, it is better to recommend talents, make politics clear and prosperous at the top, influence the people's customs below, and let the people have a sense of shame. Then who would still want to be a thief?"

Therefore, the Duke of Jin appointed Sui Hui to preside over the government affairs. Under his influence and guidance, the people gradually established a social sentiment that considers stealing shameful. Only a few recalcitrant thieves who refused to repent secretly fled to the State of Qin.

Meaning: The phrase "The wise man who delves too deeply into the abyss is cursed." implies that recognizing the evil in human nature but trying to eliminate its consequences with crude methods not only fails to address the root cause, but may also cause more trouble. Instead of using rough methods to address unhealthy social customs, it is better to make the policies clear, improve the social customs, and tackle the problem at its source.

九方皋相马《列子·说符》

秦穆公谓伯乐曰:"子之年长矣,子姓(泛指子孙后辈)有可使求马者乎?"

伯乐对曰:"良马可形容筋骨相也。天下之马者(犹言:天下无双的宝马),若灭若没,若亡若失,若比者(近来)绝尘弭辙(弥漫痕迹)。臣之子皆下才也,可告以良马,不可告以天下之马也。臣有所与共担纆(dān mò 张湛注:'负索薪菜,盖贱役者。')薪菜(拾柴)者,有九方皋,此其于马,非臣之下也。请见之。"

穆公见之,使行求马。

三月而反,报曰:"已得之矣,在沙丘。"

穆公曰:"何马也?"

对曰:"牝而黄。"

使人往取之,牡而骊。

穆公不说(悦),召伯乐而谓之曰:"败矣,子所使求马者:色物、牝牡(pìn mǔ 雌雄)当弗能知,又何马之能知也?"

伯乐喟然太息曰:"一至于此乎!是乃其所以千万臣而无数者也。若皋之所观天机也,得其精而忘其粗,在其内而忘其外;见其所见,不见其所不见;视其所视,而遗其所不视,若皋之相者,乃有贵乎马者也。"

马至,果天下之马也。

译文:秦穆公对伯乐说:"你的年龄已高,你的子孙中有没有识别良马的后人?"

伯乐回禀:"一匹优良的好马,可以从马的筋骨中看出来。天下的宝马则不然,它的神色迷离,若隐若显,奔跑时腾空而起,宛如追风逐电,不留痕迹。我的子孙都是一些庸才,可以教导他们什么是良马,却无法教导他们怎么辨别宝马。我们一同挑担拾柴的友人中,有一位名叫九方皋的人,他相马的能力不在我之下。请君主召见此人。"

秦穆公即刻下命,召九方皋觐见,派遣他前去寻找天下宝马。

三个月过后,九方皋返回禀告:"宝马已经找到,在沙丘的一个地方。"

秦穆公连忙问:"是一匹怎样的马?"

九方皋回禀:"是一匹母马,马的皮毛是黄色的。"

秦穆公随即派遣使者前去取马,却发现是一匹黑色的公马。

秦穆公接到使者禀告后很不乐意,急召伯乐说:"糟糕,你推荐的那个相马人连马的毛色、公母都分不清楚,怎能知道马的优劣呢?"

伯乐深叹了一口气,说:"竟然如此绝妙,这正是他胜过我千万倍而不止的原因。九方皋所要观察的是马的天赋。他看重马的精粹,而疏忽了马的表象;注意马匹的特质,而忽略马匹的皮毛;只看必须看的,不看不必看的;只观察必须观察的,忽略了不必仔细观察的。像九方皋这样的相马人,比一般相马人拥有更可贵的特质。

等到这匹马牵来时,果真是一匹天下宝马。

寓意:常言:"宝马常有而伯乐不常有。"相马之术胜于伯乐的九方皋之所以技高一筹在于他看重的是马匹的精髓而忽略甚至错认了它的外表。从中得到的启示:人们往往只注意外在,但真正可贵的是内在的品质。

True Discernment

Duke Mu of the state of Qin said to Bo Le who was famous for his ability to judge horses, "Sir, you are advanced in years. Is there anyone in your family I could send to look for fine steed?"

"Good horses can be judged by observing their appearance, by looking at the bones and muscles," replied Bo Le. "But for a rare horse that has no equal, its characteristics are elusive, almost impossible to pin down. It is so swift and its tread so light that when it gallops, its hoofs do not stir the dust and no prints are left behind. My sons have little ability. They could tell you what good horses are like, but they could say nothing about an incomparable steed. I have a friend who used to chop and carry firewood with me, Jiufang Gao. He is, to say the least, as good a judge of horses as I am. Please send for him."

The duke summoned Jiufang Gao and commissioned him to find an unequalled horse. After three months he reported back to the duke.

"I have found it, in a place called Shaqiu."

"What sort of a horse is it?" asked the duke.

"It is a bay mare," replied Jiufang Gao.

The duke sent some men to bring the horse back. It turned out to be a male horse black in colour. The duke was displeased. He summoned Bo Le.

"It is too bad," said the duke, "the man you recommended to send on a search for fine horses cannot even distinguish between horses and mares or the different colours of their coats. What can he know about horses?"

Bo Le heaved a sigh. "Has it come to this? This is exactly where his expertise is a thousand times better than mine and is too deep to fathom. What he sees is the mystery of Nature. He captures the essence and forgets the dross. He gets the content and forgets the form. He only sees what he is looking for and does not see what he considers unimportant. He only observes what is worthy of observation and leaves out what he deems not deserving attention. In fact, Jiufang Gao's ability is much more valuable than the mere competence to judge the merit of a horse."

When the horse arrived, it really turned out to be an incomparable steed.

Meaning: A proverb goes, "Fine horses are common, but those who can appreciate them are rare." Jiu Fanggao, a horse evaluator whose skills surpassed even Bo Le, he was excelled because he valued the essence of the horse, ignoring or even misidentifying its appearance. The lesson we can learn from this is that people often only pay attention to external appearance, but what is truly valuable is the internal qualities.

牛缺遇盗之戒《列子·说符》

牛缺者，上地（秦国地方名）之大儒也。下之邯郸（战国时赵国都城），遇盗于耦沙（水名，今，河北刑台沙河）之中，尽取其衣装车马，牛步而去。视之，欢然无忧吝之色。盗追而问其故。曰："君子不以所养，害其所养。"（前'所养'指物；后'所养'指身体）

盗曰："嘻：贤矣夫！"既而相谓曰："以彼之贤，往见赵君，使以我为，必困我。不如杀之。"乃相与追而杀之。

燕人闻之，聚族相戒，曰："遇盗，莫如上地之牛缺也！"皆受教。

俄而其弟适秦。至关下（函谷关。今，河南灵宝东北），果遇盗；忆其兄之戒，因与盗力争。既而不如，又追而以卑辞请物。盗怒曰："吾活汝弘（hóng 宽宏大度）矣，而追吾不已，迹将箸（显露）焉。既为盗矣，仁将焉在？"遂杀之，又傍（páng 牵连）害其党四五人焉。

译文：牛缺，是上地的一位大学问家。他前往邯郸，经过耦沙时遇上一伙强盗，抢尽他的衣物车马。牛缺迈步而去，看不出有丝毫吝啬的神气。盗贼追上去问他是何缘故。牛缺说："君子不因供养身体的物品，伤害它所供养的身体。"

强盗惊叹地说："噫嘻，原来你是一个贤良之士啊！"

即刻强盗们互相商讨说："凭他的贤能，拜见了赵国君主，讲起你我的行为，必然会围困你我。还不如杀了他以绝后患。于是，众强盗追上牛缺并杀了他。

燕国有人听说了此事，便召集家族亲戚互相告诫，说："遇上强盗，万不可学牛缺的做法！"大家都谨遵教训。

不久，此人的弟弟要去秦国，走到函谷关下，果然遇上强盗。他回想起兄长的告诫，便与强盗争夺财物。争夺不过，又追上强盗用卑微的言辞乞求归还他的财物。强盗大怒说："我留你活命，就已经宽宏大度了，你还要不停地追赶我们，像你这样不停地追赶，我们的行踪就会暴露。既然我们做了强盗，哪还存在什么仁善。"于是便把他杀了。并且还连累了同行的几位亲友也被强盗所杀。

寓意：不加思考地生搬硬套他人的经验，反而赔了性命。

Niu Que and the Robbers

Niu Que was a great scholar from Shangdi. He was going to Handan and met a gang of robbers when passing through Ou Sha, who rob him of his clothes, vehicles, and horses. Niu Que walked away without showing any signs of reluctance. The robbers chased after him and asked him why. Niu Que said, "A gentleman will not harm the body he supports with the things he uses to support it."

The robbers exclaimed in amazement, "Wow, you are truly a virtuous and upright scholar!"

Immediately, the robbers discussed with each other, "Given his wisdom and virtue, if he meets the king of Zhao and tells him about our deeds, we will be besieged. It's better to kill him to eliminate future troubles." So they chased after

Niu Que and killed him.

Someone from Yan State heard about this incident and gathered his family and relatives to give them a warning, saying, "When encountering robbers, never follow Niu Que's example!" Everyone took the lesson to heart.

Soon after, the younger brother of this man decided to travel to the Qin State. As he passed through the Hangu Pass, he indeed encountered robbers. Recalling his brother's warning, he attempted to fight with the robbers for his belongings. Unable to overpower them, he chased after them and begged humbly for the return of his possessions. The robbers became furious and said, "I've already shown you leniency by sparing your life, but you continue to chase us relentlessly. If you keep doing this, our whereabouts will be exposed. Since we are robbers, there is no room for kindness." So they killed him, and unfortunately, several of his relatives and friends who were traveling with him were also killed by the robbers.

Meaning: Copying others' experiences without thinking can lead to loss of life instead.

不食盗食 《列子·说符》

东方有人焉，曰爰旌目，将有适（出远门）也，而饿于道。

狐父（古地名。以盛产名戈著称）之盗曰丘，见而下壶餐（以壶盛的汤饭）以餔（bū 喂食）之。爰旌目三餔而后能视，曰："子何为者也？"

曰："我狐父之人丘也。"

爰旌目曰："嘻！汝非盗耶？胡为而食我？吾义不食子之食也。"两手据地而欧（呕吐）之，不出，喀喀（呕吐声）然，遂伏而死。

狐父之人则盗矣，而食非盗也。以人之盗，因谓食之盗而不敢食，是失名实者也。

译文：东方有个人，名叫爰旌目，他要去很远的地方，走到半路上食物殆尽饿昏在路旁。

狐父这个地方有一个强盗名叫丘，发现爰旌目饥饿待毙的样子，连忙解下随身携带的一壶汤饭喂他。爰旌目吞咽下三口饭食后，才慢慢睁开双眼看见有人扶着他，问："你是什么人？"

丘回答：我是狐父人，名叫丘。"

爰旌目惊讶地说："嘻嘻！你不是强盗吗？为什么喂饭给我？我是一个讲信义的人，不吃强盗的食物。"说罢，两手伏地使劲呕吐，吐不出来，喉咙里喀喀作声，接着趴伏在地上死了。

丘本身是强盗，可是食物并非是偷来的。因为人是盗贼，却认为食物也是偷来的，这是混淆了名声与本质的差异。（后世论者多言：求名失实，违道丧生，伪愚也哉。）

寓意：生命诚可贵，追求道义本无可厚非，但切勿求名失实。

Refusing the Food from Robbers

There was a man named Yuan Jingmu in the East. He was on his way to a distant place. In the halfway his food ran out, and he fainted by the roadside due to hunger.

In the place called Hu Fu, there was a robber named Qiu who saw Yuan Jingmu starving to death. Quickly, he took out a bowl of rice soup from his belongings to feed him. After swallowing three bites of soup, Yuan Jingmu slowly opened his eyes and saw someone supporting him. He asked, "Who are you?"

Qiu replied, "I am a man from Hu Fu, named Qiu."

Yuan Jingmu was surprised and said, "Huh! Aren't you a robber? Why are you feeding me? I am a man of integrity and I will not eat food from a robber." Saying this, he pressed his hands on the ground and tried to vomit, but he couldn't. His throat made a hacking sound, and then he fell onto the ground and died.

Qiu himself was a robber, but the food was not stolen. It is a confusion of reputation and essence to consider the food as stolen just because the person is a thief. (*Later commentators often said: Seeking fame at the cost of losing truth, violating morality, and then to sacrifice one's life without hesitation, this behavior is foolish.*)

Meaning: Life is indeed precious, and the pursuit of morality is not wrong in itself. However, one must not seek fame at the cost of truth.

不食盜食 Refusing the Food from Robbers

歧路亡羊《列子·说符》

杨子（即：杨朱，字子居。别名：杨子，阳生）之邻人亡羊，既率其党（亲族），又请杨子之竖（shù 旧称未成年的童仆、竖子）追之。

杨子曰："嘻，亡一羊何追者之众？"

邻人曰："多歧路。"

既反，问："获羊乎"？

曰："亡之矣。"

曰："奚（何）亡之？"

曰："歧路之中又有歧焉，吾不知所之，所以反也。"

杨子戚然（忧伤貌）变容，不言者移时（多时），不笑者竟日（整天）。

门人怪之，请曰："羊，贱畜；又非夫子（先生）之有，而损（减少）言笑者，何哉？"

杨子不答。门人不获所命。弟子孟孙阳出，以告心都子。

心都子他日与孟孙阳偕（同）入，而问曰："昔有昆弟（兄弟）三人，游（游学）齐鲁之间，同师而学，进仁义之道而归。其父曰：'仁义之道若何？'伯曰：'仁义使我爱身而后名。'仲（兄弟排行第二）曰：'仁义使我杀身以成名。'叔（兄弟排行第三）曰：'仁义使我身名并全。'彼三术相反，而同出于儒。孰是孰非邪？"

杨子曰："人有滨河而居者，习于水，勇于泅（qiú 游泳），操舟鬻渡（yù dù 以摆渡为谋生之业），利供百口。裹粮（携带干粮）就学者成徒，而溺死者几（将近）半。本学泅，不学溺，而利害如此。若以为孰是孰非？"

心都子嘿然（默然）而出。

孟孙阳让（责备）之曰："何吾子问之迂（曲折），夫子答之僻（怪癖），吾惑愈甚。"

心都子曰："大道以多歧亡羊，学者以多方丧生。学非本不同，非本不一，而末异若是。唯归同反一，为亡（没有）得丧（犹言得失）。子长先生之门，习先生之道，而不达先生之况也，哀哉？"

译文：杨子家的邻居跑丢了一只羊，即刻带领本家族的人，又邀请杨子的童仆帮助追寻丢失的那只羊。

杨子感到很惊奇说："嘻嘻，跑丢了一只羊，为什么要这么多的人去追寻呢？"

邻居家的人说："因为岔路太多了。"

过了一会，寻羊的人都回来了。杨子连忙问："找到羊没有？"

邻居家的人回答："没有找到。"

杨子又问："为何没有找到呢？"

邻居家的人回答："岔路中又有岔路，不知道该朝哪个方向去追，所以返回来了。"

杨子听了他的话，皱起眉头满脸忧伤，许久不讲话，整日不见有笑脸。

门徒觉得很怪异，以请教的口气问："羊是不值钱的牲畜，况且丢失的那只羊又不是先生您自己的，为何闷闷不乐，不见说笑，这是为什么呢？"

杨子没有回答，门徒无法理解其中的缘故。孟孙阳是杨子门下年龄最大的门徒，他外出时特意请教心都子对此事的看法。

心都子过了几天和孟孙阳一起进屋，请教杨子说："昔日，有兄弟三人，在齐国与鲁国游学，同拜一位先生门下学习礼义，把仁义道德研习完毕才回家。回到家后父亲问兄弟三人：'学习仁义道德，有何作为？'兄长说：'仁义使我爱惜自己的生命，而把名声放在生命之后。'二弟说：'学习仁义道德，使我为了名声不惜牺牲自己的生命。'三弟说：'学习仁义道德，使我的生命和名声都能够保全。'三兄弟求学之后的信仰、人生观完全相反，然而却出自同一位儒师，这究竟谁对谁错呢？"

杨子没有正面回答，反问："有一位居住在滨河之畔的摆渡人，熟习水性，善于泅渡，正因为他的水性很好，所以他能以操船摆渡谋生，他所赚的盈利可以供养家人百口，邻近许多人自带干粮前来求学。然而溺死者将近一半。原本是学习游泳，不是学溺死，其结果利害相差如此之大，你认为谁对谁错呢？"

心都子默然无语地走了出去。

孟孙阳紧跟着心都子,并以责备的口气说:"你怎么提出这样曲折复杂的问题，先生又回答地那么稀奇古怪？这更加深了我的迷惑。"

心都子看着孟孙阳不知所措的神情说："大道因为岔路太多而丢失了羊，求学的人因为学习方法的多种多样而丧失了生命。学习的知识或技能从本源上来说并非不相同，并非从根本上不一致，而是每件事情发展到末端总会出现偏差，再者从道通为一的观念思考问题，凡事没有得失之分。你长期在老师的门下，作为老师的大弟子，学习老师的学说，却不懂得老师譬喻的含意，真让人感到痛惜！"

寓意：学习就像寻找丢失在歧路中的那只羊，在通往未知的道路上，学习的意愿是一致的（寻找到心中所想的那只"羊"），可在学习的过程中有太多的可变的因素（天有不测风云，人有旦夕祸福）。大路分岔为众多小道，并且每个人对学习的悟性也不同，不同的人学习取得的成就也截然不同。唯有回到事物的本源思考，才不会迷惘于得失之间。

The Lost Sheep

The neighbor of Yangzi lost a sheep and immediately led members of his own clan, as well as inviting Yangzi's servants to help search for the lost sheep.

Yangzi felt surprised and said, "Wow, it's just one sheep gone missing. Why do you need so many people to search for it?"

The neighbor explained, "There are too many forks in the road."

After a while, all the sheep-seekers came back. Yangzi quickly asked, "Did you find the sheep?"

The neighbor replied, "Not yet."

Yangzi asked again, "Why didn't you find the sheep?"

The neighbor replied, "There were forks in the road, and we didn't know which direction to go in to chase the sheep, so we came back."

Upon hearing his words, Yangzi furrowed his brows and his face was filled with sorrow. He remained silent for a long time, without a smile on his face the whole day.

The disciples felt perplexed and asked in a respectful tone, "Sheep are not valuable livestock, besides the lost sheep is not yours, Teacher. Why are you so melancholy and without a smile? Why is that?"

Yangzi did not respond, leaving his disciples puzzled about the reason behind his mood. Meng Sunyang, the oldest disciple under Yangzi's tutelage, decided to seek the opinion of Xinduzi on the matter when he went out.

A few days later, Xinduzi and Meng Sunyang entered the room together and asked Yangzi, "In the past, there were three brothers who studied etiquette and righteousness in the states of Qi and Lu. They learned under the same master and didn't return home until they had fully mastered morality and ethics. When they came back, their father asked them, 'What have you achieved through studying morality and ethics?' The eldest brother said, 'Morality and righteousness have taught me to cherish my life and put my reputation after it.' The second brother said, 'Studying morality and ethics has made me willing to sacrifice my life for my reputation.' The third brother said, 'Studying morality and ethics has allowed me to preserve both my life and my reputation.' The three brothers' beliefs and life philosophies after studying were completely opposite, yet they all stemmed from the same Confucian master. Who is right and who is wrong in this case?"

Yangzi did not directly answer but asked instead, "There is a ferryman who lives along the river and is proficient in swimming. Because of his excellent swimming skills, he earns a livelihood by ferrying people across the river. The profits he earns are enough to support his entire family. Many people from the neighboring areas come to learn swimming from him, bringing their own food. However, nearly half of them drown. The original intention of learning to swim is not to drown, yet the consequences and benefits are so vastly different. Who do you think is right and who is wrong in this situation?"

Xinduzi walked out silently without saying anything.

Meng Sunyang followed closely behind Xinduzi and said in a reproachful tone, "Why did you raise such a complicated question, and why did the master answer it in such a bizarre way? This has only deepened my confusion."

Looking at Meng Sunyang's perplexed expression, Xinduozi said, "The sheep was lost because there were too many forks in the road, and students lost their lives because of the diversity of learning methods. The knowledge or skills learned are not fundamentally different or inconsistent in origin, but deviations always arise at the end of each development. Furthermore, from the perspective of the unity of Tao, there is no distinction between gain and loss in everything. You have been under the teacher's guidance for a long time, as the eldest disciple of the teacher, learning the teacher's theory, but you don't understand the meaning of the teacher's analogy. It's really sad!"

Meaning: Learning is like finding the lost sheep on a forked road. On the path to the unknown, the willingness to learn is consistent *(Find the "sheep" in one's heart)*. However there are too many variable factors in the process of learning *(Unexpected changes in weather or life events)*. The main road divides into many small paths, and each person's understanding of learning is different, leading to completely different achievements in learning among different people. Only by returning to the source of things to think can we avoid being confused by gains and losses.

歧路亡羊 The Lost Sheep

- 119 -

杨布打狗《列子·说符》

杨朱（即：杨子）之弟曰布，衣素衣（泛指穿白色的衣服）而出。天雨，解素衣，衣缁（zī）衣（泛指黑色衣服）而反(返回)。其狗不知，迎而吠（fèi 狂吠）之。杨布怒，将扑（杖）之。

杨朱曰："子无扑矣！子亦犹是也。向者（刚才）使汝狗白而往，黑而来（回家），岂能无怪哉？"

译文：杨朱的弟弟名叫杨布，有一天他身穿白色素衣出门。过了一会儿天下起雨来，他解下白色素衣，穿上黑色衣服回家。家中的狗没有认出他，迎上去狂叫。杨布十分恼怒，拿起杖子要打狗。

杨朱在一旁连忙阻止，说："你别打狗，你自己也会遇到此事。假如刚才你的狗离家前是白色的，而回家时成了黑色，你是不是也会觉得很奇怪？"

寓意：遇到责难时，冷静思考其中的原因，而不是由愤怒取代理智。

A Change of Colour

Yang Zhu, the famous philosopher, had a younger brother named Yang Bu who, once, went out dressed in white. It began to rain so Yang Bu took off his white clothes and returned home dressed in black. His dog, failing to recognize him, rushed forward to bark at him. Yang Bu was angry and wanted to beat the animal.

"Don't beat the dog," said Yang Zhu, "you would have acted in the same way. If your dog had gone out a white dog and then came home black all over, wouldn't you have thought it very strange?"

Meaning: When confronted with blame, we should calmly consider the reasons behind it instead of letting anger override our rationality.

杨布打狗 A Change of Colour

献 鸠 《列子·说符》

邯郸之民，以正月之旦献鸠于简子（赵简子，即赵鞅），简子大悦，厚赏之。

客问其故。简子曰："正旦（农历正月初一）放生，示有恩（恩惠）也。"

客曰："民知君之欲放之，故竞而捕之，死者众矣。君如欲生之，不若禁民勿捕。捕而放之，恩过不相补矣。"

简子曰："然。"

译文：赵国都城邯郸的民众，每年正月初一这一天向赵简子呈献斑鸠，赵简子很高兴，每年都会重赏呈献者。

前来拜见他的客人询问其中缘由。赵简子说："正月初一放生，表示我的恩惠。"

客人不以为然地说："民众知道您以放生表达您的恩惠，您的愿望是好的，但是民众互相争着捕捉它们，被杀死的斑鸠就更多了。如果您想要它们生存，不如禁止民众捕捉。捉来又放生，其中的恩惠和过错并不能互相弥补。"

赵简子诚恳地接受谏言，说："你说的很对。"从此，赵简子禁止民众呈献斑鸠。

（越国在赵简子的执政时期，成为战国时期七雄之一，这与赵简子虚心接受他人谏言，改正自己的行为有着直接关系。）

寓意：允许他人提出不同的看法，则是强身之本，也是强国之本。

Offering Turtledoves

The people of Handan, the capital city of the State of Zhao, presented turtledoves to Zhao Jianzi on the first day of the Chinese New Year. Zhao Jianzi was delighted and would generously reward those who presented the birds every year.

Guests who came to visit him inquired about the reason behind this. Zhao Jianzi said, "Releasing animals on the first day of the Chinese New Year shows my benevolence."

The guests disagreed and said, "The people know that you release animals to show your benevolence. Your intentions are good, but when they compete to capture them, more turtledoves end up being killed. If you really want them to survive, it would be better to prohibit the people from capturing them altogether. Capturing and then releasing them does not offset the harm caused."

Zhao Jianzi sincerely accepted the advice and said, "You're quite right." From then on, Zhao Jianzi banned the people from presenting turtledoves.

(During Zhao Jianzi's reign, Yue became one of the seven great powers of the Warring States period, which had a direct relationship with Zhao Jianzi's humility in accepting others' advice and correcting his own behavior.)

Meaning: Allowing others to express different opinions is the foundation of strengthening oneself, as well as the foundation of strengthening a country.

岂辱马医 《列子·说符》

齐（齐国）有贫者，常乞于城市。城市患（厌烦）其亟(qì 屡次)也，众莫之与。

遂适田氏之厩，从马医作役而假食（求食）。郭（城郭）中人戏之曰："从马医而食，不以辱乎？"

乞儿曰："天下之辱莫过于乞。乞犹不辱，岂辱马医哉？"

译文：齐国有一个穷人，常常在城里乞讨饭食。城里人厌烦他多次讨要，都不愿意再施舍饭食给他。

于是他来到田家的马厩，跟着马医干些杂活混口饭吃。城里人嘲笑他，说："跟着马医混饭吃，不觉得耻辱吗？"

乞丐说："天下的耻辱莫过于乞求施舍。乞求施舍尚且不觉得耻辱，替马医打杂求生还会感到耻辱吗？"

寓意：自力更生总比乞讨要体面，但有富有穷实乃社会常态，因此相对于乞讨若能有谋生之业便无可耻笑。人立身的尊严在于自力谋生也在于能够得到谋生的机会。

Shame for begging

There was a poor man in the State of Qi who often begged for food in the city. The city dwellers were tired of his repeated begging and were unwilling to give him any more food.

So he came to Tian's stable and did some chores with the horse doctor to make a living. People in the city mocked him and said, "Is it not shameful to work with the horse doctor for a meal?"

The beggar said, "The shame of the world is nothing compared to begging for charity. If begging for charity is not shameful, how could it be shameful to survive by doing chores for the horse doctor?"

Meaning: It is always more respectable to rely on one's own efforts than to beg, and the coexistence of the rich and the poor is a common social phenomenon. There is no shame in earning a livelihood instead of begging. The dignity of a person lies in both self-reliance and the opportunity to earn a living.

枯梧不祥《列子·说符》

人有枯梧树者，其邻父言枯梧之树不祥，其邻人遽（jù 仓促）而伐之。

邻人父因请以为薪（xīn 柴火）。

其人乃不悦，曰："邻人之父徒（tú 只）欲为薪而教吾伐之也。与我邻，若此其险，岂可哉？"

译文：有户人家，院子里一棵梧桐树枯萎了。邻居家的老人前来告诉他说："院中有枯树不吉祥。"他立即仓促地把枯树砍掉了。

邻居家的老人见他已经砍了枯树，便前来索要枯树当柴烧。

他很不愉快，说："邻居家的老人告诉我所谓枯树不祥的目的，只是想要我家的枯树当柴烧，才怂恿我砍树。与我相邻而居，却心存算计，岂能这样做事？"

寓意：一个人怂恿他人做某事若掺杂着别的目的，使人不得不怀疑其居心是否纯良。枯梧桐树是否把它作柴烧，这些都不能作为怀疑这棵树祥与不祥的依据。

Wilted Tree

There was a household where a phoenix tree in their yard had withered. An elderly neighbor came to inform them, "Having a dead tree in the yard is considered inauspicious." Upon hearing this, they immediately and hastily chopped down the dead tree.

After they had chopped down the dead tree, the old man from the neighborhood came to ask for the branches to use as firewood.

The owner of the yard was very unhappy and said, "The old man from the neighborhood told me that his supposed reason for the ominous dead tree was just to get my dead tree for firewood. He encouraged me to chop it down with ulterior motives. How can he act like this when we live next to each other?"

Meaning: When someone urges others to do something with ulterior motives, it makes people question their sincerity. Whether or not to use the dead phoenix tree as firewood should not be the basis for doubting it's auspicious or not.

亡 鈇 《列子·说符》

人有亡鈇（fū 斧头。一说：锄头。农田用具）者，视其行步，窃鈇也；颜色，窃鈇也；言语，窃鈇也；动作、态度无为而不窃鈇也。

俄而（不久），抇（hú 挖掘。一说"掘"的古字）其谷，而得其鈇。他日复（再）见其邻人之子，动作、态度无似窃鈇者。

译文：有位农夫丢失了一把锄头，怀疑是邻居家的儿子偷去了。他看见那人走路的样子，很像偷锄头的样子；再看那人的神色，也很像偷锄头的神色；听那人说话的语气，也像偷锄头的语气；反正，邻居家那个人的一举一动都像偷锄头的贼。

不久，他在自家翻地时，挖掘出自己丢失的锄头。他日，再次遇见邻居家的那个人，仔细观察那人的一举一动时，都不像是偷锄头的贼。

寓意：人的心中若存疑，这种疑惑可能会被无比放大乃至以质疑之事为真。当发现问题的真相时，疑惑顷刻消失殆尽。原来，有时一念起一念灭竟源于自身所思所想而非他人真实的所作所为。

In the Eyes of the Beholder

A man who lost his axe suspected his neighbour's son of stealing it. To him, as he observed the boy, the way the lad walked, the expression on his face, the manner of his speech-in fact everything about his appearance and behaviour betrayed that he had stolen the axe.

Not long afterwards the man found his axe while digging in his cellar. When he saw his neighbour's son again, nothing about the boy's behaviour nor appearance seemed to suggest that he had stolen the axe.

Meaning: If there is doubt in a person's heart, it can be enormously amplified to the point of considering the doubted matter as true. When the truth of the matter is discovered, the doubt disappears instantaneously. It turns out sometime that the emergence and disappearance of doubts stem from oneself, rather than from the actual actions of others.

亡鈇 In the Eyes of the Beholder

白公胜虑乱《列子·说符》

白公胜（？--前479年，芈姓，名胜，号白公，楚平王之孙）虑乱，罢朝而立，倒杖策（驱马棍），錣（zhuì 驱马棍上的刺）上贯颐（刺伤面颊），血流至地而弗知也。

郑（郑国）人闻之曰："颐之忘，将何不忘哉？"

意之所属箸（专注），其行足踬（zhì 颠踬）株坎，头抵植木，而不自知也。

译文：白公胜处心积虑地谋划叛乱之事，散朝之后，他仍然站在那里一动不动。突然靠在一旁的驱马棍倒下时，正巧刺伤了他的面颊，鲜血直淌到地面上，而他却没有感觉。

郑国人听说了此事，说："自己脸上受了伤都感觉不到痛，还有什么忘不了的呢？"

只要人的意念深度专注时，即使行走时脚绊着树根，或陷入凹坑里，脑袋撞上大树，也不会有感觉。

寓意：专心致志、心无旁骛之时可使人忘却周遭境遇、身体之伤，达到超然物外之境。

Dedication and Concentration

Bai Gongsheng plotted a rebellion with great care and attention. After the court session was over, he still stood there motionless. Suddenly, the horse-driving stick leaning against him fell down and stabbed his cheek, which causing blood to flow onto the ground, but he didn't feel it.

Upon hearing this news, the people of Zheng said, "If one doesn't even feel the pain of being injured on the face, what else could he possibly forget?"

As long as one's mind is deeply focused, even if one trips over a tree root or falls into a pit while walking, or even bumps one's head against a big tree, one won't feel it.

Meaning: When one is deeply immersed and undistracted, it can cause one to forget about surroundings and even bodily injuries, achieving a state of transcendence beyond external materials.

攫 金 《列子·说符》

昔齐人有欲金者，清旦（清晨）衣冠而之市，适鬻金者之所，因攫（jué 抓取）其金而去。吏捕得之。问曰："人皆在焉，子攫人之金何？"

对曰："取金之时，不见人，徒见金。"

译文：昔日，齐国有一人，非常渴望拥有黄金。有一天，清晨起床以后，他穿好衣物戴上帽子直奔集市，走入金店，伸手抓起一块黄金转身就走。巡查的官吏捕获了他，问他："众人都在现场，你怎么伸手拿走人家的黄金呢？"

那人回答："我拿黄金的时候，没看人，只看见黄金。"

寓意：唐人卢重玄解曰："张湛云：'嗜欲之，乱人心如此之甚也，故曰：察秋毫之末者，不见泰山之形；听五音之和者，不闻雷霆之声。'心有所存，形有所忘，皆若此者也。此章言，嗜欲不可纵，丧身灭性之大也。今以丧其身之物，意欲厚其身也。若能无其身，复何用金为？所言无身非谓灭身也，盖不厚而已矣。"

To Seize Gold

In the past, there was a man in the State of Qi who had a strong desire for gold. One day, after waking up in the morning, he put on his clothes and hat and ran straight to the market. He walked into a gold shop, reached out his hand and grabbed a piece of gold, then turned around to leave. An official who was patrolling caught him and asked, "Everyone is here, so why did you reach out and take someone else's gold?"

The man replied, "When I took the gold, I didn't see any people. I only saw the gold."

Meaning: When the mind is fixed on something, the body forgets itself. One should not indulge one's desires, as it can lead to the loss of one's body and destruction of one's nature.

攫金 To Seize Gold

《秦孝公招贤令》：

昔我缪（穆）公，自歧雍之间，修德行武，东平晋乱，以河为界，西霸戎翟（dí 古同狄。西方曰戎，北方曰狄）。广地千里，天子致伯，诸侯毕贺，为后世开业，甚光美。会往者，历、躁、简公、出子之不宁，国家内忧，未遑（无暇顾及）外事，三晋攻夺我先君河西地，诸侯卑秦，丑莫大焉。献公即位，镇抚边境，徙治栎阳，且欲东伐，复缪公之故地，修缪公之政令。寡人思念先君之意，常痛于心。宾客群臣有能出奇计强秦者，吾且尊官，与之分土。

秦孝公元年签

Qin Xiaogong's Call for Talents:

In the past, my ancestor, Duke Mu of Qin, started his career between Qishan and Yong County. He worked hard to govern and cultivate virtue and military strength. He settled the chaos in the State of Jin to the east, assisted Duke Wen of Jin in returning to his throne, and established a good relationship between Qin and Jin with the Yellow River as the boundary. To the west, he attacked the Rong and Di tribes, expanding the territory by thousands of miles. The emperor conferred upon him the title of earl, ruling over a region. All the vassal states came to him, laying a solid foundation for future generations, which was brilliant. Later, after successive reigns of Duke Li, Duke Zao, Duke Jian, and Duke Chu, internal politics were unstable, leaving no time for external expansion. This led to the Three Jin states seizing my ancestor's land in Hexi, which was a national humiliation! When my father, Duke Xian, succeeded to the throne, he pacified the borders, moved the capital to Liyang, and prepared to send troops eastward to recover Duke Mu's ancestral land and restore his political order. Whenever I think of my ancestor's unfulfilled ambitions, I feel a deep sorrow in my heart! Whether it is our own ministers or foreign guests, whoever can come up with a brilliant plan to strengthen Qin, I will reward him with high positions and land!

秦孝公招贤令 Qin Xiaogong's Call for Talents

商鞅头像铭文注解 Head Portrait of Shang Yang & Annotation of the Inscriptions

《商鞅》：

商鞅，姓公孙，名鞅。卫国公子之子。亦称卫鞅。约生于公元前 390 年，卒于公元前 305 年。《史记·商鞅列传》："鞅，初事卫相公叔痤。痤卒，惠王弗能用。鞅，遂入秦。"孝公即位，颁《招贤令》。商鞅闻知，携带李悝的《法经》，冒险入秦。

商鞅投奔秦国，向秦孝公献上三策：帝道、王道、霸道。秦孝公喜"霸道"。

《史记》："孝公既用卫鞅，鞅欲变法，恐天下议己。卫鞅曰：疑行无名，疑事无功。且夫有高人之行者，固见非于世；有独知之虑者，必见敖（笑）于民。愚者暗于成事，知（智）者见于未萌。民不可与虑始，而可与乐成。论至德者，不和于俗；成大功者，不谋于众。……令既具（完备），未布，恐民不信，已乃立三丈之木于国都市南门，募（召）民能徙（移）置北门者予十金。民怪之，莫敢徙。复曰：能徙者，予五十金。有一人徙之，辄（zhé 立刻）予五十金，以明不欺。卒下令。……秦人皆趋令。行之十年，秦民大说（悦），道不拾遗，山无盗贼，家给人足。民勇于公战，怯于私斗，乡邑大治。"

《史记·秦始皇本纪》："及至秦王（秦始皇）、续六世之余烈，振长策而御宇内，吞二周，而亡诸侯。履至尊，而制六合（天地四方），执捶拊（紧握棰柄）以鞭笞（以暴力征服）天下，威振四海，……却匈奴七百余里。胡人不敢南下而牧马，士不敢弯弓而报怨。"

从秦孝公颁发招贤令"诸侯卑秦，丑莫大焉。"到秦始皇"执捶拊以鞭笞天下"都是因为商鞅变法为秦国提升了国力，打下强盛的根基，才使秦始皇统一了天下。

Shang Yang:

Shang Yang, whose surname was Gongsun and given name was Yang, was the son of a prince from the State of Wei. He was also known as Wei Yang. He was born around 390 BCE and died in 305 BCE. When Duke Xiao ascended the throne, he issued the "Order to Recruit Talents". Upon hearing of this, Shang Yang, carrying Li Kui's "Law Classic", took the risk to enter the State of Qin.

商鞅入秦 Shang Yang's Entry into Qin

东郭敞《商君书·徕民》

周军之胜（伊阙之战。公元前293年，秦将白起率军在伊阙大破魏国、韩国联军），华军之胜（华阳之战。公元前273年，白起大破魏、赵联军于华阳，斩首15万），秦斩首而东之。东之无益，亦明矣。而吏犹以为大功，为其损敌也。今以草茅之地，徕三晋之民而使之事本（农耕），此其损敌也，与战胜同实。而秦得之以为粟，此反行两登（两得）之计也。且周军之胜、华阳之胜、长平之胜（长平之战。秦将白起坑杀，四十万赵军降卒），秦所亡民者几何？民客之兵（民兵：或称乡兵，列入兵籍，战时应召入伍。客兵：战时从外地主动前来参战的军队）不得事本（农耕）者几何？臣窃（个人）以为不可数矣。假使王之群臣，有能用之，费此之半，弱晋强秦，若三战之胜者，王必加大赏焉。今臣之所言，民无一日之繇（yáo 徭役），官无数钱之费，其弱晋强秦，有过三战之胜，而王犹以为不可，则臣愚不能知已。

齐人有东郭敞者，犹多愿，愿有万金。其徒请赒(zhōu 赒济)焉，不与，曰："吾将以求封也。"其徒怒而去之宋。曰："此爱于无也，故不如以先与之有也。"

今晋有民，而秦爱其复，此爱非其有，以失其有也，岂异东郭敞之爱非其有，以亡其徒乎？且古有尧、舜，当时而见称（称赞）；中世有汤、武，在位而民服。此四王者，万世之所称（称誉赞美）也，以为圣王也，然其道犹不能取用于后。今复之三世（移民来的三代人不参军打仗。给移民以期盼，又不迫使他们从事厌恶之事），而三晋之民可尽也。是非王贤立今时，而使后世为王用乎（移民的第四代便是秦人）？然则非圣别说，而听圣人难也。

译文：伊阙之战和华阳之战的胜利，促进了秦军向东扩张的步伐，一直向东讨伐也不会产生更多的益处，这是很明显的现实。然而，群吏则以为这是建立了大功，因为损伤了敌国的实力。当下我们以荒芜的土地招募韩、赵、魏三国无田宅的游民，使他们为秦国从事农业生产，同样也是削弱敌国的国力，这样的做法与战胜敌国的实质相同。而且，一方面为秦国增添了粮食储备，另一方面削弱了敌国的农业生产，减少了敌军的粮食储备，这是农业与军事两利的妙策。况且，秦军的伊阙之战、华阳之战、长平之战，秦国伤亡有多少？配合前方作战的民兵、客兵，又有多少人不能从事农业生产？我个人认为没有办法正确地估算出结果。假如君主身边的贤能之臣，能够用此一半的兵力与费用，削弱韩、赵、魏三国的实力，提升我国的国力，如同三次战役那样的胜利，大王一定会加大赏赐。今日微臣所讲的攻略，民众不必付出一天的徭役，官府也不需要浪费过多的经费，却能有效地削弱三晋的国力，增强秦国的实力。这样的结果远远胜过昔日的三次战役，然而大王还是不以为然，微臣愚钝真不知该作何解释。

齐国有个叫东郭敞的人，贪念很强，总是希望自己拥有万金。有一天，他的门徒家中遇上难处，请求他能赒济钱财。他不给，说："我打算用现有的钱财换取爵位，争取更多的财富回报。"他的门徒非常气愤地离开了他去了宋国。有人说："吝惜还没有得到的爵位，还不如力所能及地给予门徒已有的；没有得到封爵，反而先得到了失去了门徒的结果。"

当前，三晋有民众，秦国有大量没有开垦的国土，只在意未曾拥有的徭役赋税，却忽视了荒芜的国土所能产生的经济价值。这不正是吝惜未有，而丧失已有。这和东郭敞吝惜还没有到手的封爵，先失去门徒的做法有何区别？上古时期，尧王、舜帝在世，被当时的人们称赞；中古时期的商汤、周武王使万民信服。这四位帝王受到后世敬仰，被视为圣王。但是，他们的治国理念却无法被后世统治者所使用。因为时代不同，所应对的国策也不相同。现在为了吸引三晋民众投靠秦国，以法律条文明确规定：凡是移民秦国的人士，三代人不从军打仗，给予移民想要的富足，又不强迫移民从事厌恶的事情。这样实施国策，很可能把三晋没有田宅的游民全部招揽过来。直至移民的第四代人，他们便是秦人。到那时，他们为了保卫祖传的家业，也会为秦国的强盛流血流汗。大王的英明立于当下，为秦国未来的强盛打下坚实的基础，难道这不是为后世的秦王所能利用的吗？然而并不是我所说的有多么地离奇，而是接受我的提议却很难。

寓意：计策的目的相同，但方法不同：一则为惯用手法，即派遣精兵强将以武力制服天下，使天下归顺；另一则为招揽别国游民，为己所用，后者未伤兵动卒，却能盈充粮草以强国力。前者为惯性思维，后者为逆向思维。君王，包括大部分谋士常以惯用手法为强国之策，奇谋异士则以逆向思维提出利国之策。

Dongguo Chang

The victories of the battles at Yimen and Huayang promoted the eastward expansion of the Qin army. It was obvious that there would be no more benefits from continuing to fight eastward. However, the officials thought that this was a great feat because it had damaged the enemy's strength. Now, we use barren land to recruit vagrants without land and homes from the three countries of Han, Zhao, and Wei to engage in agricultural production for Qin, which is also weakening the enemy's national strength. This approach is essentially the same as defeating the enemy. Moreover, it not only adds grain reserves to Qin but also weakens the enemy's agricultural production and reduces their grain reserves.

This is a clever strategy that benefits both agriculture and military. Besides, how many casualties did Qin suffer in the battles at Yique, Huayang, and Changping? How many militia and guest soldiers could not engage in agricultural production while cooperating with the frontline troops? I personally believe that it is impossible to accurately estimate the outcome. If the wise and capable ministers around the King can weaken the strength of the three countries of Han, Zhao, and Wei and enhance our national strength with half of the troops and expenses, just like the victories of the three battles, the King will certainly reward them generously. The strategy I proposed today does not require the people to serve a single day of corvee, nor does the government need to waste excessive funds. Yet it can effectively weaken the strength of the three States and enhance the strength of Qin. Such a result far surpasses the three battles of the past, but the King still doubts it. I am really puzzled about how to explain it.

In the State of Qi, there lived a man named Dongguo Chang who was deeply greedy and always dreamed of possessing a fortune in gold. One day, one of his disciples came to him for assistance because of financial difficulties in his family. Dongguo Chang refused, saying, "I intend to use the money I have now to exchange for a rank and strive for greater wealth in return." His disciple was extremely angry and left him to go to the State of Song. Someone commented, "Cherishing a rank that has not yet been obtained is not as beneficial as giving what one can afford to one's disciple. By not obtaining the rank, one may end up losing one's disciple first."

Currently, there are people in the three States, and there is a large amount of uncultivated land in Qin. Only care about the corvee and taxes we haven't yet obtained but ignore the economic value that can be generated from the barren land. Isn't this just like being stingy with what one hasn't yet obtained and losing what one already has? In ancient times, when Emperor Yao and Emperor Shun were alive, they were praised by the people of their era. In the middle ancient times, King Tang of Shang and King Wu of Zhou gained the trust of the people. These four emperors are respected by later generations and are regarded as saintly kings. However, their governance philosophies cannot be applied by later rulers. This is because different times require different national policies.

Currently, in order to attract the people of the three States to defect to Qin, we have clearly stipulated in legal provisions that all immigrants to Qin will not be required to serve in the military for three generations. We will provide them with the prosperity they desire without forcing them to do anything they dislike. By implementing this national policy, we are likely to attract all the wandering people without land and houses in the three States. By the fourth generation of immigrants, they will be considered Qin people. By then, they will fight and sacrifice to defend their ancestral homes, and also contribute to the prosperity of Qin. The wisdom of the king is evident in this decision, laying a solid foundation for the future prosperity of Qin. Isn't this something that future kings of Qin can utilize? However, it is not that what I am saying is particularly extraordinary, but rather that it is difficult to accept my suggestion.

Meaning: The purpose of strategies may be the same, but the methods are different. One is a conventional approach, which is to send out elite troops and strong generals to conquer the world by force, making all the people submit. The other is to recruit emigrants from other countries to serve the country. The latter strategy does not involve casualties but can still enrich the country's food and grass supply and strengthen its national strength. The former is a habitual thinking, while the latter is a reverse thinking. Kings, including most strategists, often adopt the conventional approach as a strategy to make the country strong, while the wise men with unusual strategies propose policies beneficial to the country with reverse thinking.

《商君书·定分》

法令者，民之命也，为治之本也，所以备民也。为治，而去法令，犹欲无饥而去食也；欲无寒而去衣也；欲东而西行也；其不几亦明矣。

一兔走，百人逐之，非以兔为可分以为百，由名分之未定也。夫卖兔者满市，而盗不敢取，由名分已定也。故名分未定，尧、舜、禹、汤且皆如骛（wù 急速）焉而逐之；名分已定，贪盗不取。

译文：国家制定法令，是为了确保民众的生命与财产不受侵害，实施法律是一国之本，也是为了避免民众触犯法律。并且明文告知民众何可为，何不可为。治理国家离不开适合国情的法律。如果一个国家没有法律规范民众的行为，就好似希望不挨饿却放弃了生产粮食；希望不受寒冷的侵扰却扔掉了可以用来抵御寒冷的棉衣；希望向东方前行却朝着西方奔跑。这是很明显的道理。

田野里有一只兔子奔跑，后面有百人在追赶，这并不是一只兔子可以分给一百个人，而是这只兔子还没有确立归属权的缘故。集市上卖兔子的商贩很多，然而强盗也不敢在大庭广众的眼前强取，这是因为兔子的所有权已经确立。因此，一切事物的名分没有确立之前，即使圣明的尧、舜、禹、汤在世也会急切地去追逐。然而，名分确立之后，即使贪婪的小人或者强盗也不敢在光天化日之下强取豪夺。

寓意：万物遵循规则而生。以民为本制定法律，行而有序、逐利有法，民众自觉遵纪守法，国力也会强盛。

The Book of Shang Jun: Laws

The state formulates laws and decrees to protect the lives and property of its citizens. The enforcement of laws is the foundation of a country, and it is also aimed at preventing citizens from breaking the law. These laws clearly inform the people of what they can and cannot do. The governance of a country cannot be separated from laws that suit its national conditions. If a country does not regulate the behavior of its people through laws, it is like hoping not to starve but giving up producing food; hoping not to be disturbed by cold but throwing away the cotton-padded clothes that can be used to resist the cold; hoping to move eastward but running westward. This is a very obvious truth.

There is a rabbit running in the field, and hundreds of people are chasing after it. This is not because the rabbit can be shared by a hundred people, but because its ownership has not yet been established. In the market, there are many vendors selling rabbits, but robbers dare not steal them in broad daylight, because the rabbits' ownership has already been established. Therefore, when the ownership of things is not yet established, even wise leaders like Yao, Shun, Yu, and Tang would eagerly compete for them. However, once the ownership is established, even greedy villains or robbers dare not rob them openly.

Meaning: Everything follows rules to grow. When laws are made based on the interests of the people, there will be orderliness and legitimacy in seeking profits. When the people consciously abide by the law, the country will become strong.

慎子头像铭文注解 Head Portrait of Shen Zi & Annotation of the Inscriptions

《慎子》：

慎到，后世尊称"慎子"。约生于公元前390，卒于公元前315年。倡导："法，非从天下，非从地出，发于人间，合乎人心而已。""官不私亲，法不遗爱，上下无事，唯法所在。""民一于君，事断于法。""以道为本，以法为治。"法者，合情理也。

Shen Zi:

Shen Dao, revered as "Shenzi" in later generations, was born around 390 BCE and died in 315 BCE. He advocated: "Law does not come from heaven or earth but originates from the world and conforms to human hearts." "Officials should not be biased towards relatives, and the law should not be biased towards loved ones. If there is no trouble between the upper and lower classes, it is only because the law is in place." "The people are subordinate to the monarch, and matters are decided by the law." "Take the Dao as the foundation and the law as the governance." The law is also reasonable.

飞龙失乘《慎子·内篇》

飞龙乘云，腾蛇游雾（腾蛇：又称奔蛇，与飞龙皆象征国君）。云罢雾霁（jì 停止），而龙蛇与螾（yǐn 古同"蚓"，蚯蚓）蚁同矣，则失其所乘也。

译文：飞龙乘着云，驾云飞行；腾蛇趁着雾，在雾里穿行。等到云消雾散时，那些飞龙腾蛇就如同蚯蚓、蚂蚁一样。——这是因为它们失去了借以腾飞的条件所造成的后果。

寓意：英雄乘时而得势。依托一定外部的条件，才华得以施展，变得耀眼夺目。得势与失势的境遇天差地别、判若两人。

Flying Dragon

The dragon flies on the cloud, and the snake moves through the mist. When the cloud disappears and the mist clears, these dragons and snakes are just like earthworms and ants. This is because they have lost the conditions that allowed them to take flight.

Meaning: Heroes rise with the times and seize the opportunity. Relying on certain external conditions, their talents can be displayed and shine brightly. The contrast between being in power and out of power is vast, which can make a person seem like two entirely different individuals.

离 朱《慎子·内篇》

离朱（人名。即离娄。相传黄帝时人。另言：传说中的神兽）之，明察毫末于百步之外，下于水，尺而不能见浅深。

非目不明也，其势难睹也。

译文：离朱能在百步之外看清楚秋天鸟兽身上刚长的细毛，但是如果让他潜入水中，连一尺以内水的深浅也看不清楚。

这并不是他的眼睛不明亮，而是环境影响到他的视力，使他难以做出正确的判断。

寓意：无论圣贤还是凡夫俗子，人的能力在一定的情形、环境下才得到有效发挥。

Li Zhu

Li Zhu can clearly see the fine hair of autumn birds and beasts grown just now at a hundred paces away, but if he is asked to dive into the water, he can't even see clearly the depth of the water within one foot.

It's not that his eyes are not bright, but that the environment affects his vision, making it difficult for him to make correct judgments.

Meaning: Regardless of whether one is a sage or an ordinary person, one's abilities can only be effectively exerted under certain circumstances and environments.

西施至姣《慎子·外篇》

西施，天下之至姣（jiāo 姣美）也，衣之以皮倛（qī 古代术士驱鬼面具。周代称驱瘟疫的人为"皮倛"），则见者皆走。易之以元緆（yuán xī 精美的细布衣），则行者皆止。

由是观之，则元緆色之助也，姣者辞之，则色厌矣。

译文：西施是天下共认的越国美女，但是给她穿戴上方士驱瘟神的假面具，看见她的人都会吓跑。如果给她换上美丽的细布衣，行路的人都会停下脚步观看她。

由此看来，美丽的细布衣为她的天生丽质增添了光彩。如果再美丽的人没有漂亮的衣服来修饰和烘托，那么她的美丽也会逊色许多。

寓意：俗话说，人靠衣服马靠鞍，懂得因势利导亦是做事和治国之良策。

Xi Shi's beauty

Xi Shi is recognized as the most beautiful woman in State of Yue, but if she were dressed with a false mask used by the sorcerer to ward off evil spirits, those who saw her would be scared away. If she wore a beautiful fine cotton dress, passers-by would stop to admire her.

From this perspective, the elegant fine cotton clothes add to the radiance of her natural beauty. If a person, regardless of how beautiful she is, lacks the embellishment and enhancement of beautiful clothes, her beauty will still pale in comparison.

Meaning: As the saying goes, "A person relies on clothes and a horse relies on its saddle." Understanding how to adapt to the situation and take advantage of opportunities is a good strategy for doing things and governing a country.

申不害头像铭文注解 Head Portrait of Shen Buhai & Annotation of the Inscriptions

《申不害》：

申不害，后世尊称"申子"，生于公元前385年，卒于公元前337年。郑国京邑（今河南荥阳）人。韩昭侯任申不害为相，成就韩国与齐、楚、燕、赵、魏、秦并列为七雄之一。慎到重"势"；商轶重"法"；申不害重"术"。皆言：依法治国，才能强盛。

司马迁《史记·老子韩非列传》："申不害者，京人也。故郑之贱臣（谓在上司面前的谦称）。学术以干韩昭侯，昭侯用为相。内修政教，外应诸侯。十五年，终申子身，国治兵强，无侵韩者，申子之学，本于黄老（黄帝与老子）而主刑名。著书二篇，号曰：《申子》。

韩非子《外储说右上》："申子曰：'独视者谓明；独听者谓聪。能独断者，故可以为天下主。'"

Shen Buhai:

Shen Buhai, revered as "Shenzi" in later generations, was born in 385 BCE and died in 337 BCE. He hailed from Jingyi, Zheng State *(now Xingyang, Henan Province)*. Han Zhaohou appointed Shen Buhai as the prime minister, leading the Han State to become one of the Seven Great States, alongside Qi, Chu, Yan, Zhao, Wei, and Qin. Shen Dao emphasized "power"; Shang Yi emphasized "law"; and Shen Buhai emphasized "strategy". All three believed that governing the country according to law was the key to strength and prosperity.

叶公好龙《申子·逸文》

叶公子高（叶：旧读 shè 摄。叶公子高，名诸梁。字，子高。楚国贵族。封于叶。今河南叶县。故称叶公子高），钩（衣带钩）以写（刻画）龙，凿（záo 假借"爵"、酒杯）以写龙，屋室雕文以写龙。

于是，天龙闻而下之，窥头于牖（yǒu 窗户），施尾于堂。叶公见之，弃而还走，失其魂魄，五色无主。

是叶公非好龙也，好夫似龙而非龙者也。

译文：叶公子高非常喜好龙，他的衣带钩上刻着龙，酒杯上也刻着龙，房屋居室梁柱上全都刻满了龙。

于是，天上的真龙听说此事，便从天宫下来，把龙头伸进窗户，龙尾拖到堂屋。叶公看到真龙前来，转身而逃，直吓得失魂落魄，六神无主，面无人色。

寓意：沉迷于不切实际的幻想中，一旦遭遇现实残酷的一面，往往不知所以。

The Real Thing

Lord Ye, styled Zigao, was fond of dragons. He had dress ornaments and wine cups with the pattern of dragons, and all the carvings in the rooms of his house were in the shape of dragons. As a result, the real dragon heard about this and came down to his house, It stuck its head through a window to take a peep while trailing its tail in the hall. Lord Ye saw it and turned to flee with a terrified look on his face, frightened out of his wits.

This man was not really fond of dragons. He was only fond of what looked like a dragon but was not a dragon in reality.

Meaning: Obsessed with unrealistic fantasies, people often do not know what to do when confronted with the cruel reality.

孟子头像铭文注解 Head Portrait of Mencius & Annotation of the Inscriptions

《孟子》：

注：孟轲，字子车，另言子舆。后世尊称"孟子"。约生于公元前372年，卒于公元前289年。战国时邹国（今，山东邹城）人。继孔子之学，提出"民贵君轻"的理论。宣传法先、王道、仁政、德治的理念。孟子周游列国，未展宏图，以讲学寿终。

Mencius:

Meng Ke, revered as "Mencius" in later generations, he was born around 372 BCE and died in 289 BCE. He was from the State of Zou during the Warring States period *(now Zoucheng, Shandong)*. He followed the teachings of Confucius and proposed the theory that "the people are precious and the monarch is insignificant." He promoted the ideas of law first, kingly way, benevolent governance, and moral rule. Mencius traveled around the states but failed to realize his grand plans and ended his life by teaching.

五十步笑百步《孟子·梁惠王上》

填然（形容声势浩大）鼓之，兵刃既接，弃甲曳兵（形容：扔掉盔甲，拖着兵器）而走。

或百步而后止，或五十步而后止。

以五十步笑百步，则何如？

译文：击鼓冲锋声势浩大，交战双方即将兵刃相接。突然，一方丢盔弃甲、拖着兵器转身逃走。

有的逃了一百步后停止脚步，有的逃了五十步后停止脚步。

有人凭着只跑了五十步而耻笑别人已跑了一百步，则如何评论？

寓意：无论逃走五十步还是一百步，临阵脱逃的本质是一样的。虽然逃跑步数的多与少有别，但从本质而言没有差别。

The Pot Calling the Kettle Black

Imagine battledrums thundering and weapons clashing. At this time some soldiers abandon their armour and run away, dragging their weapons behind them.

Some stop after going one hundred paces. Others halt after fifty paces. Those who ran only fifty paces laughed at those who ran a hundred. What do you think?"

Meaning: The essence of fleeing is the same whether fifty steps or a hundred steps. Although there is a difference in the number of steps, there is no difference in essence.

五十步笑百步 The Pot Calling the Kettle Black

以羊易牛《孟子·梁惠王上》

王坐于堂上（王指齐宣王，名辟疆，齐威王之子），有牵牛而过堂下者。王见之，曰："牛何之？"

对曰："将以衅钟（xìn zhōng 古代杀牲以血涂钟行祭。赵岐注："新铸钟，杀牲以血涂其衅郄，因以祭之曰衅。"郄 xì 同"郤"、"隙"。用牲血当糊剂，密封钟上的沙眼，以达到钟声纯厚的目的）。

王曰："舍之！吾不忍其觳觫（hú sù 恐惧战栗貌），若无罪而就死地。"

对曰："然则，废衅钟与？"

曰："何可废也，以羊易之！"

译文：齐宣王端坐在朝堂上，有人牵着一次牛从堂前经过。齐宣王看见便问："牵牛干什么呢？"

那人回答："用它的血，祭祀新铸造的大钟。"

齐宣王说："放了它吧，我不忍心看它恐惧发抖的样子。它并没有罪过，却要为祭钟付出性命。"

那人不解地问："那么，因此而废除祭钟的仪式吗？"

齐宣王说："这怎么可以废除呢？以羊代替它。"

寓意：看见杀牛，心生怜悯，于心不忍；未见羊，杀之。所谓眼不见为净，名义上以'不杀'为怜悯，但同时认为衅钟仪式仍不可废，以一代一，并不是真正意义上对生灵的怜悯。

Exchange sheep for cattle

King Xuan of Qi was sitting in the court hall. Someone led a cow past the hall. King Xuan of Qi saw it and asked, "What are you doing with the cow?"

The person replied, "To use its blood to sacrifice for the newly minted bell."

King Xuan of Qi said, "Let it go. I can't bear to see it trembling in fear. It has no crime, yet it has to sacrifice its life for the bell-ringing ceremony."

The person looked puzzled and asked, "So, should we abolish the bell-ringing ceremony because of this?"

King Xuan of Qi said, "How can we abolish this? Let's use a sheep instead."

Meaning: Seeing the cow being killed, he felt compassion and could not bear to witness it. However, he did not see the sheep being killed. The saying goes, "What you don't see won't hurt you." In name, he claimed to have compassion by not killing, but he still believed that the bell-ringing ceremony should not be abolished. By replacing one life with another, this is not really compassion towards living beings in the true sense.

以羊易牛 Exchange sheep for cattle

揠苗助长《孟子·公孙丑上》

宋人有闵（mǐn 忧虑）其苗之不长而揠（yà 拔）之者，芒芒然（疲惫）归，谓其人曰："今日病矣！予助苗长矣！"

其子趋而往视之，苗则槁矣。

译文：宋国有一个人，他担心自己田里的禾苗长不快，就挨个地将禾苗拔高了一截，直到他累地疲惫不堪才回家。回到家后对家人说："今天可把我累坏了，我在田里帮禾苗窜高了许多。"

他的儿子急忙跑到田里察看，禾苗全都枯萎了。

寓意：治国理念要有高瞻远瞩的目光，审视思考未来的发展趋势，不可短视，追求表面效益。如果只追求短期效益，如同"拔苗助长"，其结果事与愿违。此寓意是孟子回答公孙丑提出的"何谓浩然正气"时所讲述的道理。

Giving the Seedlings a Hand

A man of the state of Song was worried about his seedlings growing too slowly. He pulled up the seedlings one by one and came home exhausted.

"I am tired out today. I helped the seedlings to grow," he said to his family.

His son hurried to the fields to have a look and found that all the seedlings had shrivelled up.

Meaning: The philosophy of governing a country should have a forward-looking perspective, examining and thinking about the future development trends, rather than being shortsighted and pursuing superficial benefits. If one only pursues short-term benefits, it is like "pulling up the seedlings to help them grow taller," and the result will be counterproductive. This moral lesson is the one that Mencius taught when he answered Gongsun Chou's question, "What is the meaning of the vast and magnificent righteousness?"

王良与嬖奚《孟子·滕文公下》

昔者,赵简子(春秋时晋国正卿赵鞅。公元前497年在晋国执政)使王良(善于驾车的人,先秦古籍多有称道他的记载)与嬖(bì)奚(赵简子得宠的臣子)乘(驾驭马车),终日而不获一禽。嬖奚反命曰:"天下之贱工也。"

或以告王良。良曰:"请复之!"强而后可。一朝(一个早晨)而获十禽。嬖奚反命曰:"天下之良工也。"

简子曰:"我使掌与女(汝)乘!"

谓王良,良不可,曰:"吾为之范我驰驱,终日不获一,为之诡遇(guǐyù 谓违背礼法,驱车横射禽兽),一朝而获十。诗云:'不失其驰,舍矢如破',我不贯(习惯)与小人乘,请辞!"

译文:从前,赵简子命令善于驾车的王良,为自己宠爱的臣子嬖奚驾车打猎。一整天也没有获得一个猎物。嬖奚回来后告诉赵简子,"王良是天下最烂的车夫。"

有人将此话告诉了王良。王良请求再次为嬖奚驾车打猎,经过再三请求获得许可。这次,一个清晨就获取十只猎物。嬖奚回来后对赵简子禀告,说:"王良真是天下最好的车夫。"

赵简子说:"那好吧,我派遣他专为你驾驶车马。"

而后赵简子说与王良,王良怎么也不肯接受,说:"我依照他的旨意终日不获一只猎物。我依照出奇制胜的法则,一个清晨便可获取十只猎物。古诗有言:'不违背驰驱的法则,放出的箭便可射中。'我不习惯与自以为是的小人驾车,请替我回绝他。"

寓意:王良顺从嬖奚的旨意行事时不获一物,嬖奚反而怪罪王良驰驱技艺不精;王良以驰驱的法则为准时,收获颇丰。评判技艺的标准并不是依凭自以为是的主观感受,而是做事的规律与法则。"贱工"与"良工"的评价竟然出自一人之口,其可谓毫无原则的小人。所以不要因为迁就小人,而放弃自己的做事原则。

Wang Liang and Bi Xi

In the past, Zhao Jianzi ordered Wang Liang who was good at driving, to drive for his favorite minister Bi Xi to hunt. But they didn't get any prey all day. When Bi Xi came back, he told Zhao Jianzi, "Wang Liang is the worst driver in the world."

Someone told this to Wang Liang. Wang Liang requested to drive for Bi Xi again to hunt, and after repeated requests, he was granted permission. This time, they caught ten preys in the early morning. When Bi Xi came back, he reported to Zhao Jianzi, saying, "Wang Liang is really the best driver in the world."

Zhao Jianzi said, "Alright, I will assign him to drive the chariot and horses exclusively for you."

Later, Zhao Jianzi talked to Wang Liang about this matter, but Wang Liang refused to accept the offer. He said, "When I followed his instructions, but failed to get a prey all day. However, I could get ten preys in one morning if I used my own strategies. An old poem goes: 'By following the rules of driving, the arrows can hit the target.' I am not accustomed to driving with a self-righteous person, so please refuse him for me."

Meaning: When Wang Liang obeyed the orders of Bi Xi, they did not obtain anything, yet Bi Xi accused him of being incompetent in driving. When Wang Liang followed the rules of driving, they made abundant gains. The standard for judging skills is not based on one's own subjective assumptions, but rather on the principles and laws of work. It is astonishing that the evaluation of "Poor job" and "Good job" come from the same person, who can be described as a petty individual with no principles. Therefore, we should not compromise our principles just to accommodate petty people.

一傅众咻《孟子·滕文公下》

有楚大夫于此，欲其子之齐语也。……

一齐人傅之，众楚人咻（xiū 扰乱）之，虽日挞（tà 鞭挞）而求其齐也，不可得矣。

引而置之庄岳（齐国临淄的街市名。庄：街名。岳：里名）之间数年，虽日挞而求其楚，亦不可得矣。

译文：有位楚国大夫，希望他的儿子学会使用齐国语言……

他请来一位齐国老师教导儿子学习齐国语言。可是，身旁有许多楚国人用楚语谈论是非，扰乱了他儿子的注意力。即使他每日鞭挞自己的儿子，还是无法让儿子学会说齐国的语言。

如果让他的儿子置身于齐国的闹市里，过不了几年，即使天天鞭挞要求他讲楚国语言，也是很难办到的。

寓意：人在少年时期，环境对其耳濡目染的影响，远超过刻板的口头说教。由此而言，社会环境潜移默化地改变了人们的生活习俗，影响着人们的生活习惯。

How to learn Foreign Languages

There was a minister of the State of Chu who hoped his son would learn to speak the language of the State of Qi.

He invited a teacher from the State of Qi to teach his son the language of Qi. However, there were many people around him who spoke in the language of Chu discussing gossip and rumors, which disturbed his son's concentration. Even though he whipped his son every day, he still couldn't make his son learn to speak the language of Qi.

If his son were placed in the bustling market of Qi, it would be difficult after a few years for him to speak the language of Chu even if he were whipped and forced to do so every day.

Meaning: In teenage years, the influence of the environment on people is far greater than the rigid verbal preaching. Therefore, social environment subtly changes people's customs and habits.

攘 鸡 《孟子·滕文公下》

今有人，日攘（rǎng 偷）其邻之鸡者。

或告之曰："是非君子之道。"

曰："请损之，月攘一鸡，以待来年，然后已。"

译文：现今好似有一人，每天都要偷取邻居家的鸡。

有人诚恳地劝告他，说："这样的做法，不是有正人君子所为。"

他回答说："那就减少些，以后每个月偷一次，等到来年再停止偷鸡。"

寓意：知错就改，何等来年？

Once a Month

Now there was a man who stole -a chicken from his neighbour every day.

"This is not the way a man of moral principles should behave," he was told.

"Well, then I'll reduce the number," he replied, "I'll steal one every month and next year I won't steal any more."

Meaning: Since he knew he was doing something wrong, he ought to stop at once. Why wait till next year?

齐人有一妻一妾《孟子·离娄》

齐人有一妻一妾而处室者。

其良人出，则必餍（yàn 吃饱）酒肉而后反（返回）。其妻问所与饮食者，则尽富贵也。

其妻告其妾曰："良人出，则必餍酒肉而后反，问其与饮食者，尽富贵也。而未尝有显者来，吾将瞯（jiàn 窥视）良人之所之也。"

蚤（同"早"）起，施从良人之所之，遍国中无与立谈者。卒之东郭墦间（东城门外的乱坟场），之祭者，乞其余；不足，又顾而之他。——此其为餍足之道也。

其妻归，告其妾，曰："良人者，所仰望而终身也。今若此！"

与其妾讪（shàn 抱怨）其良人，而相泣于中庭（院中）。

而良人未之知也，施施（洋洋得意）从外来，骄其妻妾。

由君子观之，则人之所以求富贵利达者，其妻妾不羞也，而不相泣者，几希矣。

译文：齐国有一人与妻妾同住一处。

他每天外出，总是吃饱酒肉才回家。妻子问他一同吃喝的都是一些什么人？他总是说都是富贵人家。

他的妻子对妾说："咱家的主人，每天外出总是吃饱酒肉才回家，问他同什么人一块吃喝，他说都是富贵人家。可是，咱家从来就没有富贵人家登门。我打算探视咱家主人的行迹，看看他到底与何等人士来往。"

第二天一早起床，她便尾随在丈夫身后，走遍全城，也没有看到有一人停下脚步与他交谈说话。最后，他来到东门外的乱坟场，直奔向上坟祭祖的人讨要剩余下的酒肉，不够吃，又东张西望地到别处讨要。——原来这就是他每天都能吃肉喝酒的办法。

他妻子回到家中，将自己看到的一切告诉了妾，说："男人，是咱们为妻为妾终身依赖的人，如今他却变成了这个样子。"

妻与妾共同抱怨着丈夫，伤心地于庭院中痛哭。

她们的丈夫还不知道家中发生的事，依然洋洋得意地回到家中，傲慢地对待自己的妻妾。

依君子之见，对于那些为了追逐名利不觉廉耻的人士而言，如果让他们的妻妾看到他们下作的嘴脸。不痛哭流涕，怕是非常少吧？

寓意：以求人施舍为食却伪装成与达官贵人同饮同食，这样的行为无异于为了追逐名利、虚荣炫耀而不觉廉耻。就连亲近之人得知事情的真相也羞愧难当。

Sense of Shame and Honour

A man from the State of Qi lived with his wife and concubine in the same place.

He would go out every day and always returned home after eating his fill of meat and drinking his fill of wine. When his wife asked him who he ate and drank with, he always said they were wealthy families.

His wife said to his concubine, "Our master always comes home after eating his fill of meat and drinking his fill of wine. When I ask him who he eats and drinks with, he says they are wealthy families. However, we never have any wealthy families visiting our house. I plan to investigate our master's whereabouts and see who he really associates with."

The next morning, as soon as she woke up, she followed her husband around the city, but she didn't see anyone stop to talk to him. Finally, he came to the cemetery outside the east gate and asked for leftover food and drink from people who were visiting their ancestors' graves. When he didn't have enough to eat, he looked around for more. So this was how he managed to eat and drink every day.

Upon returning home, his wife told the concubine everything she had seen and said, "The man is the one we rely on as wives and concubine for life, and now he has become like this."

Both the wife and the concubine complained about their husband and wept sorrowfully in the courtyard.

Their husband, unaware of what had happened at home. So he returned home confidently and arrogantly, treated his wife and concubine haughtily.

In a gentleman's opinion, for those who are shameless in pursuing fame and wealth, if their wives and concubines were to see their despicable faces, I fear that very few people would not weep bitterly.

Meaning: To pretend to eat and drink with dignitaries and wealthy families while actually depending on others' charity for sustenance is an act that is no different from pursuing fame and wealth out of vanity and shamelessness. Even those close to them would feel ashamed when they learn the truth.

齐人有一妻一妾 Sense of Shame and Honour

校人烹鱼《孟子·万章上》

昔者，有馈（kuì 馈赠）生鱼于郑子产（公孙侨的字，春秋时郑国的贤相）。子产使校人（赵岐注："校人，主池沼小吏也。"）畜之池。

校人烹之。反命曰："始舍之，圉圉（赵岐注："鱼在水羸劣之貌。"）焉；少则，洋洋焉（洋洋：舒缓摇尾之貌）；悠然而逝。"

子产曰："得其所哉！得其所哉！"

校人出曰："孰谓子产智？予既烹而食之，曰：'得其所哉！得其所哉！'"

故君子可欺以其方，难罔以非其道。

译文：昔日，有一人送给郑国子产一条活鱼，子产叫来管理池沼的小吏把鱼放生在池沼里。

那小吏来到水边架起火把鱼烤着吃了。他返回向子产禀告，说："刚才我把鱼放入池塘里，它还呆死不活的样子。过了一会，它翻动着水花钻进深水里去了。"

子产高兴地说："鱼儿找到合适的地方了，鱼儿找到合适的地方了。"

那小吏走出来对别人说："谁说子产聪明，我早已经把鱼烤着吃到肚子里了，他还说：'鱼儿找到合适的地方了，鱼儿找到合适的地方了'。"

所以说，正人君子有可能被合乎情理的话语蒙骗，难以被不合乎情理的话语所欺骗。

寓意：阳奉阴违、投机取巧式的自作聪明与学识渊博又为人正派所具备的聪明、智慧是两回事。用自以为是、表里不一的小聪明嘲讽正人君子的非投机钻营的正派和信任，并将正派与信任视作"不聪明"的行为，这样的行为一旦为他人所知，终会声名狼藉并失去他人的信任。

Cook the Fish

Once upon a time, someone gave Zichan of state of Zheng a live fish. Zichan asked the clerk who managed the pond to release the fish into the pond.

The clerk arrived at the waterside, lit a bonfire and grilled the fish over and ate it. Then he returned to report to Zichan, saying, "Just now, when I put the fish into the pond, it appeared lifeless and sluggish. But after a while, it splashed the water and swam deep into the pond."

Zichan was delighted and said, "The fish has found its proper place, the fish has found its proper place."

The clerk came out and said to others, "Who says Zichan is wise? I have already grilled and eaten the fish. And yet he still says, 'The fish has found its proper place, the fish has found its proper place.'"

Therefore, it is possible for upright and virtuous individuals to be deceived by plausible words, but it is difficult for them to be deceived by implausible ones.

Meaning: The self-cleverness of pretending obedience while actually disobeying and opportunistically exploiting situations, It is a far cry from the intelligence and wisdom possessed by someone who is both knowledgeable and upright. Mocking the uprightness and trustworthiness of a virtuous person with a self-centered and hypocritical mindset, viewing their honesty and trust as "unclever" behavior, this will lead to a tarnished reputation and loss of trust from others once discovered.

校人烹鱼 Cook the Fish

学弈《孟子·告子上》

弈（yì 围棋）秋（人名），通国（举国）之善弈者也。

使弈秋诲（教诲）二人弈。其一人专心致志，惟弈秋之为听；一人虽听之，一心以为有鸿鹄将至，思援弓缴而射之。虽与之俱（一起）学，弗若（如）之矣！

为是其智弗若与？曰：非然也。

译文：一说弈秋是人名。一说：弈棋高手叫"秋"，是举国有名的棋手。

请弈秋教导二人下围棋。其中一人专心致志地学习，认真地把弈秋每句传授的要领听在耳，记在心。另一人虽然也在听讲，心中却想着有鸿鹄从头顶飞过，想着拉弓射下鸿鹄。然而他与同窗一齐求学，却远不如他同窗所学到的棋艺。

难道他俩人的智力有太大的差别吗？我说不是这样的。

寓意：学在于心，专心致志；心不在焉，难以成焉。

Learning the Game of Go

One theory is that "Yi Qiu" refers to a person's name. Another theory is that "Qiu" is a chess master of Go, who is renowned throughout the country.

Qiu was asked to teach two students how to play Go. One of the students studied diligently, listening intently to every word of key points imparted by Yi Qiu, and storing it in his heart. While also listening, the other student had his mind wandering, imagining a swan flying overhead and visualizing himself drawing his bow to shoot it down. However, despite studying alongside his classmate, he did not learn as much about the art of chess as his classmate did.

Did they have a significant difference in intelligence? I would say no.

Meaning: Learning depends on the mind and requires dedication and concentration. If the mind is absent, it is difficult to achieve success.

学弈 Learning the Game of Go

冯妇搏虎 《孟子·尽心下》

晋人有冯妇者，善搏虎，卒为善士。则之野，有众逐虎。虎负嵎（yú 山弯处），莫不敢樱（接近）。望见冯妇，趋而迎之。冯妇攘臂（rǎng bì 捋起衣袖，押出胳膊）下车。

众皆悦之，其为士者笑之。

译文：晋国有位名叫冯妇的勇士，善于打虎。后来他改变了信仰，不再打老虎，成了一名有德之士。有一次冯妇驾车到郊外，正巧遇到一群人正在追赶老虎，老虎躲在山嵎里无人敢靠近。众人看见冯妇从此经过，连忙请他帮忙。冯妇二话不说挽起袖子下了车。

众人都很高兴冯妇帮忙，可是士大夫都嘲笑他说话不算数。

（赵歧注：笑其不知止也。后世称：复任前事为"重为冯妇"。）

寓意：士大夫以誓守诺言为重，而众人以眼前之事为重。危难面前是拔刀相助，还是固守曾经的诺言袖手旁观，则是：因人而异，不可一概而论。

Feng Fu Fight Tigers

There was a warrior named Feng Fu in the State of Jin who was skilled at hunting tigers. Later, he changed his belief and stopped hunting tigers, becoming a virtuous man. One day, Feng Fu was driving to the countryside and happened to encounter a group of people chasing a tiger. The tiger was hiding in a mountain cleft and no one dared to approach it. When the crowd saw Feng Fu passing by, they quickly asked him for help. Without hesitation, Feng Fu rolled up his sleeves and got off the carriage.

The crowd was delighted that Feng Fu had offered to help, but the scholars and officials ridiculed him for breaking his promise.

Meaning: Scholars and officials value their oaths and promises above all else, while the general public prioritizes immediate matters. Zhao Qi commented that they laughed at Feng Fu for not knowing when to stop. Later generations referred to this act of breaking promises and going back to the old business as "repeating Feng Fu's mistake."

庄子铭文头像注解 Head Portrait of Zhuangzi & Annotation of the Inscriptions

《庄子》：

庄周，名周。字子休，另言子沐。后世尊称庄子，约生于公元前 369 年，卒于公元前 286 年。曾任宋国地方漆园吏，世称漆园傲吏。提出：哀莫大于心死，而身死次之。道是宇宙精神，气质是人的精神，精神显示人格修养。

Zhuangzi:

Zhuang Zhou, courtesy name Zixiu, and sometimes referred to as Zimu, he was revered as Zhuangzi in later generations. He was born around 369 BCE and died in 286 BCE. He once served as a local official in the state of Song, known as the proud official of the lacquer garden. He proposed that the greatest sorrow is not physical death but the death of the heart, followed by physical death. He believed that Tao is the spirit of the universe, while temperament is the spirit of human beings, and the spirit reflects the cultivation of personality.

不龟手之药《庄子·逍遥游》

惠子（惠施，庄子挚友）谓庄子曰："魏王（梁惠王）贻（yí 赠送）我大瓠（hù 葫芦）之种（种籽），我树之，成，而实五石；以盛水浆，其坚不能自举也；剖之以为瓢，则瓠落无所容。非不呺然（xiāo rán 大而虚空）大也，吾为其无用而掊（pǒu 击碎）之。"

庄子曰："夫子固拙于用大矣。宋人有善为不龟手之药者，世世以洴澼絖（píng pì kuàng 在水里漂洗棉絮）为事。客闻之，请买其方百金。聚族而谋曰："我世世为洴澼絖，不过数金；今一朝而鬻（yù 卖）技百金，请与之。'客得之，以说吴王。越有难，吴王使之将；冬，与越人水战，大败越人，裂地而封之。能不龟手一也，或以封，或不免于洴澼絖，则所用之异也。今子有五石之瓠，何不虑以为大樽（zūn 即：腰舟）而浮乎江湖，而忧其瓠落无所容？则夫子犹有蓬之心也夫！"（成玄英疏："蓬，草名。拳曲不直也……言惠生既有蓬心，未能直达玄理。"）

译文：惠施对挚友庄子说："魏王赠送我大葫芦籽，我种植成功了，我将它培植起来后，结出的大葫芦有五石容积。（石：容量单位，十斗为一石。一百二十市斤为一石）。用它盛水，其硬度不足，难以拿起来；将其破开用作舀水瓢，却因太大不方便使用。因此我觉得它毫无用处，把它打碎丢弃了。"

庄子遗憾地说："你诚然太笨拙了。宋国有人善于配制可治愈因寒冷干燥而皮肤破裂的药膏，他们家族世代以漂洗棉絮为生。有一个外乡人听说此事后，请求购买此药方，并且愿意出价一百斤黄金。这人聚集全家商讨：'咱家世代漂洗所得不过数金，当下出售此药方便可获得百金，不如卖给他。'外乡人得到药方，便去游说吴王。正赶上越国内乱，吴王应邀出兵伐越，吴王派他统率部队。寒冬时节跟越军在水上交战，吴军的将士都用上了防冻裂的药膏，大胜越军而归，吴王因此割地封赏他。同样的药膏，有人用它获得封土；有人只是用它减少漂洗棉絮时手被冻皲裂的痛苦，这都是因为用法不同罢了。今日你有五石大葫芦，为何不把它用作腰舟，浮游于江河湖泊，反而以为它毫无用处？看来你的心还是茅塞未开。"

（庄子以"有无相生"的哲理论述：任何事物都存在两面性，如何扬长避短充分发挥其特长，这是处理问题的关键，而不是轻言放弃。）

寓意：一件物品，有用与无用在于使用它的情境不同。恰如其分地使用它，可使它增值百倍；忽略其特质去使用它，弃之而不知惜。

Uselessness and Usefulness

Hui Shi said to his close friend Zhuangzi, "The King of Wei gave me some big gourd seeds, and I successfully grew them. After cultivating them, the big gourds that grew from them had a capacity of five *dan* (a unit of capacity, ten *dou* equals one *dan*; one hundred and twenty *jin* equals one *dan*). When I used them to hold water, they were not strong enough and difficult to lift. When I tried to break them open to use as scoops, they were too big and inconvenient to use. Therefore, I think they are useless and broke them up to discard them."

Zhuangzi said with regret, "You are indeed very clumsy. There was a man in the State of Song who was skilled in making a medicine that could cure skin cracks caused by cold and dryness. His family had been making their livelihood by washing cotton for generations. When a stranger heard about this, he offered to buy the recipe for the medicine and was willing to pay a hundred *jin*[1] of gold for it. The family gathered to discuss it: 'Our generations of washing cotton have only yielded a few *jin* of gold. Selling this recipe can give us a hundred *jin* of gold right now. We should sell it to him.' The stranger obtained the recipe and went to persuade the King of Wu. Just at the time of internal strife in Yue, the King of Wu was invited to send troops to attack Yue. The King of Wu appointed him to command the troops. During the winter season, they fought against the Yue army on the water, and all the soldiers of the Wu army used the anti-frostbite ointment, which resulted in a great victory over the Yue army. The King of Wu then awarded him with land. The same ointment allowed someone to gain land, while someone else only used it to reduce the pain of their hands being frostbitten while washing cotton. This is all due to different uses. Today, you have a *five-shi* big gourd. Why not use it as a waist boat to float on rivers and lakes instead of thinking it's useless? It seems that your mind is still not open."

Zhuangzi expounded the philosophical theory of "mutual generation of existence and non-existence": everything has two sides. The key to handling problems is how to make the best use of advantages and avoid disadvantages, rather than giving up easily.

Meaning: The usefulness or uselessness of an object depends on the different contexts of its use. Using it appropriately can multiply its value by a hundredfold; ignoring its characteristics and misusing it can lead to discarding it without knowing its value.

庖丁解牛《庄子·养生主》

庖丁（厨师）为文惠君解牛，手之所触，肩之所倚，足之所履（踩），膝之所踦（yǐ 屈膝抵住牛），砉然（huā rán 象声词，刀割皮肉之声）向然（刀割声与皮肉分离声互相响应）奏刀騞（huō）然，莫不中音，合于《桑林》（商汤乐曲名）之舞，乃中《经首》（尧乐《咸池》中乐章之名）之会（节奏）。

文惠君曰："嘻（惊叹声），善哉，技盖至此乎？"

庖丁释（放下）刀对曰："臣之所好者道也，进（超越）乎技矣。始臣之解牛之时，所见无非牛者；三年之后，未尝（不曾）见全牛也。方今之时，臣以神遇（以神色感知）而不以目视，官知止，而神欲行。依乎天理，批大郤（xì 通"隙"。刺入骨与骨的连接处），导大窾（kuǎn 空隙），因其固然，技经肯綮（kěn qìng 筋骨结合

---

[1] Jin: a municipal weight unit. Ten liang make up one jin, equivalent to 500 grams (in the old system, sixteen liang make up one jin).

部位）之未尝，而况大軱（gū 大骨）乎！良庖岁更刀，割也；族（众）庖月更刀，折也。今臣之刀十九年矣，所解数千牛矣，而刀刃若新发于硎（xíng 磨刀石）。彼节者有间，而刀刃者无厚，以无厚入有间，恢恢乎（宽松）其于游刃必有余地矣。是以十九年而刀刃若新发于硎。虽然，每至于族（筋骨盘结之处），吾见其难为，怵然为戒，视为止，行为迟，动刀甚微。謋（huò）然已解，如土委地（散落）。提刀而立，为之四顾，为之踌躇满志（从容自得），善刀而藏之。"

文惠君曰："善哉，吾闻庖丁之言，得养生焉。"

译文：庖丁给梁惠王宰牛，他用手触牛、用肩抵牛，脚踩膝抵，手脚利落、身手不凡。走刀的沙沙声，牛骨肉的撕裂声，声声入耳，宛如殷商时期《桑林》之曲，又好似尧王时期的《经首》之鸣。

梁惠王惊叹地说："咦！好啊，手艺何以神乎其神？"

庖丁放下手中的刀，回禀梁惠王说："我尊崇'道'，所以比一般手艺人更进一步。刚开始学习宰牛时，我所看到的都是囫囵样的牛。三年以后，我再未见过完整的牛了。现在我以神色与牛相遇，不必眼观目视，我凭感觉或进或退，依牛体天生的结构，入刀割断连着骨头的筋与肉。更何况显而易见的大块骨头呢？好厨师每年更换一次刀具，因为他们用刀割肉。众多厨师每月更换一次刀具，因为他们是用刀砍骨头。我现在的这把刀已经使用了十九年，所宰的牛已有上千头。然而我的刀锋还像刚磨过的一样锋利。牛体骨与骨的间隙虽然很窄，而我的刀锋比它还要薄。用薄的刀锋刺入骨与骨之间的空隙绰绰有余。所以我的刀已经使用了十九年，还是像新刀一样锋利。虽然如此，每遇到筋骨交错的聚结处，我还是会警惕于心，目光专注，动作放缓，小心翼翼地运刀慢行。直到牛的骨肉分离，宛如泥土散地那样，我才舒缓气息提刀而起，回顾四处，心满意足地擦刀收藏。"

梁惠王说："好极了，我听了你这番话，懂得养生的道理了。"

（庄子以此讲述：人的生命是有限的，而人的欲望是无限的，以有限的生命追逐无限的欲望是危险的。所以倡导：人生在世，如果不卑不亢，不忮不求，以不贪念过多的欲望，则：可以保身，可以全生，可以养亲，可以尽年。）

另言：庄子与孟子同时代，梁惠王辞世前一年会见孟子曰："寡人不佞（犹言不才），兵三折于外，太子虏，上将死，国以空虚，以羞先君宗庙社稷，寡人甚丑之。叟（孟子），不远千里，厚幸（承蒙有幸）至弊邑之廷，将何以利吾国？"庄子借此嘲讽梁惠王："在位三十六年，兵三折于外，太子虏，上将死。"不懂如何"游刃有余"。

寓意：何为游刃有余？必然不是只视其形而略其构造，而是像庖丁解牛般心手相应。意即：依照事物内在发展规律和法则制定决策，从精神上去感知事理，不被虚文缛节所羁绊，行事和治国方能得心应手。

The Skills

Butcher Ding slaughtered a cow for King Liang Hui. He touched the cow with his hands, pressed it with his shoulders, stomped on it with his feet, and braced it with his knees. His hands and feet were nimble and his skills were extraordinary. The sound of his knife slicing through the cow's flesh and bones was like a tune from the Shang Dynasty's "Sanglin," or the melody of "Jingshou" from the era of King Yao.

King Hui of Liang exclaimed in amazement, "Wow! Amazing! How can one's skills be so incredible?"

Butcher Ding put down his knife and replied to King Hui of Liang, "I respect the 'Dao,' which is why I am able to excel beyond ordinary craftsmen. When I first started learning to slaughter cows, I saw them as whole animals. But after three years, I no longer saw complete cows. Now, when I encounter a cow, I don't even need to look at it. I can feel my way around it, following its natural structure, slicing through tendons and meat connected to the bones. And what's more, the larger bones are even more obvious! Good chefs change their knives every year because they use them to cut meat. Many chefs change their knives every month because they use them to chop bones. However, I have been using this same knife for nineteen years and have slaughtered over a thousand cows. But my knife is still as sharp as it was when it was newly sharpened. Although the gaps between the bones of the cow's body are narrow, my knife blade is even thinner. It slips easily into the spaces between the bones with ease. This is why my knife despite being used for nineteen years is still as sharp as a new one. However, whenever I encounter the intricate intersections of tendons and bones, I remain vigilant, focused, and deliberate with my movements. I carefully and slowly maneuver my knife until the cow's flesh and bones separate, much like how dirt scatters on the ground. Only then do I exhale with relief, lift my knife, survey my surroundings, and wipe it with satisfaction before putting it away."

King Hui of Liang said, "Excellent! After hearing your words, I have come to understand the principle of preserving one's health."

Meaning: What does "operating with ease and plenty of room" mean? It certainly isn't just looking at the surface without understanding the underlying structure, but rather achieving a harmony between one's mind and hands, similar to how Butcher Ding dissects a cow. In other words, it refers to making decisions based on the inherent laws and principles of things, perceiving the truth from a spiritual perspective, and not being hindered by trivialities. Only then can one act and govern with ease and confidence.

神社里的栎社《庄子·人间世》

匠石之齐，至于曲辕（地名），见栎社树（作为神社象征的栎树，栎 lì，又称 yuè 亦称"麻栎"、"橡"；通称"柞树"）。其大蔽（遮蔽）数千牛，絜（Xié 张开两臂量树身）之百围；其高临山（接近山头），十仞（rèn，古计量单位。一仞为周尺八尺，周尺一尺约合二十三厘米）而后有枝，其可以为舟（船。先秦用作"舟"，汉之后才有"船"这个字。此处言：可以制做船的旁枝）者，旁（旁枝）十数。观者如市，匠伯不顾，遂行不辍（chuò 停止）。弟子厌观（饱看）之，走乃（追上）匠石，曰："自吾执斧斤以随夫子（先生）未尝见材如此其美也。先生不肯视，行不辍，何邪？"

曰："已矣（罢了），勿言之矣！散木（无用之材）也。以为舟，则沉；以为棺椁，则速腐（腐朽）；以为器，则速毁；以为门户（门窗），则液樠（mán 脂液外渗）；以为柱，则蠹（dù 虫蛀）；是不材之木也。无所可用，故能若是（如此）之寿。"

匠石归，栎社（树）见梦（托梦）曰："女（汝）将恶乎（何以）比予（我）哉？若将比予于文木邪？夫柤（zhā 山楂）梨、橘、柚、果蓏（luǒ 孔颖达疏："木实曰果，草实曰蓏。"）之属，实熟则剥，剥则辱（折辱）；大枝折，小枝泄（yì 通"抴"，拉，牵引。后作"曳"）。此以（犹是以）其能苦其生者也，故不终其天年，而中道夭（夭折），自掊击（打击）于世俗者也，物莫不若是。且予求无所可用久矣，几死（几尽周折），乃今得之，为予（我）大用。使予也而有用，且（岂能）得有此大也邪？且（尚且）也若与予（你与我）也皆物也，奈何哉其相物（看我）也？而几死（即将近死）之散人，又恶知散木！"

匠石觉（觉醒后）诊（告诉）其梦。弟子曰："趣取无用，则为社何邪？"

曰："密！若无言！彼亦直寄焉，以为不知己者诟厉也。不为社者，且几有翦（jiǎn 同"剪"，砍伐）乎！且也彼其所保与众异，而以义喻之，不亦远乎！""

译文：有一位能工巧匠的名字叫"石"，他要去齐国。路过曲辕这个地方时，看见神社院中长着一棵硕大的栎树，树荫下可以容纳数千头牛。树身有百围粗，树高接近山顶，八丈以上才有分枝，可以用做舟船的分枝就有十多个。前来欣赏此树的人数如同赶集一样。匠石只看了一眼，直接走开了。他的徒弟围着大树仔细地看了一番，快步追上师傅说："自从我拜师学艺以来，还没有见过这么好的木材，师父为什么不肯多看几眼就走开了？"

匠石对徒弟说："罢了，不必多言，那只是一棵散木。用它制做舟船，入水便会沉没；用它制做棺椁，入土很容易腐朽；用它制做器具，很容易毁坏；用它制做门窗，木中浸出的油脂难以处理，既沾污衣物手指，又不雅观；用它制做梁柱，很容易遭受虫蛀侵蚀；这是一棵不能用做木料的大树。正因为它没有什么用处，所以才能长成如此高大。"

匠石回到家中，夜半时分栎树托梦于他说："你为何这么评价我呢？又为何要把我与可用的木材相比呢？那些山楂树、梨树、橘树、柚子树，在果实成熟的时候，就会遭受世人敲打扭曲，大树枝被折断，小树枝被扭曲，这都是因为它们结出的果实惹的祸，为此不能终其天年而中道夭折，这样的后果都是它们自己造成的。世上的一切事物都是如此而已。况且我期待自己无用已经很久了，几经周折我才明白：以无用而获大用的道理。假如我真的是可用的木料，岂能长成如此高大？况且你和我都是天地间的一物，并没有贵贱之别，为什么要把我当成无用之木呢？尤其是一个即将死去的无用之人，又怎能知道我就是无用之木呢？"

匠石觉醒后，把梦中的情景告诉了徒弟。徒弟不解地问："既然它希望自己无用，为什么还要长在神社里？"

匠石连忙说，"别声张，如果栎树心中不明白其中的道理，就不会寄匿在神社里。栎树托梦于我，只是嘲讽世间无知已而已。假如它不是生长在神社里，而是生长在荒郊野外，早被众人砍去当柴烧了。正因为它聚积了神社里的灵气得以保全，以此彰显自己于众不同罢了。如果依赖传统思维模式理解它的言行，那就太浅陋了。"

寓意：何为有用？何为无用？有用与无用往往只是一面之词。对事物判定的角度不同，结论也不同。并且事物在外界的判定中所得之利、弊可因环境与时局的变化相互转换。有用之木被折断扭曲或砍伐殆尽，而在一定条件下"无用"之木得以长成参天大树。对人的启示是：谦卑含容，收敛争强好胜的心态，以辩证的思维看待问题，有时无用方为大用。

Oak in the Shrine

There was a skilled artisan named Shi who was traveling to the State of Qi. As he passed through the place called Quyuan, he came across a massive oak tree growing in the courtyard of a shrine. The tree was so large that its shade could accommodate thousands of cattle. The trunk was so thick that it measured a hundred "*wei*" (*a traditional Chinese measurement for circumference*), and the tree was so tall that it nearly reached the summit of the mountain. Branches only emerged above eight *zhang* (*a traditional Chinese length measurement*), and among them there were more than ten branches suitable for building boats. The number of people who came to admire this tree was as numerous as those at a market. However, Shi, the artisan, only glanced at the tree and walked away. After carefully examining the tree, his apprentice quickly caught up with his master and said, "Since I became your apprentice, I have never seen such excellent lumber. Why didn't you take a closer look and just walk away?"

Shi said to his apprentice, "Alright, there's no need to say more. It's just a useless tree. If we use it to make boats, it will sink into the water; if we use it to make coffins, it will rot easily in the soil; if we use it to make utensils, it will break easily; if we use it to make doors and windows, the oil that comes out of the wood will be difficult to deal with, which will not only stain clothes and fingers, but also look ugly; if we use it to make beams, it will be easily infested by insects. This is a big tree that cannot be used as lumber. Because it's useless, it can grow so tall."

Shi returned home and in the middle of the night, the oak tree appeared in his dream. The tree said to him, "Why did you evaluate me like that? Why did you compare me to useful lumber? Those hawthorn trees, pear trees, orange trees, and pomelo trees will be beaten and twisted by people when their fruits ripen. Their big branches are broken, and their small branches are twisted. This is all because of the fruits they bear. They cannot live out their natural lifespan and die prematurely. This consequence is brought about by themselves. All things in the world are like this. Besides, I have long looked forward to my own uselessness. After several twists and turns, I finally understood the truth that uselessness leads to great usefulness. If I were really useful timber, how could I grow so tall? Moreover, both you and I are creatures of the universe, without any distinction of superiority or inferiority. Why treat me as useless wood? Especially a dying, useless person, how could he possibly know that I am useless wood?"

After waking up, Shi told his apprentice about the scene in his dream. The apprentice was puzzled and asked, "Since it wants to be useless, why does it still grow in the shrine?"

Shi quickly said, "Don't make a fuss. If the oak tree didn't understand the principle behind it, it wouldn't hide in the shrine. The oak tree dreamed of me just to mock the ignorance of the world. If it grew in the wilderness instead of the shrine, it would have been chopped down and burned as firewood long ago. It preserved itself by accumulating the spiritual energy of the shrine to show its uniqueness. It would be too shallow to understand its behavior based on traditional thinking patterns."

Meaning: What is useful? What is useless? Usefulness and uselessness are often just one-sided opinions. The conclusion about a thing's usefulness can vary depending on the perspective from which it is judged. Moreover, the advantages and disadvantages gained by things in external judgments can be mutually transformed due to changes in the environment and situation. Useful trees may be broken, twisted, or cut down almost entirely, while "useless" trees can grow into towering giants under certain conditions. The implication for humans is to embrace humility, to restrain the competitive and overambitious mindset and to view problems with dialectical thinking. Sometimes, what appears to be useless can actually turn out to be incredibly useful.

不若相忘于江湖《庄子·大宗师》

泉涸（hé 干涸），鱼相与处于陆，相呴（xǔ 嘘气）以湿，相濡以沫（彼此以呼出的气湿润对方），不若相忘于江湖。

译文：泉中的水已经干涸，鱼儿一齐被困在陆地上，彼此之间以呼出的气湿润对方，尽可能地减少日晒的痛苦。此时此刻，真不如畅游在江河湖泊的碧水中，相互忘记彼此。

寓意：人生之途是等待黄昏？还是在现实中努力拼搏，各有千秋罢了。成玄英疏："江湖浩瀚，游泳自在，各足深水，无复往还，彼此相忘，恩情断绝……亦犹大道之世，物各逍遥，鸡犬声闻，不相来往。淳风（古朴风俗）既散，浇浪（社会风气浮薄）渐兴，从理从教（听从名人说教），圣迹斯起。矜蹩躠（矜持尽心）以为仁，踶跂（勉力行之）以为义，父子兄弟，怀情相欺，圣人羞之，良有以也。故知鱼失水所以呴濡，人丧道所以亲爱之也。"

如果在生命行将终结之时，才想起来真情的重要性，是不是太晚了？

Mutual Assistance in Hard Times

The water in the spring has dried up, and the fish are stranded on land. They moisten each other with their breath to minimize the suffering of the sun's heat. At this moment, it's better to swim in the clear waters of rivers and lakes, forgetting each other.

Meaning: If one only remembers the importance of true feelings when life is coming to an end, is it too late?

浑沌之死《应帝王》

南海之帝为儵（shū 同"倏"，传说中的神名），北海之帝为忽(倏与忽都是寓意神速的名字)，中央之帝为浑沌（喻自然淳朴的状态）。

儵与忽时相遇于浑沌之地，浑沌待之甚善。

儵与忽谋报浑沌之德，曰："人皆有七窍（指人头上两眼、两耳、两鼻孔和口），以视、听、食、息，此独无有，尝试凿之。"

日凿一窍，七日而浑沌死。

译文：南海之神名叫"倏"，北海之神名叫"忽"，中央之神名叫浑沌。

倏与忽常常相遇于浑沌的领地，浑沌对待他俩很热情。

倏与忽计划报答浑沌对他俩的款待，商量着："人们都有七窍，唯独浑沌没有，我们试着给他凿出七窍来。"

于是，他俩同心协力，每天为浑沌凿出一窍，一气儿凿了七天，浑沌死了。

（庄子认为；作为帝王应当"游心于淡，合气于漠，顺物自然而无容私。"以这样的心态治理国事，国家才能治理好。如果像倏与忽那样违背浑沌的自然形态，强迫浑沌遵从他俩的意愿，则是好心办坏事。对于君主而言，过多地限制天下人的自由，则会贻害无穷。）

寓意：不应把自己的意愿强加于人。

Mean Well but Do Wrong

The god of the South Sea was named "Shu", the god of the North Sea was named "Hu", and the god of the Center was named "Hun dun".

Shu and Hu often met in Hun dun's territory, and Hun dun treated them very warmly.

Shu and Hu planned to repay Hun dun's kindness by discussing, "People all have seven apertures, but Hun dun does not. Let's try to carve seven apertures for him."

So, they worked together, carving one aperture for Hun dun every day. After seven days of continuous effort, Hun dun died.

Meaning: If one were to go against the natural form of Hun dun like Shu and Hu, forcing him to comply with their wishes, it would be a case of meaning well but doing wrong. For a ruler, excessively restricting the freedom of the people under his rule would bring endless harm.

臧谷亡羊《庄子·骈拇》

臧与谷（臧 zāng 男仆娶婢女所生之子称"臧"。谷：孺子。幼童）二人，相与牧羊，而俱（一起）亡其羊。

问臧奚事？则挟策（用胳膊夹着羊鞭）读书；问谷奚事？则博塞（赌博）以游。

二人者，事业不同，其于亡羊均也。

译文：臧和谷这两个孩童，一起外出放羊，两人都把羊丢了。

主人问臧："为何事丢了羊？"臧回答说："我夹着羊鞭看书。"主人问谷："为何事丢了羊？"谷回答说："我与他人赌博。"

两个孩童丢羊的原因虽不相同，但是对于丢失了羊的结局却是完全相同。

寓意：做事的职责没有履行到位，究其何因都已追悔莫及。掌握做事的首要目的才是最重要的。

The Reason for Losing Sheep

Zang and Gu, two children, went out to graze sheep together and both of them lost their sheep.

The master asked Zang, "Why did you lose the sheep?" Zang replied, "I was reading a book while holding the sheep whip." The master asked Gu, "Why did you lose the sheep?" Gu replied, "I was gambling with others."

Although the reasons for the two children to lose their sheep are different, the outcome of losing the sheep is exactly the same.

Meaning: If the responsibilities of doing things are not fulfilled, it is already too late to regret whatever the reasons are. Grasping the primary purpose of doing things is what matters most.

历人生子《庄子·天地》

历之人，夜半生其子，遽取火而视之，汲汲（形容急切的样子）然，唯恐其似己也。"

译文：有一位因患疠风病而毁容的人，他妻子夜半时分生下一个孩子，急忙取来火烛察看，惶恐不安地只怕孩子的长相像自己。

寓意：人生之途多无奈，生老病死难躲开，后人平安方释怀，留下真情盼未来。

The Reason for Unease

There was a man whose face was disfigured by leprosy. In the middle of the night, his wife gave birth to a baby. He quickly lit a candle to look at the baby, feeling terrified and uneasy that the baby might inherit his disfigured face.

Meaning: Life is full of ups and downs, birth, aging, sickness, and death are unavoidable. Only when our descendants are safe and healthy can we truly rest assured. People always hope to leave their true feelings for the future.

轮扁斫轮《庄子·天道》

桓公（齐桓公）读书于堂上。轮扁（制作车轮的工匠，名叫"扁"）斫轮于堂下，释椎、凿（槌子和凿子）而上，问桓公曰："敢问公之所读者，何言邪？"

公曰："圣人之言也。"

曰："圣人在乎？"

公曰："已死矣。"

曰："然则，君之所读者，古人之糟粕已夫（罢了）！"

桓公曰："寡人读书，轮人安得议乎？有说则可，无说则死！"

轮扁曰："臣也，以臣之事观之，斫轮，徐则甘，而不固；疾则苦，而不入。不徐不疾，得之于手，而应于心，口不能言，有数（心中有数）存焉于其间，臣不能以喻（教）臣之子，臣之子亦不能受之于臣。是以行年（将近）七十而，而老（还得亲自）斫轮。古之人与其不可传也，死矣。然则，君之所读者，古人之糟粕已夫？"

译文：齐桓公在殿堂上读书。匠人轮扁在殿堂前面斫削车轮，忽然放下手中的椎子和凿子，走上殿堂开口问齐桓公："可以问君主读的是些什么言论的书籍吗？"

桓公说："这是记载圣人所说的言论。"

又问："这些圣人还活在世上吗？"

桓公说："已经去世了。"

匠人轮扁说："这么说，君主所读的，不过是古人流传下来的糟粕罢了。"

桓公非常气愤地说："我在这里潜心读书，你这个制造车轮的工匠岂敢胡说乱道？你如果能说出道理来便罢，不然我将要治你的罪。"

匠人轮扁镇静地说："我是制造车轮的匠人，我就拿制造车轮的感受来说：榫卯做得松，容易制作，却不牢固；榫卯做得紧，难以安装。榫卯不松不紧，得之于手，应之于心。嘴上无法讲清楚其中的要点，虽然心中明白其中的玄妙，我却无法教导自己的儿子，我儿也不能领悟我心中的感悟。当下我已将近七十岁的高龄，还得亲手制造车轮。古人无法用文字表达清楚的奥妙，也随着古人死去而消亡了。所以我认为君主所读的圣贤之书，并不一定就是古人的精华，而是糟粕罢了。"

寓意：《庄子·外物》："言者所以在意，得意而忘言。"匠人轮扁不能传授技能给儿子，儿子也没有领悟父亲技能中的"意",是因为有些深刻的哲理只可意会不可言传。天下之道颇有深意且复杂多面,因此古书中文字所承载的为客观事物的某些方面,若要达到至高境界不能仅靠饱读诗书,还要加以自身的思考、用心体会和领悟。古籍中的文字、理论精髓指引了后人,但思想、境界重在"意蕴"。古籍中经典言论的文字载体是后人学习必备的要素,但文字表达出来的字面之意并非这世间万物的全部。世界是在发展的,如何运用古人理论的精髓还需后人在读书中秉持自身的思考,并用心体会世间大道。无论任何书籍,都要深思其中的道理,权衡再三之后,再作取舍,不应刻板读书,也不能因书中所言而被框定思维模式。

The Art of Crafting Wheel

Duke Huan of state of Qi was reading in the hall. The carpenter Lun Bian was chopping wheels in front of the hall. Suddenly, he put down his mallet and chisel, walked up to the hall, then asked Duke Huan of Qi, "May I ask what kind of books you are reading?"

Duke Huan of Qi said, "These are the words of the saints recorded in books."

He asked again, "Are these saints still alive in the world?"

Duke Huan of Qi replied, "They have passed away."

The carpenter Lun Bian said, "So, what the monarch is reading is just the dregs left over from the ancients."

Duke Huan of Qi was very angry and said, "I am deeply absorbed in reading here, how dare you, a wheel-making craftsman, speak nonsense? If you can justify your words, that's fine. Otherwise, I will punish you for your insolence."

The carpenter Lun Bian calmly said, "I am a wheel-maker, and I'll speak from my experience in making wheels. If the joints are made loosely, they are easy to make but not sturdy. If they are made tightly, they are difficult to assemble. The perfect balance between loose and tight requires skill in the hands and understanding in the heart. It's impossible to articulate the essentials of this craft with words. Although I understand its mysteries in my heart, I cannot teach them to my son, and he cannot comprehend my insights. Now, at my advanced age of nearly seventy, I still have to make wheels by myself. The mysteries that the ancients were unable to clearly express in words have vanished with their passing. Therefore, I believe that the books that the monarch reads, which are considered sacred and wise, do not necessarily contain the essence of the ancients, but rather their dregs.

Meaning: In the book "Zhuangzi: Outer Things," it is said, "Words exist to convey meanings, and once we grasp the meanings, we forget the words." The carpenter Lun Bian was unable to teach his son his skills because the profound philosophy behind them could only be understood through personal experience and intuition, rather than through words. His son did not comprehend the "intent" behind his father's skills, indicating that some profound truths can only be grasped implicitly, rather than explicitly through language.

The principles of the universe are profound and complex, and therefore the words in ancient books only carry certain aspects of objective things. To achieve the ultimate realm, one cannot rely solely on reading books, but also needs to think deeply, experience, and comprehend for oneself. The words and theoretical essences in ancient books guide future generations, however the true significance of thoughts and realm lies in their "implicit meaning." The written words of classic statements in ancient books are essential for later generations to learn, but the literal meaning expressed by the words does not encompass everything in the world.

丑女效颦《庄子·天运》

西施病心而颦（pín 皱眉）其里。

其里之丑人见而美之，归亦捧心而颦其里。

其里之富人见之，坚闭门而不出；贫人见之，挈（qiè 携带）妻子而去之走。

彼知颦美，而不知颦之所以美。

译文：美女西施患心痛病，紧皱着眉头行走在街巷里。

巷里一位丑女看见了觉得很美，回家时也学着西施，用手捂着胸口紧皱眉头。

街巷里的富贵人家看见她的模样，立刻紧闭门窗不敢上街；穷苦人家看见她，连忙携着妻子儿子快步离开。

丑女只知道紧皱眉头很美，却不知道紧皱眉头为什么美。

寓意：只学其表，而忘其本，盲目效仿他人的外表，反而迷失了自己。

Aping a Beauty

Xi Shi, a famous beauty, had a pain in her bosom, so she had a frown on her face when she went out. An ugly girl who lived nearby saw her and thought she looked very beautiful. Therefore when she went home, she also put her hands on her bosom and had a frown on her face.

When a rich man in the neighbourhood saw her, he shut his doors tightly and did not go out. When a poor man saw her, he took his wife and children and gave her a wide berth.

She only knew Xi Shi's frown looked beautiful but she did not know the reason for its beauty.

Meaning: Learning only the superficial aspects and forgetting the essence, blindly imitating others' appearances, will only lead to losing oneself.

望洋兴叹《庄子·秋水》

秋水时至，百川灌河，泾流之大，两涘（sì 两岸）渚崖之间，不辨牛马。于是焉，河伯（神话传说中的黄河之神）欣然自喜，以天下之美为尽在己。顺流而东行，至于北海，东面对视，不见水端。

于是焉，河伯始旋（改变）其面目，望洋向若（海神之名）而叹曰："野语有之，曰：'闻道百（bó 古度量衡，万分之一），以为莫己若（如）'者，我之谓也。且夫我尝闻少仲尼之闻，而轻伯夷之义者，始吾弗信；今我睹子之难穷也，吾非至于子之门，则殆（危）矣，吾长见笑于大方之家。"

北海若曰："井蛙不可以语于海者，拘于虚（住所）也；夏虫不可以语于冰者，笃（dǔ 困）于时也；曲士不可以语于道者，束于教也。今，尔出于崖涘（峡谷溪流），观于大海，乃知尔丑，尔将可与语大理矣。天下之水，莫大于海，万川归之，不知何时止而不盈；尾闾（泄海水之处）泄之，不知何时已而不虚；春秋不变，水旱不知。此其过江河之流，不可为量数。而吾未尝以此自多者，自以比形于天地，而受气于阴阳，吾在天地之间，犹小石、小木之在大山也。方存乎见少，又奚以自多！计四海之，在天地之间也，不似礨空（lěi kōng 蚁穴。一说，小洞）之在大泽乎？计中国之在海内，不似稊米（tí mǐ 比小米还小的草籽。比喻其小）之在大仓乎？号物之数谓之万，人处一焉；人卒（民众）九州，谷食之所生，舟车之所通，人处一焉，此其比万物也，不似豪末（毫毛的末端）之在于马体乎？五帝之所连（连续禅让），三王之所争，仁人之所忧，任士之所劳，尽此矣。伯夷辞之以为名，仲尼语之以为博，此其自多（自满）也，不似尔向之自多于水乎？"

译文：秋雨连绵，峡谷溪满，百川灌河，水漫丘原。望两岸，不辨牛马；叹波涛，浪花飞溅。于是乎，河伯之神欣然自喜，以天下之美尽在眼前。河伯之神顺流而下，向东奔涌到北海，抬头望远，无边无涯，不见水岸。

于是乎，河伯之神急忙收起自得的面容，向名为若的北海之神感叹地说："俗语有之：'知道万分之一的道理，就自以为无人超过，'这是说我呀！并且我曾经听到有人认为孔子的学问少，而且看轻伯夷的义行，起初我还不相信。今日，我亲眼目睹一望无际的大海，才明白我的一知半解是多么地可笑。如果不是亲自来到这里，我就危险了，为此我将会常常见笑于大道之士了。"

北海之神平和地对地说：不要在井中之蛙面前讲述大海的波澜壮阔，因为它的目光受到居住环境的限制；不要对夏季的虫子讲述冬季的寒冷，因为它的寿命拘限于时节；不要在孤陋寡闻的乡士面前讲述天下大道之理，因为信息闭塞束博了他们的认知。今日，你始于峡谷溪流，来到大海的门前方知自己渺小，认识到自己的不足之处，方可对你讲述大道之理。天下之水，莫过于大海，万川江河归大海，而不知何时满盈；尾闾泄漏，而不知何时虚空；春秋四季没有变化。天旱，不见有所减少；水涝，也不见有所增加。海可以容纳超过天下江河不计其数，我从来也不敢因此自满。我寄生于天地之间，以阴阳之气而运转，我在天地之间，犹如小石子、小树苗生存在大山之中，我总是觉得自己很渺小，又怎么能自大呢？估计，四海的辽阔在天地间不好似内空的小石子沉淀在大湖中吗？估计中国之大在四海之内，不好似米粒匿迹在米仓里吗？号称世上拥有万物，人类只是其中的一份子。民众聚集在九州，食五谷得以生存，乘舟车得以通行，人类相比万物而言，不好似马身上的一根毫毛吗？五帝在世传承天下，三王在世争执天下，仁爱之士有所担忧，救世的圣贤又过于劳烦，这些功绩在大道面前都显得微不足道。伯夷辞去王位以成全名誉，仲尼的言论看似博大精深，这些言行都是自满的表现，不好似你一开始认为你的水势天下无比吗？"

寓意：天地广阔，人若沧海一粟，切莫妄自尊大，以免贻笑大方。

Sighing Over the Vast Ocean

Autumn rain was continuous, filling up the gorges and streams. Hundreds of rivers flowed into the Yellow River, flooding the plains. Looking at the banks, one could not distinguish between cows and horses; the waves splashed and the surging torrents roared. Thus, the god of the Yellow River felt elated and pleased, believing that all the beauty of the world was spread out before his eyes. The god of the Yellow River flowed downstream and rushed eastward to the North Sea. When he looked up and gazed afar, he saw boundless and endless water, without any sight of the shore.

Thus, the god of the Yellow River quickly concealed his smug expression and exclaimed to the god of the North Sea named Ruo: "There is a saying: 'To know one tenth of a million things and consider oneself unparalleled'- this applies to me! And I have heard some people say that Confucius had little knowledge, and they looked down upon the righteous behavior of Boyi. At first, I didn't believe it. Today, after seeing the vast and boundless sea with my own eyes, I realize how ridiculous my limited understanding was. If I had not come here myself, I would have been in danger, and for this reason, I would have often been ridiculed by those who understand the true principles.

The god of the North Sea calmly replied, "Do not speak of the vastness of the sea in front of a frog in a well, as its perspective is limited by its living environment. Do not describe the cold of winter to an insect of summer, as its lifespan is confined to the season. Do not discuss the principles of the great way of the world with ignorant villagers, as their cognition is hindered by limited information. Today, you started from the valley stream and came to the gate of the sea to realize your own minuteness and recognize your own inadequacies. Only then can I explain the principles of the great way to you. The water of the world is no greater than the sea. Thousands of rivers flow into the sea, and no one knows when it will be full. The tailgate leaks, and no one knows when it will be empty. For it there are minimal changes in the four seasons of spring, summer, autumn and winter. In drought times, it does not seem to decrease; in flood times, it does not seem to increase. I can accommodate countless rivers in the world, and I have never dared to be complacent about it. I live between heaven and earth, rotating with the Yin and Yang. I am like a small stone or a seedling in the mountains. I always feel very small, so how can I be arrogant? Isn't the vastness of the Four Seas in the world like a small stone sinking in a big lake? Isn't the vastness of China in the Four Seas like a grain of rice hidden in a grain storehouse? With all the creatures in the world, mankind is just one of them. People live on grain, travel by boats and carriages. Compared with all the creatures, isn't mankind just like a hair on a horse's body? The Five Emperors inherited the world when they were alive, and the Three Kings contended for it. The virtuous ones worried, and the wise saviors were too busy. None of these achievements are worth mentioning in front of the Great Tao. Bo Yi gave up his throne for his reputation, and Confucius' words seemed profound, but these words and actions are all manifestations of self-satisfaction. Aren't they like when you first thought your power was unparalleled in the world?"

Meaning: The universe is vast, and humans are like a single chestnut in the vast sea. One should never be arrogant or conceited, lest they become a laughingstock.

埳井之蛙《庄子·秋水》

埳（kǎn 浅井）之蛙谓东海之鳖（甲鱼）曰："吾乐与！出，跳梁乎井干（井干：成玄英疏："干，井栏也。"一说"井台"）之上；入，休乎缺甃（zhòu 砖瓦砌的井壁）之崖。赴水则接腋持颐（承托腋窝与面颊）；蹶（jué 踩）泥则没足灭跗（fū 脚背）；还虷、蟹与科斗（还：环顾四周。虷 hán：即孑孓，蚊子幼虫。一说赤虫。科斗：蝌蚪），莫吾能若也。且夫擅（shàn 独占）一壑（坑谷）之水，而跨跱（陈鼓应今注："跨跱，盘据之意。"）埳井之乐，此亦至矣。夫子奚（何）不时来入观乎？"

东海之鳖左足未入，而右膝已絷（zhí 绊）矣。于是逡巡（徘徊）而却（退却），告之海，曰：夫，千里之远，不足以举其大；千仞之高，不足以报（探）其深。禹（夏禹）之时，十年九潦（涝），而水弗为加益（增加）；汤（商汤）之时，八年七旱，而崖不为加损（水位下降）。夫（彼）不为顷（短暂）久推移（改变），不以多少进退者，此亦东海之大乐也。"

于是，埳井之蛙闻之，适适然惊，规规然自失也。（陆德明释文："适适、规规，皆惊视自失貌。"）

译文：浅井里的青蛙对东海大鳖说："我很快乐。出来时我在井台上跳来跳去；进去时我在井壁的残缺处休息养神。跳入水中，水浸没我的胳肢窝托起面颊；踩入泥里，柔软的泥淹没我的脚背。环顾四周看看那些孑孓、小蟹、蝌蚪，全都无法与我相比。况且我盘踞这一片水域独自享用，这样的快乐可以算是达到极点了，你为什么不常来参观参观呢？

东海之鳖左脚还没有迈入，右膝已被绊住了。于是，它徘徊着慢慢退了下来，对井中之蛙讲述大海："用千里之遥，不足以形容它的辽阔；用八千尺的长杆，不足以探明它的深度。夏禹在世时，十年九涝，海水不见增加；商汤在世时，八年七旱，海岸线上的水位不见减退。海域的浩瀚不因时代变迁而改变，也不会因为雨水的多少而增减，这才是住在大海的快乐！"

于是，浅井里的青蛙听了东海大鳖讲述大海的情景，惊奇地瞪着双眼说不出话来。

寓意：眼界的开阔与否决定了认知的深刻或浅薄。唯有见多识广、博古通今才能克服井底之蛙般的沾沾自得的狭隘。

The Frog in the Shallow Well

Have you not heard of the frog that lived in a shallow well? It said to a turtle that lived in the East Sea," I am so happy! When I go out, I jump about on the railing beside the mouth of the well. When I come home, I rest in the holes on the broken wall of the well. If I jump into the water, it comes up to my armpits and holds up my cheeks. If I walk in the mud, it covers up my feet. I look around at the wriggly worms, crabs and tadpoles, and none of them can compare with me. Moreover, I am lord of this trough of water and I stand up tall in this shallow well. My happiness is full. My dear sir, why don't you come often and look around my place?"

Before the turtle from the East Sea could get its left foot in the well, its right knee got stuck. It hesitated and retreated. The turtle told the frog about the East Sea.

"Even a distance of a thousand *li*[1] cannot give you an idea of the sea's width; even a height of a thousand *ren*[2] cannot give you an idea of its depth. In the time of King Yu of the Xia dynasty, there were floods nine years out of ten, but the waters in the sea did not increase. In the time of King Tang of the Shang dynasty there were droughts seven years out of eight, but the waters in the sea did not decrease. The sea does not change along with the passage of time and its level does not rise or fall according to the amount of rain that falls. The greatest happiness is to live in the East Sea."

After listening to these words, the frog of the shallow well was shocked into realization of his own insignificance and became very ill at ease.

Meaning: Whether one's horizons are broadened determines the depth or shallowness of cognition. Only by being well-informed and knowledgeable about the past and present can one overcome the narrow-mindedness of being complacent like a frog in a well.

---

[1] li: a Chinese unit of length equal to half a kilometer.
[2] ren: a Chinese unit of length, approximately equal to 7/3 metres.

鹓雏与鸱 《庄子·秋水》

惠子相梁，庄子往见之。

或谓惠子曰："庄子来，欲代子相。"

于是惠子恐，搜于国中（城中）三日三夜。

庄子往见之，曰："南方有鸟，其名鹓雏（yuān chú 传说中与鸾凤同类的鸟），子知之乎？夫鹓雏，发于南海而飞于北海，非梧桐不止，非练实（竹实）不食，非醴泉（lǐ quán 甘甜的泉水）不饮。于是，鸱（chī 古书上指鸱鹰）得腐鼠，鹓雏过之，仰而视之，曰：'吓！（恐吓）！'今子欲以子之梁国而吓我邪？"

译文：惠子做了梁惠王的国相，庄子前去看望他。

有人对惠子说："庄子这次前来，是为了替代你的国相。"

于是惠子很恐慌，连忙在城内搜寻了三天三夜。

庄子听说此事，立刻去见惠子，说："南方有一种鸟，名叫鹓雏，它从南海出发，飞向北海，一路飞来不是梧桐树它不停下来栖息；不是竹实它不吃；不是甘甜的泉水它不饮。这时有一只鸱鸟抓得一只腐烂的死老鼠，它看见鹓雏飞过来，仰头瞪眼恐吓鹓雏。今日你也想用梁国恐吓我吗？"

（庄子与惠子是挚友，庄子借挚友升迁之事嘲讽当时的社会风气不良。）

寓意：妖言惑众，圣贤不免。

The Phoenix and the Owl

Huizi[1] became the prime minister of the state of Liang. Zhuangzi[2] went to visit him.

"Zhuangzi is here because he wants to be prime minister in your place," someone told Huizi.

Huizi was afraid and searched for Zhuangzi in the capital city for three days and three nights.

Zhuangzi went to see him.

"In the south is a bird called phoenix," said Zhuangzi." Have you heard of it? The phoenix starts off from the South

---

[1] Huizi: i.e. Hui Shi. The -zi suffix is attached to the last name of a person to form a polite mode of address.
[2] Zhuangzi: i.e. Zhuang Zhou.

Sea and flies to the North Sea. It does not alight on anything except the noble parasol tree; it does not eat anything except the fruit of bamboos; it does not drink except from sweet springs. At this time an owl got a decaying rat. The phoenix flew past the owl who lifted its head and screeched, 'Shoo!'"

"Are you now using your position as prime minister of Liang to 'shoo' me off?"

(*Zhuangzi and Huizi were the best of friends, and Zhuangzi used his close friend's promotion as a means to satirize the unhealthy social atmosphere of that time.*)

Meaning: Even the sages are inevitably maliciously slandered.

鱼之乐《庄子·秋水》

庄于与惠子游于濠梁之上（《字典词典》："濠梁：濠水上的桥。指别有会心，自得其乐的境地。"濠水：今安徽凤阳县境内）。

庄子曰："鯈（tiáo 白条鱼）鱼出游从容（悠游自得）是鱼之乐也。"

惠子曰："子（你）非鱼，安知鱼之乐？"

庄子曰："子非我，安知我不知鱼之乐？"

惠子曰："我非子，固不知子矣；子固（本来）非鱼也，子之不知鱼之乐，全矣。"

庄子曰："请循（顺着）其本，子曰：'汝安知鱼乐'云者，既已知吾知之而问我，我知之，濠上也。"

译文：庄子与惠子有说有笑地漫游到濠水桥上。

庄子看到水中的白条鱼悠游自得的神态，不由地感叹说："鱼在水中自在舒缓的模样是鱼的快乐。"

惠子以调侃的口气反驳："你不是鱼，怎能知道鱼的快乐？"

庄子以同样的口气反驳说："你不是我，怎能知道我不知鱼的快乐？"

惠子辩解："我虽然不是你，固然不知道你心里是怎么想的，但是你本来就不是鱼，所以你无法知道鱼的快乐，这点是很确定的。"

庄子回答："请顺着你的本意，你说：'你怎么知道鱼的快乐？'既然你问我为何知道鱼的快乐，那么我是在濠水桥上知道的。"

寓意：庄子在与惠子的对话中巧妙地将语义由否定之意转换为肯定之意。字面相同的反问句式可以因语气与意指的不同竟然有截然相反的解读。从另一个侧面来说：心若悠然，如知鱼之乐；精神超脱，应答游刃有余。

Pleasure of Fish

Zhuangzi and Huizi wandered and chatted cheerfully to the Hao Shui Bridge.

Upon seeing the white-striped fish swimming freely and comfortably in the water, Zhuangzi couldn't help but remark, "The way the fish swim freely and leisurely in the water is their happiness."

Huizi retorted in a mocking tone, "You're not a fish, so how can you possibly know the happiness of a fish?"

Zhuangzi retorted in the same tone, "You're not me, so how can you possibly know that I don't know the happiness of a fish?"

Huizi argued, "Although I'm not you, I may not know what's in your mind. But since you're not a fish, you can't possibly know the happiness of a fish. That's certain."

Zhuangzi replied, "Please stick to your original intention. You asked, 'How do you know the happiness of a fish?' Since you're asking me how I know the happiness of a fish, then I know it from standing on the bridge over the Hao River."

Meaning: In their dialogue, Zhuangzi cleverly transforms the semantics of Huizi's negation into affirmation. The identical rhetorical question can have completely opposite interpretations depending on the context, tone, and intended meaning behind the words. From another perspective, a free and easy heart knows the joy of fish; a detached spirit could answer questions with ease.

髑髅《庄子·至乐》

庄子之楚，见空髑髅（dú lóu 死人头骨），髐（xiāo）然有形，撽（qiào 敲打）以马捶，因而问之，曰："夫子贪生失理而为此乎？将子有亡国之事、斧钺之诛而为此乎？将子有不善之行，愧遗父母妻子之丑而为此乎？将子有冻馁（过度寒冷与饥饿）之患而为此乎？将子之春秋（指年纪）故及此乎？"于是，语卒（完毕），援髑髅，枕而卧。

夜半，髑髅见梦曰："子之谈者似辩士。视子所言，皆生人之累也，死则无此矣。子欲闻死之说乎？"

庄子曰："然。"

髑髅曰："死，无君于上，无臣于下，亦无四时之事，从然以天地为春秋，虽南面王（泛指王侯）乐，不能过也。"

庄子不信，曰："吾使司命（主管人间生死之神）复生子形，为（赐予）子骨肉肌肤，反（返）子父母、妻子、闾里、知识，子欲之乎？"

髑髅深矉（皱眉）蹙頞（缩鼻）曰："吾安能弃南面王乐而复为人间之劳乎！"

译文：庄子出行去楚国，半路上看见道旁有一个骷髅头。虽然骷髅头枯空破损，还是能看出原有的形状。庄子用捶敲打着骷髅头，问："你是因贪生怕死干了些违背道义的事情而落到如此下场吗？还是因为国破家亡遭受斧钺砍杀而落到这般田地呢？还是因为自己不光彩的行为，害怕给父母妻儿留下耻辱而自我了断了性命呢？还是因为你遭遇寒冷饥饿的祸患而成为这个样子呢？还是因为你寿终正寝而如此结果呢？"庄子说罢，拉来骷髅头枕在头下睡着了。

夜半时分，骷髅头来到庄子的梦中说："听你所说的，很像是一位说客。你所问我的话，都是人间才有的苦难，人死之后就没有这些烦心事了，你愿意听我给你说说人死之后的事情吗？"

庄子回答："好吧。"

骷髅头说："人死之后，再也没有君主在上，臣子在下的等级之别，也没有一年四季的劳累，从容与天地共生息，即使王侯将相也无法与我相比！"

庄子不信，说："我请求主管生死的神仙归还你的形体，赐予你骨骼肌肤，送你重回父母妻儿、乡亲面前，以及还给你原有的知识，你愿意吗？"

骷髅头深深皱眉缩鼻，愁容满面地说："我哪能放弃王侯的快乐，再受人间之苦呢？"

（庄子借此寓言讽刺：连年战乱使得天下百姓深以为生不如死。）

寓意：时代的发展趋势，决定着一代人的命运。

Skull

As Zhuangzi traveled to the State of Chu, he came across a skull by the roadside. Although it was dry, hollow, and damaged, its original shape could still be discerned. With a mallet, Zhuangzi knocked on the skull and posed a series of profound questions: "Did you end up like this because you were greedy for life and afraid of death, leading you to commit immoral acts? Or did you suffer the fate of being hacked to death with axes and swords due to the destruction of your country and the loss of your family? Or did you take your own life out of shame, afraid of bringing disgrace upon your parents, wife, and children? Or perhaps you ended up in this state due to the hardships of cold and hunger? Or did you simply reach the end of your natural lifespan?" After posing these questions, Zhuangzi placed the skull under his head as a pillow and fell asleep.

In the middle of the night, the skull appeared in Zhuangzi's dream and said, "What you said sounds very much like the words of a persuader. The questions you asked me are all the troubles of the human world. After death, there are no such worries. Would you like to hear me tell you about what happens after death?"

Zhuangzi replied, "Alright."

The skull said, "After death, there is no longer any distinction between superiors and inferiors, no more exhaustion from the cycles of the four seasons. I exist peacefully alongside the heavens and the earth, a state even kings and lords cannot compare to!"

Zhuangzi, unconvinced and said, "I ask the gods who govern life and death to restore your body, give you bones and skin, and send you back to your parents, wife, children, and fellow villagers, along with your original knowledge. Would you like that?"

The skull deeply furrowed its brow, wrinkled its nose, and said with a sorrowful expression, "How could I possibly give up the pleasures of being a king or noble, and suffer the hardships of the human world again?"

(Zhuangzi used this fable to satirize the situation where years of continuous warfare had made life so miserable for the people of the world that they would consider death a preferable option.)

Meaning: The trend of historical development determines the fate of a generation.

鲁侯养鸟《庄子·至乐》

颜渊（即：颜回）东之齐，孔子有忧色，子贡下席（离席）而问曰："小子（先秦称：学生）敢问：回东之齐，夫子（老师）有忧色，何邪（耶）？"

孔子曰："善哉汝问（你问的好），昔者管子有言，丘（我）甚善之，曰：'褚（zhǔ 古同"储"，囊袋）小者，不可以怀（装）大，绠（gěng 汲水绳）短者，不可以汲（吸取）深。'夫若是者，以为命有所成，而形有所适也，夫（彼）不可损益。吾恐回与齐侯言尧、舜、黄帝之道，而重以燧人、神农之言。彼（指齐侯）将内求于己而不得，不得则惑，人惑则死（齐侯疑惑就会治罪于颜回）。且女（汝）独不闻邪？昔者海鸟止于鲁郊，鲁侯御而觞（shāng 举觞称贺）之于庙，奏《九韶》（传说中的舜乐名）以为乐，具（备）太牢（古代祭祀等级：牛、羊、豕三牲具备的宴请为"太牢"。也是最高级别）以为膳。鸟乃眩视忧悲，不敢食一脔（luán 小块肉），不敢饮一杯，三日而死。此以己养，养鸟也；非以鸟养，养鸟也。夫以鸟养，养鸟者，宜栖之深林，游之坛陆（水中陆地），浮之江湖，食之鳅（泥鳅）鲦（白条鱼），随行列（同类）而止，委蛇而处（顺势而为）。彼（指海鸟）唯人言之恶闻（害怕），奚（何）以夫譊譊（náo 喧嚣）为乎！《咸池》、《九韶》之乐，张之洞庭之野（成玄英疏："洞庭之野，天地之间，非太湖之洞庭也。"），鸟闻之而飞，兽闻之而走。鱼闻之而下入，人卒（民众）闻之，相与还（环）而观之。鱼处水而生，人处水而死。彼必相异，其好恶故异也。故先圣不一其能，不同其事。名止于实，义设于适，是之谓条达（条理通达）而福持（福份常存）。

译文：颜回向东去齐国，孔子面有忧愁之色。子贡起身离开坐席来到孔子面前问："学生敢问：颜回向东去齐国，老师多有忧愁之色于面颊，这是为什么呢？"

孔子说："你问得很好！昔日管仲曾经说过的话，我很赞同，他说：'囊袋小，不可装大的物件；吸水绳太短，吸不到深井里的水。'由此可言：人的性格是天生的，不同的性格适合不同的行业，人的天资不会随意改变。我担心颜回向齐侯谈论尧、舜、黄帝的治国理念，以及燧人氏、神农氏的言论。齐侯听了颜回的说教，必将尝试着去实现理想的目标。然而沧海桑田世事无常，先祖的治世之道，并不一定适合当下的发展趋势。不切实际地生搬硬套先祖的治世理念，很难取得理想的效果。如果达不到预想的效果，齐侯便会怀疑颜回的意图，齐侯疑惑就会治颜回的罪。况且古人云：'君子藏器于身，待时而动。'何时藏身？何时而动？所以'谋事在人，成事在天'。事情规划的再好，也需要天意的配合才容易成功。我害怕以颜回正直的性格，会招惹意想不到的坎坷。难道你不曾听过那个传说吗？从前，有一只海鸟在鲁国都城的郊外栖息，鲁侯为了迎接海鸟在宗庙里设宴款待，并奏起《九韶》乐章，备"太牢"为膳食。海鸟见此景眩晕忧愁，不敢吃一小块肉，也不敢饮一小杯酒，过了三天海鸟死了。这是用养人的方法养鸟，而不是用养鸟的方法养鸟。使用养鸟的方法养鸟，就应该把鸟儿放归深山野，游乐于江河湖畔、水中陆地，啄食水中泥鳅鱼虾，搜觅田间草虫稻粒，随群鸟栖息，乘轻风盘旋，顺势而为，悠然自得地翱翔在天地间。为何要剥夺鸟儿的天性，奏起《咸池》、《九韶》之乐，喧嚣于天地之间？鸟儿听到人间的吵闹声，就会惊飞半空；野兽听到人间的吵闹声，就会飞奔逃离；鱼儿听到人间的吵闹声，就会潜入深水；民众听到人间的吵闹声，就会环绕圈观。鱼在水中才能生存，人在水中就会淹死。鱼和人的天性不同，其好恶也不相同。因此古代圣贤提倡人尽其才、物尽其用。名誉要建立在事实之上，道义要设立在民生之上，这样才能称谓：通情达理，福份常存。"

寓意：顺应天性、顺应自然、顺势而为。

Follow nature

Yan Hui left for the State of Qi to the east, and Confucius looked worried. Zi Gong got up from his seat and came to Confucius, asking, "I dare to ask, Teacher, why do you look worried when Yan Hui is leaving for the State of Qi to the east?"

Confucius said, "You've asked a good question. I quite agree with what Guan Zhong once said: 'A small pouch cannot hold big things; a short rope cannot draw water from a deep well.' Therefore, it can be said that people's characters are innate, and different characters are suitable for different professions. People's innate abilities do not change at will. I am worried that Yan Hui will discuss with the King of Qi the governance ideas of Yao, Shun, and Huangdi, as well as the speeches of Sui Renshi and Shen Nong. If the King of Qi listens to Yan Hui's preaching, he will undoubtedly try to achieve his ideal goals.

However, the world is constantly changing, and the governance strategies of our ancestors may not necessarily suit the current development trends. It is difficult to achieve desired results by blindly applying the governance philosophies of our ancestors in an impractical manner. If the desired results are not achieved, the King of Qi may doubt Yan Hui's intentions, and such doubts may lead to Yan Hui being punished. Moreover, as the ancients once said, "A gentleman conceals his abilities and waits for the right moment to act." But when is the right time to hide, and when is the right time to act? Hence, "Man proposes, but God disposes." Even if plans are well-made, the cooperation of destiny is still needed for success. I fear that Yan Hui, with his upright character, may encounter unexpected obstacles. Have you not heard of that legend?

Once upon a time, a *yuanju*, a fabulous bird from the sea, rested in the suburbs of the state of Lu. With great pomp and ceremony the Marquis of Lu escorted the bird to his ancestral temple where a toast was respectfully drunk to it. The ancient music of *jiushao* usually reserved for grand occasions was played. Beef, pork and lamb which were used as sacrificial offerings for important events were spread before the bird. The bird became dizzy and pined away, not daring to touch a morsel of meat or a cup of wine. After three days it was dead. The Marquis treated the bird in the way he himself would want to be treated, not in the way the bird would like to be treated.

Using the method of bird keeping to raise birds, we should release them into the deep mountains and wilderness, allowing them to roam freely around the rivers, lakes, and fields, pecking at mud carp, fish, and shrimp in the water, searching for insects and rice grains in the fields, nesting with other birds, hovering in the gentle breeze, following the natural flow, and freely soaring in the universe. Why deprive birds of their natural instincts and play music like "Xianchi" and "Jiushao" in between heaven and earth? When birds hear the noisy sounds of humans, they will fly up into the air in fright; when wild animals hear the noisy sounds of humans, they will flee; when fish hear the noisy sounds of humans, they will dive into deep water; when people hear the noisy sounds of humans, they will gather around to watch. Fish can survive in water, but humans will drown in it. Fish and humans have different instincts and preferences.

Therefore, ancient wise men advocated that people should give full play to their talents and things should be used to their utmost capacity. Reputation should be built on facts, and morality should be established with the welfare of the people as the priority. This is what it means to be rational and sensible, and only then can one enjoy constant blessings."

Meaning: To follow one's natural instincts, to adapt to nature, and to act in accordance with the situation.

佝偻者承蜩《庄子·达生》

仲尼适楚，出于林中，见佝偻者承蜩（tiáo 蝉），犹掇（duō 拾取）之也。

仲尼曰："子巧乎，有道邪？"

曰："我有道也。五六月，累丸二而不坠，则失者锱铢（旧制锱为一两的四分之一，铢为一两的二十四分之一。喻微小数量）；累三而不坠，则失者十一（十分之一）；累五而不坠，犹掇之也。吾处身也，若厥株拘（枯树根）；吾执臂也，若槁木（枯树）之枝。虽天地之大，万物之多，而唯蜩翼之知。吾不反不侧，不以万物易（改变）蜩之翼，何为而不得！"

孔子顾（回头）谓弟子曰："用志不分，乃疑于神，其佝偻丈人（古时对老年男人的尊称）之谓乎！"

译文：孔子前往楚国，从树林里走出来，看见一位驼背老人手持一根长杆粘蝉，如拾取一样容易。

孔子感叹地问："你如此灵便，有什么技巧吗？"

驼背老人回答："我是有技巧的，经过五六个月的练习，我把两颗粘丸固定在长杆顶端，想要粘的蝉很少能跑掉；如果放置三颗粘丸，十只蝉只能落掉一只；如果放置五颗粘丸，粘蝉如同在地上拾取一样方便。再者，我的身体好似竖立的枯树，举杆子的手臂如同枯树枝。虽然天地之大、万物众多，在我的眼里只看到蝉的翅膀。我不转身也不侧望，更不会因其它万物分散我对蝉翼的注意力，这样做还会捉不到吗？"

孔子回过头对弟子们说："用心专一，就会像神明一样灵巧，这就是驼背老人所讲的道理。"

寓意：专心致志地做事，熟能生巧的境界犹如神助。

Catching Cicadas

Confucius was on his way to the State of Chu. As he emerged from the woods, he saw an old man with a hunchback holding a long pole to catch cicadas. The old man caught the cicadas as easily as picking them up.

Confucius asked in amazement, "You are so nimble. Is there any skill behind it?"

The old man with a hunchback replied, "I do have a skill. After practicing for five or six months, I place two sticky pills at the end of the long pole, and few cicadas can escape from my grasp. If I use three sticky pills, only one cicada in ten will escape. And if I use five sticky pills, catching cicadas is as easy as picking them up from the ground. Moreover, my body feels like a withered tree standing still, and my arm, gripping the pole, resembles a feeble tree branch. Although the world is vast and there are many creatures, in my eyes, I only see the wings of the cicadas. I do not turn around or glance sideways, and I am not distracted by other creatures. How could I fail to catch them?"

Confucius turned back and said to his disciples, "If you are devoted to one thing, you will be as agile as a deity. This is what the hunchback old man taught us."

Meaning: Doing things with concentration and dedication, the realm of proficiency through familiarity is like being assisted by a deity.

心有沉浮《庄子·达生》

颜渊（颜回）问仲尼曰："吾尝济（渡）乎觞深（渊名）之渊，津人（船夫）操舟若神。吾问焉，曰：'操舟可学邪？'曰：'可，善游者数能（善于游泳的人多数都能驾驶船只）。若乃（至于）夫（那些）没人（潜水之人），则未尝见舟，而便操之也。'吾问焉（为什么）？而不吾告，敢问何谓也？"

仲尼曰："善游者数能，忘水也（忘却对水的恐惧）。若乃夫没人之，未尝见舟，而便操之也，彼（他）视渊若陵（丘陵），视舟之覆（回旋）犹其车却（进退）也。覆却万方（进退自如，宛如在水中游泳），陈乎前而不得入其舍（眼前的浪涛不会造成内心恐慌），恶（何）往而不暇（闲暇），以瓦注（赌注）者巧（轻松）；以钩（衣带钩上的佩饰）注者惮（胆怯）；以黄金注者殙（hūn 心智昏乱）。其巧一也（世间的技巧相通为一），而有所矜（拘谨），则重外也。凡外重者内拙。"

译文：颜回请教孔子说："我曾经乘船摆渡于觞深之渊，驾船的船夫技巧如神。我问他：'驾驶船只可以学吗？'他说：'可以，善于游泳的人大多数都能驾驶船只。至于那些能够潜入深水里的人，不曾见过船只也能操控船只。'我问他：'为什么呢？'他不回答我。敢问老师这是什么原因呢？"

孔子说："善于游泳的人，大多数可以驾驶船只，这是他们心中不怕水的缘故。至于那些能潜水的人，虽然他们不曾见过船只也能操控船只，这是因为在他们的眼里渊水如丘陵，浪涛翻滚也不会触动他们心中的恐慌，心中有沉浮就会显现出神态自如的面容。用瓦片当作赌注，下注者的心态轻松，因为心中没有负担；用钩佩当作赌注，下注者心中惧怕失手，因此思前想后；用黄金作赌注，由于物品太贵重，下注者生怕追悔莫及，因此由于心志昏乱更容易出错。天下的技巧都是相通为一，做事怀着拘谨的心态，都是因为太在意外部环境从而影响到自己的心志。由此而言：在意外部因素的人，内心很脆弱。"

寓意：所谓心有沉浮，即言一个人对事情的结果能够预料、承担和防备之时方能处之泰然；反之，过于忧心得失以致心志不稳、惊惶失措，更容易导致事情的结果偏离意愿。

The Heart Has Ups and Downs

Yan Hui asked Confucius, "I was once ferrying across the deep waters of *Shangshen* Lake, and the boatman was skilled like a god. I asked him, 'Can one learn to drive a boat?' He said, 'Yes, most people who are good at swimming can drive a boat. As for those who can dive deep into the water, they can control a boat even without never seeing it.' I asked him, 'Why is that?' But he didn't answer me. I would like to ask you, Teacher, what's the reason for that?"

Confucius said, "Most people who are good at swimming can drive a boat, because they have no fear of water in their hearts. As for those who can dive, even if they have never seen a boat before, they can still control it, because in their eyes, the deep water is like a hillock, and the rolling waves cannot shake their inner panic. Having ups and downs in one's heart will manifest as a calm and composed demeanor. Using tiles as bets, the gambler feels relaxed because there is no burden in his heart; using hooks and pendants as bets, the gambler fears making mistakes, so he thinks twice before making a decision; using gold as bets, the gambler is afraid of regretting it later because the item is too valuable, so he is more likely to make mistakes due to his confusion. Skills in the world are all interconnected, and the reason why people are hesitant in doing things is because they are too concerned about external factors which affect their minds. Therefore, people who care about external factors are very fragile in their hearts."

Meaning: The phrase "having ups and downs in one's heart" refers to a person's ability to predict, bear, and prepare for the consequences of situations, enabling them to remain calm and composed. Conversely, being overly worried about gains and losses can lead to instability in one's mind and a state of panic, which can easily cause the results of things to deviate from one's intentions.

祝宗人说猪《庄子·达生》

祝宗人（祭祀官，亦称"祝史"）玄端（穿黑色礼仪之服）以临牢策，说彘（猪）曰："汝奚恶死？吾将三月豢（豢养）汝，十日戒，三日齐（斋），藉（铺垫）白茅（一种洁白柔滑的草，表示圣洁），加（架）汝肩尻（肩膀和屁股，借指全体）乎雕俎（diāo zǔ 木制雕绘的礼器）之上，则汝为之乎？"

为彘谋，曰：不如食以糠糟，而错之牢策之中。

自为谋，则苟生有轩冕之尊，死得于滕楯（zhuàn shǔn 具有画饰的殡车）之上、聚偻（柩车之饰）之中则为之。

为彘谋，则去之；自为谋，则取之；所异彘者何也？

译文：主持祭祀的官吏身穿礼服来到猪圈旁，对猪说："你为何害怕死亡？我将好生喂养你三个月，等到祭祀时的前十天，为你梳浇沐浴；前三天为你斋荤腥；等你死去，我会为你垫上圣洁的白茅，架起你的全身装入雕满花饰的祭盘上，你觉得如何呢？"

为猪打算，不如让猪吃糠咽菜，自由地生活在大自然中。

为自己打算，生时为了享有高官厚禄苟生，死时躲入纹饰的棺椁里厚葬。

为猪谋划，放其回归大自然。为自己谋划：贪求轩冕柩车。这与猪有什么不同呢？

寓意：以即将被作为贡品的猪来比喻人生：若一味贪求高官厚禄、锦衣玉食而殚精竭虑甚至苟且偷生，不正若被视作"贡品"吗？

Talks About Pigs

The official in charge of the sacrifice, dressed in his robes, came to the pigsty and said to the pig, "Why are you afraid of death? I will feed you well for three months, and on the tenth day before the sacrifice, I will comb and bathe you; The first three days before the sacrifice, I will abstain from eating meat. And when you die, I will place you on a sacred white mat and lay your entire body on a beautifully carved sacrificial plate. What do you think of that?"

It is better for pigs to live freely in nature, eating bran and vegetables, than to be killed for sacrifice.

For ourselves, we strive for high positions and rich salaries in life, and we are buried in fancy coffins when we die.

Planning for the pig, we let it return to nature. Planning for ourselves, we greedily pursue positions of honor and elaborate funeral carriages. How is this any different from the pig?

Meaning: Using the pig that is about to be offered as a sacrifice as a metaphor for life: If one relentlessly pursues high positions, wealth, and luxury, and even stoops to survive, isn't it exactly like being seen as a "sacrifice"?

祝宗人说猪 Talks About Pigs

心病还须心药医《庄子·达生》

桓公（齐桓公）田于泽（田猎于湖泽），管仲御，见鬼焉。

公抚管仲之手曰："仲父何见？"

对曰："臣无所见。"

公反，诶诒（ēi yí 神魂不宁而乱语）为病，数日不出。

齐士有皇子告敖者曰："公则自伤，鬼恶能伤公？夫忿滀（fèn chù 郁结）之气，散而不反，则为不足；上而不下，则使人善怒；下而不上，则使人善忘；不上不下，中身当心，则为病。"

桓公曰："然则，有鬼乎！"

曰："有。沈有履（山岭上的积水潭里有履鬼）；灶有髻（灶神）；户内之烦壤，雷霆处之（成玄英疏："门户内粪壤之中，其间有鬼，名曰雷霆。"）；东北方之下者，倍阿、鲑蠪（guī lóng）跃之；西北方之下者，则泆阳处之。水有罔象（水怪），丘有莘（shēn 山怪），山有夔（传说中的龙形异兽），野有彷徨（成玄英疏："其状如蛇，两头，五采。"），泽有委蛇（传说中的人面蛇身之神）。"

公曰："请问，委蛇之状何如？"

皇子曰："委蛇，其大如毂（车轮中心插车轴的部件）其长如辕（车前驾牲畜的直木），紫衣而朱冠（象征皇权）。其为物也，恶闻雷车之声（寓：雷神的车驾惊动了水神），则捧其首而立，见者殆（接近）乎霸。"

桓公辴（chǎn）然而笑曰："此寡人之所见者也。"于是正衣冠与之坐，不终日而不知病之去也。

译文：齐桓公田猎于湖泽，管仲亲自为他驾驭马车。忽然，湖泽上空出现异常的景象，齐桓公连忙抚着管仲的手喊到："仲父快看，那是什么？"

管仲抬头望去诧异地说："我什么也没有看见呀。"

齐桓公回到宫中，神魂不安地胡言乱言，数日不出宫门。

齐国的贤士皇子告敖听说了此事，特意进宫劝说齐桓公："你是自己忧伤成疾，鬼怪怎能伤害到你呢？你是忧虑过度，郁结的气散而不返回，造成你的精神萎靡不振；忧虑烦心郁气上头，容易使人发怒，郁气下行不返上，则容易使人健忘；郁气不上不下，聚结于心，则容易患病。"

齐桓公问："世上有鬼吗？"

皇子告敖说："有，高山积水潭中有履鬼；炉灶里有灶神；院肉秽杂之物中有雷霆；室内东北角有倍阿、鲑蠪跳来跳去；西北角墙下，有名叫泆阳的神居住在那里。水中有罔象神；丘陵有峷神；山中有夔神；野外之神名叫彷徨；湖泊之神名叫委蛇。"

齐桓公连忙问："请问，委蛇神是什么样子？"

皇子告敖回答："委蛇有车毂那么粗，身长如同车的辕木，身着紫色衣服，头戴大红冠帽。这样的异兽最厌恶雷霆般的车声，听到就会抬头观看，看见这种异兽的人，就要成为霸主了。"

齐桓公听后高兴地笑了起来，说："这正是寡人看到的。"于是齐桓公整好衣冠，端庄地坐下来与皇子告敖交谈起来。不到一天的时间，齐桓公不知不觉地痊愈了。

（庄子借"君权神授"言说时代特征。）

寓意：心理暗示对人的精神状态、身体产生着无以名状的作用。

To Cure Mental Disorder

Duke huan of Qi went hunting in the marsh, and Guan Zhong drove the carriage for him. Suddenly, there was an unusual sight in the sky above the marsh. Duke huan of Qi quickly took Guan Zhong's hand and shouted, "Uncle Guan, look! What is that?"

Guan Zhong looked up and said in surprise, "I can't see anything."

Duke Huan of Qi returned to the palace, his mind in turmoil and speaking incoherently, refusing to leave his chambers for days.

The sage Prince Gaoao of the State of Qi heard about this and deliberately entered the palace to persuade Duke Huan of Qi, saying, "Your illness is caused by your own sorrow, not by ghosts or spirits. You have overindulged in worry, causing your vital energy to stagnate and not circulate properly, leading to your lethargy. Excessive worry can cause anger and frustration, which in turn can lead to forgetfulness. When the stagnant energy neither rises nor descends, it accumulates in the heart, making you susceptible to illness."

Duke Huan of Qi asked, "Do ghosts exist in the world?"

The prince Gaoao said, "Yes, indeed. There is ghost called *Fu Gui* in tall mountains and deep pools. There is kitchen god residing in the stove. There is thunder god among the filthy and messy things in the yard. There are gods named *Beia* and *Gui Long* hopping around in the northeast corner of the room. Beneath the northwest wall, there is a god named *Yi Yang* residing there. There is god called *Wang Xiang* in the water. There is god named *Shen* on the hillocks. There is god named *Kui* in the mountains. The god of the wilderness is named *Pang Huang*; and the god of the lake is named *Wei She*."

Qi Huan Gong quickly asked, "May I ask, what does the god *Wei She* look like?"

The prince Gaoao replied, "*Wei She* is as thick as a cart hub, with a length comparable to the length of a cart's pole. It wears purple clothes and has a bright red crown on its head. This exotic beast hates the sound of thunderous cart wheels and will raise its head to look when it hears them. Whoever sees this exotic beast will become a dominant ruler."

Duke Huan of Qi smiled happily after hearing this and said, "This is exactly what I saw." So he tidied up his robes, sat down calmly, and began to converse with the prince. Within less than a day, Qi Huan Gong recovered unconsciously.

Meaning: Psychological suggestion plays an unspeakable role in people's mental state and physical condition.

纪渻子养斗鸡《庄子·达生》

纪渻（"省"的古字）子为王(据《列子·黄帝篇》中称：周宣王。一说指：齐王）养斗鸡。

十日而问："鸡已乎？

曰："未也，方虚憍而恃气（好意气用事）。"

十日又问。曰："未也。犹应向景（不能克制环境对它的影响）。"

十日又问。曰："未也。犹疾视而盛气。"

十日又问。曰："几矣（差不多了）。鸡虽有鸣，已无变矣，望之似木鸡矣，其德全矣，异鸡无敢应者，反走矣。"

译文：纪渻子为周宣王驯养斗鸡。

过了十日，王问他："斗鸡驯养好了吗？"

纪渻子回答："还不行。正处在虚而不实、意气用事的状态。"

过了十日，王又问他。他回答："不行，它听到别的鸡叫就响应，看见别的鸡就上前应战。"

过了十日，王又问他，他回答："还不行，它看到鸡，怒目而视，气势汹涌。"

又过了十日，王再次问他。他回答："差不多了，它看见别的鸡或听到别的鸡叫，仡然无动于衷，看上去像是一只木鸡，神色自如地站在那里，别的鸡都不敢向前应战，转身逃离到一旁。"

寓意：心中有章法的人，沉稳内敛，遇事不会自乱阵角。不怒自威的气场先胜一等，使他人折服。

The Fighter

Ji Shengzi raised fighter cocks for the king.

After ten days the king asked," Is the cock ready?"

"Not yet. It is still puffed up with arrogance and puts on airs."

After another ten days the king asked about the cock again.

"Not yet," was the reply." It still reacts violently to the merest sound or shadow."

Another ten days passed and the king pressed his question a third time.

"Not yet," said Ji." It still glowers and looks down on everyone."

Ten days passed. The king again asked about the cock.

"It is almost ready," replied Ji." Even though other cocks make a noise, it shows no reaction. The bird looks like a wooden cock but it is fully equipped to win in a fight. No cock dares to fight with it. They all turn and flee."

Meaning: People who have principles in their hearts are calm and reserved, and they will not panic when faced with problems. Their authoritative presence, which does not require shouting, gives them an edge, convincing others.

吕梁丈夫《庄子·达生》

孔子观于吕梁（水名。一说：黄河龙门山。一说：吕梁洪。今江苏徐州东南），悬水三千仞（周尺八尺为一仞），流沫（水势急流翻腾泡沫）四十里，鼋（yuán 鳖的一种）鼍（tuó 即扬子鳄，俗称：猪婆龙）鱼鳖之所不能游也。见一丈夫游之，以为有苦而欲死也，使弟子并流而拯之。数百步而出，被发（披发）行歌而游于塘下（堤岸）。

孔子从而问焉，曰：吾以子为鬼，察子（仔细看）则人也。请问，蹈水有道乎？"

曰："亡，吾无道。吾始乎故，长乎性，成乎命。与齐（古通"脐"，肚脐。借指水中的旋涡似肚脐）俱入，与汩（向上翻涌的水流）偕出，从水之道而不为私焉。此吾所以蹈之也。"

孔子曰："何谓始乎故，长乎性，成乎命？"

曰："吾生于陵而安于陵，故也；长于水而安于水，性也；不知吾所以然而然，命也。"

译文：孔子来到吕梁观看瀑布的景色，高悬的瀑布接近三千仞，浪花飞溅达四十余里，龟龙鱼鳖不能游过去。突然，看见一男子漂浮在水面上，孔子以为那个人因生活困苦而寻短见，急忙叫弟子顺着水流去营救。那个人顺着水流漂出数百步之后从急流中钻出来，披着头发唱起歌游到堤岸边。

孔子走上前去问他："刚开始我还以为见到了鬼，仔细一看才知道是个人。请问，你这么好的水性是否有什么诀窍？"

那个人回答："没有什么诀窍，开始的时候是出于习性。长久的习性成就了我的禀赋。我与旋涡一起潜入水底，又同涌流一齐翻滚到水面，顺着水流的惯性，不强加主观的意愿，这就是我能够自由出入水中的缘故。"

孔子又问："什么叫做始于习惯,长于禀性,成于自然？"

那个人回答："我生于山陵，因而安于山陵的环境，这就是习惯；我生长在水边，乐于在水中游来游去，这叫禀性；我说不出游泳的道理却善于游泳,如同自然的本性一样,这就是命。"

(孔子曰："少成若天性，习惯如自然。")

寓意：生长环境决定习惯，习惯成就禀赋，禀赋顺应天命。

Habits Turn into Nature

Confucius came to Luliang to see the scenery of the waterfall. The high waterfall was nearly 3000 *ren*[1] above the ground, and the spray splashed for more than 40 miles, which was so strong that even turtles, dragons, fish, and turtles could not swim through it. Suddenly, he saw a man floating on the water surface. Confucius thought that the man might have committed suicide because of his hard life, so he quickly ordered his disciples to rescue him by following the water

---

[1] ren: an ancient measure of length equal to seven or eight chi.

flow. After floating hundreds of metres downstream, the man emerged from the rapid current, with his hair flying, singing and swimming to the embankment.

Confucius walked up to him and asked, "At first, I thought I saw a ghost, but when I looked closely, I realized it was a person. May I ask, do you have any tricks for swimming so well?"

The person replied, "There's no trick to it. It all started as a habit. Over time, this habit has become my natural ability. I dive with the vortex to the bottom of the water and roll with the surge to the surface. I follow the inertia of the water flow without forcing my own will. This is why I can swim freely in and out of the water."

Confucius asked again, "What do you mean by 'starting with habit, growing with nature, and maturing with instincts'?"

The person replied, "I was born in the mountains, so I am accustomed to the environment of the mountains. That's habit. I grew up by the water and enjoy swimming around in it. That's my nature. I can't explain the principles of swimming, but I am good at it, just like how my natural instincts guide me. That's fate."

Confucius said, "What we learn in our youth gradually becomes our innate nature, and habits become our second nature."

Meaning: The growth environment determines habits, habits shape instincts, and instincts follow destiny.

梓庆为鐻《庄子·达生》

梓庆（鲁国木匠。梓人：古代专门负责制作乐器悬架、饮器和箭靶等的木工。庆：人名）削木为鐻（jù 用来悬挂钟鼓架子两侧的立柱），鐻成，见者惊犹鬼神。

鲁侯见而问焉，曰："子何术以为焉？"

对曰："臣，工人，何术之有！虽然，有一焉。臣将为鐻，未尝敢以耗气也。必齐（斋）以静心。齐三日，而不敢怀庆赏爵禄；齐五日，不敢怀非誉巧拙；齐七日，辄然忘吾有四枝形体也。当是时也，无公朝，其巧专而外骨消（世俗之念消散）；然后入山林，观天性，形躯至矣，然后成见鐻（心中有焉），然后加手焉；不然则已。则以天合天，器所以疑神者，其是与！"

译文：鲁国有一位善于制做乐器支架的工匠，名叫"庆"。他制做的支架，好似鬼爷神工所为。

鲁侯看见后惊奇地问他："你使用什么法术制成的呢？

木匠庆回答："我只是一个木匠，没有什么法术。虽然如此，我还是有所感触可以一说：我将要开始制作时，首先不敢损气伤神，必先斋戒多日，达到心平气和的状态时，才考虑如何动手。斋戒到第三天，便不再期盼赏赐官爵、俸禄后的喜悦；斋戒到第五天，便不再思考是非、名誉、议论纷纷的批评，或者众人的夸赞之词；斋戒到第七天，我的意念进入忘我的境域。当时是：无君无臣、无公无私，悠然地思寻天地之真。然后，进入山林信步而行，静观树木的天性，搜寻理想的木材，仔细推敲制成之后的形状。然后小心翼翼地施工制作。不做则已；要做，就以匠心的天真与木材的天性合二为一，借天造地设的神奇，凝结于器物之中。可能这就是其中的道理吧！"

寓意：抛弃杂念，专心致志，感悟天地之真，达到以天人合一的境地，由此制作出来的物品便有了灵气。

Devoted and Concentrated

There was a skilled craftsman named Qing in Lu State, who excelled at making instrument brackets. The brackets he made seemed to be the work of gods.

When the marquis of Lu saw it, he was amazed and asked Qing, "What magic did you use to make it?"

Carpenter Qing replied, "I am just a carpenter and do not possess any magic. Nevertheless, I have some thoughts that I can share: Before I begin a project, I first refrain from wasting my energy and spirit. I must fast and purify myself for many days, achieving a state of tranquility and peace before considering how to proceed. During the third day of fasting, I no longer anticipate the joy of receiving an official rank or salary; by the fifth day, I no longer dwell on criticisms of right and wrong, fame, gossip, or the praise of others; by the seventh day, my thoughts enter a state of selflessness, where there is no distinction between lord and servant, no consideration of public versus private, and I calmly search for the true essence of heaven and earth. Then I enter the mountains and wander freely, calmly observing the natural character of the trees, searching for the ideal wood, and carefully contemplating the final shape. Finally, I proceed with the construction, working diligently and with great care. If I'm not going to do it, then I won't. But if I do, I want to merge the innocence of a craftsman's heart with the natural character of the wood, harnessing the wonders of nature to condense them into the artifact. Perhaps this is the underlying principle behind it."

Meaning: Abandon distractions, focus the mind, and perceive the true essence of nature, achieving a state of harmony between man and the universe. The artifacts made in such a state are endowed with a sense of spirituality.

林回弃璧《庄子·山木》

假（国名）人之亡，林回（人名。假国的贤士）弃千金之璧，负赤子而趋（逃亡）。

或曰："为其布（古代钱币）与？赤子之布寡矣；为其累与？赤子之累多矣。弃千金之璧，负赤子而趋，何也？"

林回曰："彼以利合，此以天属也。"

夫以利合者，迫穷祸患害相弃也；以天属者，迫穷祸患害相收也。夫相收之，与相弃亦远矣。

译文：假国遭遇晋国侵犯，假国人都在逃亡。假国贤士在逃亡时抛弃千金之璧，背负刚出生的婴儿逃亡。

有人不解地问他："若为钱财，婴儿不如玉璧值钱；若为自己不受累赘，背负婴儿要比玉璧更受累。丢弃价值千金的玉璧，却背负婴儿逃亡，这是为什么呢？"

林回说："这块玉璧只不过因为值钱才常佩于身，这个孩子却是我的亲骨肉。"

凡是以利益相结合的，面临灾难时就会相互抛弃；以亲情相结合的，遭遇灾难时就会相互依靠。相互依靠与相互抛弃，这之间存在着天壤之别。

寓意：中华民族的天性：亲情重于身外之物的信仰由来已久。

Lin Hui Abandoning the Jade

When the country of Jia was invaded by the country of Jin, all its citizens fled. Among them, a wise man from Jia abandoned a jade worth a thousand gold coins to carry a newly born baby on his back as he fled.

Someone didn't understand and asked him, "If it's for money, the baby is not worth as much as the jade. If it's to avoid being burdened, carrying the baby would be more tiring than carrying the jade. Why would you abandon the jade worth a thousand gold coins and instead carry the baby while fleeing?"

Lin Hui said, "The jade is just worn on the body because it's valuable, but this baby is my own flesh and blood."

Those who are united by interests will abandon each other when faced with disasters; those who are united by kinship will rely on each other when they encounter disasters. There is a vast difference between relying on each other and abandoning each other.

Meaning: The belief that family ties are more important than external possessions has a long history in the Chinese people's nature.

贫穷与疲惫《庄子·山木》

庄子衣大布而补之，正緳（xié 麻绳）系履而过魏王（即：魏惠王）。

魏王曰："何先生之惫邪？"

庄子曰："贫也，非惫也。士有道德不能行，惫也；衣弊履穿，贫也，非惫也。此所谓非遇时也。王独不见夫（那些）腾猿乎？其得楠、梓（梓树）、豫章（樟树）也，揽蔓（攀缘）其枝，而王长（称王）其间，虽羿（后羿，善于射箭）、逢蒙（后羿弟子）不能眄睨（miǎn nì 不敢轻慢）也。及其得柘、棘、枳枸（zhǐ gǒu 即：枳枸。叶有锯齿）之间也，危行侧视，振动悼慄（dào lì 惊恐战栗）。此筋骨非有加急而不柔也，处势不便，未足以逞其能也。今处昏上乱相之间，而欲无惫，奚可得邪？此，比干之见剖心征也夫！"

译文：庄子身穿补丁的粗布衣，用麻绳绑扎鞋子，前来拜访魏惠王。

魏惠王看见庄子如此落魄，奇怪地问："先生为何如此疲惫不堪？"

庄子回答说："我这样都是因为家中贫穷，并不是疲惫。（庄子寓意：贫穷的原因是衣食住行中的物质匮乏，疲惫的含义则是人的精神面貌萎靡不振）当今之世，有志向的人士不能推行道德理想，因此精神面貌疲惫不堪。衣破鞋透是生活贫穷的表现，不是精神面貌的展现。此可称谓：生不逢时罢了。大王你不曾看见森林里跳来跳去的猿猴吗？猿猴在高大的楠木树上、梓树林、樟树林中攀枝飞跃，在森林中称王称霸。即使后羿、蓬蒙在世，也不能轻意射中它们。然而，当它们遇到柘、辣、枳棋这些带有尖刺的灌木丛，则会小心翼翼地放慢脚步，胆战心惊地以柔弱的动作缓慢前行。这不是因为它们收紧筋骨失去灵活性，而是因为它们所处的环境不允许它们发挥自己的特长。当下正处于乱世时期，有志向的人士希望施展自己的才能，怎么可能呢？由此而言：比干被剖心的事实就能证明这一切。"

寓意：时代发展趋势，左右着每个国民的精神状态。

Poverty and Exhaustion

Zhuangzi, who dressed in patched clothes and tied shoes with hemp ropes, visited King Hui of Wei.

When King Hui of Wei saw Zhuangzi in such a destitute condition, he asked curiously, "Why does the gentleman look so exhausted?"

Zhuangzi replied, "I am like this because my family is poor, not because I am tired. *(Zhuangzi intended to imply that poverty results from a lack of material resources for basic needs such as clothing, food, shelter, and transportation, while fatigue refers to a person's spiritual malaise.)* In today's world, individuals with aspirations cannot pursue their moral ideals, leading to a state of spiritual exhaustion. Being dressed in patched clothes and worn-out shoes is a manifestation of poverty, not a reflection of one's spiritual state. This can be summarized as: one is born at an untimely hour. Haven't you ever seen the monkeys jumping around in the forest, Your Majesty? The monkeys climb and leap from branch to branch in tall nandou trees, zi trees, and camphor trees, ruling over the forest. Even if Hou Yi and Peng Meng were alive, they could not easily shoot them down. However, when they encounter thorny shrubs such as the cudrania, the mulberry, and the Chinese boxthorn, they cautiously slow down their pace and advance cautiously with delicate movements. This is not because they have tightened their muscles and lost their flexibility, but because the environment they are in does not allow them to exert their strengths. We are now living in a troubled time, and those who have aspirations want to exercise their talents, but how can they? From this perspective, the fact that Bi Gan's heart was cut out is sufficient to prove everything."

Meaning: The trend of the times determines the mental state of every citizen.

庄周逐异鹊《庄子·山木》

庄周游于雕陵之樊（篱笆），睹一异鹊自南方来者，翼广七尺，目大运寸，感（碰）周之颡（sǎng 额头）而集于栗林。庄周曰："此何鸟哉，翼殷不逝，目大不睹？"蹇裳（提衣）躩步（快速行走），执弹而留之。睹一蝉，方得美荫而忘其身；螳螂执翳（yì 遮蔽）而搏之，见得而忘其形；异鹊从而利之，见利而忘其真（自己）。庄周怵然曰："噫！物固相累，二类相召也。"捐弹而反走，虞人（管理山泽苑囿之官）逐而谇（责骂）之。

庄周反入，三月不庭（一说三日不愉快）。蔺且（庄子的弟子）从而问之："夫子何为顷间甚不庭乎？"

庄周曰："吾守形而忘身，观于浊水而迷于清渊。且吾闻诸夫子曰：'入其俗，从其俗。'今吾游于雕陵而忘吾身，异鹊感吾颡，游于栗林而忘真，栗林虞人以吾为戮（责骂），吾所以不庭也。"

译文：庄周闲游于雕陵栗树林的篱笆下，看见一只奇异的鹊鸟从南方飞来。它的翅膀有七尺多长，眼睛的直径有一寸那么大，从庄周面前飞过时，它的翅膀碰到庄周的额头，随后落在栗树上。庄周感叹地说："这是一只什么鸟？翅膀很大，飞的却不快；眼睛很大却看不见地上的人？"庄周提起前襟紧跟过去，拿出弹丸守候在一旁。此时，庄周看见一只蝉在树叶的阴影下乘凉而忘乎所以。一只螳螂借着遮蔽突然扑向蝉，螳螂得到了蝉，却忘其自身的安全。异鹊张开大口，一口吞下螳螂与蝉。异鹊只看到眼前利益，而忘了自己的安危。庄周看到眼前所发生的一切，怵然惊心地说："唉呀！天地间物与物都是互相制约，互相招引啊！"于是，扔下手中的弹丸转身走开。看守栗林的官吏还以为庄周是在偷栗子，追着大声责骂着庄周。

庄周回到家中，一连三天都不愉快。弟子蔺且不解地问他："先生为什么近日以来都不愉快呢？"

庄周说："往日我在意表面现象，而忽略了内在的本质。看见混浊的污水而遗忘了清澈的甘泉。况且，我曾听过众夫子说：'每到一处，都要遵守当地的习俗。'今日，我游览雕陵栗林时有些得意忘形，突然异鹊碰到我的额头，我只关注异鹊的一举一动，却忘了我离栗林的篱笆墙太近，看守栗林的官吏又认为我在偷栗子而追着责骂我。所以我心灰意冷，难以高兴起来。"

寓意：只顾眼前利益，使人忘乎所以，危险也就靠近了。

Forget about Dangers

Zhuangzi was casually wandering under the fence of the orchard of chestnut trees in Diao Ling when he saw a strange magpie flying from the south. Its wings were more than seven *chi*[1], and its eyes were an *cun*[2] in diameter. When it flew past Zhuangzi, its wings grazed his forehead, and then it landed on the mulberry tree. Zhuangzi exclaimed, "What kind of bird is this? Its wings are so big, but it doesn't fly fast; its eyes are so big, but it can't see people on the ground?" Zhuangzi picked up his hem and followed closely, ready with his marbles. At this moment, Zhuangzi saw a cicada taking a nap in the shade of the leaves, lost in its own world. A mantis suddenly lunged at the cicada, using the foliage for cover. The mantis had captured the cicada but forgot about its own safety. The strange magpie opened its beak and swallowed both the mantis and the cicada. The strange magpie only saw its immediate gain, forgetting about its own safety. Zhou Zhuang saw everything that was happening before his eyes and exclaimed in horror, "Alas! Everything in the universe is mutually restrained and attracted!" So he dropped the marbles in his hand and turned to walk away. The official guarding the chestnut grove thought that Zhou Zhuang was stealing chestnuts and chased after him, shouting and scolding loudly.

When Zhuang Zhou returned home, he was unhappy for three consecutive days. His disciple Lin Ju was puzzled and asked him, "Why have you been unhappy recently, sir?"

Zhuang Zhou said, "In the past, I focused on superficial appearances and overlooked the underlying essence. I saw the muddy sewage and forgot about the clear, sweet springs. Besides, I have heard the wise men say, 'Wherever you go, follow the local customs.' Today, when I was wandering in the chestnut grove of Diaoling and feeling a bit too confident and elated, suddenly a strange magpie hit my forehead. I was so focused on the magpie's every move that I forgot how close I was to the hedge of the grove. The official guarding the grove thought I was stealing chestnuts and chased after me, scolding loudly. That's why I feel disheartened and can't be happy."

Meaning: Focusing only on immediate interests can make people forget themselves, and danger is then approaching.

---

[1] Chi: a unit of length. The system of measurement has varied across different dynasties. Currently, one chi is equivalent to ten cun.
[2] Cun: a unit of length equal to about one-third of a decimeter.

恶贵美贱《庄子·山木》

阳子（即：杨朱）之宋，宿于逆旅（旅店）。

逆旅人有妾二人，其一人美，其一人恶（丑），恶者贵，而美者贱。

阳子问其故。

逆旅小子（旅店主人）对曰："其美者自美，吾不知（觉）其美也；其恶者自恶，吾不知其恶也。"

阳子曰："弟子记之，行贤而去自贤之行，安往而不爱哉！"

译文：杨朱要去宋国，半路上入住一家旅店。

旅店主人有两个妾，其中一位长相美丽，另一位长相丑陋。旅店主人看重长相丑陋的妾，不看重长相美丽的妾。

杨朱觉得奇怪，问店主是何原因。

旅店主人说："长相美丽的妾总是不在意他人的感受，使我难以接受她自以为是的性格，所以无法体会她的美丽；长相丑陋的妾总是自谦自己的言行，使我忽略了她外表的缺陷，让我不觉她的长相丑陋。"

杨朱深情地说："学生们要记住，行贤施德的时侯，一定要摒弃自傲的心态，不论到何处，怎能不受他人爱戴？"

寓意：内在的品德修养，胜过外在的美丽。

Beauty and Plainness

On his way to the state of Song Yangzi stayed at an inn. The innkeeper had two concubines. One was pretty and attractive while the other was homely and plain. The plain one was made much of by her husband but the pretty one was slighted.

Yangzi asked the innkeeper why he treated his concubines differently.

"The pretty one," said the young husband," is very conscious of her good looks. And she always doesn't care about others' feelings, making it difficult for me to accept her self-righteous personality. That is why I do not find her beautiful. The plain one is very conscious of her homeliness. And she always remains modest about her words and actions, causing me to overlook her looks. That is why I do not find her unattractive."

Yangzi said to his disciples, "You must remember this lesson. If you are virtuous in your conduct without being constantly conscious of your own worth, you will find favour with people wherever you go."

Meaning: Inner moral cultivation outweighs outer beauty.

鲁 少 儒《庄子·田子方》

庄子见鲁哀公（庄子与魏惠王、齐威王同时代，距鲁哀公已有一百二十年，两人未曾相见。庄子借"鲁哀公"言说曾经的传说）。

哀公曰："鲁多儒士，少为先生方（道术）者。"

庄子曰："鲁少儒。"

哀公曰："举鲁国而儒服，何谓少乎？"

庄子曰："周闻之，儒者冠圜（通"环"）冠者，知天时；履句屦（古代一种鞋，鞋端有绦制之鼻的方形鞋）者知地形；缓佩玦（有缺口的佩玉）者事至而断。君子有其道者，未必为其服也；为其服者，未必知其道也。公固以为不然，何不号于国中曰：'无此道而为此服者，其罪死！'"

于是哀公号之五日，而鲁国无敢儒服者。独有一丈夫，儒服而立乎公门。公即召而问以国事，千转万变而不穷。

庄子曰："以鲁国而儒者一人耳，可谓多乎？"

译文：庄子前去拜见鲁哀公。

鲁哀公对庄子说："在我们鲁国有许多儒士，学你道术的却很少。"

庄子回答："在鲁国真正可称谓儒士的也很少。"

鲁哀公说：鲁国处处可以见到身穿儒服的人士，岂能说儒士少呢？"

庄子回答："我听说，能够称为儒士的人，头戴环形帽子，表示上知天文；脚穿方形鞋子，表示下知地理；身上佩带玉玦，表示遇事果断。真正的儒士不在意穿着；身穿儒服的人未必了解天下大道。如果你不相信，何不发出王令于国中：'凡是不懂儒术而身穿儒服的人士，一律处于死刑。'"

于是，哀公在鲁国发布命令。过了五日，鲁国不再有人身穿儒服上街。唯独有一位老者，身穿儒服站立在宫殿大门前。哀公立刻召见他，问其治国大纲、天文地理，这位老者一一对答如流。

庄子说："以鲁国之大，真正称为儒士的只有这一位老者罢了，怎能说鲁国儒士很多呢？"

寓意：所谓表里如一，是外在与内在的统一。由表及里，由内向外的一致才能称得上名副其实，否则即是徒有其表和徒负虚名。

True Confucian scholars are rare

Zhuangzi went to visit Duke Ai of Lu.

Duke Ai of Lu said to Zhuangzi, "There are many Confucian scholars in our state of Lu, but few learn your way of thinking."

Zhuangzi replied, "In Lu, there are very few who can truly be called Confucian scholars."

Duke Ai of Lu said, "You can see people dressed in Confucian robes everywhere in Lu. How can you say there are few Confucian scholars?"

Zhuangzi replied, "I have heard that those who can be called Confucian scholars wear circular hats, symbolizing their knowledge of astronomy; square shoes, symbolizing their knowledge of geography; and jade pendants, symbolizing their decisiveness in handling affairs. True Confucian scholars do not care about their attire; those who wear Confucian robes do not necessarily understand the great way of the world. If you do not believe it, Why not issue a royal decree throughout the kingdom stating that 'anyone who does not understand Confucianism but wears Confucian robes shall be sentenced to death'?"

So, Duke Ai issued a decree in the state of Lu. Five days later, no one wore Confucian robes on the streets of Lu anymore. Except for an old man who stood before the palace gate dressed in Confucian robes. Duke Ai immediately summoned him and asked about the principles of governing the country, as well as knowledge of astronomy and geography. The old man answered each question fluently and coherently.

Zhuangzi said, "Given the vastness of the state of Lu, there is only this one old man who truly qualifies as a Confucian scholar. How can you say that there are many Confucian scholars in Lu?"

Meaning: The so-called consistency between appearance and reality refers to the unity of the outer and inner. Only when the inside is consistent with the outside can it be called worthy of the name, otherwise it is just an empty shell or a false reputation.

匠石运斤《庄子·徐无鬼》

庄子送葬，过惠子之墓，顾（回头）谓从者曰："郢人(借指楚国的一位工匠)垩（白土）漫其鼻端，若蝇翼，使匠石斲（zhuó 砍）之。匠石运斤成风，听而斲之，尽垩而鼻不伤，郢人立不失容。宋元君闻之，召匠石曰："尝试为寡人为之。"匠石曰："臣则尝能斲之，虽然臣之质（对象）死久矣.'自夫子之死也，吾无以为质矣，吾无与言之矣。"

译文：庄子送葬，途中经过惠子的坟墓，回头对随从说："楚国有一位工匠，施工时一滴白灰溅到他的鼻尖上，形似苍蝇翅膀大小，他让好友匠石帮他砍下来。匠石挥起斧头呼呼作响，任凭斧头砍去，把白灰砍的干干净净而鼻子一点也没有损伤，工匠站立不动神色不变。宋元君听说此事，召来匠石说：'请你也尝试着为我砍削鼻尖上的泥点。'匠石说：'我曾经有过如此技能。但是能够让我施展技巧的对象已经去世很久了。'自从惠子死后，我就失去了能够争辩的对象，我也失去了知心的朋友。"

（庄周与惠施是知己老友，虽然行事不同，也有分歧，友情却很深厚。）

寓意：亲情与友情，均建立在互相信任的基础之上。

The Carpenter and His Axe

Zhuangzi passed the grave of Huizi while he was taking part in the funeral procession of a friend.

He turned and said to those following him," In Ying, the capital city, a man had a bit of chalk as tiny as the wings of a fly smeared on the tip of his nose. He asked a carpenter named Shi to chop it off. Shi brandished his axe, quick as wind, and with great ease chopped off all the chalk without hurting the nose, while the man stood there calmly with no change of expression on his face."

This came to the ears of King Yuan of the state of Song. He had the carpenter brought to him.

"Do it again for me," said the king.

"It is true that I was able to do it once," replied the carpenter." But not any more. The other partner has been dead for a long time."

"Ever since the death of my friend Huizi, I too have lost a partner. I have no one to hold discussions with."

Zhuang Zhou and Hui Shi were close friends who knew each other well. Although they had different ways of acting and disagreed on some issues, their friendship was very deep.

Meaning: Both family affection and friendship are built on the foundation of mutual trust.

一狙搏矢《庄子·徐无鬼》

吴王浮（行船）于江，登乎狙（古书记载的一种猴子）之山，众狙见之，恂（恐惧）然弃而走，逃于深蓁（榛树林）。有一狙焉，委蛇攫抓，见巧乎王。王射之，敏给搏捷矢。王命相者（随从）趋射之，狙执死。

王顾谓其友颜不疑曰："之狙也，伐其巧，恃其便以敖予，以至此殛（jí 诛）也。戒之哉！嗟乎！无以汝色骄人哉！"

颜不疑归而师董梧（吴国贤人），以助（锄）其色，去乐辞显（显贵），三年而国人称之。

译文：吴王乘船出游大江之上，登上一座猴山，众猴见有人来，纷纷逃进榛树林。有一只猴得意地跳来跳去，好似有意在吴王面前炫耀自己的灵巧。吴王拿起弓箭向它射去，那只猴敏捷地接住了飞箭。吴王大怒，下令左右随从共同射杀，那猴被众箭射死。

吴王回头对好友颜不疑说："这只猴，炫耀它的灵巧，依赖自己的敏捷，以傲慢的神态展现于我，以此招来杀身之祸。要引以为戒，千万不可以傲慢的态度对待他人。"

颜不疑回到家，立即拜贤士董梧为师，除去傲态，摒弃享乐和显摆。三年后，国人都称赞他的性情平易近人。

寓意：狂妄自大的行为容易招祸。《老子》曰"企者不立。"

The arrogant monkey

King Wu boarded a boat to cruise on the river and landed on a monkey mountain. As soon as the monkeys saw someone coming, they fled into the hazelnut forest. One monkey jumped around proudly, as if deliberately showing off its cleverness in front of King Wu. King Wu took out his bow and arrow and shot at it, but the monkey cleverly caught the flying arrow. Enraged, King Wu ordered his attendants to shoot it together, and the monkey was killed by multiple arrows.

King Wu turned to his good friend Yan Buyi and said, "This monkey showed off its cleverness and relied on its agility to show its arrogance to me, which led to its own death. We should learn from this and never treat others with arrogance."

Upon returning home, Yan Buyi immediately took Dong Wu, a wise man, as his mentor, and eliminated his arrogant attitude, abandoning pleasures and showiness. Three years later, the people of the country praised him for his affable temperament.

Meaning: Arrogant and overbearing behavior is prone to disaster. Laozi said, "He who tries to stand on tiptoe will not be able to maintain his balance."

触蛮战争《庄子·则阳》

有国于蜗之左角者，曰触氏；有国于蜗之右角者曰蛮氏。时相与争地而战，伏尸数万，逐北旬（十日）有五日而后反（返回）。

译文：蜗牛的左触角上有个国家，称谓触氏国；蜗牛的右触角上有个国家，称谓蛮氏国。两个国家时常为了争夺国土而发动战争。每次战场上都会遗留下数万死尸。追亡逐北需要十天半月才能返回。

寓意：古时的帝王将相，只顾扩张自己的国土，不顾苍生涂炭。据史书记载：二百多年的战国时期，共发生战争二百二十二次。庄子借此寓言讽刺那些好战者没有胸襟。

The War between Chu and Man

There is a country on the left antenna of a snail, called Chu's Kingdom, and another country on the right antenna, called Man's Kingdom. The two countries often fight wars over territory. Each battle leaves tens of thousands of corpses. Pursuing the fleeing enemy takes ten days or half a month to return.

Meaning: Ancient emperors and ministers only cared about expanding their own territory, regardless of the suffering of the people. According to historical records, there were two hundred and twenty-two wars during the more than two-hundred-year Warring States period. Zhuangzi used this fable to satirize those warmongers for being ungenerous.

盗之祸《庄子·则阳》

柏矩学于老聃（即老子，姓李名耳），曰："请之天下游。"

老聃曰："已矣！天下犹是也。"

又请之，老聃曰："汝将何始？"

曰："始于齐。"

至齐，见辜人（受车裂之刑者）焉，推而强之（合拢被撕裂的尸体），解朝服而幕（覆盖）之，号天而哭之曰："子乎子乎！天下有大菑（zāi 古同"灾"），子独先离之。！"

曰："莫为盗，莫为杀人？荣辱立，然后睹（显露）所病（祸害）；货财聚，然后睹所争。今，立人之所病，聚人之所争，穷困人之身使无休时，欲无至此。得乎（算了吧）！古之君人者，以得为在民，以失为在己；以正为在民，以枉为在己；故（因此）一形（一个人）有失其形（犯错）者，退而自责。今则不然，匿为物，而愚不识；大为难，而罪不敢；重为任，而罚不胜；远其涂，而诛不至。民知（智）力竭，则以伪继之。日出多伪，士民安取不伪。夫（彼）力不足则伪，知（智）不足则欺，财不足则盗。盗窃之行，于谁责而可乎？"

译文：柏矩在老聃门下求学，有一天他请示老师说："请老师允许我到天下各地游历一番。"

老聃对他说："算了吧，天下处处都是一样的。"

过了几日柏矩再次提出请求。老聃问他说："你要从什么地方开始游历天下呢？"

柏矩回答："我从齐国开始游历天下。"

柏矩来到齐国，看见一具暴露于街头的罪人尸体，遭车裂之刑的尸体分散一地。他费力地将分散的尸骨收拢到一起摆放整齐，然后脱下自己的朝服为死者盖上。盖好尸体他仰天号哭，说："你呀，你呀！天下的大灾大难让你给遇上了，残遭杀戮悲惨地离开了人世间。"

柏矩痛哭后，对着尸体无奈地说："你落到如此下场，是因为盗窃？还是因为你杀了人？今日的世道，统治者以荣耀与耻辱树立标杆，然后激励民众追逐荣耀；统治者为了敛财，然后目睹天下万民以利相争。今日的君主立于荣耀之上，居钱财之中，以名誉与利益困扰百姓，而使百姓永无宁日。在这样的社会环境之下，民众能做什么呢？古时的君主，将功德归于民众，把过失归于自己；将正确的归于民众，把过失归于自己。因此，有一人犯罪，不责备罪人，而是责备自己。今世的治国理念不是这样，而是故意隐匿真相而愚弄无知，提升处理事物的难度，而加罪不敢作为的人；加重权责，而惩罚难以胜任的人；规划远大宏图，而诛杀无法实现的人。民众的智慧与力气已经用尽了，只能用弄虚作假的手段应对当局。统治者的骗术层出不穷，天下的百姓岂能不虚伪？民众的能力不足的时候，就会出现造假之事；民众的智力不足的时候，则会出现欺骗之事；民众的财力不足的时候，就会出现偷盗之事。当下社会上的盗窃行为猖獗，应该由谁承担责任呢？"

寓意：社会风气的肃清往往由上至下，溯本清源，以正视听。

Misery

Bo Ju studied under Lao Dan. One day, he asked his teacher, "Please allow me to travel around the world."

Lao Dan replied, "Forget it. The world is the same everywhere."

A few days later, Bo Ju made the request again. Lao Dan asked him, "Where do you want to start your journey around the world?"

Bo Ju answered, "I want to start from Qi."

Bo Ju arrived in Qi and saw the corpse of a criminal exposed on the street, torn to pieces by carts. He struggled to gather the scattered bones and arrange them neatly, then took off his court robes to cover the dead body. After covering the corpse, he wept loudly towards the sky, saying, "Oh you, oh you! You have encountered the great disaster of the world and left this world tragically through slaughter."

After weeping bitterly, Bo Ju helplessly said to the corpse, "Did you end up like this because of theft? Or did you kill someone? In today's world, rulers set benchmarks of glory and shame, encouraging people to chase after glory. Rulers collect wealth and watch the people compete for their own interests. Today's monarch stands above glory and amid wealth, troubling the people with fame and profits, never giving them a moment of peace. What can people do in such a social environment? In ancient times, monarchs attributed merit to the people and the blame to themselves; they attributed correctness to the people and the blame to themselves. Therefore, when someone committed a crime, they did not blame the culprit but blamed themselves. However, the governance philosophy of today's world is not like that. Instead, it deliberately hides the truth to fool the ignorant, increases the difficulty of handling matters, and blames those who dare not act; it imposes heavier responsibilities and punishes those who are difficult to compete; it plans grand ambitions and executes those who cannot achieve them. The wisdom and strength of the people have been exhausted, and they can only respond to the authorities with fraudulent means. The deceitful tactics of rulers are endless, and how can the people of the world not be hypocritical? When the people lack ability, they will resort to fraud; when they lack intelligence, they will deceive; and when they lack financial resources, they will steal. With the rampant theft in today's society, who should bear the responsibility?"

Meaning: The purification of social ethos often starts from the top and goes down to the bottom, tracing back to its roots and clarifying the truth to correct people's views.

辙中有鲋《庄子·外物》

庄周家贫，故往贷栗于监河侯（刘向《说苑》作"魏文侯"）。监河侯曰："诺！我将得邑金，将贷子三百金，可乎？"

庄周忿然作色曰："周昨来，有中道而呼者。周顾视车辙中，有鲋（即：鲫鱼）鱼焉。周问之曰：'鲋鱼来！子何为者邪？'对曰：'我，东海之波臣也。君岂有斗升之水而活我哉？'周曰：'诺。我且东游吴越之王，激西江之水而迎子，可乎？'鲋鱼忿然作色曰：'吾失我常与，我无所处。吾得斗升之水然活耳，君乃言此，曾不如早索我于枯鱼之肆（店铺）！'"

译文：庄周家中遭遇生活困难，因此去监河侯那里借粮。监河侯对他说："好吧。我将要收到封邑的赋税，到那时我借给你三百金的粮食，可以吗？"

庄周沉下脸生气地说："我昨天来的时候，走到半路时听到喊救命的声音。我四顾查看，只见车辙中有一条鲫鱼。我低下身子问：'鲫鱼呀，你在喊什么呢？'鲫鱼说：'我是东海水族中的臣子，你可有一斗或一升的水救救我吗？'我说：'好吧。我正要去南方游说吴国与越国的两位国君，请他们引来西江之水迎接你，你看可以吗？'鲫鱼生气地说：'我失去赖以生存的水源片刻难以活命。如果现在能够得到一升半斗的水便可活下去。依照你所说的，简直就是要与我在干鱼铺中相见。'"

寓意：营救与帮助讲究时效，以不切实际的承诺代替当务之急的救助，无异于见死不救。

A Fish in Straits

Zhuang Zhou's family was poor so he went to the Marquis of Jianhe[1] to ask for a loan of grain.

"Sure," said the marquis." I will soon get the taxes from my fief. Then I will lend you three hundred pieces of gold. Will that be all right?"

Zhuang Zhou was pale with anger. "On my way here yesterday, I heard cries coming from the middle of the road. I turned round to take a look and found a crucian carp lying in a rut."

"'Crucian carp,' I said, 'what are you doing here?'"

"'I am a minister serving the king of the East Sea,' it replied. 'Sir, do you have a little water to save my life?'"

"'Sure, 'I said.' I am about to go to the south where I will persuade the kings of the states of Wu and Yue to channel the waters of the Xijiang River here to escort you back to the sea. Will that be all right?'"

"The crucian carp was pale with anger. 'I am out of my proper element and have no place of refuge. A little water will save my life, but you have the effrontery to say such things. You would have done better to hurry along to the dried fish shop and look for me there.'"

Meaning: Timeliness is the key to rescue and assistance. Substituting impractical promises for urgent help is tantamount to leaving people to their fate.

---

[1] Jianhe: Some sources say this refers to the Marquis Wen of the state of Wei while others speculate that this person is merely a magistrate.

任公子钓大鱼《庄子·外物》

任公子为大钩巨缁（zī 粗大的黑绳），五十犗（jiè 阉割过的牛）以为饵（鱼饵），蹲乎会稽（山名。今绍兴东南），投竿东海，旦旦（天天）而钓，期年（一年）不得鱼。已而（后来），大鱼食之，牵巨钩陷没而下，骛扬而奋鳍，白波若山，海水震荡，声侔鬼神，惮赫千里。

任公子得若鱼，离而腊之（干制），自制河（制河：即浙江）以东，苍梧（苍梧山。岭南）以北，莫不厌若鱼者。已而，后世辁才（quán cái 浅薄之才）讽说（道听途说）之徒，皆惊而相告也。

夫揭竿累（细绳）趣灌渎（灌溉用的小沟渠），守鲵鲋（ní fù 泛指小鱼），其于得大鱼难矣。饰小说以干县（悬）令，其于大达亦远矣。是以未尝闻任氏之风俗（风度），其不可与经于世亦远矣。

译文：任公子制做了一个大鱼钩，又制做了一条黑色的粗绳当钓鱼线，再用五十头犍牛当做鱼饵。他登上会稽山顶，把钓鱼竿投向东海。每天都在那里垂钓，过了一年也不曾钓到鱼。后来一条大鱼吞下鱼钩，牵动巨大的鱼钩沉入水下。不多时只见水流翻滚，掀起如山的白浪，海水猛烈震荡着，发出阵阵鬼神般的声响，千里之内的人听到此声都感到震惊。

任公子钓得大鱼，分割成块制成鱼干，分享给千里之内的百姓。从浙江以东，再到岭南以北，人人饱尝了这一美味。而后才疏学浅之人听说了此事，都觉得惊奇而奔走相告。

那些手举小鱼竿，走进小渠沟钓得如鲇、鲫一类小鱼的人士，如果想钓到大鱼那是很难的。由此而言：凭借浅薄荒诞的言论谋求崇高的声誉，相比那些通晓大道之理的人士而言相差的太远了，所以不曾听说过任氏风度的人，也不必与他谈论治世的大道理，因为彼此之间的差距太大了。

寓意：用大鱼饵可钓得大鱼，小鱼饵只能钓到小鱼，这譬如人与人的度量、风度、学识相差甚远，所以治世之大道与道听途说的口耳之学怎能相提并论。

A Big Fish

Ren Gongzi crafted a large fishhook and a thick black rope to serve as fishing line. He then used fifty strong oxen as bait. Ascending to the peak of Kuiji Mountain, he cast his fishing rod towards the East China Sea. Fishing there day after day but did not catch any fish for a year. Later a big fish swallowed the hook and pulled the huge hook into the water. Soon, the water began to roll and white waves rose like mountains. The sea was shaking violently, making god-like noises that shocked people within a thousand miles.

Ren Gongzi caught a big fish, cut it into pieces and made it into fish jerky, which was shared with the people within a thousand miles. From the east of Zhejiang to the north of Lingnan, everyone tasted the delicacy. Then people who are incompetent and shallow heard of this, all felt amazed and ran to tell each other.

Those who hold small fishing rods and go to small streams to catch small fish like catfish and crucian carp will find it difficult to catch big fish. In the same way, those who seek a high reputation through absurd and shallow arguments are far from those who understand the principles of the great Tao. Therefore, those who have never heard of Ren's style do not need to discuss the great principles of governing the world with them, as there is a huge gap between them.

Meaning: Using big bait can catch big fish, while small bait can only catch small fish. This is similar to the vast differences in people's mettle, demeanor, and knowledge. Therefore, how can the great principles of the world be compared to gossip and hearsay?

儒以诗礼发冢《庄子·外物》

儒以诗礼发冢。

大儒胪传（lú chuán 对下传告）曰："东方作矣（天要亮了）！事之何若？"

小儒曰："未解裙襦（裙：古称下裳，男女相同。襦：短衣。指：还没有解开衣裤）。口中有珠！"

"《诗》固有之曰：'青青之麦，生于陵陂（山坡）。生不布施，死何含珠为！'接其鬓（揪起鬓角两侧），压其颥（下巴），儒（你）以金椎控其颐，徐别其颊（缓缓别开面颊），无伤口中珠。"

译文：儒士用《诗经》、《礼经》的教养偷坟掘墓。

大儒在上面对坟坑里的小儒传告："太阳就要出来了，事情进展的怎么样了？"

小儒在坟坑里说："还没有解开衣裤哩。嘿，口中含着一颗大珍珠。"

大儒在坑上感叹地说："《诗》中固有其说：'青油油的麦苗，生长在山坡上。活在世上不知道施舍财物，死后含着珍珠有何用！'揪起他的两侧鬓角，压他的下颏，你用铁锤轻敲他的上颌，缓缓分开他的两颊，不要损坏口中的宝珠。"

寓意：儒生表面以诗、书、礼教见长，而其中一些儒生打着儒家学说的幌子，暗地里却在行窃盗墓。寓言借此讽刺表里不一的人士。

Inconsistency in Appearance vs Reality

Confucian scholars, despite their education in the "Book of Songs" and "Book of Rites," engage in the unseemly task of tomb raiding.

The senior Confucian scholar calls out to the junior one in the grave pit, "The sun is about to rise. How is the progress?"

The junior Confucian scholar replies from the grave pit, "I haven't even undone the clothes yet. Hey, look, there's a big pearl in his mouth."

The senior Confucian scholar sighed and said from above the grave pit, "Indeed, there is a saying in 'The Book of Songs': 'Green wheat grows on the hillside. What use is there in holding onto pearls in mouth after death if one does not know how to give in life?' Grab hold of his temples, press down on his chin, and gently tap his upper jaw with an iron hammer to slowly separate his cheeks. Be careful not to damage the pearl in his mouth."

Meaning: The Confucian scholars seemed to excel in poetry, books and etiquette, but some of them used Confucianism as a guise to commit crimes such as tomb raiding. This fable satirizes those hypocritical people.

老莱子《庄子·外物》

老莱子（楚国隐士）之弟子出薪（外出打柴），遇仲尼。反以告，曰："有人于彼，修上而趋下（谓上身长下身短），末偻（后背微驼）而后耳（双耳贴近脑后），视若营四海（营四海：形容瞻视高远），不知其谁氏之子。"

老莱子曰："是丘也。召而来！"

仲尼至，曰："丘，去汝躬矜与汝容知（智），斯（就）为君子矣。"

仲尼揖而退。蹙（拘谨）然改容而问曰："业可得进乎？"

老莱子曰："夫（你），不忍一世之伤，而骜（ào傲）万世之患，抑固窭（jù浅薄）邪，亡其（还是）略（智略）弗及邪？惠以欢为骜，终身之丑，中民（平庸）之行进焉耳。相引以名，相结以隐（平庸之辈相互吸引的是名望，相互结盟的是私恩）。与其誉尧而非桀，不如两忘而闭其所誉。反（违背）无非伤也，动（妄动）无非邪也。圣人踌躇（反复思量）以兴事，以每成功。奈何哉（为什么）其载（行为）焉终矜（总是自以为是）尔（呢）！"

译文：老莱子的学生外出打柴时，走在半道上遇到孔子。回来后告诉老师说："有一位先生，上身长下身短，后肯微驼，双耳贴近脑后，看他的面容多有忧世之思，不知道这位先生是谁。"

老莱子说："是孔丘。把他请来。"

孔子应老莱子的邀请前来拜访。老莱子说："孔丘，去掉你身上的傲气与睿智的面容，就可称谓君子了。"

孔丘听了后谦恭地作揖而退，告辞走了。过了几日，他改变了往日的神态，再次来到老莱子的身边请求指教，说："我听从先生教诲，每日闭门思过，敢问先生现在是否有所改进？"

老莱子说："你只知道忧虑一世的伤痛，却骜然不顾万世的隐患，是因为你的见识浅薄？还是因为你的智略不及呢？以施惠于人而得其欢心自傲，是终身丑陋的行为，这些都是平庸之辈所为。他们以名声互相招引，以私恩互相结盟。与其赞美尧王而非议桀纣，不如放弃诋毁与赞美。违世异俗者，无不自伤；轻举妄动者，无不邪僻。圣人谋事都是经过反复推敲之后才实施，所以每每获得成功。为什么，你的行为总是自以为是呢？"

寓意：诚挚地接受他人建议并修正言行，善莫大焉。

Lao Laizi

When Lao Laizi's student went out to collect firewood, he met Confucius on the way. When he came back, he told his teacher, "There was a gentleman who had a long upper body and a short lower body, with a slightly hunchback posture and ears close to the back of his head. His face seemed full of concern for the world, but I don't know who this gentleman is."

Lao Laizi said, "It's Confucius. Invite him over."

Confucius came to visit Laozi upon invitation. Laozi said to him, "Confucius, if you can rid yourself of your arrogance and wise demeanor, you would truly be called a gentleman."

After hearing this, Confucius humbly bowed and retreated, bidding farewell. A few days later, he appeared again beside Lao Laizi with a changed demeanor, seeking guidance. He said, "I have followed your advice and reflected on myself every day. I would like to ask if there has been any improvement in me now?"

Lao Laizi said, "You only know to worry about the sorrows of one lifetime, yet arrogantly ignore the hidden dangers of countless generations. Is it because your knowledge is shallow? Or is it because your wisdom is insufficient? To boast of granting favors to others in order to gain their favor is a lifetime of ugliness, something only ordinary people would do. They use their reputation to attract each other, and form alliances through private favors. Instead of praising King Yao and condemning King Jie and King Zhou, it is better to abandon both criticism and praise. Those who oppose the world and oppose customs always hurt themselves; those who act lightly and recklessly always behave deviously. Saints plan their affairs through repeated deliberation before implementing them, which is why they often succeed. Why is it that your behavior is always self-righteous?"

Meaning: It is the best thing to sincerely accept others' advice and correct our words and deeds.

神龟《庄子•外物》

宋元君（即宋元公，宋平公之子）夜半，而梦人被发窥阿门（旁门），曰："予（我）自宰路（洲名）之洲，我为清江（疑：长江）使河伯（黄河）之所，渔者，余且得予。"

元君觉（醒后），使人占（占卜）之。曰："此神龟也。"

君曰："渔者有余且乎？"

左右曰："有。"

君曰："令余且会朝。"

明日，余且朝。君曰："渔何得？"

对曰："且之网得白龟焉，其圆五尺。"

君曰："献若之龟。"

龟至。君再欲杀之，再欲活之，心疑，卜之。曰："杀龟以卜，吉。"

乃刳（kū 剖开再挖空）龟，七十二钻，而无遗策。

仲尼曰："神龟能见梦于元君，而不能避余且之网；知能七十二钻而无遗策，不能避刳肠之患。如是，则知有所困，神有所不及也。虽有至知，万人谋之。"

译文：宋元君在夜半时分，梦见一位披头散发的老者正在旁门窥视，并且对他说："我来自宰路深洲，我作为清江使臣出使河伯，半道上被渔夫余且捕获。"

宋元君醒来后，立刻派人占卜此梦。卜辞说："这是一只神龟，给你托梦求救。"

宋元君问左右侍臣："渔夫中有没有名叫余且的人？"

左右侍臣回答："有。"

宋元君说："传令余且来朝。"

第二天，余且应召前来朝见。宋元君问他："你捕鱼时，捕到了什么？"

余且回答："我捕到一只白龟，直径有五尺长。"

宋元君说："你把白龟献来。"

余且将白龟献给了宋元君。宋元君面对白龟又想杀，又想供养，心中迟疑不决，只好再次问卦。卜辞说："杀白龟，用龟甲占卜，大吉。"

于是杀了白龟，用龟甲占卜七十二卦，卦卦灵验，无一差错。

孔子听说了此事，说："神龟能托梦于宋元君，却无法躲避余且的鱼网；占卜七十二卦，无一差错，却不能避开杀身之祸。如此而言，智者也有困惑的时候，神灵也有法力不及的缺陷。即使至高无上的智者，也无法与万人谋略相比。"

寓意：虽然"人算不如天算"。然则，万般谋划只怕偶然。

Divine Turtle

In the middle of the night, King Yuan of Song saw an old man with disheveled hair peering through the side gate and said to him, "I come from the deep reaches of Zailu. I am a envoy of Qingjiang River to Hebo. But I was captured halfway by the fisherman Yu Qie."

After waking up, King Yuan of Song immediately had someone cast a divination spell to interpret the dream. The oracle said, "This is a divine turtle who has appeared in your dream to ask for help."

King Yuan of Song asked his attendants, "Is there a fisherman named Yu Qie among you?"

The attendants replied, "Yes, there is."

Song Yuanjun said, "Summon Yu Qie to come to court tomorrow."

The next day, Yu Qie came to the court as summoned. King Yuan of Song asked him, "What did you catch when you were fishing?"

Yu Qie replied, "I caught a white turtle with a diameter of five feet."

King Yuan of Song said, "You shall present me with the white turtle."

Yu Qie presented the white turtle to King Yuan of Song. King Yuan of Song hesitated when faced with the turtle, torn between killing it and keeping it. Unable to make a decision, he turned to divination again. The oracle said, "It is auspicious to sacrifice the white turtle and use its shell for divination."

So the white turtle was sacrificed, and its shell was used to cast divination for seventy-two hexagrams. Every hexagram came out accurate, without a single mistake.

Confucius heard about this matter and said, "The divine turtle could appear in King Yuan's dreams, but it couldn't avoid Yu Qie's fishing net. It could cast seventy-two accurate hexagrams for divination, but it couldn't escape its own demise. Thus, even the wisest among us have moments of confusion, and even the most divine powers have limitations. Even the wisest and most supreme among us cannot compare to the collective wisdom of many."

Meaning: Although "man's plans are not as good as God's plans", yet in the end, all sorts of plans may still be undone by chance.

心服与口服《庄子·寓言》

庄子谓惠子曰："孔子行年（经历）六十，而六十化（言论有变化）。始时所是，卒（后来）而非之，未知今之所谓是之，非五十九非也。"

惠子曰："孔子勤志服知（真知）也。"

庄子曰："孔子谢（放弃）之矣，而其未之尝言。孔子云：'夫，受才乎大本（天地），复灵以生。鸣而当律（天律），言而当法。利义陈乎前，而好恶是非直服人之口而已矣。使人乃以心服，而不敢蘁（wù 违背）立，定天下之定。'已乎，已乎！吾且不得及彼乎！"

译文：庄子对惠子说："孔子到了六十岁时，不断修正过去的言论。开始认为正确的，到后来又否定了以前的观点。不知他今日肯定的言论，正是他五十九岁时所否定的言论？"

惠子感慨地说："孔子勤奋努力一心想要实现自己的志向，不正是追寻人世间真正的智慧吗？"

庄子说："有人说孔子放弃了自己的志向，我却没有听到过。孔子说：'禀受才智于天地，回复灵性以全生。声音要合乎天律，言语要合乎法律。如果天下以利当先，夸夸其谈好坏曲直的道理，强迫天下人遵守，天下人也只能是口头服从罢了。如果存在能使人们能够内心诚服而且不敢有丝毫违逆的规定，便可称其为天下的定律。'算了！算了！我的才智还是赶不上孔子。"

寓意：使人心服口服的规律与法则，乃天下之定律。以利为先的规定，立意非正，即使强迫他人遵守，也只是口头服从。《孟子·公孙丑上》："以力服人者，非心服也，力不赡也。"

Sincerely Convinced

Zhuangzi said to Huizi, "Confucius continued to revise his past statements when he reached his sixties. What he had once thought was correct, he later denied. I don't know if what he affirmed today is what he denied at age fifty-nine?"

Huizi commented with emotion, "Confucius's diligent efforts to fulfill his aspirations are precisely seeking the true wisdom of the world, isn't he?"

Zhuangzi said, "Some say that Confucius gave up his aspirations, but I have never heard of such a thing. Confucius said, 'Receiving wisdom from heaven and earth, we restore our inherent nature to live fully. Our voices must conform to the laws of nature, and our words must abide by the laws of society. If the world were to prioritize profit and enforce everyone to spout empty rhetoric about morality, people would only comply outwardly. However, if there are rules that truly captivate people's hearts and make them dare not disobey, then they can be called the immutable laws of the world.' Alas! Alas! My wisdom still falls short of Confucius's."

Meaning: The laws and principles that truly win people's hearts are the immutable laws of the world. Rules that prioritize profit and have ulterior motives are not righteous, and even if they force others to comply, it will only result in superficial obedience. As Mencius said in "The First Book of the Analects of Mencius: Gongsun Chou (Part One)": "Those who use force to subdue others do not truly win their hearts; they only do so because they lack the means to resist."

曾子心悲《庄子·寓言》

曾子（即：曾参）再仕，而心再化（心情有转变），曰："吾及亲仕（做官），三釜（古代以六斗四升为一釜）而心乐；后仕，三千钟（十釜为一钟）而不洎（及），吾心悲。

弟子问于仲尼曰："若参（曾子）者，可谓无所县（古通"悬"。牵挂。挂念）其罪乎？"

曰："既已县矣。夫，无所县者，可以有哀乎？彼（他）视三釜、三千钟，如观雀蚊虻相过乎前也。"

译文：曾子再次出仕做官，然而他的心境变化却很大，他说："父母双亲健在时，出仕做官的俸禄只有三釜，心中也很快乐。再次出仕做官，俸禄高达三千钟，如此丰厚俸禄却无法赡养双亲了。因此我的心中很悲伤。"

孔子的学生请教老师说："像曾参这样的人士，可以称谓不为利禄所牵挂吧？"

孔子说："曾参心中是有所牵挂，如果他没有牵挂，为何如此悲伤呢？他所牵挂的是当自己挣得三千钟的俸禄时，却不能与父母分享他的富有，再也没有机会报答父母的养育之恩，这就是他悲伤的原因。对于那些超凡脱俗的人，无牵无挂地飘逸在自己的精神世界里，他们看待三釜、三千钟的俸禄，如同看见鸟雀蚊虫在眼前飞过一样，没有任何感受罢了。"

寓意：心有挂碍与心无挂碍是两种截然不同的思想境域。

Two States of Mind

Zeng Shen took up public office again, but his mood had changed significantly. He said, "When both my parents were alive, I was content with a salary of just three *fu*[1] of grain. Now, as I take up public office again, my salary has increased to three thousand *zhong*[2] of grain, yet I cannot use this generous salary to support my parents. Therefore, I am deeply saddened."

A student of Confucius asked his teacher, "Can we say that a person like Zeng Shen is not bothered by profit and position?"

Confucius said, "Zeng Shen indeed has something that he cannot let go of. If he didn't, why would he be so sad? What he cannot let go of is the fact that when he earns a salary of three thousand *zhong*, he cannot share his wealth with his parents and no longer has the chance to repay their nurturing grace. This is the reason for his sadness. For those who are transcendent and detached, floating freely in their own spiritual world, they view a salary of three *fu* or three thousand *zhong* as if they were seeing birds and insects flying past them, without any feelings whatsoever."

Meaning: Having attachments in one's heart versus being detached from all attachments represent two vastly different states of ideological realm.

杨朱与老子《庄子·寓言》

阳子居（即：杨朱）南之沛。老聃（老子）西游于秦。邀于郊，至于梁（沛郊地名）而遇老子。老子中道仰天而叹曰："始以汝为可教，今不可也。"

阳子居不答。至舍，进盥漱巾栉（zhì 梳子、篦子等），脱屦户外，膝行而前，曰："向者（刚才）弟子欲请夫子，夫子行不闲，是以不敢。今闲矣，请问其过。"

老子曰："而睢睢盱盱（飞扬跋扈），而谁与居（相处）？大白（完全显露）若辱，盛德若不足。"

阳子居蹴然（cù rán 惊惭不安）变容曰："敬闻命矣！"

其往也，舍者迎将（迎接），其家公（店家主人）执席，妻（店主之妻）执巾栉，舍者避席（让出坐席），炀

---

[1] fu; zhong: The ranks and units of measurement for salaries. The fu is usually used to measure less grain, while the zhong is used for larger capacity.

[2] fu; zhong: The ranks and units of measurement for salaries. The fu is usually used to measure less grain, while the zhong is used for larger capacity.

者（灶下烧火的伙夫）避灶（让出灶火的温暖）。其反也，舍者与之争席矣。

译文：阳子居南下前往沛地。老子西行漫游在秦国。阳子居邀请老子在沛地相见。阳子居走到沛地郊外梁地时，才迎上老子。在返回沛地的半路上，老子仰天长叹，说："起初，我以为你是可教导的人，见到你才知道你是不可受教的。"

阳子居没有回答。二人来到旅店后，阳子居端着洗漱用具，把鞋子脱在门外，跪行到老子面前说："刚才在半路上，我原本想要请教先生，看到先生忙于赶路，所以不敢冒然启齿。现在先生已然闲暇，请问先生，学生错在什么地方？"

老子说："我来与你相见，还认为你可教，见到后，看到你飞扬跋扈的神态，谁愿意与自命不凡的人相处呢？完全显露自己志向，宛如向人展示耻辱。品德高尚的人，常以自谦的言行举止示人。"

阳子居惊讶而渐愧地说："谨遵先生教诲，学生铭记在心。"

阳子居送别老子返回旅店，旅店里所有人都热情地迎接他。店主亲自为他安排了坐席，店主的妻子为他拿来毛巾和梳子，旅客们主动为他让出席位，灶下烧火的厨工也让出炉火。等到阳子居离开旅店返家时，店内所有人都争着坐一坐阳子居曾经坐过的席位，都想亲自感受阳子居的气息。

寓意：自谦的人，时时在意他人的感受，因此容易与人相处，也容易赢得他人的尊重。

Yang Zhu and Laozi

Yang Zhu traveled southward to Pei, while Laozi traveled westward to Qin. Yang Zhu invited Laozi to meet in Pei. Yang Zhu met Laozi only when he arrived at Liang, which was outside of Pei. On the way back to Pei, Laozi looked up at the sky and sighed, saying, "At first, I thought you were someone who could be taught, but now I see that you are not."

Yang Zhu did not respond. After they arrived at the inn, Yang Zhu carried his toiletries, took off his shoes outside the door, and knelt down to approach Laozi, saying, "On the halfway there, I originally intended to ask you for advice, but seeing that you were busy on the road, I dared not speak. Now since you are free, could you please tell me where I went wrong?"

Laozi said, "When I came to meet you, I still thought you were someone who could be taught. However, after meeting you and seeing your arrogant demeanor, who would want to associate with someone who thinks they are exceptional? To fully reveal your ambitions is like displaying shame to others. A virtuous person always demonstrates humility in their words and actions."

Yang Zhu, surprised and ashamed, said, "I will follow your wise advice, Mr. Laozi. Your words are deeply imprinted in my heart."

After bidding farewell to Laozi, Yang Zhu returned to the inn. Everyone there warmly welcomed him. The innkeeper personally arranged a seat for him, and his wife brought him a towel and comb. Fellow travelers offered up their seats, and even the kitchen staff gave him the prime spot next to the fire. When Yang Zhu left the inn and returned home, everyone in the inn competed to sit in the seat he had once occupied, eager to experience a bit of his aura.

Meaning: A modest person always takes others' feelings into consideration, which makes it easy to get along with others and win respect from them.

大王亶父《庄子·让王》

大王亶父（dǎn fù 即：古公亶父。周文王的祖父）居邠（今作"彬县"），狄人攻之。事之（给予）皮帛而不受，事之以犬马而不受，事之以珠玉而不受，狄人之所求者土地也。

大王亶父曰："与人之兄居，而杀其弟；与人之父居，而杀其子，吾不忍也。子皆勉（勉强）居矣！为我臣与为狄人臣，奚（何）以异！且吾闻之，不以所用养害所养。"因杖策（柱杖）而去之。民相连（相续）而从之，遂成国于岐山之下。

夫大王亶父，可谓能尊生矣。能尊生者，虽贵富，不以养伤身；虽贫贱，不以利累形（累身）。今世之人居高官尊爵者，皆重（多）失之，见利轻亡其身，岂不惑哉！

译文：大王亶父居住在邠地，狄人前来侵犯。大王亶父为了避免百姓受到伤害，向狄人提出以物质求和的提议。给予狄人兽皮丝织品，他们不接受；给予良狗名马，他们也不接受；给予珍珠宝玉，他们仍不接受；狄人所要的是占有这里的土地。

大王亶父说："和人家的兄长住在一起，却要杀害兄长的弟弟；和人家的父母住在一起，却要杀害父母的儿子。我不忍心做这样的事情。你们就勉强留在这里，反正做我的臣民与做狄人的臣民，没有太大区别。况且我听说：不以养活百姓的土地去伤害土地上生活的百姓。"于是大王亶父拄着拐杖离开了邠地。邠地的百姓相继跟随着他离开了此地，漂泊到岐山脚下重新建起国家。

此大王亶父，可称谓尊重生命的典范。能够尊重生命的人，虽然在意富贵，也不会为了追求富贵而伤害他人的性命；虽然贫贱，也不会为了追求利益而伤害他人的身体。当今之人，那些占居高官厚禄者，多数都不是这样的价值观，而是为了追逐利益不顾他人的生命安危，这样的价值观岂能不使人感到困惑吗？

寓意：人的生命高于一切，高尚的品德源于尊重他人的生命。

King Danfu

King Danfu resided in the region of Bin when the Di tribe came to invade. In order to protect his subjects from harm, King Danfu proposed a peace offering to the invaders. He offered them animal hides and silk fabrics, but they refused; he offered fine dogs and renowned horses, but they still declined; he even offered pearls and precious stones, yet they remained unmoved. What the Di tribe truly desired was possession of the land.

King Danfu said, "It is unacceptable to live with someone's elder brother yet intend to kill his younger brother, or to live with someone's parents yet intend to kill their son. I cannot bear to do such things. You may stay here if you wish, as there is not much difference between being my people and being people of the Di tribe. Besides, I have heard that one should not harm the people who live on the land in order to own the land that sustains them." With these words, King Danfu left Bin on his crutches. The people of Bin followed him in succession, wandering to the foot of the Qi Mountain and rebuilding their country there.

King Danfu can truly be called a paradigm of respecting life. Those who respect life, although they care about wealth and status, will not harm others' lives in pursuit of them; and although they may be poor, they will not harm others' bodies in pursuit of profit. In contrast, many of today's individuals in positions of high power and privilege do not hold such values. Instead, they prioritize their own interests, disregarding the safety and well-being of others. Cannot such values leave people feeling perplexed and concerned?

Meaning: Human life is above everything, and noble character comes from respecting the lives of others.

王子搜之惧《庄子·让王》

越人三世弑其君（越王翳被儿所杀；越人又杀他儿；立无余为君，又杀）。王子搜（即：无颛）患之，逃乎丹穴（山洞）。而越国无君，求王子搜不得，从（追）之丹穴。

王子搜不肯出，越人薰之以艾（艾草）。乘以王舆（车）。王子搜援绥（suí 登车时手挽的绳索）登车，仰天而呼，曰："君乎，君乎！独不可以舍我乎！"

王子搜非恶为君也，恶为君之患也。若王子搜者，可谓不以国伤生矣，此固越人之所欲得为君也。

译文：越国三代的君主连续遭到弑杀。王子搜非常害怕，逃于丹山的洞穴里躲藏起来。然而，越国不能没有国君。众大臣下令四处搜寻，一直追到丹山，才发现王子搜躲在山洞里。

众官吏在洞外无论怎样呼喊，王子搜就是不敢走出来。无奈之下，众官吏烧起艾草烟熏洞穴，王子搜实在难以忍受烟熏的痛苦，只好走了出来。众官吏立刻拥戴他登上王车，他手挽着登车的绳索，仰天呼喊说："王位啊，王位啊，唯独不能放弃我吗！"

王子搜并不是害怕登上王位，而是害怕王位带来的隐患。像王子搜这样的人，可以说是不因贪求国君的地位而伤害自己的生命，这正是越国人希望他登上王位的原因。

寓意：不贪求名望和地位的人，有时反而更容易得到声誉和与官爵。

Prince Sou's Fear

Three generations of the monarchs of Yue were assassinated consecutively. Prince Sou was so terrified that he fled and hid in a cave on Danshan Mountain. However, Yue could not be without a monarch. The ministers ordered a search, and eventually found Prince Sou hiding in the cave on Danshan Mountain.

No matter how loudly the officials shouted outside the cave, Prince Sou just wouldn't come out. In desperation, the officials set fire to artemisia to smoke out the cave. Unable to bear the pain of the smoke, Prince Sou finally emerged. Immediately the officials escorted him onto the royal chariot. Holding onto the rope, he looked up to the sky and cried out, "Oh throne, throne, why can't you leave me alone!"

It was not the throne that Prince Sou was afraid of, but the hidden dangers it brought. A person like Prince Sou, who was not willing to jeopardize his life for the position of the king, was precisely the reason why the people of Yue hoped for him to ascend the throne.

Meaning: People who do not covet fame and status are sometimes more likely to gain reputation and official positions.

子华子谏言《庄子·让王》

韩魏相与争侵地。子华子（魏国贤人，思想接近道家学派）见昭僖侯（韩昭侯）。昭僖侯有忧色，子华子曰："今使天下书铭于君之前，书之言曰：'左手攫之，则右手废（砍下），右手攫之，则左手废，然而攫之者必有天下。'君能攫之乎？"

昭僖侯曰："寡人不攫也。"

子华子曰："甚善！自是观之，两臂重于天下也，身亦重于两臂。韩之轻于天下亦远矣。今之所争者，其轻于韩又远。君固愁身伤生，以忧戚（忧愁）不得也！"

僖侯曰："善哉！教寡人者众矣，未尝得闻此言也。"

子华子可谓知轻重矣。

译文：韩国与魏国为了争夺土地而发动战争。魏国贤人子华子为此事前来拜访韩国昭僖侯。进宫后，他看出昭僖侯面有忧愁的神色。子华子说："假如当下有天下书的契约摆在君主的面前，契约铭言：'左手攫取天下，则砍去右手；右手攫取天下，则砍去左手。'君主你是否为了拥有天下，而甘愿失去一只手呢？"

昭僖侯说："寡人不会为了取得天下而失去一只手。"

子华子说："很好，由此看来，你的双臂比拥有天下重要，你的生命比双臂重要。韩国与天下相比，轻于后者。现在所争夺的土地，又轻于韩国。然而君主为了边境上的国土得失，忧愁苦恼以致伤害到自己的生命，这样的忧愁才是得不偿失啊！"

僖侯爽朗地说："说的好！开导我的人很多，却没有人能把其中的利害关系讲的如此透彻。"

寓意：说服他人的根本在于对事态发展趋势有清晰的认知，讲利弊、判得失，有理有据，使对方心悦诚服。

Zi Huazi's advice

To compete for land, both the State of Han and the State of Wei launched a war. As a wise man in Wei, Zi Huazi visited the King Zhao Xi of Han for this matter. After entering the palace, he noticed that the King Zhao Xi had a worried look. Zi Huazi said, "If there were a contract of the world's books in front of you now, stating that 'if you seize the world with your left hand, you will lose your right hand; if you seize the world with your right hand, you will lose your left hand,' would you be willing to lose one of your hands in order to possess the world?"

King Zhao Xi said, "I would not lose a hand in order to gain the world."

Zi Huazi said, "Excellent, from this, it can be seen that your arms are more important than possessing the world, and your life is more valuable than your arms. Han compared to the world is less important. The land being contested now is even less valuable than Han. However, the king worries and suffers to the point of hurting his own life because of the gains and losses of territory on the border. Such worry is truly a loss greater than the gain."

King Zhao Xi responded with a cheerful laugh, "Well said! I have had many advisers, but none have been able to explain the pros and cons so thoroughly as you."

Meaning: The fundamental of persuading others lies in having a clear understanding of the trend of events, analyzing advantages and disadvantages, and judging losses and gains in a reasonable and well-grounded manner, so that the other party can be convinced.

颜阖守陋闾《庄子·让王》

鲁君（即：鲁哀公。一说鲁定公）闻颜阖（鲁国隐士）得道之人也，使人以币先焉（慰问）。颜阖守陋闾（陋巷），苴布之衣，而自饭牛（喂牛）。鲁君之使者至，颜阖自对之。

使者曰："此颜阖之家与？"

颜阖对曰，"此阖之家也。"

使者致币，颜阖对曰："恐听者谬，而遗使者罪，不若审之。"

使者还，反审之，复来求之，则不得已。故若颜阖者，真恶富贵也。

故曰：道之真，以治身；其绪余（残余），以为国家；其土苴（土芥）以治天下。由此观之，帝王之功，圣人之余事也，非所以完身养生也。今，世俗之君子，多危身弃生以殉（追逐）物，岂不悲哉！凡圣人之动作也，必察其所以之，与其所以为。今且有人于此，以随侯之珠（指：周时汉中随侯得到的一颗明珠）弹千仞之雀，世必笑之。是何也？则其所用者重（贵重），而所要者轻也。夫生者，岂特随侯之重哉！"

译文：鲁哀公听说颜阖是一位得道的圣贤人士，特意派遣使臣送去财物以示慰问。颜阖居住在狭窄巷子里，身穿麻布粗衣，自己动手喂牛。鲁哀公的使臣来到他家，颜阖亲自接待他。

使臣问他说："这里是颜阖先生的家吗？"

颜阖回答说："这是颜阖的家。"

使臣拿出鲁君送给他的礼物。

颜阖连忙说："恐怕是你听错了，如果因为你没有听明白而造成失误，鲁君一定会怪罪你，不如回去核实一下。"

使臣返回再三核实，确认无误又来到颜阖的家，颜阖此时已经搬迁到别的地方去了。所以，像颜阖这样的人，才是真正厌恶富贵的人。

因此，《道》的精华在于修身养性；《道》的残余用于治国；《道》的糟粕用于治天下。由此看来，帝王的功绩只是圣人的残余之事，并不用于养生。反观当下的世俗君子，多以危害身体的方式，不顾生命极限追逐财富，岂能不让人感到悲哀吗？大凡圣人做事，必先思考为什么要做，还要思考怎么做更有价值。现在，如果有人在此时用随侯之珠，去射杀千仞高空里的麻雀，世人一定会嘲笑他。这是因为什么呢？是因为所使用的东西太珍贵，而收获的东西太轻贱了。请问，人的生命，岂能如随侯之珠的价值吗？

寓意：何为轻重缓急？何为修身养性？明晓大道之理，便能分清事情的轻重与主次。

The Simple Virtue of the Sage

Duke Ai of Lu heard that Yan He was a sage who had attained enlightenment, and specifically sent an envoy to deliver financial gifts as a gesture of consolation. Yan He resided in a narrow alley, dressed in coarse hempen clothing, and fed his own cows. When the emissaries of Duke Ai arrived at his humble abode, Yan He greeted them personally.

The envoy asked, "Is this the residence of Master Yan He?"

Yan He replied, "Yes, this is the home of Yan He."

The envoy then presented the gifts sent by Duke Ai of Lu.

Yan He quickly said, "Perhaps you have misunderstood. If your lack of clarity leads to a mistake, Duke Ai of Lu will surely blame you. It would be better for you to go back and verify the information."

The envoy returned to double-check and confirm that there were no mistakes, and then came to Yan He's house again. However, by then, Yan He had already moved to another place. Consequently, individuals like Yan He genuinely despise wealth and status.

Therefore, the essence of the Tao lies in self-cultivation; the remnants of the Tao are used to govern the country; and the dregs of the Tao are used to manage the world. From this perspective, the achievements of the emperor are merely remnants of the saints and are not used for self-nourishment. On the contrary, looking at the present secular gentlemen, many of them pursue wealth at the cost of their health, ignoring the limits of their lives. Isn't it sad? Great saints always consider the reasons and values of their actions before taking any actions. Nowadays, if someone were to use the Pearl of Suihou to shoot a sparrow flying thousands of feet in the air, people would certainly laugh at him. Why is that? It's because the tool used is too precious, while the reward is too insignificant. May I ask, is human life comparable to the value of the Pearl of Suihou?

Meaning: What is the priority of things? What is self-cultivation? Understanding the way of Tao, one can distinguish the importance and priority of things.

客之言《庄子·让王》

子列子（即：列御寇）穷，容貌有饥色。客有言之于郑子阳（郑国国相，名叫子阳）者曰："列御寇，盖有道之士也，居君之国而穷，君无乃为不好士乎？"

郑子阳即令官遗之粟。子列子见使者，再拜而辞。

使者去，子列子入，其妻望（失望）之，而拊心（fǔ xīn 拍胸。表示哀痛）曰："妾闻为有道者之妻子，皆得佚乐。今有饥色，君过而遗先生食，先生不受，岂不命邪！"

子列子笑，谓之曰："君非自知我也，以人之言而遗我粟，至其罪我也，又且以人之言，此吾所以不受也。"

其卒（后来），民果作难而杀子阳。

译文：列子因家中贫困，面带饥饿的神色。有位过客看到列子的脸色不好，便对国相子阳谏言说："列御寇，是一位有道的人士，居住在君主的国家里忍受贫穷的煎熬，君主岂不是不惜有道之士吗？"

国相子阳即刻下令馈送财物于列子。列子见到使臣，再三拜谢推辞馈送的财物。

使臣离开后，列子走进屋内，其妻失望地拍着胸口说："我听说做有道人士的妻子，都能过上不愁吃喝的日子，谁想到今日还得挨饿。国相得知后自觉有愧，特意馈送财物，你却拒不接受，岂不是命该受穷吗？

列子微笑地对妻子说："国相并不是亲眼看到我们的处境，他只是凭着传言而馈送财物。等到他要治我的罪时，也会凭着传言治我的罪，所以我不敢接受因传言带来的馈送。"

后来，郑国民众果然发难杀了子阳。

寓意：圣贤之士懂得为人处世的原则，明晓传言并不牢靠，从而避免了不必要的灾祸，真可谓是趋吉避凶。

Words of the Guest

Due to his poverty, Liezi's face looked hungry. When a passerby noticed his poor complexion, he advised the Prime Minister Ziyang, " Liezi is a man of wisdom, but he has to endure poverty in our country. Doesn't the king cherish wise men?"

Upon hearing the guest's words, Prime Minister Ziyang immediately ordered to send gifts to Liezi. When Liezi saw the envoy, he refused the gifts by bowing and thanking them repeatedly.

After the envoy left, Liezi went inside his house, and his wife was disappointed and patted her chest, saying, "I've heard that wives of wise men live comfortably without worrying about food and drink, but who would have thought that we would still have to starve today? The Prime Minister felt guilty and intentionally sent gifts, but you refused to accept them. Isn't it fate that we should be poor?"

Liezi smiled and said to his wife, "The Prime Minister did not witness our situation personally. He only sent the gifts based on rumors. And when he wants to punish me, he will also do so based on rumors. Therefore, I dare not accept gifts brought by rumors."

Later, the people of Zheng indeed revolted and killed Ziyang.

Meaning: The wise and virtuous understand the principles of life and know rumors are not reliable, thus avoiding unnecessary disasters. They can truly be described as seeking good fortune and avoiding misfortune.

屠羊说《庄子·让王》

楚昭王失国（昭王：名轸，楚平王的儿子。失国：吴伐楚，楚昭王逃亡，因而失去国土），屠羊说（以屠羊为业。名叫"说"）走而从于昭王。昭王反(返)国，将赏从者，及屠羊说。

屠羊说曰："大王失国，说失屠羊；大王反国，说亦反屠羊。臣之爵禄已复矣，又何赏之有！"

王曰："强之（强令接受）。"

屠羊说曰："大王失国，非臣之罪，故不敢伏其诛；大王反国，非臣之功，故不敢当其赏。"

王曰："见之。"

屠羊说曰："楚国之法，必有重赏大功而后得见。今，臣之知（智）不足以存国；而勇不足以死寇。吴军入郢（楚国都城），说畏难而避寇，非故随大王也。今大王欲废法毁约而见说，此非臣之所以闻于天下也。"

王谓（对）司马子綦曰："屠羊说居处卑贱，而陈义甚高，子綦为我延（yán 引）之以三旌之位。"

屠羊说曰："夫三旌之位，吾知其贵于屠羊之肆也；万钟之禄，吾知其富于屠羊之利也；然岂可以贪爵禄而使吾君有妄施之名乎？说不敢当，愿复反吾屠羊之肆。"遂不受也。

译文：吴国举兵侵犯楚国，并且攻占了楚国都城。楚昭王逃亡在外失去了国土，屠羊者说也跟随着楚昭王逃走。后来楚军战胜吴军，楚昭王返回祖国，赏赐跟随的臣子，其中也包括屠羊者说。

赏赐轮到屠羊者说的时候，他言道："大王失去国土，我失去屠羊的职业；大王收复国土，我也恢复屠羊的职业。我的俸禄已经恢复了，哪里还有领赏的道理呢？"

昭王听了回禀，下令："必须接受赏赐。"

屠羊者说又言："大王失去国土，并不是我的过错，因此我不敢认其罪；大王收复国土，也不是我的功劳，所以我也不敢领赏。"

昭王听了再次回禀，觉得屠羊者说讲的有道理，于是下令："召屠羊者说进见。"

屠羊者说再言："楚国的法律规定，必先有重大立功表现的人士而后得以召见。当下我的智商不足以保卫国土，我的勇敢不足以杀敌建功。吴国的军队侵入都城时，我只是因为恐慌而躲避敌寇，并不是故意追随大王而去。今日大王不顾法律的严谨而召见我，因我之过而传遍天下，并非我之本意。"

昭王对司马子綦说："屠羊者说虽然地位卑微，然而他陈述的道理却很恰当。你替我邀请地担任三公职位。"

屠羊者说接到旨意回禀说："此三公之位，我知道其尊贵于屠羊的职业；万钟棒禄，要比屠羊的收益丰厚；但是我怎能为了贪图爵禄，而使得我的君主背负妄施恩惠的名声呢？我真的不敢当，甘愿重返屠羊的职业。"屠羊者说最终也没有接受昭王给予的赏赐。

寓意：人有自知之明，不失为一种高尚的品德。此种品德不仅可避祸就福，亦能使人钦佩。

Noble Character of Self-Awareness

Wu army invaded the State of Chu and captured its capital. King Zhao of Chu fled and lost his country, so did butcher Shuo who followed him in exile. Later Chu army defeated Wu army, and King Zhao of Chu returned to his country. He rewarded his followers, including butcher Shuo.

When it was Shuo's turn to be rewarded, he said, "When the king lost his country, I lost my job as a butcher; when the king recovered his country, I also resumed my job as a butcher. Now my salary has been restored, so why should I accept any more rewards?"

After hearing the report, King Zhao ordered, "The reward must be accepted."

Butcher Shuo replied again, "It is not my fault that the king lost his country, so I dare not claim the guilt; it is not my merit that the king recovered his country, so I dare not accept the reward."

After hearing the report again, King Zhao agreed with Shuo's reasoning and ordered, "Summon butcher Shuo to come and see me."

Butcher Shuo spoke once more, "According to the laws of Chu, only those who have made significant contributions are eligible to be summoned. My intelligence is not sufficient to defend the country, and my bravery is not enough to kill enemies and establish achievements. When the army of Wu invaded our capital, I only fled from fear, not deliberately following the king. Today, if the king summons me despite the rigidity of the law, it will be because of my fault and it is not my intention for this to be known throughout the world."

King Zhao said to Sima Ziqi, "Although butcher Shuo's status is humble, the principles he has stated are quite appropriate. Please invite him to serve as one of the Three Ministers."

Butcher Shuo responded to the imperial decree by saying, "I am aware that the position of one of the Three Ministers is more honorable than my trade as a butcher, and that the generous salary offered exceeds the profits I could ever make from slaughtering sheep. However, how could I possibly accept such a position out of greed for rank and riches, knowing that it would cast my king in the light of bestowing favors indiscriminately? I am truly unworthy and prefer to return to my humble trade as a butcher." In the end, butcher Shuo declined the reward offered by King Zhao.

Meaning: A person who has self-awareness is indeed possessed of a noble moral character. This moral character can not only avoid disasters and seek good fortune, but also win the admiration of others.

商汤伐夏桀《庄子·让王》

汤（商汤：商朝开国元勋，又称成汤）将伐桀（夏朝最后君主，相传为暴君），因（就与）卞随（商代隐士）而谋。卞随曰："非吾事也。"

汤曰："孰（谁）可？"

曰："吾不知也。"

汤又因瞀（wù 即：务光）光而谋，瞀光曰："非吾事也。"

汤曰："孰可？"

曰："吾不知也。"

汤曰："伊尹何如？"

曰："强力忍垢（忍辱负重），吾不知其他也。"

汤遂（于是）与伊尹谋伐桀，剋（克）之。以让卞随。卞随辞曰："后（指商汤）之伐桀，也谋乎我，必以我为贼也；胜桀而让我，必我为贪也。吾生乎乱世，而无道之人，再来漫（玷污）我以其辱事，吾不忍数闻也。"乃自投椆水（水名，在颍川）而死。

汤又让瞀光，曰："知者谋之，武者遂之，仁者居之，古之道也。吾子胡（hú 文言文疑问词，意指：为什么；何故。）不立乎？"

瞀光辞曰："废上，非义也；杀民，非仁也；人犯其难，我享其利，非廉也。吾闻之曰：'非其义者，不受其禄；无道之世，不践其土。'况尊我乎！吾不忍久见也。"乃负石而自沉于庐水（地名，今辽宁西，一说古北平郡界）。

译文：商汤要出兵征伐夏桀，就此事与隐士卞随谋划，卞随说："出兵征伐不是我应该做的事情。"商汤请教他："此事可以与谁商议？"

卞随回答："我不知道。"

商汤又与瞀光协商。瞀光说："这不是我该做的事情。"

商汤连忙问："可以与谁协商？"

瞀光回答："我不知道。"

商汤又问："伊尹如何？"

瞀光说："我只知道他具有忍厚负重的能耐，别的我就不知道了。"

商汤于是与伊尹联手谋划征伐夏桀，获得成功。成功之后，商汤要把天下让给卞随，卞随辞谢说："你在征伐之初与我谋划，一定认为我是一个残暴的人；取得成功之后，你又要把天下让给我，一定认为我是一个贪婪的人。我生活在乱世中，已经非常无奈，然而无道义的人士屡次玷污我的名声，迫使我从事有辱身份的事情，我实在难以多次听到如此言辞。"于是他投入椆水自杀身亡。

商汤只好把天下让给瞀光，说："有谋之士谋划天下大业，勇敢的将士完成平定天下的大业；有德之士，居天子之位匡正天下大业。这是自古以来的道理。先生为何不肩负天下的重任呢？"

瞀光辞谢说："推翻自己的君主是不义；发动战事使百姓遭殃是不仁；将士在战场上冒死拼杀，我却坐享其成，这是不知廉耻的行为。我听说：'对于不合乎道义的人，不能接受他的爵禄；对于不讲道义的国家，不能踏入他的国土。'何况，还要尊我为天子？我再也不想见到你。"于是，瞀光把石头捆在自己身上投进庐水自尽了。

寓意：卞随与瞀光以死铭志，将仁与义建立在功名利禄之上的行为与商汤截然相反。孔子《论语·子罕》："子曰：三军可夺帅也，匹夫不可夺志也。"从另一面而言此为当时社会普遍的信仰。

Shang Tang Overthrew Xia Jie

Shang Tang planned to march against Xia Jie and consulted the recluse Bian Sui on this matter. Bian Sui replied, "It is not my place to decide on military campaigns." Shang Tang inquired further, "With whom should I discuss this matter?"

Bian Sui answered, "I don't know."

Shang Tang then turned to consult Wu Guang. Wu Guang said, "This is not something that I should do."

Shang Tang asked quickly, "With whom should I consult?"

Wu Guang replied, "I don't know."

Shang Tang persisted, "What about Yi Yin?"

Wu Guang said, "I only know that he possesses the patience and endurance to bear heavy burdens. Other than that, I don't know much about him."

Shang Tang then joined forces with Yi Yin to plan the conquest of Xia Jie, and they were successful. After their victory, Shang Tang offered the rule of the nation to Bian Sui. Bian Sui declined and saying, "When you first consulted me about the campaign, you must have thought of me as a cruel person. And now, after succeeding, you want to offer me the rule of the nation, surely thinking me a greedy one. I already feel helpless living in this troubled era. However unethical individuals have repeatedly tarnished my reputation, forcing me to do things that are degrading to my status and dignity. All this is something I cannot bear to hear about again. With these words, he threw himself into the Chou Shui River and drowned.

Shang Tang had to give the nation to Wu Guang, saying, "Men of counsel plan great affairs for the nation, brave soldiers accomplish the great tasks of pacifying the world; men of virtue sit on the throne of the emperor to rectify the great affairs of the nation. This has been the truth since ancient times. Why doesn't Mr. Wu Guang shoulder the great responsibility of the world?

Wu Guang refused with these words: "To overthrow one's own monarch is immoral; to initiate a war and bring disasters to the people is unkind; and it is shameless for me to sit back and enjoy the fruits of soldiers' efforts on the battlefield. I have heard that, 'One who does not abide by morality cannot accept his rank or salary; One should not set foot on the land of a country that does not abide by morality.' Moreover, how could you consider me as the emperor? I don't want to see you again." Then Wu Guang tied a stone to his body and threw himself into the Lu River to commit suicide.

Meaning: Bian Sui and Wu Guang died to uphold their principles, prioritizing benevolence and righteousness above fame and fortune, in stark contrast to the behavior of Shang Tang. Confucius once said in "The Analects of Confucius: "A commander can be deposed of his army, but a common man cannot be deprived of his will." In another perspective, this statement reflects the common belief in society at that time.

伯夷与叔齐《庄子·让王》

昔，周之兴，有士二人处于孤竹（古代诸侯国名。今，河北卢龙南），曰：伯夷、叔齐。二人相谓曰："吾闻西方有人，似有道者，试往观焉。"

至于岐阳（岐山之南），武王闻之，使叔旦往见之，与盟曰："加富二等，就官一列。"血牲而埋之。

二人相视而笑曰："嘻，异哉，此非吾所谓道也。昔者，神农之有天下也，时祀（四季的祭祀）尽敬（敬天），而不祈喜（福）；其于人也，忠信尽治，而无求焉。乐与政，为政；乐与治，为治；不以人之坏，自成也；不以人之卑，自高也；不以遭时，自利也。今，周见殷之乱，而遽（仓猝）为政。上谋，而下行货（贿赂），阻兵（倚仗军力）而保威（淫威），割牲而盟以为信，扬行（张扬）以说（取悦）众，杀伐以要利，是推乱以易暴也。吾闻古之士，遭治世不避其任，遇乱世不为苟存。今，天下暗，周德衰，其并乎周，以涂吾身也，不如避之以絜（xié 通"洁"）吾行。"二子北至于首阳之山（今，山西永济南），遂饿而死焉。

若伯夷，叔齐者，其于富贵也，苟可得已，则必不赖。高节戾行（砥砺操行），独乐其志，不事于世，此二士之节也。

译文：昔日，商朝渐渐衰败，周朝缓缓兴起。孤竹国公子伯夷与叔齐，为了把皇权让给三弟，相伴离家出走。兄弟二人相对而言："我听说西方国土好似有位得道人士，咱们前去拜访。"

由此，二人来到岐山之南，寻访有道人士。周武王听说了此事，特意派遣其弟周公旦前去拜见，并邀约："赐予你们二等俸禄，任官一等爵位。"并且许诺：杀牲涂盟书埋于盟坛之下。

兄弟二人相对而笑："唉，差异了，这不是我们寻找有道人士的本意。昔日，神农氏治理天下，遵循时节祭祀天地，是向天地感恩，而不是为自己祈福；对天下百姓诚实守信尽心维护社会公平，而不是为了维护自己的统治。天下百姓，乐于推行政令就实施政令；乐于推行法治就实施法治。从不趁他人衰败之机，窃取自己的成功；不以他人卑微的行为，而吹捧自己品德高尚；也不会因为时局发展趋势，而放纵自利的欲望。当前，周朝看到殷商内乱，而仓猝收买人心突显自己的政德。对上天，窥视天机；对天下百姓行贿许愿，倚仗军事力量保障自己的淫威。杀牲盟誓只是展示诚信；张扬替天行道只是为了取悦天下百姓。杀戮讨伐只是为了争权夺利，这是推动乱世以便自己实施暴行。我听说古代的仁人志士遇到治世时代，不躲避自己应尽的责任；遇到乱世时代，不为苟且偷生。今日，天下昏暗，周朝的德行已经衰败，我们怎能以周朝衰败的德行玷污我们的名节，不如避开是非之地，以维护你我的信仰与言行。"二人相伴来到首阳山下，因不食周朝食物而饿死在首阳的深山中。

像伯夷、叔齐这样的贤士，如果想过上富贵生活，放低自己的姿态便可获得。然而，二人不想违背良知而苟且偷生。高节清风、自乐其志、不从世俗，这就是二位贤士的节操。

寓意：时代的价值观和倡导的道德品行、社会风尚，指引着社会或蓬勃向上或堕落腐化，也决定着人们的生存环境。世风日下，伯夷与叔齐宁愿弃生以明志。

Bo Yi and Shu Qi

In the past, the Shang Dynasty was decaying gradually, while the Zhou Dynasty was emerging slowly. Bo Yi and Shu Qi, the princes of Gu Zhu State, decided to leave home together to cede the throne to their third younger brother. The two brothers said to each other, "I heard that there is a sage in the western land. Let's go there to visit him."

Therefore, the two brothers went to the south of the Qishan Mountain to seek the sage. King Wu of Zhou heard about this and sent his younger brother, Zhou Gongdan, to meet them, inviting them to accept the position of the second-class salary and the first-class rank. He also promised to write an alliance document, and smear the alliance document with blood of animals, then bury it under the altar of the alliance.

The two brothers smiled at each other and said, "Alas, you have misunderstood our intention. This is not our original intention in searching for the sage. When Shen Nong governed the world in the past, he sacrificed to Heaven and Earth according to the seasons as a way of giving thanks to them, not for his own blessing; He was honest and trustworthy to the people of the nation, striving to maintain social justice, not to maintain his own rule; The people of the nation were happy to implement the policies when they were willing to do so, and happy to implement the rule of law when they were ready for it. He never took advantage of others' decline to steal his own success, did not praise his own virtue based on others' humility, and did not indulge his own selfish desires due to the trend of the times. Currently, the Zhou Dynasty observed the internal turmoil within the Yin Dynasty and hastily sought to win over the hearts of the people, displaying its supposed political virtues. They sought to divine the secrets of the heavens, bribed and made promises to the people, and relied on military strength to guarantee their own power. The slaughtering of animals for oaths was merely a show of sincerity, while preaching righteousness was done solely to please the masses. Their wars and killings were motivated solely by the desire for power and profit, fueling the chaos in order to carry out atrocities. I have heard that virtuous men of ancient times, in times of peace, did not shirk their duties, and in times of tumult, they did not merely seek survival. Today, the world is dark, and the moral integrity of the Zhou Dynasty has declined. How can we taint our reputation with the decaying morality of the Zhou Dynasty? It is better to avoid the place of trouble and uphold our beliefs, words, and actions." So the two people went to the foot of the Shouyang Mountain together and starved to death in the deep mountains of Shouyang, because of refusing to eat the food of the Zhou Dynasty.

Such wise men as Boyi and Shuqi could have led a wealthy life if they had chosen to lower their standards. However, they chose not to compromise their conscience and live a life of comfort without principles. They preferred to uphold their high moral standards, follow their own convictions, and resist the temptations of the world. This is the integrity of the two wise men.

Meaning: The values of the era, advocated moral character, and social trends guide the society either towards prosperity or decadence, and also determine people's living environment. As social morality declines, Boyi and Shuqi preferred to sacrifice their lives to demonstrate their principles.

伯夷与叔齐 Bo Yi and Shu Qi

舐痔得车《庄子·列御寇》

宋人有曹商（人名）者，为宋王（宋偃王）使秦。其往也，得（感恩）车数乘。王（秦王）说（悦）之，益车百乘。反（返回）于宋，见庄子曰："夫处穷闾陋巷，困窘织屦（用麻、葛做鞋换钱求生），槁项黄馘（xù面黄肌瘦）者，商（我）之所短也；一悟万乘之主，而从车百乘者，商之所长也。"

庄子曰："秦王有病召医，破痈溃痤者，得车一乘，舐痔者，得车五乘，所治愈下（下作），得车愈多。子岂治其痔邪，何得车之多也？子行矣！"

译文：宋国有一位名叫曹商的人，为宋偃王出使秦国。宋偃王特意为秦王筹办数车乘礼物，以此向秦王表达敬意。秦王收到宋偃王奉送的礼物，又加上曹商能言善道的赞美之词，使得秦王一时兴起，回馈宋王百乘礼物。曹商看着秦王回馈的礼物，想象着回到宋国将会得到重赏，不由地欣喜若狂。返回途中遇上庄子，说："那些住在穷街陋巷里的人，以依靠编草鞋谋生，过着脖颈干枯、面黄肌瘦的苦日子，我曹商是做不到的。一旦说动万乘大国的君主，就能得到百乘的赏赐，这才是我曹商的长处啊。"

庄子看着洋洋得意的曹商，说："我听说，秦王患病，招聘天下名医，能够破除毒疮的人，可获得一车乘的赏赐；用舌头舔舐秦王痔疮的人可获得五乘的赏赐。治疗的手法越下作，得到的赏赐越多。难道你给秦王治痔疮？为何得到如此多的赏赐呢？你真行啊！"

寓意：以溢美之词、溜须拍马赢得他人欢心从而获得赏赐的说客，却自认为高人一等而贬低辛勤劳作的穷苦人家，这样的行径不仅不明智反遭他人耻笑。

Shameless Behavior of Flattering

There was a man named Cao Shang in the State of Song who was dispatched to the State of Qin as an envoy of King Song Yan. King Song Yan prepared several carts of gifts to show his respect to King Qin. King Qin was pleased with the gifts and Cao Shang's eloquent praise, so he sent a hundred carriages full of gifts back to King Song Yuan as a reward. Cao Shang, looking at the gifts from King Qin, imagined that he would be highly rewarded when he returned to the State of Song, and felt extremely happy. On his way back, he met Zhuangzi and said, "Those who live in poor neighborhoods and make a living by making sandals, leading a hard life with yellowish complexion and emaciation, I Cao Shang could never do that. But once I persuade the king of a great country with a million chariots, I can get a hundred carriages of gifts as a reward. This is my strength."

Zhuangzi looked at Cao Shang who was full of pride and said, "I heard that when the Qin Emperor fell ill, he recruited doctors from all over the world. Those who could cure his venomous sores would receive a reward of one carriage, while those who licked his piles with their tongues would get five carriages. The more demeaning the treatment method was, the more rewards one could get. Did you treat the Qin Emperor's piles? Why did you get so many rewards? You are really good!"

Meaning: A speaker who wins others' favor with overstated praise and flattering remarks to gain rewards. But he considers himself superior than others and belittles poor people who work hard, this is not only unwise but also ridiculed by others.

说剑《庄子·说剑》

昔，赵文王（即赵惠文王）喜剑，剑士夹门而客三千余人，日夜相击于前，死伤者岁百余人，好之不厌。如是三年，国衰，诸侯谋之。

太子悝（kuī）患之，募左右曰："孰能说王之意，止剑士者，赐之千金。"

左右曰："庄子当能。"

太子乃使人以千金奉庄子。庄子弗受，与使者俱往见太子，曰："太子何以教周，赐周千金？"

太子曰："闻夫子明圣，谨奉千金以币从者。夫子弗受，悝尚何敢言！"

庄子曰："闻太子所欲用周者，欲绝王之喜好也。使臣上说大王，而逆王意，下不当（不从）太子，则身刑而死，周尚安所事金乎？使臣上说大王，下当太子，赵国何求而不得也！"

太子曰："然。吾王所见，唯剑士也。"

庄子曰："诺。周善为剑。"

太子曰："然，吾王所见剑士，皆蓬头突鬓，垂冠，曼胡之缨，短后之衣，瞋（chēn 瞪）目而语难，王乃说（悦）之。今夫子必儒服而见王，事必大逆（败露）。"

庄子曰："请治剑服。"

治剑服三日，乃见太子。太子乃与见王，王脱白刃（拔出佩剑）待之。庄子入殿门不趋（趋行），见王不拜。

王曰："子欲何以教寡人，使太子先？"

曰："臣闻大王喜剑，故以剑见王。"

王曰："子之剑何能禁制？"

曰："臣之剑，十步一人，千里不留行。"

王大悦之，曰："天下无敌矣！"

庄子曰："夫为剑者，示之以虚，开之以利，后之以发，先之以至。愿得试之。"

王曰："夫子休就舍待命，令设戏（比试）请夫子。"

王乃校（比较）剑士七日，死伤者六十余人，得五六人，使奉剑于殿下，乃召庄子。王曰："今日试士敦剑

- 252 -

（击剑）。"

庄子曰："望之久矣。"

王曰："夫子所御杖（剑），长短何如？"

曰："臣之所奉皆可。然臣有三剑，唯王所用，请先言而后试。"

王曰："愿闻三剑。"

曰："有天子剑，有诸侯剑，有庶人剑。"

王曰："天子之剑何如？"

曰："天子之剑，以燕溪石城为锋（刀锋），齐岱（齐国泰山）为锷（剑锷），晋魏为脊，周宋为镡（xín 剑环），韩魏为夹（剑柄），包以四夷（四方），裹以四时（四季），绕以渤海，带以常山（北岳恒山），制以五行，论以刑德，开以阴阳，持以春夏，行以秋冬。此剑，直之无前，举之无上，案之无下，运之无旁，上决浮云，下绝地纪。此剑一用，匡诸侯，天下服矣。此天子之剑也。"

文王芒然自失，曰："诸侯之剑何如？"

曰："诸侯之剑，以知（智）勇士为锋，以清廉士为锷，以贤良士为脊，以忠圣士为镡，以豪桀士为夹。此剑，直之亦无前，举之亦无上，案之亦无下，运之亦无旁；上法圆天，以顺三光；下法方地，以顺四时；中和民意，以安四乡。此剑一用，如雷霆之震也，四封之内，无不宾服而听从君命者矣。此诸侯之剑也。"

王曰："庶人之剑何如？"

曰："庶人之剑，蓬头突鬓，垂冠，曼胡之缨，短后之衣，瞋目而语难；相击于前，上斩颈领，下决肝肺。此庶人之剑，无异于斗鸡，一旦命已绝矣，无所用于国事。今，大王有天子之位，而好庶人之剑，臣窃为大王薄之。"

王乃牵而上殿。宰人上食，王三环之。

庄子曰："大王安坐定气，剑事已毕奏矣。"

于是，文王不出宫三月，剑士皆服毙其处也。

译文：昔日，赵国的惠文王喜好剑术，聚于门下的剑士多达三千多人。剑士在惠文王面前日夜拼杀，每年都有百余人死伤。然而，惠文王总是百看不厌。这样的情境持续了三年，国运衰弱，各诸侯图谋攻伐赵国。

太子悝对此很忧虑，招募左右侍从说："谁能说服大王改变心意，制止剑士拼杀，赏赐他千金酬谢。"

众侍从说："庄子当能做到。"

于是，太子派使臣以千金奉送庄子。庄子不敢轻意接受，随同使臣前来拜见太子，说："太子有何指令于我，为什么赏赐大礼？"

太子说："我听说先生明达圣哲，我谨奉千金跟随先生受学。如果先生不接受此礼，我怎么敢言说呢？"

庄子说："听说太子欲让我阻止惠文王沉溺剑术之事。我上劝大王，违背王意；下不从太子，就会落个受刑而死，我哪里还能用上您赐予的赏金？如果，我说服大王，又能顺从太子之意，我在赵国何种赏赐得不到呢？"

太子说："确实如此，只要你为赵国的未来尽力而为，我当然要答谢你。不过，我父王乐意召见的唯独是剑士。"

庄子不介意地说："可以，我就以剑士身份拜见大王。"

太子难为情地又说："然而，我父王所要召见的剑士，都是一些蓬头突鬓、帽沿压眉，用粗带子扎紧帽子的人。他们身穿后襟超短衣，瞪目怒视而言语艰涩，我父王乐见如此。今日，如果先生身穿儒士服拜见我父王，恐怕会败露。"

庄子答应："就依照您父王的喜好装扮成剑士。"

三天之后，特意为庄子制作的剑士服做好了，庄子穿上剑士服拜见太子。太子引领庄子上殿拜见惠文王，惠文王拔出佩剑等待庄子前来。庄子进入殿门，没有小步疾行，看见惠文王也不行拜见礼。文王不高兴地问："你有何剑术教导寡人？还敢请太子为你举荐？"

庄子沉着地说："我听说大王喜好剑术，所以，以我的剑术见于大王。"

惠文王问："你的剑术有何妙招制胜对手？"

庄子说："我的剑，十步取人头，千里不留生。"

惠文王欣喜，说："天下无敌啊！"

庄子自信地说："我使用的剑术，先示人以虚，开启对自己有利的势位，让对方出手露出破绽。然后，突发一剑封喉的招数结束对抗，大王是否愿意尝试一下？"

惠文王连忙说："先生请去馆舍休息，等我安排好比试事宜再请先生。"

惠文王即刻发出王令，所有剑士互相角逐，优胜者挑战庄子。一时间，剑士们以死拼搏七日，死伤者高达六十余人，优胜者有五六人，持剑聚于殿前等候召唤。惠文王召来庄子，说："今日尝试与剑士比试如何？"

庄子说："我盼望已久了。"

惠文王不经意地问："先生使用的剑，对长短有没有要求？"

庄子大气地说："我使用的剑长短皆可。我有三把剑，唯主者所用，请让我把这三把剑的由来讲给您听，然后再比试剑术可以吗？"

惠文王说："当然可以，我愿意听你讲一讲。"

庄子说："有一把天子剑；有一把诸侯剑，有一把庶人剑。"

惠文王急切地问："什么是天子剑？"

庄子说："天子剑，以燕国塞外石城山峰为剑锋；以齐国的泰山为剑刃；以晋国、卫国为剑脊；以周地、宋国为剑鼻；以韩国、魏国为剑柄；包以天地四方、裹以天时四季于剑鞘；剑的穗带环绕渤海与北岳恒山。遵从五行相生相克之本；以德刑并施平定天下。出剑，应和阴阳之变；行剑，符合天地之理，始于春夏，止于秋冬。此剑，一往无前。向上，至高无上；向下，至深无下；运行，无物可随，上可劈开浮云，下可斩断地根。此剑一旦出鞘，便可匡正诸侯，让天下万民臣服。这就是天子之剑。"

惠文王茫然自失，又问："诸侯剑，应该是怎样呢？"

庄子回答："诸侯剑，以智勇双全的人士为剑锋；以清廉的人士为剑刃；以贤良的人士为剑脊；以忠圣的人士为剑鼻；以豪杰的人士为剑柄。此剑，勇往直前无阻挡。举起，至高无上；按下，至深无下；运行，无物可随。上遵天时，以顺日、月、星三光；下守地利，以应四季之变；中顺民意，以平安无事定四方。剑出鞘，如雷霆万钧，四境之内无不臣服遵从君令者。这就是诸侯之剑。"

惠文王再问："什么是庶人剑？"

庄子回答："手握庶人剑的人士，都是蓬头垢面，突显着鬓发，以展示与众不同的身份；压低帽沿隐起目中寒光，遮掩心中的残忍，用粗劣的长缨把帽子勒在脑袋上，只怕丢盔显露败象；身穿后襟超短上衣，只是为了方便窜来窜去躲避刀锋；只顾怒目瞪眼，却妨碍了口齿伶俐。相对拼杀，剑朝上，狠不得一刀砍下对方的头；剑向下，妄图一剑劈开对方的心肝肺。庶人常用的剑术，犹如公鸡相斗，一旦命绝身亡，对国家长治久安无任何作用。当下，大王身居天子之位，却喜好庶人之剑，我私下里很为大王的行为感到惋惜。"

惠文王若有所悟地慢步引领着庄子走进大殿。命令掌管膳食的官吏为庄子盛上美食，庄子看见如此款待，悬着的那颗心终于放下。然而，惠文王面无表情地绕着庄子的席位踱步三圈。

庄子看看美食，又看看惠文王，自己又不好意思先吃，情急之下说："大王安心地坐下来定定神，论剑的事情已经结束了。"

于是，惠文王自从听罢庄子论剑之后，三个月没有走出宫门，剑士们都自刎在住所里。

寓意：所谓玩物丧志，可言：无论沉溺于何种消遣之事忘乎所以，皆会荒废正道。一个国家中：王有王道、民有民生，其国运才能处于正轨，不至于衰靡。修身治国的道理震耳发聩、发人深省。

The Sword

In the past, the King Huiwen of Zhao had a great fondness for swordsmanship and had gathered more than three thousand swordsmen under his roof. These swordsmen would fight day and night in front of the king, and every year there would be over a hundred casualties. Nevertheless, the king never seemed to tire of watching them. This situation lasted for three years, leading to the decline of the country's fortune. The various feudal lords plotted to attack and conquer the state of Zhao.

Prince Kui was deeply worried about this situation and recruited his attendants, saying, "Whoever can persuade the king to change his mind and stop the swordfighters from battling will be greatly rewarded with a thousand gold coins."

The attendants replied, "Zhuangzi should be able to accomplish this."

So, the prince sent an envoy with a thousand gold coins to offer them to Zhuangzi. Zhuangzi, hesitant to accept such a generous gift, accompanied the envoy to meet the prince.

Upon arriving, he said to the prince, "What orders do you have for me, and why such a generous reward?"

The prince replied, " Sir, I have heard that you are wise and enlightened. I humbly offer these thousand gold coins to learn from you. How dare I speak if you refuse such a token of my respect and gratitude?"

Zhuangzi said, "I have heard that Prince Kui wishes for me to stop King Huiwen from indulging in swordsmanship. If I advise the king, it would be against his wishes. If I disobey the prince, I may face the consequence of death. How could I possibly use the reward you have offered? If I persuade the king and also comply with the prince's wishes, what reward in the state of Zhao could I not receive?"

The prince replied, "Indeed, as long as you do your best for the future of Zhao, I will certainly reward you. However, the only type of person my father king is willing to summon are swordfighters."

Without hesitation, Zhuangzi replied, "Alright, I will meet the king as a swordsman."

The prince, feeling embarrassed and added, "However, the swordfighters my father king summons are those with unkempt hair, bushy eyebrows, and hats tied tightly with a coarse cord. They wear short tunics with their backs exposed, stare angrily, and speak in a gruff manner. This is what my father king enjoys seeing. If you, Sir, were to meet him today dressed in your scholar's robes, it might reveal your true identity."

Zhuangzi agreed, "I will dress as a swordfighter according to your father king's preferences."

Three days later, the swordfighter's costume specifically made for Zhuangzi was ready. Zhuangzi put it on and went to meet the prince. The prince escorted Zhuangzi to the throne room to meet with King Huiwen. King Huiwen drew his sword and awaited Zhuangzi's arrival.

As Zhuangzi entered the throne room, he did not hurry his steps or bow to King Huiwen. This caused the king to ask angrily, "What swordsmanship do you have to teach me? And why did you dare ask the prince to recommend you?"

Zhuangzi calmly said, "I heard that the king is fond of swordsmanship, so I have come to show my swordsmanship to the king."

King Huiwen asked, "What is the secret of your swordsmanship that allows you to defeat your opponents?"

Zhuangzi replied, "My sword can take a person's head in ten steps, leaving no chance of survival even a thousand miles away."

King Huiwen was delighted and said, "You are truly unmatched in the world!"

Zhuangzi confidently replied, "The swordsmanship I use involves first showing my opponent a false move, creating a favorable position for myself. This induces them to make a mistake. Then, with one sudden stroke, I strike at their throat, ending the confrontation. Would the king like to try it?"

King Huiwen quickly responded, "Please, sir, go to the guest quarters and rest. I will arrange everything for the competition and summon you when it's ready."

King Huiwen immediately issued a royal command, ordering all swordsmen to compete against each other, with the winners challenging Zhuangzi. For seven consecutive days, the swordsmen fought fiercely, leaving over sixty dead or injured. Five or six of the most skilled survivors gathered in front of the palace with their swords, waiting for the summons.

King Huiwen summoned Zhuangzi and said, "How would you like to try a competition with our swordsmen today?"

Zhuangzi said, "I have been looking forward to this for a long time."

King Huiwen casually asked, "Does the sword you use have any specific requirements regarding its length or weight?"

Zhuangzi replied with grandeur, "I can use swords of any length. I possess three swords, and only the master knows which one to use. Allow me to explain the origin of these three swords to you before we proceed with the swordsmanship competition."

King Huiwen said, "Of course, I would be delighted to hear your explanation."

Zhuangzi replied, "There is the sword of the emperor, the sword of the feudal lord, and the sword of the commoner."

Eagerly, King Huiwen asked, "What is the sword of the emperor?"

Zhuangzi said with grandeur, "The sword of the emperor has and Shicheng of Yanxi as its edge, Mount Taishan as its point, Jin and Wei as its spine, Zhou and Song as its guard, and Han and Wei as its flanges. It is wrapped in the Four Barbarians, clothed in the Four Seasons, surrounded by the Bohai Sea, and girded by Changshan Mountain. Its forging follows the Five Elements, and its use is governed by punishment and reward. It opens with Yin and Yang, and is wielded in Spring and Summer, and used in Autumn and Winter. This sword cuts straight ahead without impediment, lifts up without limit, presses down without boundary, and moves without obstruction. It can pierce the floating clouds above and split the earth below. With a single swipe of this sword, the feudal lords are corrected, and the entire world submits. This is the sword of the emperor."

King Huiwen felt lost and asked again, "And what about the sword of the feudal lord? What should it be like?"

Zhuangzi replied: "The sword of the feudal lord is sharpened by wise warriors, its edge honed by upright officials, its spine strengthened by virtuous men, its guard adorned by loyal saints, and its scabbard protected by valiant heroes. This sword also cuts straight ahead without impediment, lifts up without limit, presses down without boundary, and moves without obstruction. Above, it follows the laws of heaven. Below, it respects the advantages of the land, responding to the changes of the four seasons. In the middle, it harmonizes with the will of the people, ensuring peace and stability in all directions. When this sword is drawn, it's like the thunder of heaven shaking the earth. Within its domain, all submit and obey the commands of the king. This is the sword of the feudal lord."

King Huiwen asked again, "What is the sword of the commoner?"

Zhuangzi replied, "Those who wield the sword of the commoners are usually unkempt with dirty faces and prominent sideburns to show their uniqueness." They pull down their hat brims to conceal the chill in their eyes, shielding their cruel intentions. They tie their hats securely on their heads with crude and long tassels, fearing to lose their helmets and reveal signs of defeat. They wear super-short tunic is solely for the convenience of dodging and weaving around to avoid the blade; however, focusing solely on glaring angrily with one's eyes prevents one from speaking eloquently. When engaging in combat, they would brandish their swords upwards, intent on slicing off the enemy's head with a fierce swipe. Or they would swing their swords downwards, aiming to slash open the enemy's heart, liver, and lungs. The swordsmanship commonly practiced by commoners is akin to the fighting of chickens. Once one of them is fatally injured, it serves no purpose for the long-term stability and prosperity of the country. Now, Your Majesty occupies the throne of the heavens, yet you find pleasure in the swordplay of the commoners. I truly lament Your Majesty's actions in private."

Huiwen King slowly led Zhuangzi into the palace with an enlightened expression. He ordered the official in charge of catering to serve Zhuangzi delicious food. Upon seeing such treatment, Zhuangzi finally let his hanging heart rest. However, Huiwen King walked around Zhuangzi's seat three times with an expressionless face.

Zhuangzi looked at the delicious food and then looked at King Huiwen, feeling embarrassed to eat first. In a moment of urgency, he said, "King, please take your seat and compose yourself. The matter of discussing swords has already come to an end."

After listening to Zhuangzi's discussion on swordsmanship, King Huiwen did not step out of the palace for three months, and the swordsmen all committed suicide in their lodgings.

Meaning: The saying goes that indulging in pleasures will ruin one's ambition. In other words, whatever kind of pastime one indulges in to the point of forgetting everything will cause one to neglect the right path. In a country, the king should uphold the royal way, and the people should take care of their livelihoods. Only then can the country's fortune stay on track and avoid decline. The principles of self-cultivation and governance are striking and thought-provoking.

蝴蝶梦《庄子·内篇·齐物论》

南郭子綦，隐机而坐，仰天而嘘（缓缓呼吸），苔焉（dá yān 相忘貌）似丧其耦（ǒu 躯体）。颜成子游（颜成，名偃。字，子游）立侍乎前，曰："何居乎（何故）？形固，可使如槁木（枯木）；而心固，可使如死灰乎（冷灰）？今之隐机（将身体依托在案几上），非昔之隐机者也。"

子綦曰："偃，不亦善乎，而问之也？今者，吾丧我(无我)，汝（你）知之乎？女（汝）闻人籁，而未闻地籁，女（汝）闻地籁，而未闻天籁夫！"

译文：（南郭：南外城。南郭子綦：指南外城处士子綦。成玄英疏："楚昭王之庶弟，楚庄王之司马。字，子綦。古代多以居所为'号'，故，号'南郭'。此人怀道抱德，虚心妄淡。庄子羡其清高，托为论首。"后世多以南郭子綦倚靠在案几旁的仪态，形容物我两忘、清高淡泊的精神仪态。）

南郭子綦倚靠在案几旁，仰首向天缓缓呼吸。若即若离的神色犹如魂魄出窍、躯体无主。他的学生颜成子游陪伴在子綦面前，惊讶地问："这是何故？您的形体似枯木，您的神情恍惚似冷灰，今日靠在案几旁不同于往日的状态啊！"

子綦说："偃，这不是很好吗？今日我忘却了自己，你可知道吗？你听过"人籁"，而没有听说"地籁"吧？你如果知道"地籁"的由来，也可能没有听说过"天籁"吧！"

Butterfly Dream

Nanguo Ziqi leaned against the table and breathed slowly towards the sky. His expression was as if his soul had left his body, leaving his flesh without a master. His student, Yan Chengzi You, who was accompanying him, asked in surprise, "What's the matter? Your body looks like wilted wood, and your expression seems vacant like cold ashes. Today, leaning against the table, you look different from usual!"

Ziqi said, "Yan, isn't this wonderful? Today, I have forgotten myself. Do you know that? You have heard of 'human sounds', but have you ever heard of 'earthly sounds'? If you understand the origin of 'earthly sounds', you might not have heard of 'heavenly sounds'!"

蝴蝶梦 Butterfly Dream

子游曰："敢问其方（其中的道理）？"

子綦曰："夫（假借为'彼'），大块噫气（吐气），其名为'风'。是唯无作，作则万窍怒呺。而独不闻之翏翏（liù liù 远远袭来的风气）乎？山林之畏佳（wèi zhuī 高峻貌），大木（树）百围之窍穴，似鼻、似口、似耳、似枅（jī 柱子上支承大梁的方木）、似圈、似臼（舂米的凹坑）、似洼者、似污者，激者、謞（xiào 大叫）者，叱（大声呵斥）者、吸者、叫者、譹（háo 号哭）者、宎（yǎo 风吹入深谷发出的声音）者、咬者，前者唱于，而随者唱喁（yú 应和之声。成玄英疏：'于、喁，皆是风吹树动前后相随之声'）。泠（líng）风（小风）则小和，飘风（暴风）则大和。厉风济，则众窍为虚（暴风过后或称停止，山间众窍为空）。而独不见之调调之，刁刁乎？（向秀注：调调：树枝大动。刁刁：树枝微动。）"

译文：子游说："敢问其中的道理？"

- 261 -

子綦说："天地间吐出的气，称之谓'风'。清风、微风，可视为无害。风一旦发作成为厉风、暴风，大地上的一切孔穴、山谷皆在怒吼。你唯独没有听过那呼啸而过的山风吗？山林畏惧，参天大树之间的空隙，有的似鼻、有的似口、有的似耳，有的好似圆柱顶端插横木的方孔，有的宛如围起的木栅栏，有的又像舂米的凹坑，有的像深水潭，有的又好似浅水湾。它们发出的声音宛如湍急的流水声，又好似迅疾的箭镞声。又像大声呵叱，又像细细呼吸；又好像放声叫喊，又好像嚎啕大哭，皆在山谷里回荡。犹如：鸟儿叫喳喳，大地也随和。轻风凉意随小和，狂风怒吼随大和。暴风哑然而止，大地寂静无声。难道你不曾看见：呼啸的狂风袭来万物摇曳，柔弱的清风吹来嫩枝悠摆的景色吗？"

Zi You said, "I dare ask, what is the principle behind this?"

Ziqi said, "The breath exhaled between heaven and earth is called 'wind'. Gentle and soft winds can be considered harmless. But when the wind becomes fierce and violent, all the holes and valleys on the earth are roaring. Have you ever heard the howling mountain wind? The mountains are afraid, and the gaps between towering trees are like noses, mouths, ears, square holes for inserting crossbars on top of columns, fenced enclosures, mortaring pits, deep pools, or shallow bays. The sounds they emit are like the rush of torrential water, or the whistle of speeding arrows. They are also like loud shouts, soft breaths, or loud cries, all echoing throughout the valleys. It's like the chirping of birds, and the earth joins in. Cool, gentle breezes accompany the minor harmonies, while furious winds howl in the major keys. When the storm suddenly ceases, the earth falls silent. Haven't you ever seen the scene where the roaring wind causes everything to sway, and the gentle breeze causes tender branches to sway gracefully?"

蝴蝶梦 Butterfly Dream

子游曰："地籁，则众窍是已。人籁，则比竹（吹奏管乐）是已。敢问天籁？"

子綦曰："夫吹万不同，为而使其自己也。咸（皆）其自取，怒者其谁邪？"

译文：子游说："地籁，是大地万种窍穴发的风声。人籁，是吹奏各种管式乐器发出的器乐声。我冒昧地请教何为天籁之声？"

子綦说："天籁之声，风，唯一体。窍，为万种。风为一，吹奏万种不同的空穴，使风发出万种不同的声音。发动者，停止者，皆是大自然中风所造成的自然现象。"（风起云涌，翻滚着云层，云层经过摩擦产生出电能。电闪雷鸣的自然现象，称谓天籁之声。《白虎通》：'雷者，阴中之阳也。'）

Zi You said, "Earthly sounds are those produced by the ten thousand holes and cracks in the ground. Human sounds are those made by various wind instruments. I venture to ask, what are the 'heavenly sounds'?"

Zi Qi said, "The 'heavenly sounds', or varieties of wind, is a unity of wind. There are ten thousand kinds of holes and cracks, but the wind is one. As it blows through these various voids, it produces ten thousand different sounds. Both the initiator and the terminator of these sounds are natural phenomena caused by the wind in nature."

大知闲闲（大智者斤斤自守）；小知间间（繁杂琐碎）。大言炎炎；小言詹詹（成玄英疏：炎炎，猛烈也；詹詹，词费也。后世从"詹詹炎炎"形容喋喋不休之状）。其寐（睡觉）也魂交，其觉（醒）也形开（身心不一）。与接为构，日以心斗。缦（同"慢"，傲慢）者，窖（善于算计）者，密（慎密）者，小恐惴惴（惴惴不安），大恐缦缦（沮丧）。其发若机括（jī kuò 弩上发矢的机关），其司是非之谓也。其留如诅盟（誓约），其守胜之谓也。其杀若（如）秋冬，以言其日消（弱）也。其溺之，所为之，不可复之也。其厌也如缄（捆扎），以言其老洫（xù 空虚）。近死之心，莫使复阳也。

译文：大智者斤斤自守；小智者繁杂琐碎。善于论辩者的言辞，盛气凌人；拘俗守常的言论，平庸烦琐。他们在梦中也神魂交错，醒来时身心不一。与人交谈总爱搬弄是非，整日钩心斗角不得安宁。傲慢者，不懂谦让；善于算计者，不露声色，伺机行事；潜志行事者，谨小慎微。小恐惴惴不安，大恐灰心丧气。他们的争议，犹如箭出弦又快又尖刻，据是非而力争，好似坚守心中的誓言，实则是以守胜为目的。他们的辩议宛如秋冬时节的草木日见枯萎，沉溺于其中，自以为是，不求改变。他们的精神闭锁，好似早已被绳索捆扎。他们的言辞空虚无聊，拼死力争也难以使他们复阳。

The wise man is self-disciplined while the petty wise man is full of trivialities. The words of those who are good at arguing are overbearing, and the words of those who adhere to conventions are mediocre and tedious. They are also confused in their dreams and wake up with inconsistent minds and bodies. When communicating with others, they always love to gossip with intrigue and never rest in peace all day long. Arrogant ones do not know how to be humble; those who are good at scheming do not show their cards and wait for an opportunity to act; those who act with concealed intentions are cautious.

The little frightened ones are anxious and apprehensive, while the greatly frightened ones are discouraged and despondent. Their disputes are like arrows flying out of the bowstring, sharp and keen. They argue based on right and wrong, seemingly adhering to their convictions, but in reality, their aim is to win by defending their positions. Their debates are like the plants and trees in autumn and winter, withering day by day, indulging in their own opinions, stubbornly refusing to change. Their minds are closed and locked, as if they have been tied up with ropes for a long time. Their words are empty and boring, and it is difficult to revive them even if they argue vigorously.

喜怒哀乐，虚叹变慹（zhí 恐惧），姚佚（轻浮）启态。乐出虚，蒸成菌，日夜相代乎前，而莫知其所萌。已乎！已乎！旦暮得此，其所由以生乎？

译文：他们欣喜、愤怒、悲伤、快乐，叹息过往的得失而又装出不在意的姿态。他的轻浮的心态，犹如乐管发出的嘘叹声，又好似潮湿的土地上萌生的蘑菇菌。天地间，日月交替，他们却不知其中的缘故。罢了，罢了，一旦明白其中的道理，不就明白万事万物形成的原因吗？

They are delighted, angry, sad, and happy, sighing over past gains and losses while pretending to be indifferent. His frivolous attitude is like the sound of a whistle from a musical instrument, or a mushroom sprouting from damp soil. Between heaven and earth, the sun and moon alternate, but they do not know the reason for it. Alas, once one understands the principle behind it, one will understand the reasons for the formation of all things in the universe.

非彼，无我；非我，无所取。是亦近矣，而不知其所为使。若有真宰（宇宙主宰），而特（独）不得其朕（zhèn 迹象）。可行己信（已知），而不见其形，有情（实）而无形。

译文：没有我的对应面，就无法展现我的自身；没有我自身的存在，也无法展现我的对应面。从这个角度思考事物的发展规律，就容易接近事物的本质。然而却无法确认形成这样认识的原因何在，倘若宇宙有真宰，我却难以感悟其中的真谛。用已知的验证它却不见其形，真乃：自有真情在，难得其形态。

Without my corresponding aspect, I cannot reveal myself; without my own existence, I cannot show my corresponding aspect. Thinking about the laws of development from this perspective makes it easier to approach the essence of things. However, it is impossible to confirm the reason for such understanding. If there is a true creator in the universe, I cannot comprehend the true meaning behind it. When verifying it with what is known, its form cannot be seen. It is truly said that true feelings exist, but it is difficult to grasp their form.

百骸、九窍、六藏、赅（gāi 兼）而存焉？吾，谁与为亲？汝（我）皆说（悦）之乎？其有私（偏爱）焉？如是皆有为臣妾乎？其臣妾不足以相治（抗衡）乎？其递相（互相）为君臣乎？其有真君存焉？如求得其情与不得，无益损乎其真。一受其成形，不亡以待尽。

译文：百骸（成玄英疏："百骸，百骨节也。"）、九窍（指耳、目、口、鼻及尿道、肛门，九个孔道。《周礼·天官·疾医》："两之以九窍之变。"郑玄注："阳窍七，阴窍二。"）、六藏（成玄英疏："六藏，六腑也，谓大肠、小肠、膀胱、三焦也。"或以心、肝、脾、肺、肾、命门为"六藏"。），这些人体器官都完备地存在于我的身体内吗？我对它们中的哪个最亲近？还是我都喜欢？还是存有偏爱？如此这样，有无"臣妾"之分？其中的"臣与妾"是否相互抗衡？或者轮番替代"君臣"之位？是否存在"真君"？无论求得其"真"，还是无法求得其"真"，都无法否定其"真"的存在。人一旦禀承天地之"气"而形成躯体，躯体也随着时光流逝而消亡殆尽。

Are all the human organs such as the hundred bones, the nine apertures, and the six organs completely present in my body? Which of them am I closest to? Do I like them all equally, or do I have preferences? If so, is there a distinction between "subjects and favorites"? Do the "subjects and favorites" compete with each other, or do they take turns replacing the " sovereign and subject" position? Is there a "true monarch" among them? Whether we seek the "truth" or fail to find it, we cannot deny the existence of the "truth". Once a person inherits the "Qi" of heaven and earth to form a body, the body will also dissipate with the passage of time.

与物相刃相靡，其行尽如驰，而莫之能止，不亦悲乎！终身役役而不见成功，苶然（nié rán 疲惫）疲役而不知其所归，可不哀邪！人谓之不死，奚益（何益）？其形化，其心与之然，可不谓大哀乎！人之生也，固若是芒（迷茫）乎？其我独芒，而人亦有不芒者乎？

译文：物与物之间互相违逆，或者递相消亡，它们的行径犹如飞驰的快马，而哀莫能制止，这样的结局是不是太可悲？终身忙忙碌碌却看不到成功，苶然沮丧而不知归宿在何方，怎能使人不哀伤？有人说：人的精神不会死，何益？人的躯壳随着时光流失渐渐衰竭，人的精神与情感也随着身体衰竭而消失，可不谓大悲吗？人生于世，固然迷茫无知，还是唯我迷茫，而也有不迷茫者？

When things oppose each other or disappear one after another, their actions are like galloping horses, and no one can stop their tragic endings. It's too sad to be busy all one's life without seeing success, feeling lost and not knowing where to go. Some people say that a person's spirit will not die, but what's the use? As time goes by, a person's body gradually wears out, and their spirit and emotions also disappear with their body. Isn't it a great sadness? In life, are we all confused, or am I the only one who is confused, while there are those who are not?

夫，随其成心（成见）而师之，谁独且无师乎？奚（何）必知代而心自取者有之？愚者与有焉。未成乎心，而有是非，是今日适越（去越国），而昔至也。是以无有为有。无有为有，虽有神禹且不能知，吾独且奈何哉！

译文：以自己主观判断当作评判是非的标准，那么，这样的标准谁会没有呢？何必要以自己的认知替代真知？再糊涂的人也会有。心中没有原则而论是非对错，好似今日去越国，昨天就已经到达。把还没有发生的事情说成有。没有的说成有，就是神明的大禹在世也无法讲清楚，我怎么能讲清楚呢？

If one uses one's own subjective judgment as the criterion for evaluating right and wrong, then who doesn't have such a criterion? Why replace true knowledge with one's own cognition? Even the most foolish person would do so. If there is no principle in one's heart to judge right and wrong, it's like going to Yue today and arriving there yesterday. Saying what hasn't happened has happened, or saying what doesn't exist exists, is something even the divine Yu the Great could not clarify. How can I clarify it?

夫，言非吹也。言者有言，其所言者特（却）未定也。果有言邪？其未尝有言邪？其以为异于鷇（kòu 初生的小鸟）音，亦有辩乎？其无辩乎！

译文：与人讲道理，并非如刮起的风。虽然言者有话说，然而所说的道理是非未定好像飘忽不定的"风"。果真是在讲道理，还是不曾讲道理？其言犹如初生雏鸟的叫声，有所辨别？又无所辨别。

When explaining a reason to someone, it's not like a gust of wind. Although the speaker has something to say, the truth of what he says is as uncertain as the fleeting "wind". Is he really explaining a reason, or is he not? His words are like the cries of a newly hatched chick, somewhat distinguishable yet indistinguishable.

《道》，恶乎（何处）隐而有真伪？言（理），恶乎（何处）隐而有是非？《道》，恶乎往而不存？言，恶乎存而不可？《道》，隐于小成；言，隐于荣华。故（因此）有儒、墨之是非，以是其所非，而非其所是。欲是其所非而非其所是，则莫若以明。

译文：天下之道，何处隐藏起真假？天下的常理，何处隐藏着是非？天下的正道为何名存实亡？天下的常理为何有人还在讲却已面目全非？天下正道被一孔之见所隐匿；天下的常理被浮华之辞所淹没。因此，有了儒家、墨家的是非之辩，把对方的"是"，认作"非"，把对方的"非"，当做"是"。欲求所是所非，莫过于：揭开隐者的面纱，以见日月之明。

Where does the truth and falsity hide in the way of the world? Where does right and wrong hide in the common sense of the world? Why do the righteous paths of the world exist in name only? Why do some people still talk about the common sense of the world, but it has already changed completely? The righteous paths of the world are hidden by narrowmindedness; the common sense of the world is drowned by flashy words. Therefore, there are debates about right and wrong between Confucianism and Mohism, treating the other's "right" as "wrong" and the other's "wrong" as "right". To seek what is right and what is wrong, the best way is to reveal the veil of the hidden and see the brightness of the sun and the moon.

物无非彼，物无非是。自彼则不见，自知则知之。故曰：彼出于是，是亦因彼。彼是方生之说也（彼是：彼此。方生之说指：惠施"方生方死"之说）。虽然，方生方死，方死方生；方可方不可，方不可方可；因是因非，因非因是。是以圣人不由，而照之于天，亦因是也。

译文：事物没有这一面与那一面的划分，因为这一面出自那一面，那一面又来自这一面，皆是相对而言。虽然新生命的出生，是走向死亡的开始，但死亡也意味着新生命的开始。可与不可，相遇而生；因是因非，相待为一。这些都不是圣人能够操控的，而是归于天地间的自然进化，仅此而已。

There is no distinction between this side and that side of things, because this side comes from that side, and that side comes from this side, all are relative. Although the birth of a new life is the beginning of its journey towards death, death also marks the beginning of a new life. What can be done and what cannot be done arise from each other's existence; what is right and what is wrong, true and false, coexist as one. These are not something that can be manipulated by saints, but rather belong to the natural evolution of the universe, that's all.

是亦彼也，彼亦是也。彼亦一是非，此亦一是非，果且（果真）有彼是亦哉，果且无彼是乎哉？彼是莫得其偶，谓之道枢（中枢）。枢，始得其环中，以应无穷。是亦一无穷，非亦一无穷也。故曰：莫若以明。

译文：是亦彼；彼亦是。没有纯粹的是，也没有纯粹的彼。彼也包含是与非，此也包含着是与非。果真有彼此吗？果真无彼此吗？在彼此还没有分离的起点，称之谓道枢。枢，始于《道》的中心点，掌控了《道》的中心点以应无穷。"是"也变化无穷，"非"也变化无穷。所以，从物体的根源思考物体进化过程中的因果关系，才能真正明白物体进化过程中的奥秘。

This is also That; That is also This. There is no pure This, nor pure That. That also contains Yes and No, and This also contains Yes and No. Is there really a distinction between This and That? Or is there no distinction at all? At the starting point where This and That have not yet separated, it is called the Pivot of the Tao. The Pivot starts from the center of the Tao and controls the center of the Tao to respond to infinity. "Yes" also has infinite variations, and "No" also has infinite variations. Therefore, only by considering the causality in the evolutionary process of an object from its origin can we truly understand the mysteries of its evolution.

以指喻，指之非指，不若（如）以非指喻，指之非指也。以马喻：马之非马；不若（如）以非马喻：马之非马也。天地一指也，万物一马也。

译文：物体的表象，不等于物体的本质，以马来说明白马不是马，不如说：白马不是马属物种的总名称。从道通为一的观点而言，天地一指，万物中无论白马、黑马都是马。

The appearance of an object does not equal its essence. To illustrate this with a horse, saying that a white horse is not a horse is not as accurate as saying: a white horse is not the general name for the species of horse. From the perspective of the unity of the Tao, the heavens and earth are one, and all things, whether white horses or black horses, are horses.

可，乎可；不可，乎不可。道，行之而成；物，谓之而然。恶乎（何所）然？然于然。恶乎（何所）不然？不然于不然。物固有所然，物固有所可。无物不然，无物不可。故为是：举莛与楹（yíng 堂屋前部的柱子），厉（古同疠、癞，恶疮，借指丑妇）与西施，恢恑憰怪（huī guǐ jué guài 谓离奇怪异），道通为一。

译文：大众认可的，我也认可；大众不认可的，我也不认可。因为，道路是众人走出来的，名称是大众叫出来的。为何是这样？众人认为是这样，我也认为是这样。为何不是这样呢？众人不认为是这样，我也不认为是这样。因为，一切事物都存在共同点，也存在不同点。由此而言，天下万物有共认的因素，也有不共认的因素。所以小草的茎杆与厅前的大柱；丑妇与美女西施；以及离奇古怪的事与物，以"道"的观点而言都是相通为一。

What is accepted by the masses, I also accept; what is not accepted by the masses, I also do not accept. Because the path is created by people, and names are given by the masses. Why is it like this? Because the masses believe it to be so, I also believe it to be so. Why is it not like this? Because the masses do not believe it to be so, I also do not believe it to be so. Because everything has both similarities and differences. From this perspective, all things in the world have commonalities and non-commonalities. So, the stem of a grass and the big pillar in the hall; the ugly woman and the beautiful Xi Shi; as well as bizarre and extraordinary things and objects, from the perspective of the "Tao," are all interconnected and one.

其分也，成也；其成也，毁也。凡物无成与毁，复通为一。唯达者知通为一，为是不用，而寓诸庸（犹言：寄于庸）。庸也者，用也；用也者，通也；通也者，得也；适得而几矣。因是已，已而不知其然，谓之道。

译文：天地间万物的分解与消亡，也是新生命诞生的开始，新生命的诞生，也是走向消亡的起点。因此，天地间的万物，在《道》的理论中没有"成与毁"。生与死的划分，复通为一，唯有通达的圣人明白复通为一的道理。凡事不强加于"是"，而寄于庸。庸者，中庸之道也；用者，万事通达；通达者，万事得道也。由此而言：顺其自然而不知所以然，称之谓：道法自然。

The decomposition and disappearance of all things in the universe are also the beginning of the birth of new life, and the birth of new life is also the starting point of moving towards disappearance. Therefore, in the theory of "Tao," there is no concept of "creation and destruction" among all things in the universe. The distinction between life and death is reunited into one, and only the enlightened saints understand the principle of reunification. One does not forcibly impose their own opinions on things, but rather lets them flow naturally. This natural flow is the Taoist principle of "zhongyong," which leads to the understanding and mastery of all things. In this sense, following the natural flow of things without trying to understand the reasons behind them is called "following the natural law of Tao."

劳神明为一，而不知其同也，谓之"朝三"。何谓"朝三"？狙公赋茅，曰："朝三而暮四"众狙皆怒。曰："然则，朝四而暮三。"众狙皆悦。名实未亏，而喜怒为用，亦因是也。是以圣人和之以是非，而休乎天钧，是之谓两行。（郭象注："任天下之是非。"）

译文：众辩者，劳神费力地争辩唯一，而不谈论其中的统一。这就是所谓的"朝三"，何谓"朝三？"有位养猴人给猴子橡子时，说："早上给你们三颗，晚上给四颗。"众猴听罢皆怒。养猴人便改口："那么，早上给你的四颗，晚上给三颗。"众猴听罢皆喜，供给猴子橡子的总数没有改变，只改变了供给方式，其结果大不相同。因此圣人以变通为手段，推行均平之理笼络人心，是之谓：各得其所。

Those who argue are laboriously disputing for uniqueness, rather than discussing the unity within it. This is what is called "three in the morning". What is "three in the morning"? A keeper of monkeys was giving acorns to the monkeys, saying, "Three for you in the morning, and four in the evening." All the monkeys were angry. So, the keeper changed his words and said, "Then four for you in the morning, and three in the evening." All the monkeys were happy. The total number of acorns given to the monkeys didn't change, only the way of giving them changed, and the result was completely different. Therefore, the sage uses flexibility as a method to promote the principle of equality and unite people's hearts. This is called: everyone gets what they deserve.

古之人，其知（智）有所至矣。恶乎（何所）至？有认为，未始有物者，至矣，尽矣，不可以加矣。其次以为有物矣，而未始有封也（犹言：分类）。其次以为有封焉，而未始有是非也。

译文：远古时期的先祖，他们的智慧已经达到至高的境界，什么是至高的境界？有的人认为宇宙从一开始并不存在具体的事与物，这样的认知是很了不起的，也是不容质疑的。其次，有人认为有物而没有分类罢了；再次，有人认为有物与物的分类，而未有是非之别。

Ancestors in ancient times had reached the supreme level of wisdom. What is the supreme level? Some people believe that the universe did not exist with specific things and matters from the very beginning. Such cognition is remarkable and should not be doubted. Secondly, some people think that there are things, but they are not categorized; thirdly, some people believe that there are things and categories of things, but without right or wrong.

是非之彰（彰显）也，道之所以亏也。道之所以亏，爱之所以成。

译文：宇宙元气未分时期的状态，称谓：浑沌时期。《易经》"元气未分，浑沌为一。"三国魏曹植《七启》："夫，太极之初，浑沌无分。"从"浑沌未分"进化为"太极之初"，也是"是非之彰显"之时。正因为《道》在进化过程中首先做到"亏"，或称"包容"、"谦和"，才能成就"赢"，再由"亏与赢"进化成"阴阳"。也可以说：爱是宇宙进化的基础。换而言之：青年男女甘愿为对方付出毕生真挚的感情不离不弃的行为，方可称谓：

爱情。爱情也是人类进化的根本，或称：爱是人类进化的基础。

The state of the universe during the period when primal energy had not yet separated is known as the Age of Chaos. The Book of Changes states, "Before primal energy separated, chaos reigned supreme." In the "Seven Exhortations" by Cao Zhi of the Three Kingdoms period, it states, "In the earliest days of the Supreme Ultimate, chaos reigned without distinction." The transition from "Chaos Undivided" to "The Beginning of the Supreme Ultimate" was also the time when "right and wrong became evident." It is because the Tao first achieved "deficit" or "tolerance" and "humility" during the process of evolution that it could achieve "victory." Then, from "deficit and victory," it evolved into "yin and yang." One could also say that love is the foundation of the universe's evolution. In other words, the act of young men and women willingly sacrificing their sincere affection for each other throughout their lives, never leaving each other's side, could be described as love. Love is also the fundamental basis of human evolution.

果且（果真）有成与亏乎哉，果且无成与亏乎哉？有成与亏，故昭氏之鼓琴也；无成与亏，故昭氏之不鼓琴也。

译文：天地间的阴阳之气有变化？还是没有变化？若有变化，则昭文的弹琴声才能借助空气的流动性传播（或称：琴声通过声波传达至人的听觉，才能听到弹琴声。）若没有变化，甚至连昭文也没法听到自己弹奏的琴声。

Is there a change in the Yin and Yang energies between heaven and earth? Or is there no change? If there is a change, then Zhao Wen's piano playing can only be transmitted through the fluidity of the air (or one could say that the sound of the piano is transmitted to human hearing through sound waves, allowing us to hear the piano playing). If there is no change, even Zhao Wen himself would be unable to hear the sound of his own piano playing.

昭文之鼓琴（弹琴）也；师旷之枝策（举杖以击节奏）也；惠子之据梧（jù wú 司马云："梧，琴也。"崔云："琴瑟也。"）也。三子之知（智），几乎皆其盛者也。故（因此）载之末年。

译文：昭文善于弹琴；师旷精通乐律；惠施善奏琴瑟。这三人的才智，借阴阳之气的流动性，将器乐声融合成悦耳的和协之声，几乎盛名远扬。因此，他们的事迹被载入史册，流传于后世。

Zhao Wen excelled at playing the qin, Shi Kuang was proficient in music theory, and Hui Shi was skilled at playing the qin and se. With the help of the fluidity of Yin and Yang energy, these three individuals merged their instrumental sounds into harmonious melodies that were pleasant to the ears, earning them widespread fame. Consequently, their deeds were recorded in annals of history, and passed down through the ages.

唯其好之也，以异于彼；其好之也，欲之明之彼。非所明而明之，故以坚白之昧终。而其子又以文之纶终，终身无成。若是而可谓成乎？虽我亦成也。若是而不可谓成乎？物与我无成也。是故（因此）滑疑之耀，圣人之所图（古含"鄙"之意）也。为是不用，而寓诸庸，此之谓以明。

译文：他们各有所长，又别于彼此。各自的观点都希望得到对方认同，彼此不太清晰的理念也要力争取胜。所以，才有了迷惑的"坚白论"。他的儿子又以此论点绪余，终身也没有取得成功。如果这些人所讲述的理念可称作成功，那么我的理论也可以称作成功。如果这些人讲述的理念不可以称作成功，那么我所坚守的理念，也许参杂着不确切的言辞。因此，滑乱疑惑的炫耀之辞，圣人是鄙视的。对于自然之道而言，不能强加于是非对错，而是采取中庸之道的原则，才能称谓：大道之明。

Each of them had their own strengths and differed from each other. They each hoped to gain recognition for their respective viewpoints and strove to prevail in their somewhat unclear beliefs. Thus, the confusing "theory of firmness and whiteness" arose. His son continued with this argument and never achieved success in his lifetime. If the ideas preached by these individuals can be considered successful, then my theory can also be considered successful. If the ideas preached by these individuals cannot be considered successful, then perhaps my beliefs are mixed with inexact words. Therefore, the confused and boastful words are despised by the saints. As for the principles of nature, we cannot impose our own notions of right and wrong, but rather should embrace the principle of the Golden Mean. This is what we call "the clarity of the great way".

今且（犹：今夫。我）有言于此，不知，其与是类乎？其与是不类乎？类与不类，相与为类，则与彼无以异矣。虽然，请尝（尝试）言之：有始也者，有未始（未曾）有始也者；有未始，有夫未始，有始也者。有"有"也者，有"无"也者，有未始（未曾）"有无"也者。有未始，有夫未始"有无"也者。

译文：今我有言于此，不知道我的言语与他人的谈论是否类同？还是不相同？类同与不类同，大致归类，恐怕与他人的观点相差不大吧。虽然如此，请让我尝试而言：宇宙万物最初进化出"有"，也有未曾开始的"有"，还有未曾开始进化的"无"，也包含着未曾开始进化的"有与无"。

Now I have something to say. I do not know whether my words are similar to or different from others'. In general, the differences between mine and others' opinions are probably not so great. Nevertheless, let me have a try: The universe and all things evolved from the "being", there is also the "being" that has not yet begun, as well as the "non-being" that has not yet begun to evolve. It also contains the "being and non-being" that has not yet begun to evolve.

俄而（突然）"有无"矣，而未知"有无"之，果孰（谁）"有"，孰"无"也？今我则已有谓（有所评说）矣，而未知吾所谓之，其果有谓乎？其果无谓乎？

译文：突然间，"大道为一"进化出"有与无"，却难以确认谁是"有"，谁是"无"。今天我已经有所评说，而不知我的评说果真是这样，还是果真不是这样呢？

Suddenly, the " All being one from the viewpoint of Tao " evolves into "being and non-being", but it is difficult to determine who is "being" and who is "non-being". Today, I have already commented on this, but I don't know whether my comments are truly accurate or not.

天下莫大于秋毫之末，而太（泰）山为小。莫寿于殇子，而彭祖（传说中的仙人）为夭。天地与我并生，而万物与我为一。既已为一矣，且得有言乎？既已谓之一矣，且得无言乎？一与言，为二；二与一，为三。自此以往，巧历不能得，而况其凡乎！故，自"无"适"有"，以至于"三"，而况（何况），自"有"适（往）"有"乎！无适焉，因是已。

译文：天下莫大于秋毫之末，而泰山为小。世上没有比夭折的孩子更长寿，因为夭折的孩子与天地共生。而传说中的仙人彭祖都是短命的。天地与我共生存，而万物与我为一。既然我与天地为一，尚且无话说？客观存在的"一"，加上我们言论就成了"二"，"二"再加上未知的"一"，就成了"三"。以此类推，再精妙的历算师，也难以求得最终答案，更何况凡夫俗子呢？由此而言：从"无"到"有"，推演计算到"三"，又何必从"有"推算到"有"呢？不必劳神费力地下功夫，还是顺其本然吧！

In the world, nothing is greater than the tip of an autumn hair, while Mount Tai is regarded as small. There is no longer-lived being than a prematurely deceased child, because this child coexists with heaven and earth. Legendary immortal Pengzu is also short-lived. Heaven and earth coexist with me, and all things are integrated with me. Since I am integrated with heaven and earth, how can I have no words to say? The objective existence of "One" plus our speech becomes "Two", and "Two" plus the unknown "One" becomes "Three". Extending this logic, even the most skilled calendar calculator would find it difficult to arrive at a final answer, let alone an ordinary person. Hence, why bother calculating from "something" to "something" when one can simply deduce from "nothing" to "something" through a calculation of "three"? It is unnecessary to exert oneself unnecessarily; it is better to simply let things be as they are.

夫,《道》,未始(未曾)有封;言(理),未始(未曾)有常(规定),为是(是非)而有畛(zhěn 界线)也。请言其畛:有左(指在下)。有右(指在上)。有伦(人伦)。有义(仪制)。有分(分封)。有辩(辩驳)。有竞(竞劝)。有争(争议)。此之谓八德。

译文:天地之道,未曾有过划分;天下之理,也不曾有过不可逾越的界限。为"是非"划分标准(《增韵》:"左,人道尚右,以右为尊。故,非正之术曰:左道"。),在左,为下、为卑。在右,为上、为尊。有人伦。有仪制。有分封。有辩驳。有竞劝。有争议。此称谓:八德。

The laws of heaven and earth have never been divided, and the principles of the universe have never had insurmountable boundaries. The criteria for distinguishing "right and wrong" are determined by human customs. *("Zeng Yun" states that, " The left is considered inferior in the culture, while the right is regarded as superior and respected. Hence, those who deviate from the right path are said to be on the left path.")* When one is on the left, one is considered inferior and humble. When one is on the right, one is considered superior and respected. There are human relations, rites and regulations, feudal appointments, arguments, competition, disputes. These eight elements are collectively known as the Eight Virtues.

六合(天、地、东、南、西、北,六个方位)之外,圣人存(察)而不论。六合之内,圣人论而不议。《春秋》经世先王之志,圣人议而不辩。故,分也者,有不分也;辩也者,有不辩也。曰:何也?圣人怀(存)之,众人辩之,以相(互相)示也。故曰:辩也者,有不见也。

译文:六合之外,圣人察而不论。六合之内,圣人论而不争议。《春秋》经世之志,治国大纲,圣人议而不辩。因此,有可分,就有不可分;有可辩,就有不可辩,为什么?圣人把自己的认知藏于怀中,而众夫子则是争辩不休夸耀于外。所以说，常常夸耀于外的人，并不了解事物发展的本来面目。

Beyond the six boundaries, the sage observes but does not discuss. Within the six boundaries, the sage discusses but does not argue. The "Spring Autumn Annals" is a record of governance principles and the outline for ruling a country. The sage discusses without debating. Therefore, there are things that can be distinguished and cannot be distinguished; there are things that can be debated and cannot be debated. Why? The sage hides his knowledge in his heart, while the scholars argue endlessly and boast externally. Therefore, those who often boast externally do not understand the true nature of things.

夫，大道不称（说）。大辩不言。大仁不仁。大廉不嗛（qiān 通"谦"）。大勇不忮（zhì 逆）。《道》，昭而不道。言（理），辩而不及。仁，常而不成。廉，清而不信。勇，忮而不成。五者，圆而几向方矣！故，知止其所不知，至矣。孰（谁）知不言之辩，不道之道？若有能知，此之谓"天府"，注焉而不满，酌焉而不竭，而不知其所由来，此之谓葆光。（成玄英疏："葆，蔽也。至忘而照，即照而忘，故能韬敝其光，其光弥朗。"）

译文：至高无上的大道之理不必宣传，最了不起的理念不必争辩。仁爱之士不必向人展示仁爱。廉洁之士不必叫嚷自己清白。至勇之士从不叛逆。所谓"大道之理"招摇过市，则是不道。强辩之词总有过犹不及的缺陷。仁爱之词常挂嘴边反而称不上仁爱。廉洁到清白的极致，反而使人感到不真实。将叛逆当作勇敢，就不能称谓勇敢。这五种行为，宛如着意求"圆"，却几近成了"方"。因此，懂得收敛自己的言行，便是明智之举。谁能不用言辞便可讲清楚"不道之道"？若有能知，便可称谓"天府之才"。无论注入多少也无法满盈、无论酌取多少也不会竭尽，然而却不知其中的缘故何在，此可称谓"葆光"。

The supreme Truth of the Universe doesn't need to be preached, and the greatest principles don't require debate. The benevolent don't need to show their kindness, and the honest don't need to proclaim their integrity. The bravest people never rebel. When the "Supreme Truth" is flaunted in public, it ceases to be true. Forceful arguments often have flaws of overdoing it. Kind words constantly spoken lose their genuine kindness. Perfect honesty can appear inauthentic. To mistake rebellion for bravery is not truly brave.

These five behaviors, which are intended to pursue "perfection," have almost become "rigid." Therefore, it is wise to know how to restrain one's words and actions. Who can explain the "Tao of not-speaking" without words? If someone knows it, he can be called a "talent of Heaven." No matter how much is poured in, it cannot be filled; no matter how much is taken out, it will not be exhausted. Yet, no one knows the reason why. This can be called "treasuring light."

故昔者，尧问于舜曰："我欲伐宗、脍、胥敖，南面而不释然，其故何也？"

舜曰："夫，三子者，犹存乎蓬艾（蓬蒿与艾草，泛指草野）之间。若不释然，何哉？昔者，十日并出，万物皆照，而况（何况）德之进乎日者乎！"

译文：昔日，尧曾经对舜说："我想征伐宗、脍、胥敖这三个小国家。每当上朝理事，总是不能释放心中的烦扰，这是为什么？"

舜回答："这三个小国的国君，犹如生存在蓬蒿、艾草之间。倘若你无法释怀，为什么？远古时代曾经有十个太阳并出，普照天下万物。何况，高尚的品德超越太阳的恩惠。"

In the past, Yao once said to Shun, "I want to conquer the three small countries of Zong, Kuai, and Xu'ao. Whenever I attend the court and deal with affairs, I always cannot release my heart from trouble. Why is that?"

Shun replied, "The kings of these three small countries are like living among reeds and wormwood. If you cannot release your heart from trouble, why? In ancient times, there were ten suns shining together, illuminating everything under heaven. Moreover, noble character surpasses the favor of the sun."

啮缺（niè quē 传说中的上古贤圣。《庄子·天地》：'尧之师曰许由，许由之师曰啮缺，啮缺之师曰王倪。'）问乎王倪，曰："子知物之，所同是乎？"

曰:"吾恶乎知之!"

"子知子之所不知邪?"

曰:"吾恶乎知之!"

"然则,物无知邪?"

曰:"吾恶乎知之!虽然,尝试言之。庸讵（yōng jù 何以）知吾所谓知之,非不知邪?庸讵知吾所谓不知之,非知邪?且吾尝试问乎女（汝、你）:民湿寝则腰疾偏死（患半身不遂）,鳅（泥鳅）然乎哉?木处（人居住在树上）则惴栗恂惧（因恐惧而战栗）,猿猴然乎哉?三者,孰（谁）知正处?民食刍豢（chú huàn 家畜）；麋鹿食荐（草）；蝍蛆（jí qū 蜈蚣）甘带（爱食小蛇）；鸱鸦（chī yā 鹞鹰）嗜鼠。四者孰知正味?猿,猵狙以为雌。麋与鹿交（交配）。鳅与鱼游。毛嫱（qiáng）、丽姬（古代美女）,人之所美也；鱼见之,深入；鸟见之,高飞；麋鹿见之,决骤（迅速逃离）。四者,孰知天下之正色（美色）哉?自我观之,仁义之端（条理）,是非之涂（途）,樊然殽乱（纠纷混乱）,吾恶（何）能知其辩!"

译文:啮缺问王倪:"你知道物与物之间存在共同点吗?"

王倪说:"我何以知道!"

啮缺又问:"你知道你不知道的原因是什么吗?"

王倪说:"我何以知道呢?"

啮缺再问:"那么,物与物之间的差异也不清楚吗?"

王倪说:"我何以知道!虽然如此,我还是要尝试着回答你提出的问题。何以知道我所知道的就是他人不知道的,何以认为我所不知道的,正是他人已知的?我也尝试着问问你:人睡在潮湿的地方,最容易患腰部疾病,甚至会酿成半身不遂,泥鳅常年生活在湿泥中,为什么不叫喊腰痛?人爬到树枝的高处,就会感到恐惧战栗,猿猴在树枝上睡大觉,怎么就不惊恐失色?人、泥鳅、猿猴,三者谁最懂得居住环境?人以家禽牲畜的肉为食物；麋鹿爱吃草芥；蜈蚣爱吃小蛇；鹞鹰爱吃老鼠。人、麋鹿、蜈蚣、鹞鹰,谁真正懂得天下美味?猿猴把猵狙当配偶。麋喜欢与鹿交配。泥鳅与鱼交尾。毛墙、丽姬,是人人称道的美女。可是,鱼儿看见她们,深潜水底；鸟儿看见她们,惊飞高空；麋鹿看见她们,飞奔逃离。人、鱼、鸟、麋鹿,谁真正懂得天下美色?以我看来:仁义之端倪,是非之途径,都是纠纷混乱错综复杂,我何以知道其中的差异在那里呢?"

Nie Que asked Wang Ni, "Do you know if there are commonalities between things?"

Wang Ni replied, "How would I know?"

Nie Que asked again, "Do you know the reason why you don't know?"

Wang Ni said, "How would I know that?"

Nie Que inquired further, "So, are the differences between things also unclear to you?"

Wang Ni said, "How would I know? Nevertheless, I will still try to answer the questions you raised. How do we know that what I know is unknown to others, and how do we assume that what I don't know is already known to others? I will also ask you this: when people sleep in damp places, they are most susceptible to developing waist ailments, which can even lead to paralysis. Why don't loaches which live in wet mud all year round, complain of back pain? When humans climb up high on tree branches, they feel fear and tremble, but why don't monkeys which sleep on tree branches, show any signs of alarm? Which of the three - humans, loaches, and monkeys - knows the best about their living environment? Humans eat the meat of domestic animals and livestock; deer prefer to graze on grass and weeds; centipedes prefer to eat small snakes; and eagles prefer to prey on mice. Among humans, deer, centipedes, and eagles, who truly knows what the best food in the world is? Monkeys mate with macaques, deer mate with other deer, and loaches mate with fish. Mao Qiang and Li Ji are praised as beautiful women by everyone. However, when fish see them, they dive deep into the water; when birds see them, they fly up into the sky; and when deer see them, they flee in terror. Who among man, fish, bird, and deer truly knows the beauty of the world? As I see it, the beginnings of righteousness and morality, and the paths of right and wrong, are all tangled and intricate, how can I possibly know the difference between them?"

啮缺曰："子不知利害，则至人固不知利害乎？"

王倪曰："至人神矣！大泽焚而不能热；河汉（指上天银河）冱（hù 冻结）而不能寒；疾雷破山、厉风振海，而不能惊。若然（如此）者，乘云气，骑日月，而游乎四海之外，死生无变于已，而况利害之端乎！"

译文：啮缺说："你不知道利害，那些修炼高深的至人也不知道利害吗？"

王倪说："物我两忘的至人神妙难测！大湖焚烧不能使至人感到炎热；银河冻结而不能使至人感到寒冷；疾

雷破山、厉风震海而不能使至人受惊。如此至人，乘云驾雾，骑日月，而云游于四海之处，死生也不会伤害到至人，何况利与害这类凡俗琐事呢？"

Nie Que said, "You don't know about the advantages and disadvantages. Don't those supreme beings who have reached a high level of cultivation also know about them?"

Wang Ni replied, "The supreme Being who forgets both himself and the world is mysterious and inscrutable! Even a blazing lake cannot make him feel hot, and a frozen Milky Way cannot make him feel cold. Thunder that breaks mountains and gale that shakes the sea cannot frighten him. Such a Supreme Being rides on clouds, drives the sun and moon, and floats freely throughout the Four Seas. Neither death nor life can harm him, so how could trivial matters like advantages and disadvantages affect him?"

瞿（qú）鹊子问长梧子曰："吾闻诸夫子：'圣人不从事于务（指俗事），不就利，不违害，不喜求，不缘道。无谓，有谓；有谓，无谓。而游乎尘垢之外。'夫子以为孟浪之言（言语轻率），而我以为妙道之行也。吾子以为奚若（和何）？"

译文：瞿鹊子问长梧子说："我听众先生言说：'圣人不从事凡俗琐事，不趋利，不避害，不喜求索，不以攀缘之心行虚通之道。无所为，有所为；有可为，无可为，而云游于尘世之外。'众先生认为是荒诞无稽之谈，而我却认为是妙道之言，先生您认为如何？"

Qu Quezi asked Chang Wuzi, "I have heard the wise man say, 'The sage does not engage in trivial affairs, does not pursue profits, does not avoid harms, does not delight in seeking, and does not follow a false path of aspiration. They act without purpose and with purpose; they can act and cannot act, floating freely beyond the world of dust and mortals.' Many wise men consider this talk absurd and baseless, but I find it profound and meaningful. What do you think, sir?"

长梧子曰："是黄帝之所听荧（tīng yíng 疑惑）也，而丘（孔丘）也，何足以知之，且女（汝）亦大早计？见卵而求时夜（看见鸡蛋就想到打鸣的公鸡），见弹而求鸮炙（xiāo zhì 想到以炙鸮鸟为食）。予尝为女（汝）妄言之，女（汝）以妄听之。奚旁日月，挟宇宙，为其吻合，置其滑涽(huá hūn 纷乱不定。郭象注："滑涽纷乱，莫之能正。")以隶相尊。众人役役（奔走钻营），圣人愚芚（yú tún 无知貌）参（参验）万岁而一成纯，万物尽然，而以是相蕴（积聚）。予恶乎（我何以）知，说生之非惑邪！予恶乎知，恶（厌恶）死之，非弱丧（少年失其居）而不知归者邪？

译文：长梧子说："你的这些话语，黄帝听了也会疑惑，而孔丘怎么能说的清楚？况且，你所考虑的是否太超前了？就像是刚看到鸡蛋，就想到鸡蛋变成报晓的公鸡；刚看到弓弹，就想着打猎归来正吃烤熟的鸮鸟肉？我姑且与你妄言，你也妄听罢了。什么傍日月，挟宇宙，与天地吻合，任其纷乱不安，以卑贱为尊。众人奔走钻营，圣人愚笨迟钝，参验万年之纯真，万物尽了然，而以是非相互蕴含积聚。我何以知道，厌恶死亡贪求活在世上的困惑？又何以知道，小小年纪失去故土，流落他乡而不知其所归的迷茫？"

Chang Wuzi said, "Even Huangdi would be puzzled by your words, how could Confucius ever clarify them? Besides, are you thinking too far ahead? It's like seeing an egg and immediately thinking of it hatching into a crowing cock or seeing a bow and arrow and imagining coming back from a hunt with roasted owl meat. I will speak freely with you, and you can listen freely as well. What about being alongside the sun and moon, embracing the universe, aligning with the heavens and earth, embracing their chaos, and regarding humility as dignity? While the masses scramble and strive, the sage remains foolish and sluggish. Verifying the purity of tens of thousands of years, understanding everything in the universe, and embodying the accumulation of right and wrong. How could I know the confusion of hating death and craving to live in the world? And how could I know the confusion of losing a childhood home, wandering in a foreign land, and not knowing where to go?"

丽之姬，艾（地名）封人之子（女）也。晋国之始得之也，涕泣沾襟；及其至于王所，与王同筐床（大方床），食刍豢，而后悔其泣也。

译文：丽之姬，是艾地封疆大臣的女儿。晋国征伐艾地时俘获了她，当时她哭地泪湿衣襟。等到把她带入晋王宫殿宠为夫人，同晋王共寐方床，共享美味佳肴时，她后悔当初的哭泣。

Li Ji, the daughter of the governor of the Aidi area, was captured by the State of Jin when it invaded Aidi. She wept bitterly at that time. But when she was brought into the palace of the King of Jin and was given the honor of being the King's wife, she shared a bed and delicious food with the King, she regretted crying at that time.

予恶乎（我何以）知，夫死者，不悔其始之蕲（qí 祈）生乎！梦饮酒者，旦而哭泣；梦哭泣者，旦而田猎。方其梦也，不知其梦也；梦之中又占其梦焉，觉而后，知其梦也。且有，大觉而后知此其大梦也。而愚者自以为觉，窃窃然知之。君乎，牧乎，固哉！丘（孔丘）与女（汝，你），皆梦也；予（我）谓女（汝，你）梦，亦梦也。是其言也，其名为吊诡（犹怪异）。万世之后而一遇大圣，知其解者，是旦暮遇之也。"

译文：我何以知道，那些死者不后悔当初的求生？梦中饮酒作乐的人，早晨起床后可能就在痛哭流涕；睡梦中哭泣的人，醒来后可能就在田野里愉快地守猎。在梦中，不知在其梦；梦之中，又占卜其梦。觉醒后才知道自己是在做梦。尚且大觉之后才知：人生犹如一场梦。然而，愚昧之人以苛察（以繁琐苛刻为明察）小事来显示精明，以求心中欣慰，自己是命运的主宰者吗？还是命运的奴仆呢？这其中固然有差别。孔丘与你是在梦中呢，还是我和你亦在做梦？以上所言，可谓是"奇谈怪论"吧。万世之后倘若遇上一位大圣人，悟出其中的道理，恐怕也是偶然。

How do I know that those who have passed away do not regret their desire to survive in the past? A person who drinks and enjoys himself in a dream may wake up crying in the morning; Someone who cries in a dream may wake up to hunt happily in the field. In a dream, one does not know that he is dreaming; In the middle of a dream, one divines his

- 285 -

dream. Only after waking up do we realize that we were dreaming. Even so, we only know after waking up from a deep sleep: life is like a dream. However, foolish people try to show their wisdom by scrutinizing trivial matters, seeking a sense of satisfaction in their hearts. Are they masters of their own fate, or slaves to it? There is indeed a difference. Are Confucius and you dreaming, or am I dreaming with you? What I have said above can be considered as "strange talk" perhaps. If a great sage comes across it thousands of years later and understands the truth behind it, it will probably be by chance.

既使我与若（你）辩矣，若（你）胜我，我不若胜，若果是也，我果非也邪？我胜若，若不吾胜，我果是也，而果非也邪？其或是也，其或非也邪？其俱是也，其俱非也邪？我与若不能相知也，则人固受其黮暗（dǎn àn 蒙昧），吾谁使正之，使同乎若者正之，既与若同矣，恶（何）能正之？使同乎我者正之，既同乎我矣，恶能正之？使异乎我与若（你）者正之，既异乎我与若矣，恶（何）能正之？使同乎我与若者正之，既同乎我与若矣，恶能正之？然则，我与若与人，俱（皆）不能相知也，而待彼也邪！

译文：即使我与你辩论，你胜我，我没有胜道你，那么你果真是对的，而我果真是错吗？我胜过你，你没有胜过我，我果真就是对，你果真就是错？或者，有一人对，有一人错；或者，咱俩都对，也许咱俩都错了。我和你并没有办法知道真相。世人姑且受其蒙昧，我可以让谁作出正确的裁定呢？让同意你观点的人来评判，既然他们与你的看法相同，怎知裁决是公正的？让同意我观点的人来评判，既然与我的看法相同，怎能知道结论是公正的？让不同意你、我观点的人来评判，既然与你、我的观点不相同，怎么知道裁定就是正确的？让同意你、我观点的人来评判，既然与你、我的观点相同，怎么知道结论是无误呢？然则，我、你与他人都无法知道正确的答案是什么。只能等待彼此的自然之分吧。

Even if I argue with you, and you win over me, does it mean you are really right and I am really wrong? If I win over you and you fail to win over me, does it mean I am really right and you are really wrong? Or is it that one of us is right and the other wrong? Or are we both right, or maybe we are both wrong? You and I cannot know the truth. The world is temporarily blinded by ignorance, so who can I ask to make the right decision?

If we let those who agree with you judge, since they share the same opinion with you, how can we know if the decision is fair? If we let those who agree with me judge, since they share the same opinion with me, how can we know if the conclusion is fair? If we let those who disagree with both of us judge, since they don't share the same opinion with either of us, how can we know if the verdict is correct? If we let those who agree with both of us judge, since they share the same opinion with us, how can we know if the conclusion is flawless? In the end, neither you, me, nor anyone else can know what the truth is. We can only wait for the natural separation between us.

何谓和之以天倪？（郭象注："天倪者，自然之分也。"）

曰："是，不是；然，不然。是，若果（如果）是，则是之，异乎不是，亦无辩；然，若果（如果）然也，则然之，异乎不然也，亦无辩。化声（郭象注："是非之辩为化声。"）之相待，若其不相待，和之以天倪（没有边际）因之以曼衍（延伸变化），所以穷年（终其天年）也。忘年忘义，振于无竟（没有穷尽；没有边际），故寓诸无竟。"

译文：瞿鹊子问："什么是'和之以天倪'？"

长梧子说："是，也包含着'不是'；然，也包含着'不然'。是，如果是'是'，就算做'是'，异乎不是，也无话可说；因为是与不是的界线怎么区分，并不清楚。然，如果是'然'，就称谓'然'，异乎不是'然'，也无话可说；因为然与不然的边界在哪里，也不清楚。只能依赖是非之辩以此类推。如果还不能得出正确的判定，也只能顺其自然，忘却时光，忘却争议，寄于无穷天尽没有边际的境域中，随着时光磨砺则会自然分晓。"

Qu Quezi asked, "What is meant by 'harmonizing with the natural distinction'?"

Chang Wuzi replied, "Yes, it also contains 'no'; and sure, it also contains 'not sure'. If 'yes' is 'yes', it is 'yes'. There is nothing to say if it is different from 'no', because the boundary between 'yes' and 'no' is not clear. Similarly, if 'sure' is 'sure', it is called 'sure'. There is nothing to say if it is different from 'not sure', because the boundary between 'sure' and 'not sure' is also unclear. We can only rely on the debate between right and wrong to infer. If we still cannot make a correct judgment, we can only let nature take its course, forget about time, forget about disputes, and entrust ourselves to the boundless realm of infinity. With the passage of time, things will naturally become clearer."

罔两（影子边缘的阴影）问景（影）曰："曩（nǎng 以往）子行，今子止，曩子坐，今子起，何其无特操（独立的操守）与？"

景曰："吾有待而然者邪（耶）。吾所待，又有待，而然者邪。吾待蛇蚹蜩翼邪。恶识（冒犯）所以然？恶识（得罪）所以不然？"

译文：影子边缘的阴影问影子，说："以往你行，今日你停止；以往你坐，今日你又起来，你怎么就没有自己独立的操守呢？"

影子回答："我是有所依托才是这样的。我所依托的，又有所依托，仅此而已。我所依托的犹如蛇、蝉蜕化后留下的外壳。我怎么知道为什么会是这样？为什么不是这样呢？"

The shadow at the edge of the shadow asked the shadow, saying, "You used to move, but now you stop; you used to sit, but now you rise up. Why don't you have your own independent moral principles?"

The shadow replied, "I am like this because I rely on something. What I rely on also relies on something else, and that's all there is to it. What I rely on is like the shell left behind by a snake or a cicada after it molts. How do I know why it is like this? Why not like that?"

昔（古同"夕"、"夜"）者，庄周梦与胡蝶（蝴蝶）。栩栩（忻畅貌）然胡蝶也，自喻适志与。俄然觉，则蘧蘧（qú qú 悠然自得）然周也。不知，周之梦与胡蝶与；胡蝶之梦为周与？周与胡蝶，则必有分矣。此之谓物化。

译文：夜间，庄周梦见自己变成一只蝴蝶。栩栩如生的蝴蝶，自以为得志而不知庄周的存在。突然感觉到，悠然自得的蝴蝶就是庄周。不知道是庄周在梦中化作蝴蝶？还是蝴蝶托梦于庄周？庄周与蝴蝶必然有区别，此可谓自然物化吧。（物化：成玄英疏："夫，新新变化，物物迁流，譬彼穷指，方兹交臂。"李善注："化，谓变化而死也，不忍斥言其死，故言：随物而化也。"）

寓意：梦幻中：心旷神怡，悠然自得。现实中：硝烟弥漫，朝不保夕。

烽火连年断炊烟，
群雄逐鹿踏关山，
期盼苍天开道眼，
夜半寻梦蝴蝶还。

During the night, Zhuangzi dreamed that he turned into a butterfly. The vivid butterfly thought that it had achieved its goal and did not know the existence of Zhuangzi. Suddenly, it felt that the content butterfly was Zhuangzi. Was it Zhuangzi who turned into a butterfly in his dream, or was it a butterfly who appeared in Zhuangzi's dream? There must be a difference between Zhuangzi and the butterfly. This can be called natural materialization.

Meaning: In dreams: relaxed and content, feeling at ease. In reality: smoke-filled, and life is precarious.

Years of war, smoke from kitchens cut off,
Heroes compete for power, marching over the mountains and rivers,
Hoping the heavens would open its eyes,
At midnight, dreaming of a butterfly returning.

尹文子头像铭文注解 Head Portrait of Yinwenzi & Annotation of the Inscriptions

《尹文子》：

尹文，尊称尹文子，齐国人。约生于公元前360年，卒于公元前280年。为稷下学派代表人物。倡导：大道容众，大德容下。道，不足以治，则用法；法，不足以治，则用术；术，不足以治，则用权；权，不足以治，则用势。实现自治。

另言：尹文子，周人。约生于公元前350-285年。齐宣王时游学齐国，与一班辩士同住稷下，并纳儒、墨、道。不求做官，而论议天下是非，形成"稷下学风。"崇尚仁、义、礼、乐、名、法、刑、赏，维护三皇五帝建立的治世之道。

《庄子·天下》以宋钘（jiān 人名用字。战国有宋钘。又见《荀子·非十二子》）、尹文为一家："不累于俗，不饰于物，不苛于人，不忮（zhì 违逆）于众，愿天下之安宁，以活民命，人我之养，毕足而止。以此白心，古之道术，有在于是者，宋钘、尹文闻其风而悦之。"

Yinwenzi:

Yin Wen, known as Yin Wenzi, was a native of Qi. He was born around 360 BCE and died in 280 BCE. He was a representative figure of the Jixia School. He advocated: 'The great way accommodates all, and great virtue accommodates the humble. If the way is not enough for governance, then use laws; if laws are not enough for governance, then use tactics; if tactics are not enough for governance, then use power; if power is not enough for governance, then use influence. Achieve self-governance.'.

Another note: Yin Wenzi was a person from the Zhou Dynasty. He was born around 350-285 BCE. During the reign of King Xuan of Qi, he studied in the state of Qi, lived with a group of debaters in Jixia, and embraced Confucianism, Mohism, and Taoism. He did not seek official positions, but discussed the rights and wrongs of the world, forming the "Jixia style of learning." He advocated benevolence, righteousness, propriety, music, fame, law, punishment, reward, and maintained the way of governing established by the Three Sovereigns and Five Emperors.

"In 'Zhuangzi: The World,' Song Jian and Yin Wen are identified as belonging to the same school of thought: 'They are not fettered by worldly conventions, do not adorn themselves with external trappings, do not impose harsh demands on others, do not go against the general sentiment, and hope for world peace to preserve human life. Satisfaction with basic salaries is sufficient, as it expresses the sincerity of their hearts. Such content exists in ancient Daoism, and Song Jian and Yin Wen greatly admired this scholarly atmosphere upon hearing it.'"

晋国苦奢《尹文子·卷上》

昔，晋国苦奢（穷奢极欲），文公以俭矫之，乃衣不重帛，食不兼肉。

无几时，人皆大布之衣，脱粟之饭。

译文：从前，晋国风行穷奢极欲的恶习。晋文公很担忧，以身带头节俭，期待改变社会风气。他不穿两件以上的丝绸衣，每餐不食两种肉食。

不久，人们便兴起穿粗布衣、食糙米饭的习俗。

寓意：移风易俗需身体力行、以身作则，推而广之方能见效。

Luxury Problem in the State of Jin

In the past, the bad habit of excessive luxury prevailed in the State of Jin. The Duke of Jin was very worried about this and took the lead in practicing thrift in order to change the social atmosphere. He did not wear more than two silk clothes and did not eat two kinds of meat at each meal.

Soon, people began to wear coarse cloth and eat brown rice.

Meaning: Changing social atmosphere requires setting an example through one's own actions and leading by this example. Only by widely promoting and adopting these practices can we achieve visible results.

宣王好射《尹文子·卷上》

宣王（齐宣王）好射，说（悦）人之谓己能用强（强弓）也。其实所用不过三石，以示左右，左右皆引试之，中关而止。皆曰："不下九石，非大王孰能用是？"

宣王悦之。

然则，宣王用不过三石，而终身自以为九石。三石，实也；九石，名也。宣王悦其名，而丧其实。

译文：齐宣王喜好射箭，乐于听到人们夸他能拉动强弓。其实他所拉动的只是三石之弓，以示左右近臣，左右近臣都来试拉，近臣们每拉到一半时，都故意停下表示力不从心，并且都说："这是一把需有九石力气之人才能拉开的强弓，除非大王能拉的动，谁还能拉的动呢？"

齐宣王听了很高兴。

然而，齐宣王拉开的只是三石之弓，直到他死之前都认为自己拉动的是九石之弓。三石是实，九石是虚，齐宣王爱好虚名，而丧失实际。

寓意：喜欢虚名，丢弃了实际，岂不让人叹息！

King Xuan's Love for Archery

King Xuan of Qi had a great fondness for archery and delighted in hearing praises about his strength to pull a powerful bow. In reality, he could only pull a *three-dan* bow. He showed it to his ministers and attendants to demonstrate his skill. When the attendants tried to pull the bow, each of them deliberately stopped halfway, pretending that they couldn't do it, and said, "This is a powerful bow that requires *nine-dan* of strength to pull. Who else can pull it apart except the King?"

King Xuan of Qi was very pleased to hear this.

However, what he was able to pull was only a *three- dan* bow, and he believed until his death that he was pulling a *nine- dan* bow. The former was real, the latter was illusion. King Xuan of Qi loved vanity and thus lost sight of reality.

Meaning: Liking vanity and discarding reality, how can one not sigh over it!

献山雉为凤凰《尹文子·卷上》

楚人担山雉（zhì 鸟名。一名"鸐"。郭璞注："尾长者。"俗称"山鸡"），路人问："何鸟也?"

担雉者欺之曰："凤凰也。"

路人曰："我闻有凤凰，今始见之，汝贩之乎？"

曰："然。"

则十金，弗与。请加倍，乃与之。

将欲献楚王，经宿而鸟死。路人不遑（无暇），惟恨不得以献楚王。

国人传之，咸（皆）以为是真凤凰，贵欲以献之，遂闻楚王。

楚王感其欲献于己，召而厚赐之，过于买鸟之金十倍。

译文：楚国有人担着一只山鸡赶路，过路人问他："这是什么鸟？"

挑担山鸡的人欺骗他，说："这是一只凤凰。"

过路人说："我只是听说过有凤凰，今天才亲眼所见，你愿意卖它吗？"

回答："卖"。

出价十金，不卖。再添一倍的价钱，才卖给他。

过路人买下山鸡，想把山鸡献给楚王，没想到，过了一夜那只鸟便死了。他顾不上痛惜买鸟的花费，只婉惜没能及时献于楚王。

国内人很快传开了，都说那是一只真凤凰。正因为它极为珍贵，过路人一心想要献给楚王。不久，楚王也听说了此事。

楚王感慨此人出高价购买传说中的凤凰只是为了献给自己，便召过路人进宫给予厚赏。那赏赐要超过买鸟花费的十倍还多。

寓意：过路人以诚心赢得厚赏；楚王以厚赏赢得民心。

Offering the Phoenix

A man from the State of Chu was carrying a pheasant on his shoulder as he walked. A passerby asked him, "What kind of bird is this?"

The man carrying the pheasant deceived him and said, "This is a phoenix."

The passerby said, "I've only heard of the phoenix before, but today I've seen it with my own eyes. Are you willing to sell it?"

The man replied, "Yes, I am willing to sell it."

The passerby offered ten gold coins, but the man refused. When the offer doubled, he finally sold it to him.

The passerby bought the pheasant and intended to present it to the King of Chu. Unexpectedly, the bird died overnight. He did not lament the cost of buying the bird, but only regretted that he had not presented it to the King of Chu in time.

The news spread quickly throughout the country, and everyone said that it was a real phoenix. Because it was so rare and precious, the passerby was determined to present it to the King of Chu. Soon, the King of Chu also heard about it.

The King of Chu was moved by the fact that the passerby had spent a great deal of money to purchase the legendary phoenix just to present it to him. Therefore, he summoned the passerby to the palace and awarded him generously, giving him a reward that was more than ten times the cost of buying the bird.

Meaning: The passerby earned a generous reward for his sincerity, and the King of Chu won the hearts of his people through his generous reward.

盗与殴《尹文子·卷下》

庄里丈人，字，长子曰"盗"，少子曰"殴"。

"盗"出行，其父在后追呼之，曰："盗！盗！"

吏闻之，因缚之。

其父呼"殴"喻吏，遽而声不转，但言："殴！殴！"

吏因殴之，几殪（yì 死）。

译文：乡村里有位大爷，给自己大儿子起名叫"盗"，给小儿子起名叫"殴"。

有一天，"盗"出门远行。其父在后一边追赶一边喊着"盗！盗！"

此时，官吏正巧路过，听到喊叫声，就把"盗"捆绑起来。

这位大爷急忙喊叫小儿子向官吏解释实情，由于心急声调没有转过来，只喊出："殴！殴！"

官吏以为是让殴打，于是狠狠殴打"盗"。"盗"几乎被打死。

寓意：名声与实际不相符，容易造成相反的结果。

Theft and Assault

In the countryside, there was an old man who named his eldest son "Dao" and his youngest son "Ou". *("Dao" means "theft" in Chinese, while "Ou" means "assault" in Chinese.)*

One day, "Dao" went out for a long journey. His father chased after him shouting, "Dao! Dao!"

At that moment, an official passed by and heard the shouting. He tied up "Dao" thinking he was a thief.

The old man quickly called out to his youngest son to explain the truth to the official, but because he was so anxious, he didn't manage to change his tone, only shouting out, "Ou! Ou!"

The official misunderstood this as a command to beat "Dao", so he brutally beat him on the road. "Dao" was almost beaten to death.

Meaning: When reputation does not match reality, it can easily lead to opposite results.

公孙龙子头像铭文注解 Head Portrait of Gongsun Long & Annotation of the Inscriptions

- 297 -

《公孙龙》：

公孙龙，字子秉。另言：子石。约生于公元前 320 年，卒于公元前 250 年。后世尊称公孙龙子。赵国（今，河北邯郸）人。以诡辩学著称。提出：任何事物皆有个性于共性之别。冯友兰著《中国哲学史》称公孙龙为"离坚白"派系。

另言：公孙龙约生于公元前 325 年-250 年，与荀卿同时代，略早些。同辈人还有魏牟，邹衍等。

Gongsun Long:

Gongsun Long, courtesy name was Zibing, In some sources, he was also referred to as Zishi. He was born around 320 BCE and died around 250 BCE. He was revered as Gongsun Longzi by later generations. He hailed from the State of Zhao *(present-day Handan, Hebei)*. He was renowned for his skill in sophistry and proposed that everything has its individuality as opposed to commonality. In the book "A History of Chinese Philosophy," Feng Youlan described Gongsun Long as a member of the "Li Jian Bai" faction.

Another note: Gongsun Long was born around 325 BCE - 250 BCE, and was contemporary with Xun Qing, slightly earlier. His peers also included Wei Mu and Zou Yan.

白马非马《公孙龙·白马论》

〈关吏〉曰："白马非马，可乎？"

〈公孙龙〉曰："可。"

〈关吏〉曰："何哉？"

〈公孙龙〉曰："马者，所以命形也。白者，所以命色也。命色者，非命形也。故曰：白马非马。"

〈关吏〉曰："有白马，不可谓无马也。不可谓无马者，非马也？有白马为有马。白之非马，何也？"

〈公孙龙〉曰："求马，黄、黑马皆可致。求白马，黄，黑马不可致。使白马乃马也，是所求一也；所求一者，白马不异马也。所求不异，如黄、黑马有可，有不可。何也？可与不可，其相非明。故，黄、黑马一也，而可以应'有马',而不可以应'有白马',是白马之非马审矣。"

〈关吏〉曰:"以马之色为非马,天下非有无色之马也。天下无马,可乎?"

〈公孙龙〉曰:"马,固有色,故有白马。使马无色,有马如已耳,安取白马?故,白者,非马也。白马者,马与白;马与白马也,故曰:白马非马也。"

〈关吏〉曰:"马,未与'白'为马;白,未与'马'为白。合:马与白,复名,白马,是相与以不相与为名,未可。故曰:白马非马,未可。"

〈公孙龙〉曰:"以有白马,为有马;谓有白马,为黄马,可乎?"

〈关吏〉曰:"未可。"

〈公孙龙〉曰:"以有马,为异有黄马,是异黄马于马也。异黄马于马,是以黄马为非马。以黄马为非马,而以白马为有马;此飞者入池,而棺椁异处。此天下之悖言乱辞也。"

〈公孙龙〉曰:"有白马,不可谓无马者,离白之谓也。是离者,有白马不可谓有马也?故,所以为有马者,独以'马',有马耳,非有'白马',为有马。故其为'有马'也,不可以谓'白马'也。白者,不定所白,忘之而可也。白马者,言定所白也,定所白者,非白也。马者,无去取(没有舍弃或保留)于色,故黄、黑皆所以应(应召)。白马者,有去取于色,黄、黑马皆所以色去(因马的色泽不可应召),故,唯白马独可以应耳。无去者,非有去也(有选择与没有选择,这本身就存在着差别)。故曰:白马非马。"

译文:关吏说:"依照你的意思'白马不是马',可以吗?"

公孙龙说:"可以。"

关吏问:"为什么?"

公孙龙说:"'马'这个词,是命名物种属性的,'白'是命名色泽的。不可以将命名色泽的词语用来命名属性。所以,白马不可以称作'马'。"

关吏说:"有白马,就不能称为'没有马'。既然,不能称为'没有马',那么白马就不是马么?(确定地说)有白马就是有马。你把白马不当作马,这是为什么呢?"

公孙龙说:"如果你需要马,那么黄马、黑马都可以应召。你只要求白马,那么黄马、黑马都不能应召。你把白马当作马,是追求唯一色泽的马,只要这唯一色泽的马匹,马群中就不能混杂其它色泽的马匹。如果你不强调马匹的色泽,那么黄马、黑马也可以应召,也不可以应召。这是为什么呢?可以与不可以,这不是很明白的道理吗?因为,有黄马、黑马时,只能应召:有马;而不能应召:有白马。由此而言:'白马'是专属物种的命名，不是'马'的命名。"

关吏说："以马匹外表的色泽评判是不是马，天下并没有无色泽的马。依你的观点：天下没有马，可以吗？"

公孙龙说："天下的马匹固然有色泽，其中也包括有白马。假如世上的马匹无需以色泽区分种群，有'马'就可以了，为什么还要另外标明'白马'？所以色泽的白，并不能代表马匹的本质。白马，只是'马'与'白'的合称，'马'与'白'不可以单独称'白马'。因此，白马不可称作'马'。"

关吏反驳说："马匹，并不是因为它长着白色皮毛才称它为马；白色，也不是马匹专用色而称作白。不能把马匹的本质与外在的特征分割，任何物种的属性与内在的基因是相辅而成。所以你说白马不是马，不可以。"

公孙龙说："依你的观点，有白马就是有马。那么，有白马就是有黄马？可以吗？"

关吏连忙说："不可以。"

公孙龙说："既然，你也明白'有马'，不等同'有黄马'，你是把黄马与马分开而言。如果黄马不等同马，就是把黄马不当作马。把黄马不当作马，反而要把白马当作马。由此好比：鸟在水中尽翱翔，棺椁东西各自葬，这不是天下悖论乱辞吗？"

公孙龙接着说："你认为有白马就不能称为没有马，这是不考虑白马与马之间的差别，脱离马匹特征，只强调有白马就是有马？故然，所以为有马，唯独以'马'为'有马'，并不是以'白马'为'有马'。故其为称作有马，不能称为有'白马'。白者，这个词含意很广，抽象的'白'与限定的'白'有很大区别，有时可以忽略。白马，称呼马匹的皮毛是白色的，但是着重点不在'白'而在'马'。征召马匹的时候，没有强调马匹色泽时，黄马、黑马都可以应召。征召时规定必须是白马，那么黄马、黑马因它们的毛色不能应召，唯独只有白马才能应召。有选择与没有选择，这本身就存在很大的差别，所以白马不是马。"

（中国春秋战国时期，国与国频繁发动战争，当时的马匹属于军用物资。因此，公孙龙牵马出关，遭到守关官吏阻拦。公孙龙为了保住自己的坐骑，情急之下充分发挥辩士的口才，以《白马非马》的理论反驳官吏，使官吏难以应答，不得不许可公孙龙牵马出关。公孙龙因临场发挥出色，成就了千古奇谈。）

寓意：辩证思维方法：由共性之中找到个性，由个性之中找到共性。而诡辩论则是利用事物之间可以相互转化的属性来偷换概念使局势利于自身。

White Horse is Not a Horse

The guard at the checkpoint said, "According to your logic, 'white horse is not a horse', is that correct?"

Gongsun Long replied, "Yes, it is."

The guard asked, "Why?"

Gongsun Long explained, "'Horse' is a term used to designate the species, while 'white' is a term used to designate color. We cannot use a term for color to designate the species. Therefore, a white horse cannot be called a 'horse'."

The guard retorted, "If there is a white horse, it cannot be said that there is 'no horse'. So if it's not 'no horse', then is a white horse not a horse? (Clearly) Having a white horse means there is a horse. Why do you refuse to consider a white horse as a horse?"

Gongsun Long said, "If you need a horse, then both yellow and black horses can be summoned. But if you only ask for a white horse, then neither yellow nor black horses can be summoned. You treat a white horse as a horse, but you are seeking a horse of a single color. In this case, there cannot be any horses of other colors mixed in the group. If you do not emphasize the color of the horse, then both yellow and black horses can or cannot be summoned, depending on the context. Why is that? Shouldn't it be obvious whether something can or cannot be done? Because when there are yellow and black horses, you can only summon 'a horse' but not 'a white horse'. From this perspective, 'white horse' is a designation for a specific species, rather than just a horse."

The guard continued, "If we judge whether a horse is a horse based on its color, then there is no horse in the world without color. Following your logic, does it mean there are no horses in the world?"

Gongsun Long said, "Although all horses in the world have colors, including white horses, if horses do not need to be distinguished by color, then simply calling them 'horses' would suffice. Why is there a need to separately label them as 'white horses'? Therefore, the color white does not represent the essence of a horse. A white horse is simply a combination of 'horse' and 'white,' and 'horse' and 'white' cannot be referred to as ' white horse' alone. Hence, a white horse cannot be called a 'horse'."

The guard countered, "A horse is not called a horse because it has white fur; likewise, white is not exclusively used to describe horses. We cannot separate the essence of a horse from its external characteristics, as the attributes and internal genetics of any species complement each other. Therefore, your assertion that a white horse is not a horse is invalid."

Gongsun Long asked, "According to your view, if there is a white horse, then there is a horse. So, does the existence of a white horse also imply the existence of a yellow horse? Is that acceptable?"

The official promptly replied, "No, it is not acceptable."

Gongsun Long said, "Since you also understand that 'there is a horse' is not the same as 'there is a yellow horse', you separate yellow horses from horses when speaking. If a yellow horse is not the same as a horse, then you do not consider a yellow horse as a horse. If you do not consider a yellow horse as a horse, but consider a white horse as a horse, then it's like saying birds are flying freely in the water, or coffins are buried separately in the east and west. Isn't this a confusion of words and paradoxes in the world?"

Gongsun Long continued, "You believe that the existence of a white horse cannot be considered as the absence of a horse. This is because you fail to take into account the difference between a white horse and a horse, ignoring the characteristics of a horse and only emphasizing that the existence of a white horse is the same as the existence of a horse. Hence, the reason why it is considered as a horse is solely because of the term 'horse' being used, not because of the term 'white horse'. Therefore, when referring to the existence of a horse, it cannot be called the existence of a 'white horse'. The term 'white' has a broad meaning, and there is a significant difference between the abstract 'white' and the specific 'white', which can sometimes be overlooked."

He went on, "A white horse refers to a horse with white fur, but the emphasis is not on the "white" but on the "horse." When horses are summoned without emphasizing their color, yellow horses and black horses can all respond. However, if the summons specifies that it must be a white horse, yellow horses and black horses cannot respond due to their color, and only white horses can be summoned. There is a significant difference between having a choice and not having a choice, which is why a white horse is not considered a horse in this context."

During the Spring and Autumn and Warring States periods in China, wars between states were frequent, and horses were military materials. Therefore, when Gongsun Long tried to lead his horse out of the gate, he was stopped by the official guarding the gate. To protect his horse, Gongsun Long quickly utilized his eloquence as a debater and rebutted the official with his theory of "White Horse is Not a Horse," leaving the official speechless and having no choice but to allow Gongsun Long to lead his horse out of the gate. Gongsun Long's excellent improvisation has become a legendary story through the ages.

Meaning: Dialectical thinking: to find individuality from generality and generality from individuality. While sophistry is to take advantage of the convertible attribute between things to play on words so as to make the situation favorable to oneself.

白马非马 White Horse is Not a Horse

先教而后师之《公孙龙·迹府》

公孙龙，赵（赵国）平原君之客也。孔穿，孔子之叶（后裔）也。穿与龙会。穿谓龙曰："臣居鲁，侧闻下风，高先生之智，说（悦）先生之行，愿受业之日久矣，乃今得见。然所不取先生者，独不取先生之以白马为非马耳。请去白马非马之学，穿请为弟子。"

公孙龙曰："先生之言悖。龙之学，以白马为非马者也。使龙去之，则龙无以教；无以教，而乃学于龙也者，悖。且，夫欲学于龙者，以智与学焉为不逮（及）也。今，教龙去白马非马，是先教而后师之也；先教而后师之，不可。"

译文：公孙龙，是赵国平原君的门客。孔穿，是孔子的后裔。孔穿来到赵国与公孙龙相会。孔穿对公孙龙说："我在鲁国的时候久闻先生大名，仰慕先生的才智，钦佩先生的德行，愿接受先生教诲很久了。今日才得以相见。然而，鄙人唯独不赞同先生的'白马非马'理论。请先生放弃'白马非马'之学说，我愿作先生的弟子。"

公孙龙说："先生所言如此昏乱，我的学识就是'白马那马'之学说。你要求我放弃它，我便没有可以教导你的理论。我无可教，你才愿意向我求学，这是很荒唐的事情。况且你向我求学，是表示你的才智与学识不及我。现在，你教导我放弃'白马非马'之学说，你是先教导我，然后才拜我为师。先教我，后拜师，这是不可以的。"

寓意：求学之本是信服，自己不信服，岂能虚心求学？

Teach First

Gongsun Long was a retainer of the Prince of Pingyuan in the State of Zhao. Kong Chuan, a descendant of Confucius, traveled to the State of Zhao to meet with Gongsun Long. Kong Chuan said to Gongsun Long, "When I was in the State of Lu, I had heard of your esteemed name for a long time, admired your wisdom, and held your virtues in high esteem. I have longed to receive your guidance for quite some time. Today, I am finally able to meet you. However, there is one theory of yours that I do not agree with, and that is the theory of 'white horse is not horse'. I kindly request that you abandon this theory, and I am willing to become your disciple."

Gongsun Long replied, "Your words are quite confusing. My scholarship is founded on the theory of 'white horses are not horses'. If you ask me to abandon it, then I have nothing to teach you. It is absurd that you would willingly seek my guidance when I have nothing to offer. Furthermore, by seeking my guidance, you are acknowledging that your wisdom and knowledge are inferior to mine. Now, for you to ask me to abandon my theory of 'white horses are not horses' would mean that you are teaching me before becoming my disciple. It is not acceptable to teach me first before you are becoming my disciple."

Meaning: The foundation of seeking knowledge is belief. If one does not believe, how can they humbly seek knowledge?

楚人得弓《公孙龙·迹府》

楚王，张繁弱（古良弓名）之弓，载忘归（古良箭名），以射蛟兕（jiāo sì 蛟龙与犀牛）于云梦之囿（yòu），而丧其弓。左右请求之。王曰："止！楚人遗弓，楚人得之，又何求乎？"

仲尼闻之，曰："楚王仁义，而未遂也。亦曰人亡弓，人得之而已，何必楚？"

译文：楚王，张开繁弱大弓，搭上忘归快箭，在云梦囿苑里狩猎时，把良弓丢失了。众随从请求返回寻找。楚王说："算了吧，楚国人丢失了弓，楚国人拾得，又何必寻找呢？"

孔子听说此事，说："楚王算是仁义，却没有达到至仁之境。应该说：人丢失了弓，人拾得就是，何必加上楚国人？"

寓意：心有所想，口有所言。在孔子看来，人若想表达真正的大仁大义，不必强调人与人之间的区别，否则就是狭隘的仁义了。

Chu People Found a Bow

The King of Chu, armed with his *Fanruo* great bow (*Name of a famous ancient bow*) and loaded with his *Wanggui* speedy arrows (*Name of a famous ancient arrow*). When he was hunting dragons and rhinoceroses in the *Yunmeng* Garden, he lost his precious bow. His attendants begged him to go back and search for it. "Forget it," said the king. "If a Chu citizen loses his bow, it will be found by another Chu citizen. Why should we look for it?"

Confucius heard about this and said, "King of Chu is benevolent, but he has not reached the ultimate state of benevolence. He should say: 'A man lost his bow, and another man found it. Why add the nationality of Chu?'"

Meaning: What one thinks, one speaks. In Confucius' view, if one wants to express true great benevolence and righteousness, there is no need to emphasize the differences between people; otherwise, it would be narrow-minded benevolence and righteousness.

荀子头像铭文注解 Head Portrait of Xunzi & Annotation of the Inscriptions

《荀子》：

荀子，名况，字卿。另言号卿。约生于公元前313年，卒于公元前238年。赵国人。曾三任齐国稷下学宫祭酒。两任兰陵（今，山东枣庄）县令。晚年蛰居此处著书立说。倡导："礼法并施"、"制天命而用之。"提倡重习俗，重教育，树正气。

另言：荀子，又称孙卿。时人尊称荀卿。孔子中心思想为"仁"，孟子中心思想为"义"，荀子继二人后提出"礼"、"法"并重的理论，进而推动了法家思想的成熟。

Xunzi:

Xunzi, whose given name was Kuang, courtesy name was Qing. He was born around 313 BCE and died in 238 BCE. He was from Zhao. He served three times as the offering wine of the Jixia Academy in Qi. He served two terms as the county magistrate of Lanling *(now, Zaozhuang, Shandong)*. In his later years, he lived here and wrote books. He advocated: "Implementing both etiquette and law", "Controlling the mandate of heaven and using it." He advocated valuing customs, education, and fostering righteousness.

Another note: Xunzi, also known as Sun Qing. People at the time respected him as Xun Qing. Confucius' central idea is "benevolence", Mencius' central idea is "righteousness", and Xunzi, following the two, proposed the theory of equal importance of "ritual" and "law", which further promoted the maturity of Legalist thought.

蒙鸠为巢《荀子·劝学》

南方有鸟焉，名曰蒙鸠（鹪鹩鸟），以羽毛为巢，而编之以发，系之苇苕（芦苇）。风至苕折，卵破子死。巢非不完也，所系者然也。

译文：南方有一种小鸟，名叫鹪鹩。它用柔软的羽毛作巢，并且用长发把巢系在芦苇上，大风吹来把芦苇吹断了，鸟巢摔在地上，卵破子死。

鸟巢做的并不是不完美，而是筑巢的地方选择错了。

寓意：要实现心中的理想，最初的选择很重要。

The Fragility of a Nest

There is a kind of small bird called Jiaoliao in the south. It builds its nest with soft feathers and ties it to reeds with long hair. When a strong wind blows and breaks the reeds, the nest falls to the ground, breaking the eggs and killing the chicks.

The nest is not imperfectly built, but the place where it is built is wrongly chosen.

Meaning: To achieve one's ideals, the initial choice matters greatly.

处女遇盗《荀子·富国》

处女婴（系在颈上）宝珠，佩宝玉，负戴黄金，而遇中山之盗也。虽为之逢蒙视（不敢正视），诎要桡腘（弯腰曲膝），若卢屋妾，由将不足以免也。

译文：有一位少女，脖子上着戴着珍珠项链，腰上佩着宝玉，肩上背着黄金，在荒山野岭遇上强盗。虽然她两眼不敢直视，弯腰曲膝，宛如他人家中的婢妾，还是不能免于灾祸。

（荀子倡导："必将修礼以齐朝，正法以齐官，平政以齐民。"实施这样的治国理念，才能使得国家强盛。国家强盛，他国才不敢轻意侵犯，否则国弱宛如"处女遇盗"。）

寓意：力不及，反而炫耀财富，最容易招来横祸。

The Maiden Encountering Robbers

There was a young girl wearing a pearl necklace around her neck, wearing jade on her waist, and carrying gold on her shoulder. She met robbers in the wilderness. Although she didn't dare to look straight at them and crouched like a servant in another's house, she still couldn't avoid the disaster.

Meaning: To show off wealth while lacking the ability to protect it is the easiest way to invite disasters.

欹 器《荀子·宥坐篇》

孔子观于鲁桓公之庙，有欹器（qī qì 古代盛水器，设置在君王座位右方，以此为戒）焉。孔子问于守庙者，曰："此为何器？"

守庙者曰："此盖（大概）为宥坐之器。"

孔子曰："吾闻，宥坐之器者，虚则欹（倾斜），中则正，满则覆。"

孔子顾谓弟子曰："注水焉。"

弟子挹（yì 舀）水而注之。中而正，满而覆，虚而欹。

孔子喟然而叹曰："吁，恶（wū 安）有满而不覆者哉！"

译文：孔子一行人来到鲁桓公的庙中参观，看到一个形体倾斜的器物。孔子问守庙官吏，说："这是什么器物？"

守庙官吏回答："此物大概是宥坐之器。"

孔子说："我听说宥坐之器内部空空如也时就倾斜，内部不空不满时就端正，盈满时就会颠覆。"

孔子转过身对弟子说："朝里面舀些水试试看。"

弟子们连忙舀水灌入。果然，水灌到一半不空不满时它就保持端正，灌满水就时它就颠覆，倒空水时它就会倾斜。

孔子看到此景，深深地叹了一口气，说："唉，哪有满盈不颠覆的道理呢？"

寓意：满招损，谦受益，为人处事不可自满。

An Admonitory Vessel

On a visit to the temple of Duke Huan of the state of Lu, Confucius came upon a "leaning vessel". He asked the keeper of the temple about it.

"What vessel is this?"

The keeper replied, " This vessel is put on the right-hand side of one's seat to serve an admonitory purpose."

Confucius said, " I have heard that such an admonitory vessel would lean to one side when it is empty, stand upright when its contents are just the right amount, and fall down when it is full."

He turned to his disciples. "Pour water into it."

His disciples ladled water into the vessel. When the amount was neither too little nor too much the vessel stood upright; when the vessel was full it fell down; when it was empty it leaned to one side.

Confucius heaved a sigh. "Alas! A fall is inevitable for one who is full of his own worth."

Meaning: Haughtiness invites losses while modesty brings profits. One should not be complacent when dealing with people and handling affairs.

东野毕之马失《荀子·哀公》

定公（鲁定公）问于颜渊曰："东野毕之善驭乎？"

颜渊对曰："善则善矣！虽然，其马将失。"

定公不悦，入谓左右曰："君子固谗人乎！"

三日，而校来谒（校人：养马官。谒：禀告），曰："东野毕之马失，两骖（cān 古代驾在车前两侧的马）列（裂），两服（中间夹车辕的两马）入厩。"

定公越席而起，曰："趋驾！召颜渊！"

颜渊至，定公曰："前日寡人问吾子，吾子曰：'东野毕之驭，善则善矣！虽然，其马将失。'不识吾子何以知之？"

颜渊对曰："臣以政知之。昔，舜巧于使民，而造父巧于使马。舜不穷其民，造父不穷其马，是以舜无失民，造父无失马也。今，东野毕之驭，上车执辔（pèi 嚼子），衔体正矣；步骤驰骋，朝礼毕矣；历险致远，马力尽矣。然，犹求马不已，是以知之也。"

定公曰："善！可得少进乎？"

颜渊对曰："臣闻之，鸟穷则啄，兽穷则攫（攫取），人穷则诈。自古至今，未有穷其下，而能无危者也。"

译文：鲁定公问颜渊说："东野毕善于驾驭马车吗？"

颜渊回答："善长是善长，可是他驾驭的马匹将要跑掉了。"

鲁定公很不高兴，回宫时对左右侍臣说："所谓的君子，原来是一个谗言之人。"

三天后，养马人前来报告说："东野毕驾驶的马匹都跑了。外侧的两匹马挣脱缰绳跑丢了，驾辕的两匹马跑回马棚。"

鲁定公听了，从坐席上跳了起来，喊着："快驾车，速召颜渊进见。"

颜渊来到宫中，鲁定公急切地说："前几日我问你，你说：'东野毕驾驶马车的技术好是好，不过他所驾驭的马匹就要跑掉了。'你是怎么知道的？"

颜渊回答："我是依照处理政务的道理想到的。从前，舜帝明白如何统治天下百姓，而车夫造父知道如何驾驶马匹。舜帝不困窘天下百姓，造父不困窘他的马匹。所以，舜帝不失其民，造父不失其马。如今东野毕驾车，一上车就拉紧缰绳，马口中的嚼子已经拉到与他的体形一样高。在他的操控之下，马匹已经用尽全部力气，他仍然不满意地狠狠抽打马匹。因此，从他的行为上，我就知道事情的结果。"

鲁定公说："说的好，你能更进一步讲讲吗？"

颜渊回答："我听说，鸟儿困窘时就会啄；野兽困窘时就要攫取；人困窘时就会诈生。从古到今，没有因困窘属下的人而不遭受危险的。"

寓意：依赖刁难下属向上邀功的行为，都不会持续很久。

Horses Lost

Duke Ding of Lu asked Yan Yuan, "Is Dong Yebi good at driving horses?"

Yan Yuan replied, "He is indeed skilled, but his horses are about to run away."

Duke Ding was displeased and said to his attendants, "So a gentleman is actually a man of calumny."

Three days later, the horse keeper came to report, "Dong Yebi's horses have all run away. The two horses on the outside broke their reins and escaped, while the two driving horses returned to the stables."

After hearing this, Duke Ding of Lu jumped up from his seat and shouted, "Hurry up and prepare the carriage! Summon Yan Yuan to come see me immediately!"

When Yan Yuan arrived at the palace, Duke Ding eagerly said, "A few days ago, when I asked you about Dong Yebi's horse driving skills, you said, 'Dong Yebi is indeed skilled at driving horses, but the horses he drives are about to run away.' How did you know that?"

Yan Yuan replied, "I inferred it based on the principles of governing affairs. In ancient times, Emperor Shun understood how to rule over the people of the nation, while the charioteer Zao Fu knew how to drive horses. Emperor Shun did not overburden the people, and Zao Fu did not overburden his horses. Therefore, Emperor Shun did not lose his people, and Zao Fu did not lose his horses. Nowadays, Dong Yebi drives his carriage, tightening the reins as soon as he gets on. The bit in the horse's mouth is already pulled up to the same height as his body. Under his control, the horse has already exerted all its strength, yet he still beats the horse harshly, unsatisfied. Therefore, from his actions, I knew the outcome."

Duke Ding of Lu said, "That's well said. Can you elaborate further?"

Yan Yuan replied, "I have heard that when birds are distressed, they peck; when beasts are distressed, they grab; and when people are distressed, they resort to deceit. Throughout history, no one has escaped danger by oppressing their subordinates."

Meaning: The behavior of relying on making things difficult for subordinates to seek credit from superiors will not last long.

韩非子头像铭文注解 Head Portrait of Hanfeizi & Annotation of the Inscriptions

《韩非子》：

韩非，后世尊称韩非子。战国时期韩国公子。约生于公元前281年，卒于公元前233年。师从荀子。中国古代杰出的哲学家、思想家、政治家和散文家。集礼、法、道、德于大成。并将法、术、势相容，达到先秦治世的顶端。

司马迁《史记•老子韩非列传》："韩非者，韩之诸公子也。喜刑名法术之学，而其归本于黄老。非（韩非）为人口吃（习惯性言语缺陷），不能道说，而善著书。其与李斯俱（一起）事荀卿（拜荀子为师），斯，自以为不如非……

非见韩（韩国）之削弱，数以书谏韩王，韩王不能用。于是，韩非疾（痛疾）治国不务修明其法制，执势（以权势）以御其臣下。富国强兵，而以求人任贤，反举浮淫之蠹，而加之于功实之上。以为儒者，用文乱法；而侠（侠士）者，以武犯禁。宽则，宠名誉之人；急则，用介胄（武力）之士。今者，所养非所用，所用非所养。悲，廉直不容（如）于邪枉之臣。观往者，得失之变，故作《孤愤》、《五蠹》、《内外储》、《说林》、《说难》十余万言……

人或传其书至秦。秦王（秦始皇）见《孤愤》、《五蠹》之书，曰：'嗟乎，寡人得见此人与之游，死不恨矣！'李斯曰：'此韩非之所著书也。'秦因急攻韩。韩王始不用非，及急，乃遣非使秦。秦王悦之，未信用。李斯姚贾害（嫉妒）之，毁之曰：'韩非，韩之诸公子也。今王欲并诸侯，非终为韩，不为秦，此人之情也。今王不用，久留而归之，此自遗患也，不如以过法（超过正常法律）诛之。'秦王以为然，下吏治非。李斯使人遗非药，使自杀。韩非欲自陈，不得见。秦王后悔之，使人赦之，非已死矣……

申子、韩子皆著书，传于后世，学者多有。余独悲韩非子为《说难》而不能自脱耳。"

韩非死于秦国牢狱，这一年是秦王嬴政十四年，即：公元前233年，时年48岁。

Hanfeizi:

Han Fei, He was revered as Han Feizi by later generations. was a prince of the State of Han during the Warring States period. He was born around 281 BCE and died in 233 BCE. He studied under Xunzi and was an outstanding philosopher, thinker, statesman, and essayist in ancient China. He integrated ritual, law, Daoism, and morality into a comprehensive system. He also harmonized law, tactics, and power, reaching the pinnacle of governance during the pre-

Qin era.

In Sima Qian's "Historical Records: Biographies of Laozi and Han Fei," it is written: "Han Fei was a nobleman from the state of Han. He was fond of the study of legalism. The theoretical foundation of his doctrine came from the Yellow Emperor and Laozi. Han Fei had a stutter and was not good at speaking, but he was adept at writing and formulating theories. He and Li Si were both students of Xunzi, and Li Si considered himself intellectually inferior to Han Fei. Han Fei saw the state of Han gradually weakening, and repeatedly submitted official petitions to persuade the King of Han, but the King did not accept his advice. At that time, Han Fei hated the governance of the country without focusing on improving the legal system, the monarch could not use the power to control his ministers, nor could enrich the country and strengthen the military by seeking and appointing capable people. Instead, the monarch appointed and praised frivolous and incompetent parasites and gave them higher status than those who were pragmatic and effective. He believed that some Confucian scholars used classical texts to disrupt national laws, while chivalrous men violated national prohibitions by force. When the country was at peace, the monarch favored those who had only false reputation and praise, and when the situation was critical, he used those armored warriors. Now the people supported by the state were not what they needed, and the people they needed were not what they supported. He lamented that honest and upright people were not tolerated by crooked and treacherous ministers. He examined the gains and losses of ancient and modern times, so he wrote works such as 'Loneliness and Indignation,' 'Five Wormwood,' 'Internal and External Reserves,' 'Talks,' 'Difficulties of Persuasion,' and others with more than 100,000 words. However, Han Fei deeply understood the difficulties of persuasion.

The book he wrote, 'Difficulties of Persuasion,' spoke very highly of persuasion, but he eventually died in the state of Qin. He was killed due to the slanderous accusations of Li Si, unable to escape the scourge of persuasion. After his death, the King of Qin regretted it deeply.

侵官之害甚于寒《韩非子·二柄》

昔者，韩昭侯醉而寝。典冠（主管君主王冠）者，见君之寒也，故，加衣于君之上。觉寝而说（悦）。问左右曰："谁加衣者？"

左右曰:"典冠。"

君因兼罪典衣(主管君主衣服的人)与典冠。其罪典衣,以为失其事也;其罪典冠,以为越其职也。非不恶寒也,以为侵官之害,甚于寒。

故,明主之畜臣,臣不得越官而为功,不得陈言而不当。越官则死,不当则罪。守业其官,所言者贞也,则群臣不得朋党相为矣。

译文:从前,韩昭侯酒醉后睡着了。管理君主王冠的近侍典冠,眼见韩昭侯寒冷,拿来君主衣服盖在韩昭侯身上。韩昭侯醒来后心情很愉悦,问左右侍臣说:"谁给我盖的衣服?"

左右侍臣说:"是典冠。"

韩昭侯因此治罪典衣与典冠。怪罪典衣,是因为典衣失职;怪罪典冠,是因为典冠越权。韩昭侯并不是不怕寒凉,而是越权行为之害甚于自身的寒冷。

因此,圣明的君主蓄养臣子,臣子不得越权夺功,不能讲述不合身份的话语。越权夺功则罪死;不当之言则有罪。各自严守职责,慎言慎行,这才是为臣的品行。这样的做法,都是为了防止臣子结党营私以乱朝纲。

寓意:放任官吏的越权行为,则会造成架空皇权的结局。

Exceeding Authority: Worse than the Cold

Once upon a time, Duke Zhao of Han fell asleep after drinking too much. The attendant who was in charge of the king's crown, saw that Duke Zhao of Han was feeling cold, so he took the king's robe and covered him with it. When Duke Zhao of Han woke up, he felt very pleased and asked his attendants, "Who covered me with this robe?"

The attendants on the left and right said, "It is the hat keeper."

So Duke Zhao of Han punished both the clothes keeper and the hat keeper. He blamed the clothes keeper for negligence of duty and blamed the hat keeper for exceeding his authority. Duke Zhao of Han was not afraid of the cold, but he knew that the harm of exceeding authority was greater than his own discomfort.

Therefore, wise monarchs cultivate their ministers who must not exceed their authority or steal credit, and they should not speak words inappropriate to their status. Those who exceed their authority or steal credit deserve punishment by death; those who speak improperly are guilty. Each minister should strictly adhere to their duties, speak and act cautiously, and this is the conduct expected of them. Such practices are all aimed at preventing ministers from forming cliques and disrupting the order of the court.

Meaning: If the officials are allowed to exceed their authority, it will result in the weakening of the emperor's power.

宋有富人《韩非子·说难》

宋有富人，天雨墙坏。其子曰："不筑，必将有盗。"其邻人之父亦云。

暮而，果大亡其财。

其家甚智其子，而疑邻人之父。

译文：宋国有户富人家，天下雨淋坏了他家的院墙。他儿子说："不修好院墙，必将遭坏人偷窃。"邻居家中的大爷也是这样说的。

夜幕降临，果然家中遇盗被坏人偷去大量财物。

这户富人家，着实夸赞儿子有先见之明，却怀疑邻居家的大爷与此事有关。

寓意：只认私情，不讲理性，将无法得出正确的评判，并且很难以此为戒。

Prejudice and Rationality

There was a wealthy family in the State of Song. One day, a heavy rain damaged their courtyard wall. Their son said, "If we don't fix the wall, it will certainly be vulnerable to thieves." The elderly neighbor echoed the same sentiment.

As night fell, the family was indeed robbed of a large amount of property by thieves.

The wealthy family praised their son for his foresight but suspected that the elderly neighbor might be involved in the robbery.

Meaning: If one only recognizes private affection and ignores rationality, he will not be able to make a correct judgment and it will be difficult to learn from it.

和氏之璧 《韩非子·和氏》

楚人和氏（一作"卞和"），得玉璞（pú 未经琢磨的玉石）楚山中。奉而献之厉王。

厉王使玉人相之，玉人曰："石也。"王，以和为诳（kuáng 欺骗）而刖（yuè 砍）其左足。

及厉王薨（hōng 死），武王即位，和又奉其璞，而献之武王。武王使玉人相之，又曰："石也"。王，又以和为诳，而刖其右足。

武王薨，文王即位，和乃抱其璞而哭于楚山之下，三日三夜，泣尽而继之以血。

王闻之，使人问其故。曰："天下之刖者多矣，子奚（何）哭之悲也？"

和曰："吾非悲刖也，悲夫宝玉，而题（说成）之以石，贞士而名之，以诳，此吾所以悲也。"

王乃使玉人理其璞，而得宝焉，遂命曰："和氏之璧。"

译文：楚国有一位名叫和氏的乡下人，在楚国深山得到一块玉璞，前来献给厉王。

厉王指使制玉工匠察验，工匠说："这是一块石头。"厉王认为和氏欺骗他，因此，砍了和氏的左脚。

等到厉王死后，武王登上王位，和氏又向武王献玉璞。武王派工匠察验，工匠说："这是一块石头。"武王也认为和氏欺骗他，因此令人砍了和氏的右脚。

武王死后，文王登上王位。和氏便抱着这块玉璞在楚山脚下痛哭三天三夜，眼泪哭尽直到眼睛流出血来。

文王听说此事，特派人前去问他，说："天下被砍去脚的人很多，为何唯独你哭得如此伤心呢？"

和氏说："我并不是为砍去双脚而痛哭，我悲痛的是把宝玉当作石头，把贞洁之士当成骗子，这才是我最悲痛的。"

文王立刻指派工匠打开玉璞，果真是一块宝玉。于是，文王命名宝玉：和氏之璧。

寓意：和氏之璧象征忠心赤诚，将其献之的行为亦复如是。可若频频因他人一言蔽之，而误将此忠贞之举视作欺君罔上的罪过，并处以刑罚，其使人寒心的程度甚于罪罚所带来的痛苦。

The Jade of He

A man of the state of Chu named Bian He found a piece of uncut jade in the *Chu* mountain. Holding the jade with both hands he respectfully presented it to King Li. The king ordered a jade craftsman to examine it.

"This is stone," said the craftsman.

The king thought that Bian He was trying to deceive him so he gave orders to cut off his left foot.

After the death of King Li, King Wu ascended the throne. Again Bian He came with the jade in his hands to present it to King Wu. King Wu ordered a jade craftsman to examine it.

"This is stone," said the craftsman again.

The king also thought Bian He was trying to deceive him, so he gave orders to cut off his right foot.

After the death of King Wu, King Wen came to the throne. Bian He took the piece of uncut jade in his arms and wept at the foot of the Chu mountain. He wept for three days and three nights. When he had no more tears he wept blood.

This came to the ears of the king and he sent some one to ask Bian He the reason for his grief.

"There are many men who had their feet cut off as punishment," said the king's messenger, "why do you weep so bitterly?"

"I am not sad because my feet were cut off," replied Bian He. "I grieve because a precious stone is considered a common rock and an upright and loyal man is branded a liar. This is the cause of my sorrow."

The king ordered jade craftsmen to cut open the stone. They discovered a piece of precious jade which was thereupon named the Jade of He.

Meaning: The Jade of He Shi symbolizes loyalty and sincerity, just as does the act of presenting it. However, if the king is frequently blinded by the words of others and mistakenly views such loyal and virtuous actions as crimes of deceit towards him, and subjects those who offer precious gifts to punishment, the degree of disappointment it causes is far greater than the pain brought by the punishment itself.

春申君之妾 《韩非子·奸劫弑臣》

楚庄王（即：楚顷襄王）之弟春申君，有爱妾曰余，春申君之正妻，子（正妻生的孩子）曰甲。余欲君之弃其妻也，因（因此），自伤其身以视君而泣，曰："得为君之妾，甚幸。虽然，适夫人非所以事君也，适君非所以事夫人也。身故不肖，力不足以适二主，其势不俱适，与其死夫人所者，不若赐死君前。妾以赐死，若复幸于左右，愿君必察之，无为人笑。"

君因信妾余之诈，为弃正妻。余又欲杀甲，而以其子为后，因自裂其亲身衣之里（内衣），以示君而泣，曰："余之得幸君之日久矣，甲非弗知也，今乃欲强戏余。余与争之，至裂余之衣，而此子之不孝，莫大于此矣。"

君怒，而杀甲也。

故，妻以妾余之诈弃；而子以之死。从是观之，父之爱子也，犹可以毁而害也。君臣之相与也，非有父子之亲也，而群臣之毁言，非特一妾之口也，何怪，夫贤圣之戮死哉！此（因此），商君之所以车裂于秦，而吴起之所以枝解于楚者也。

凡人臣者，有罪固不欲诛，无功者皆欲尊显。而圣人之治国也，赏不加于无功，而诛必行于有罪者也。然则，有术数者（圣贤之人）之为人也，固左右奸臣之所害，非明主弗能听也。

译文：楚庄王之弟名叫春申君，他宠爱的妾，名叫余。春申君正妻所生的儿子，名叫甲。余，希望春申君抛弃正妻，立自己为妻。于是，余故意弄伤自己的身体给春申君察看。并且哭泣着说："我有幸成为您的妾，我感到非常荣幸。虽然，全心顺从您的妻子，就无法全心奉侍您；顺从您的心愿，又无法全心奉侍您的妻子，妾身力不从心，很难做到同时奉侍两位主人。并且，还要做到使两位主人都满意。与其日后死在您妻子面前，不如今日赐死在君主的面前。倘若，君赐死妾，再宠爱他人时，希望君主明察她的德行，不要再被世人耻笑。"

春申君相信了余的谎话，抛弃了前妻，另立余为妻。

余，登上正妻之位，又设法陷害春申君与前妻所生的太子甲，欲立自己的孩子为太子。于是，余自己撕裂贴身内衣，拿去给春申君察看，并且哭泣着说："我得到您的宠爱已经很久了，太子甲不是不知道。今日，他要强行调戏我，我与他抗争，他竟然撕裂了我的内衣，如此不孝之举，莫过于他的行为。"

春申君大怒，杀了自己的长子甲。

因此，妻子被妾余的欺诈所抛弃；儿子被妾余的谎言所杀。以此看来，父子亲情是天性所属，尚且被谎言所伤害。君与臣之间没有血缘关系的牵扯，而朝中众臣的诽谤之言要远远大于妾余的一家之言。何怪圣贤被错杀？如此，便是商鞅被车裂于秦国；吴起被肢解于楚国的原由所在。

大凡为人臣者，有了过错不希望被追究；没有建立功勋也希望得到尊贵显赫。然而圣明的君主治理国家，行赏不赐予无功的臣子，而刑法必用于有罪之臣。然则，有能力治理国家的圣贤之士，必然会遭受奸邪之臣的陷害；不是圣明的君主，难以听取他人的劝诫。

寓意：兼听则明，偏听则暗。

The Disaster of Treasonous Ministers

The younger brother of King Zhuang of Chu was known as Chun Shen Jun. His beloved concubine was named Yu. The son born to Chun Shen Jun's wife was named Jia. Yu hoped that Chun Shen Jun would abandon his wife and marry her. So, Yu deliberately hurt herself and showed Chun Shen Jun. She wept and said, "I am very honored to be your concubine. Although I am willing to obey your wife, I cannot serve you wholeheartedly; if I follow your wishes, I cannot serve your wife wholeheartedly. It is difficult for me to serve two masters at the same time. Moreover, I also have to satisfy both masters. It's better to be executed by you today than to die in front of your wife later. If you decide to execute me, when you fall in love with someone else, I hope you will see through her character and not be laughed at by the world again."

Chun Shen Jun believed Yu's lies, abandoned his legitimate wife, and instead made Yu his principal wife.

Yu, having ascended to the position of principal wife, then schemed to frame the Crown Prince Jia, the son born of Chun Shen Jun and his former wife, with the intention of naming her own child as the Crown Prince. Consequently, Yu tore her underwear and showed it to Chun Shen Jun, weeping and saying, "I have been favored by you for a long time, and Crown Prince Jia is not unaware of this. Today, he attempted to forcibly assault me, and I resisted him. He tore my underwear in the process, displaying such impiety and disrespect. There is no greater sin than his behavior."

Chun Shen Jun was enraged and killed his eldest son, Crown Prince Jia.

Thus, the legitimate wife was discarded due to the fraud perpetrated by concubine Yu; the son was killed because of Yu's lies. From this perspective, even the natural bond of fatherly love and sonly affection can be harmed by deceit. Between a monarch and his ministers, there is no blood tie, yet the malicious gossip and rumors spread by ministers far outweigh the lies of a single concubine. It is no wonder that wise and virtuous individuals are wrongly executed. This is precisely the reason why Shang Yang was cruelly executed by the chariot-splitting punishment in Qin, and Wu Qi was dismembered in Chu.

Generally speaking, ministers of a state do not wish to be punished for their mistakes, meanwhile they hope to be respected and honored even though they have not yet earned any merit. However, wise monarchs govern their countries by rewarding only those who have contributed and punishing those who have committed crimes. However, capable and virtuous ministers are bound to be framed by treacherous and wicked ministers; and it is difficult for a monarch who is not wise to listen to the advice of others.

Meaning: Listening to all sides leads to enlightenment, while listening to only one side leads to blindness.

黑牛白角《韩非子·解老》

先物行，先理动，之谓前识。前识者，无缘而妄意（臆）度也。何以论之？

詹何（楚国人，善道术）坐，弟子侍，有牛鸣于门外。

弟子曰："是黑牛也，而白在其题（额头）。"

詹何曰："然，是黑牛也，而白在其角。"

使人视之，果黑牛而以布裹其角。

以詹子之术，婴（婴触）众人之心，华焉殆矣！故曰："道之华也。"

尝试释詹子之察，而使五尺之愚童子视之，亦知其黑牛而以布裹其角也。故以詹子之察，苦心伤神，而后与五尺之愚童子同功，是以曰："愚之首也。"故曰："前识者，道之华也，而愚之首也。"

译文：在事情还没有发生之前，就能对事情做出评判，称谓先见之明。先见之明是根据主观意识猜测的结果。何以见得？

詹何坐在堂屋里，弟子在一旁奉侍他。有一头牛在门外鸣叫。

弟子说："这是一头黑牛，它的额头上有一块白色印迹。"

詹何说："对，是一头黑牛，牛角上是白色的。"

指使弟子查看，果然是一头黑牛，而且用白布缠着牛角。

詹何以自己的道术，触动众弟子的心，华而不实几乎殆尽。因此，先见之明是扭曲了《道》的根本，而弥漫出浮华之术。

请试想一下，放弃詹何的先见之明，指派一名顽童前去看一下，也知道这是一头黑牛，以白布裹着牛角。由此而言，以詹何劳神总结出的先见之明，与顽童的认知无异，这样的言行称谓"愚蠢的开始。"所以说："先见之明，是《道》的一种浮华之术，也是头等的愚蠢。"

寓意：在道通为一的理论中，华而不实的言论，则是无知的显现。

Black Cow with White Horns

To judge the rightness or wrongness of a matter before it happens is called foresight. Foresight is based on subjective guesses and predictions. How can this be seen?

Zhan He sat in the main room of the house, while his disciple waited at his side. Outside the door, a cow was mooing.

The disciple said, "That's a black cow with a white mark on its forehead."

Zhan He replied, "Yes, it's a black cow with white horns."

He instructed the disciple to go check, and indeed, it was a black cow, with its horns wrapped in white cloth.

Zhan He moved his disciples' hearts with his own daoist skills, but they were almost entirely showy and lacked substance. Therefore, foresight distorted the essence of the "Dao" and gave rise to ostentatious techniques.

Imagine it, if we had given up Zhan He's foresight and instead sent a naughty child to have a look, the child would also have known that it was a black cow with its horns wrapped in white cloth. In this sense, Zhan He's labored foresight is no different from that of a child's cognition. Such words and actions can be described as a "foolish beginning." Therefore, it can be said that "foresight is a flashy technique of the 'Dao' and also the utmost foolishness."

Meaning: In the theory of "All being one from the viewpoint of Dao", flowery but hollow speech is a manifestation of ignorance.

扁鹊说病 《韩非子·喻老》

扁鹊见蔡桓公，立有间（观察片刻）。

扁鹊曰："君有疾在腠理（còu lǐ 中医指皮肤的纹理与皮下肌肉之间），不治将益深。"

桓侯曰："寡人无疾。"

扁鹊出。桓侯曰："医之，好治不病，以为功。"

居十日，扁鹊复见曰："君之病在肌肤，不治将益深。"

桓侯不应。扁鹊出。桓侯又不悦。

居十日，扁鹊复见曰："君之病在肠胃，不治将益深。"

桓侯又不应。扁鹊出。桓侯又不悦。

居十日，扁鹊望桓侯而还走，桓侯故使人问之。

扁鹊曰："疾在腠理，汤熨（用热敷患处）之所及也；在肌肤，针石之所及也；在肠胃，火齐（汤剂）之所及也；在骨髓，司命之所属，无奈何也。今在骨髓，臣是以无请也。"

居五日，桓侯体痛，使人索（寻）扁鹊，已逃秦矣。桓侯遂死。

译文：扁鹊觐见蔡桓公，站在一旁观察了片刻。

扁鹊对桓侯说："君主患有疾病于皮肤，如果不及时治疗恐怕加重。"

桓侯说："我没有病。"

扁鹊无奈地退出宫门，桓侯不悦地对左右侍臣说："医生好医治没有病的人，借此显示自己有功。"

过了十日，扁鹊又来觐见蔡桓侯，说："君主的疾病已经发展到肌肉里，再不医治恐怕加重。"桓侯不理睬，扁鹊只好退出宫门，桓侯又大为不悦。

又过了十日，扁鹊百次觐见桓侯，说："君主的疾病已经蔓延到肠胃，如果再不治疗将会严重。" 桓侯仍然不理睬。扁鹊走出宫门，桓侯极为不悦。

再过了十日，扁鹊看见桓侯转身就走，桓侯不解地派侍从追问扁鹊。

扁鹊对侍从说："病灶侵入人体皮肤的表层，用汤药清洗或者用药热敷，便可以治愈。病灶在人体肌肤，用针灸疗法便可治愈。疾病蔓延到了肠胃，使用"火剂汤"便可治愈。如果疾病侵入骨髓，就是掌管生死的神仙也无可奈何。现在，君主的疾病已经侵入骨髓，我能有什么办法？"

过了五日，桓侯浑身疼痛，指派人寻找扁鹊。扁鹊却已经逃到秦国去了。桓侯在痛苦中死去。

（相传：扁鹊是黄帝时期的名医，又传是春秋时期的名医。蔡桓公与鲁桓公同时代，与扁鹊相距二百年。韩非子借"扁鹊"之名，言说当时的良医。大凡良医治疗"病之初"，以此讲述《老子·第六十三章》："天下之难事，必作于易，天下之大事，必作于细。"防患于未然。）

寓意：在情况未变危急和严重的时候，采取相应的措施往往行之有效。

Bian Que's Analysis of Diseases

One day, the miracle-working doctor Bian Que saw Huan Gong, King of the State of Cai, and said: "Your Majesty, I think you are ill. But your illness is only under the skin and can be easily cured. If you do not treat it now, I'm afraid your condition will become serious."

Huan Gong did not believe him. He said: "I am not ill."

After Bian Que left, Huan Gong said to his subjects around him: "These doctors always like to treat people who are not ill in order to brag about their superb medical skill."

Ten days later, Bian Que saw Huan Gong again. He said: "Your Majesty, your illness has invaded your muscles. If you do not treat it now, your condition will become more serious."

Huan Gong was displeased with what he heard and did not listen to Bian Que. Then Bian Que left.

Another ten days later, Bian Que saw Huan Gong and said anxiously: "Your Majesty, your illness has invaded your stomach and intestines. If your do not treat it, your condition will worsen."

Huan Gong was extremely displeased, and he would not listen to Bian Que. Then Bian Que left.

Another ten days later, when Bian Que saw Huan Gong, he turned round at once and left. Huan Gong was surprised and sent someone to catch up Bian Que to ask him for the reason.

Bian Que said: "When a person gets ill and his illness is only under the skin, it can be easily cured with medical plaster or decoction. When it is between the skin and the flesh, it can still be cured by acupuncture; even if it develops into the stomach and intestines, medical decoctions will still be effective. But when it reaches them marrow, then one can only resign to one's fate, for the doctor can no longer do anything about it. Now His Majesty's illness has penetrated into the marrow. I can do nothing to cure him."

Five days afterwards, Huan Gong felt pain all over his body. He sent for Bian Que.

Since Bian Que had anticipated that Huan Gong would ask him for treatment and that he would get into trouble if he couldn't cure the illness, he had escaped to the State of Qin a few days before.

(Legend: Bian Que was a famous doctor during the period of Huangdi, while another legend claimed that he was a renowned doctor in the Spring and Autumn period. Cai Huang gong lived in the same era as Lu Huang gong, and was separated by two hundred years from Bian Que. Han Feizi borrowed the name "Bian Que" to discuss the virtues of good

doctors in his time. Generally speaking, good doctors treat diseases at their earliest stages. This passage uses this analogy to illustrate the wisdom in Laozi's Chapter 63: "The difficult things in the world must begin with the easy, and the great things in the world must begin with the small." Prevention is better than cure.)

Meaning: Taking appropriate measures when the situation is not yet critical and serious is often effective.

纣为象箸 《韩非子·喻老》

昔者，纣为象箸（象牙制成的筷子），而箕子（商代贵族，封于箕，曾劝谏纣王，被囚禁）怖（恐怖）。以为象箸必不加于土铏（xíng 陶器），必将犀玉之杯；象箸玉杯必不羹菽藿（shū huò 粗劣的杂粮）。必旄、象、豹胎；旄、象、豹胎必不衣短褐（粗布短衣），而食于茅屋之下，则锦衣九重，广室高台。吾畏其卒，故怖其始。

居五年，纣为肉圃（肉林），设炮烙，登糟丘，临酒池，纣遂以亡。

故，箕子见象箸，以知天下之祸。故曰："见小曰明。"

译文：从前，商朝纣王做了一双象牙筷子，太师箕子看见后感到无比恐惧。他觉得使用象牙筷子决不会再用陶土制做的器皿，必将用犀牛角或者玉器制做的酒杯。用象牙筷子和玉杯，决不会再喝豆汁或食用杂粮做的饭食，必然要吃牦牛、大象、豹胎；食牦牛、大象和豹胎，决不会穿着粗麻短衣在茅草屋用餐；必然要身穿锦衣绸缎，坐在广室高台里享用美食。箕子害怕出现这样的结果，所以对这样的开端感到恐惧。

过了五年，商纣王摆设肉林，设炮格刑具，登上酒糟堆成的山，俯临酒池。于是纣王被灭，断送了商朝五百多年的辉煌。

因此，箕子看见纣王使用象牙筷子，便预知天下将会出现大祸临头的局势。所以说："从细微之思考未来的发展趋势，叫做明察。"

（韩明子以此讲述《老子·第五十二章》："见小曰明。"）

寓意：奢靡之始，危亡在即。

Ivory Chopsticks for a Start

In the ancient times Emperor Zhou of the Shang dynasty used chopsticks made of ivory. On observing this, *Jizi*[1], a respected minister, was filled with anxiety.

He reasoned thus: "Ivory chopsticks would not be used with earthenware dishes. There would surely be wine cups made from rhinoceros' horns and jade. Ivory chopsticks and jade cups would not go with simple fare. There would surely be delicacies such as the embryos of the yak, elephant and panther. One who tastes such delicacies would not wear clothes made of rough material or dwell in a thatched cottage. He would be clothed in layers of beautiful brocade and live in a mansion, big and imposing. I am afraid for his end. That is why the beginnings of luxurious living fill me with anxiety."

After five years, the emperor built a garden where he hung slabs of meat and set up copper grills. Grains from distilleries piled up like hillocks and there was enough wine to fill pools. As a result of such extravagances, Emperor Zhou was overthrown.

Meaning: The beginning of extravagance leads to danger and destruction.

涸泽之蛇 《韩非子·说林上》

泽涸，蛇将徙。有小蛇谓大蛇曰："子行而我随之，人以为蛇之行者耳，必有杀子。不如相衔负我以行，人以我为神君也。"

乃相衔，负以越公道。人皆避之，曰："神君也。"

译文：湖泽里的水已干涸，蛇将迁徙。有条小蛇对一条大蛇说："你在前面游走，我在你后面尾随，人们看见了，一定认为这是两条蛇正在逃走，必会遭到截杀。你不如把我衔起，背着我行走，人们以为我是神"蛇"。"

于是，大蛇衔起小蛇，背负着它在大道上游走，人们惊奇避开，说："这是一条神蛇。"

寓意：违背常态的行为，有时会取得截然不同的结果。

---

[1] Jizi: i.e. Ji Xu Yu, the uncle of Emperor Zhou.

Snake in a Dried-Up Lake

The water in the lake and marsh has dried up, and the snakes will migrate. A small snake said to a big snake, "You go ahead, and I'll follow you. If people see us, they will definitely think that two snakes are escaping and will try to kill us. Why don't you pick me up and carry me on your back? People will think that I am a divine snake."

So, the big snake picked up the small snake and carried it on its back, walking on the road. People were surprised and avoided them, saying, "This is a divine snake."

Meaning: Behavior contrary to the norm sometimes achieves completely different results.

不死之药 《韩非子·说林上》

有献不死之药于荆王者（荆王，即：楚王。荆：楚国别称），谒者（古官名。掌管宾赞受事）操之以入。

中射（侍卫官）之士问曰："可食乎？"

曰："可。"

因夺而食之。王大怒，使人杀中射之士。

中射之士使人说王曰："臣问谒者，曰'可食'，臣故食之，是臣无罪，而罪在谒者也。且，客献不死之药，臣食之，而王杀臣，是死药也，是客欺王也。夫，杀无罪之臣，而明人之欺王也，不如释臣。"

王乃不杀。

译文：有人向楚王进献不死之药，为天子传达宾赞受事的官吏手捧不死药进宫。

宫中侍卫官问："这个可以吃吗？"

传达宾赞受事的官吏说："可以吃。"

于是，侍卫官拿过来便吃了下去。楚王怒，令人杀侍卫官。

侍卫官便托人对楚王说："我问传达宾赞受事的官吏：'可以吃吗？'他说：'可以。'所以我才吃了。我这样做并没有罪，而是他有罪。况且，客人献的是不死之药，我吃下去，却要遭受君主的杀戮，说明这药是死药，这证实客人是在欺骗我王。并且，让我王背负乱杀无辜的名声，这说明我王很容易被欺骗。真不如释放我这样的无罪之臣。"

楚王听了他的解释，下令不杀。

寓意：抓住事物之间的矛盾点与相互制约之处，从而巧言辩驳。从另一个侧面说明从不同角度将文字字面含义引申出不同的解读，可以巧妙地达到辩解的目的。

Elixir of Life

Someone presented the king of Chu with the elixir of life. The official who was responsible for receiving guests and presents carried the elixir into the palace.

The palace guard asked, "Can this be eaten?"

The official replied, "Yes, it can be eaten."

So the guard took it and ate it. The king of Chu was furious and ordered the guard to be killed.

The guard then asked someone to convey a message to the king of Chu, saying, "I asked the official in charge of receiving guests and presents, 'Is this edible?' He replied, 'Yes, it is.' So I ate it. I am not guilty, but he is. Besides, the guest presented the elixir of life, yet after eating it, I am being killed by the king. This proves that the medicine is not life-giving but a fake. It also verifies that the guest is deceiving our king. Furthermore, by killing an innocent person like me, our king will bear the reputation of killing innocent people, indicating that our king is easily deceived. It would be better to release a guiltless minister like me."

After hearing his explanation, the king of Chu ordered not to kill him.

Meaning: Grasp the contradictions and mutual constraints of things, so as to argue cleverly and achieve the purpose of speaking. It also shows from another perspective that different interpretations can be derived from the literal meaning of words, which leaves room for negotiation.

失日之危《韩非子·说林上》

纣为长夜之饮，欢以失日，问其左右，尽不知也。乃使人问箕子。

箕子谓其徒曰："为天下主，而一国皆失日，天下其危矣。一国皆不知，而我独知之，吾其危矣。"辞以醉，而不知。

译文：商纣王不分昼夜地饮酒作乐，忘记了时日，询问身边侍从，侍从都不清楚。纣王便派人询问箕子。

箕子听到此事后，对自己门徒说："作为一国之君，而使一国人都忘记时日，这样的国家将会面临危险。一国人都不知道时日，而唯独我一个人知道，那么我将面临危险。告诉来使，说我已经醉了，什么也不知道。"

寓意：举国上下毫无节制地饮酒作乐，则使国家陷入危险的境地。而众人皆醉，唯一人独醒，此人亦身处危险之境。时也，运也；运也，命也，时运之命也。国运与个人的命运是相辅相成的。

Danger of Forgetting the Time

King Zhou of Shang drank and made merry day and night, forgetting the time. When he asked his attendants, none of them knew the answer. So he sent someone to ask Jizi.

After hearing this news, Jizi said to his disciples, "If a king makes all the people in his country forget the time, the country will be in danger. If all the people in the country don't know the time, but I am the only one who knows, then I will be in danger. Tell the messenger that I am drunk and don't know anything."

Meaning: If the whole country drinks and carouses without restraint, it will put the country in a dangerous situation. And if everyone is drunk, but only one person is sober, this person will also be in a dangerous situation. The national fortune and the fate of individuals complement each other.

卫人嫁其子《韩非子·说林上》

卫人嫁其子（女儿。秦之前儿女统称"子"，秦之后才有儿女之分）而教之曰："必私积聚。为人妇而出（休妻），常也；其成居，幸也。"

其子因私积聚，其姑（古称婆婆为姑）以为多私，而出之。其子所以反（返）者，倍其所以嫁。其父不自罪于教子非也，而自知其益富。

今，人臣之处官者，皆是类也。

译文：卫国有一个人，在嫁女时对女儿说："到了婆家须要私下积攒财物。身为别人的妻子，常会被婆家休妻。成为终身伴侣，那只是侥幸的事。"

他女儿嫁到婆家之后私下积攒财物，她的婆婆见她私心太重，让儿子休了她。她返回娘家时所带回的财物，超过她的嫁妆一倍还多，其父不怪罪自己教育女儿的方法失误，反而以为女儿聪明，增加了家中的财富。

今，身处官位的臣子，都是这类人。

寓意：以卫人嫁女为例，在其位者若不谋其政却狭私钻营，为一己私欲牟利，此为不诚也。若这种习气蔚然成风，长者以此教导下一辈，不以为耻反以为荣，可谓颠倒是非，祸乱朝政。

Narrow Self-Interest

There was a man in Wei State who said to his daughter on the day of her wedding, "When you get to your husband's family, make sure to accumulate wealth secretly. As a wife, a woman may often face the risk of being divorced by her husband's family, and achieving a lifelong partnership is only a matter of chance."

After she married into her husband's family, she secretly accumulated wealth. Her mother-in-law saw how selfish she was and persuaded her son to divorce her. When she returned to her parents' home, she brought back more wealth than what she had received as dowry, even more than double. Her father did not blame himself for failing to educate his daughter properly. Instead, he praised her for her cleverness, as she had increased the family's wealth.

Nowadays, the officials who hold positions in the government are all these kinds of people.

Meaning: Taking the marriage of a daughter of a family in Wei as an example, if those in power do not fulfill their duties but are selfish and scheming, seeking profits for their own personal gain, this is considered dishonest. If this bad habit becomes widespread, with the elders teaching the younger generation in this way, not regarding it as shameful but instead as glorious, it can be said that they are reversing right and wrong, and causing chaos in the government.

鸟有翢翢者《韩非子·说林下》

鸟有翢翢者（《字典词典》注：dào dào《汉语号典》注：tào tào 又注：zhōu zhōu）者，重首而屈尾，将欲饮于河，则必颠，乃衔其羽而饮之。

人之所有饮不足者，不可不索其羽也。

译文：古时候有一种鸟名叫翢翢，头大而尾巴短。如果要到河边饮水，必将栽进河里。因此，每次饮用河水，都要请同伴衔着它的羽毛才能饮到水。

人有欲望无法得到满足时，也会寻求同伙协助。

（陈奇猷《韩非子集释》："此谓人之所有饮，而不能巩固其足者，则必索其羽以衔之。度韩非之意，盖以喻：奸邪之臣为奸私之行，则必求党羽，以此周相为也。"）

寓意：人的欲望难以实现时，就会结党营私践踏公共道德。

Origin of "Party Cronies"

In ancient times, there was a bird named *Dao Dao*, which had a big head and a short tail. If it wanted to drink water at the river, it would inevitably fall into the river. Therefore, every time it drank river water, it had to ask its companion to hold its feather so that it could drink water.

When people cannot satisfy their desires, they will also seek help from their companions.

Meaning: The term "party cronies" originated from this. When people find it difficult to satisfy their desires, they will form cliques and seek private gains, trampling on public morality.

与悍者邻《韩非子·说林下》

有与悍者邻，欲卖宅而避之。人曰："是其贯将满矣，子姑（姑且）待之。"

答曰："吾恐，其以我满贯也。"遂去之。

故曰:"物之几者,非所靡也。"

译文:有户与凶悍之人为邻的人家,想要卖了自家房产搬到别处。有人对他说:"这户凶悍人家,很快就要恶贯满盈了,你姑且等待一时。"

这户人家说:"我怕他以伤害我来满足他的恶。"于是这户人家想办法早早搬了家。

所以说:"感到灾难将要来临,就要及早想办法躲开是非之地,不可拖延。"

寓意:趋吉避凶,生存之道。

Unwise to Wait

A man had a neighbour who was a malicious brute. He wanted to sell his house and get away from the fellow.

"His sins will soon come to a head and he will have his just deserts," he was told, "why not wait a little while?"

"I am afraid," he replied, "that his sins will come to a head through me." So he moved.

So it is said, "When one senses that disaster is impending, one should seek ways to avoid the troubled place early on, without delay."

Meaning: Seeking fortune and avoiding misfortune is the way of survival.

中行文子出亡《韩非子·说林下》

晋,中行(háng)文子(即:荀寅,晋国执政的六卿之一)出亡(逃),过于县邑,从者曰:"此啬夫(sè fū 官吏名。检束群吏百姓的官吏),公之故人。公奚不休舍,且待后车?"

文子曰:"吾尝好音,此人遗我鸣琴;吾好珮(佩),此人遗我玉环;是振我过者也,以求容于我者,吾恐其以我求容于人也。"乃去之。

果收文子后车二乘而献之其君矣。

译文:晋国执政的六卿之一中行文子出逃,路过一处县城时,他的随从说:"这个县城里的啬夫官吏,曾经在您的手下做事，您何不在他那里休息片刻，等待后面的车马？"

文子说："我曾经喜好音乐，他就送给我鸣琴；我喜好佩戴玉环，他就送给我玉环；他的行为助长了我的过错，以求得我对他的好感。我担心，他会把我当做礼物一样送人，以求得他人对他的好感。"随即，快速离开了此地。

果然，这个啬夫收缴了中行文子身后两辆车的财物和他的随从，献给了国君。

寓意：阿谀奉承的人本性难改，容易改变的是所要奉承的对象。

Friend or Foe?

When Zhonghang Wenzi of the state of Jin became a fugitive he passed a certain county.

"The magistrate of this place is an old friend of yours," said his attendants. "Why don't you stay here and rest a bit while waiting for the carriages that are coming behind us?"

"At one time when I was fond of music," replied Wenzi," this man gave me a beautifully tuned *qin* (*a stringed instrument*). There was another time when I became fond of jade ornaments, then he gave me jade rings. He was ready to abet me in my wrongdoings. Since he put himself out to win my favour, I am afraid that he will use me to win someone else's favour."

Immediately, Wenzi quickly left this place. It turned out that the magistrate did stop two carriages that came after Wenzi and offered them as a gift to his new master.

Meaning: People who flatter others are hard to change their nature, while it is easy to change the objects of their flattery.

荆王伐吴《韩非子·说林下》

荆王伐吴（当指公元前537年楚灵王伐吴之事）。吴使沮卫、蹶融（吴王余祭之弟）犒于荆（楚）师，而将军曰："缚之，杀以衅鼓。"

问之曰："女（汝）来，卜乎？"

答曰："卜。"

"卜吉乎？"

曰："吉。"

荆人曰："今，荆将欲女（你）衅鼓，其何也？"

答曰："是故（因此），其所以吉也。吴使臣来也，固视将军怒。将军怒，将深沟高垒；将军不怒，将解怠。今也，将军杀臣，则吴必警守矣。且（况且），国之卜，非为一臣卜。夫杀一臣而存一国，其不言吉，何也？且（尚且）死者无知，则以臣衅鼓无益也；死者有知也，臣将当战之时，臣使鼓不鸣。"

荆人因不杀也。

译文：楚灵王以诸侯及东夷之兵共同伐吴。吴王派遣沮卫、蹶融以酒肉前去慰劳楚军。然而，楚军将令却下令，说："把他们绑起来，杀了他们用血祭鼓。"

楚军将令问："你们来时有没有占卜？"

回答说："占过卜。"

将令又问："你们占的卦是吉兆还是凶兆呢？"

回答说："是吉兆。"

将令再次问："现在，我军将要用你们的鲜血祭祀战鼓，还是吉兆吗？"

回答说："这正是吉兆的缘故。吴王派遣使臣前来，就是要看看将军是否会发怒。如果将军发怒杀了我们，吴国将会捉高警惕，深挖战壕，高筑壁垒；如果将军不发怒，我军则会懈怠。当下，你们杀了吴王的使臣，那么吴国必然会加紧备战。况且，国之卜，不是为我一人卜，杀一个使臣，而保存一个国家，岂能不是吉兆吗？尚且，我的死，在天无灵，以我的鲜血祭祀战鼓并无益处；如果，我的死在天有灵，我将在你的鸣鼓冲锋时，使你们的战鼓不鸣。"

楚军将令听了他们的陈述，没有杀吴国使臣。

寓意：文官的善辩之辞，既可保命又可救国。

The Eloquent Envoy of Wu

King Ling of Chu led troops from various states and the eastern barbarians to attack Wu. King of Wu sent Ju Wei and Jue Rong to comfort the Chu troops with wine and meat. However, the general of the Chu troops ordered, "Bind them up and sacrifice them with blood to the drum."

The Chu general asked, "Did you consult divination before coming here?"

They replied, "Yes, we did."

The general asked again, "Was the omen auspicious or inauspicious?"

They replied, "It was auspicious."

The general asked again, "Now, as our army is about to sacrifice your blood to the war drum, is it still a good omen?"

They replied, "That's exactly why it's auspicious. King of Wu sent his envoy here to see if the general would lose his temper. If the general were to become angry and kill us, Wu would become vigilant, dig deep trenches, and build tall fortifications. If the general remains calm, our troops will become lax. Now, if you kill the envoy of the King of Wu at this moment, Wu will undoubtedly intensify its preparations for war. Moreover, the divination was not just for me alone. Killing one envoy to save a whole country, how could it not be a good omen? Besides, if my death has no divine significance, offering my blood as a sacrifice to the war drums will be useless. However, if my death does have divine significance, I will ensure that your war drums remain silent when you charge forward."

After hearing their statement, the general of the Chu army decided not to kill the envoy from Wu.

Meaning: The eloquent arguments of civil officials can save both their lives and the country.

知伯铸大钟 《韩非子·说林下》

知伯（即：智伯。晋国六卿之一）将伐仇由（晋国邻近的一个小国。今，山西盂县境内），而道难不通，乃铸大钟遗仇由之君。仇由之君大说（悦），徐道（开道）将内之。赤章曼枝（仇由国大臣）曰："不可。此小之所以事大也，而今也，大以来，卒必随之，不可内也。"

仇由之君不听，遂内之。

赤章曼枝因断毂（gǔ）而驱，至于齐。七月而仇由亡矣。

译文：晋国执政的六卿之一智伯，将要攻伐仇由国。因道路狭窄，无法通行大型战车。于是智伯铸造一口大钟赠送仇由国的君主。仇由国的君主很高兴，准备开道架桥迎接赠送的大钟。大臣赤章漫枝说："不可以，这是小国奉献大国的礼物。当下大国反而奉献小国，这样的馈赠不合常理，他的军队必定尾随而来，所以，不可以让大钟进入国内。"

仇由国的君主不听劝告，执意开道架桥迎接大钟。

赤章曼枝因此截短了车毂，急速逃亡到齐国。七个月之后，仇由国被晋国智伯所灭。

寓意：遇事要三思而治行，大凡险恶的事情往往隐藏在违背常态的情景之中。

Zhi Bo Casts a Huge Bell

Zhi Bo, one of the six ministers of the State of Jin, was about to attack the State of *Qiuyu*. However, due to the narrow roads, large war chariots could not pass through. Therefore, he cast a huge bell and presented it to the ruler of the State of *Qiuyu*. The ruler of the State of *Qiuyu* was delighted and prepared to clear the road and build bridges to receive the bell. The minister Chi Zhang Manzhi said, "This is not advisable. This should have been a gift from a small country to a big country. Now a large country is presenting this gift to a small country, which is unusual. Their army will surely follow, so it is not advisable to allow the bell to enter our country."

The ruler of *Qiuyu* ignored the advice and stubbornly decided to clear the road and build bridges to receive the huge bell. Consequently, Chi Zhang Manzhi shortened the hub of his carriage and fled to the State of Qi at a rapid pace. Seven months later, the State of *Qiuyu* was destroyed by Zhi Bo of the State of Jin.

Meaning: When confronted with situations, one should think twice before acting. Generally speaking, perilous matters often lurk in scenarios that deviate from the norm.

韩赵相难 《韩非子·说林下》

韩、赵相与为难。韩索兵于魏曰:"愿借师以伐赵。"

魏文侯曰:"寡人与赵兄弟,不可以从。"

赵又索兵以攻韩,文侯曰:"寡人与韩兄弟,不敢从。"

二国不得兵,怒而反(返回)。

已乃知文侯以构与己也,皆朝魏。

译文:韩国与赵国相与为敌。韩国君主向魏文侯借兵,说:"希望借你的兵力讨伐赵国。"

魏文侯说:"我与赵国是兄弟之国,不能顺从你的请求。"

赵国也派遣使者,向魏文候借兵攻伐韩国。魏文候说:"我和韩国是兄弟之邦,不敢听从你的请求。"

两国都没有借到兵,怨然离去。

事后,两国都知道,魏文侯依此希望两国和解。于是,两国都派遣使臣前来答谢魏文侯的恩惠。

寓意:以智慧赢得两国和睦相处的成就,功德无量。

Conflict between two States

Both the Kingdom of Han and the Kingdom of Zhao were enemies of each other. The king of Han wanted to borrow troops from the Duke of Wei, saying, "I hope to borrow your troops to attack the Kingdom of Zhao."

The Duke of Wei replied, "My country and the Kingdom of Zhao are brotherly states, and I cannot comply with your request."

Later, the Kingdom of Zhao also sent emissaries to the Duke of Wei, requesting troops to attack the Kingdom of Han. The Duke of Wei said, "My country and the Kingdom of Han are brotherly states, and I dare not obey your request."

Both countries failed to borrow troops and left angrily.

Later, both countries realized that the Duke of Wei hoped for reconciliation between them through this tactic. Therefore, both countries sent emissaries to express their gratitude for the Duke of Wei's kindness.

Meaning: To achieve the accomplishment of peaceful coexistence between the two countries through wisdom is infinitely meritorious.

韩咎为君《韩非子·说林下》

韩咎（即：韩釐王）立为君，未定也。弟在周，周欲重之，而恐韩咎不立也。

綦母恢（姓綦母，名恢。西周大臣）曰："不若以车百乘送之。得立，因曰为戒；不立，则曰来效贼也。"

译文：韩咎将被立为韩国的国君，但还没有最终确定下来。韩咎在西周王城时，西周君王想借此机会向他表示友善，又怕韩咎登不上王位。

西周大臣綦母恢献策，说："不如以百辆车乘护送回国。如果，韩咎立为君主，就说是为了他的安全采取的警戒；如果，他没有登上君主之位，就说是向韩国献贼的。"

寓意：所谓成王败寇，正如寓言所示。王权是一种地位的象征，它具有摄人心魄的能量，既能使他人臣服，又能让争夺它的人拼死搏杀。成与不成是两种截然相反的结局，境遇可谓是天差万别。

Winners Rule, Losers Pay

Han Jiu will be elected as the king of Han, but it hasn't been finally determined yet. When Han Jiu was in the capital of the Western Zhou Dynasty, the king of the Western Zhou Dynasty wanted to seize the opportunity to show him friendship, but he was afraid that Han Jiu might not ascend the throne.

Qi Mu Hui, a minister of the Western Zhou Dynasty, proposed a strategy, saying, "It would be better to escort him back with a hundred carriages. If Han Jiu is elected as the king, we can say it's for his safety; if he fails to ascend the throne, we can say it's to present the enemy to Han."

Meaning: The proverb goes, "The Victor is the king, the loser is the enemy." Just as shown in the fable, royal power is a symbol of status, and it has the power to fascinate people. It can make others submit, and also make people fight for it. Success and failure are two completely different outcomes, and the situations can be vastly different.

海大鱼《韩非子·说林下》

靖郭君（即：田婴。齐国之相）将城薛，客多以谏言。靖郭君谓谒者（传令官）曰："毋为客通。"

齐人有请见者曰："臣请三言（三个字）而已。过三言，臣请烹。"

靖郭君因见之。

客趋（小步快走）进曰："海大鱼。"因反走。

靖郭君曰："请闻其说。"

客曰："臣不敢以死为戏。"

靖郭君曰："愿为寡人言之。"

答曰："君闻大鱼乎？网不能止，缴不能挂也，荡而失水，蝼蚁得意焉。今夫，齐亦君之海也。君长有齐，奚以薛为？君失齐，虽隆薛城至于天，犹无益也。"

靖郭君曰："善"乃辍，不城薛。

译文：齐国贵族靖郭君要在薛地建筑新的都城，许多客卿都来劝谏他。靖郭君嫌烦对传令官说："不要再为前来劝谏的人士通报。"

齐国有一人请求拜见说："我只讲三个字，超过三个字就把我煮了。"

靖郭君便同意接见他。

这个人恭敬地小步快走，进宫便说："海大鱼。"说罢转身就走。

靖郭君连忙说："请把你的意思讲完再走。"

这人回过头说："我不敢拿自己的生命开玩笑。"

靖郭君说："我乐意听你的解释。"

这人回答说："君主您听说过海里的大鱼吗？渔网捕不住它，带绳的长箭挂不住它。但是当它任性游到浅滩时，蝼蚁也会在它的身上为所欲为。当下齐国好比君主的大海，君主长期拥有着齐国，为何还需要再建一座薛城？假如您失去齐国为根基，即使筑薛城高于天，也没有什么益处。"

靖郭君说："讲得好。"于是，停止建筑新城，不再把薛城当作都城。

寓意：善意劝谏，也需要别出心裁的说道。

The Giant Sea Fish

The noble Jingguo Jun of Qi wanted to build a new capital in Xue. Many guests came to advise him, but Jingguo Jun was tired of it and told the messenger, "Don't report any more people who come to advise me."

A man from Qi State requested to see Jingguo Jun and said, "I will only speak three words. If I exceed that, you can boil me alive." Jingguo Jun agreed to meet him.

The man respectfully approached the palace and said, "Sea Big Fish," before turning and walking away.

Jingguo Jun quickly called out, "Please finish what you mean to say before you leave."

The man turned back and said, "I dare not jest with my own life."

Jingguo Jun replied, "I am willing to listen to your explanation."

The man replied, " Your Majesty, Have you ever heard of the giant sea fish? Fishermen cannot capture it with their nets, and long spears with ropes cannot hook it. However, when it swims recklessly into shallow waters, even small ants can do whatever they want on its body. Right now, Qi State is like your own sea. You have owned Qi State for a long time. Why do you need to build another city of Xue? If you lose Qi State as your foundation, even if you build capital in Xue which is higher than the sky, it will not bring any benefit."

Jingguo Jun said, "Well spoken." So he stopped building the new city and no longer considered Xue as the capital.

Meaning: Friendly advice also requires ingenious ways of expression.

急与慢《韩非子·观行》

古之人，目短于自见，故以镜观面；智短于自知，故以道正己。故，镜无见疵之罪，道无明过之怨。目失镜，则无以正须眉；身失道，则无以知迷惑。西门豹之性急，故佩韦（柔韧的皮带）以缓己；董安于之心缓，故佩弦以自急。

故，以有余补不足，以长续短之谓明主。

译文：自古以来的人类，自己的眼睛看不见自己脸，因此必须借助镜子才能看清自己面部的污渍；鉴于超出自身认知局限难以理解的事物，要以大道之理权衡是非进而端正自己的行为。所以，镜子没有照出污渍的过错，大道之理也不应因彰显出人的过失而受到抱怨。眼睛看不到镜子里的自己，就无法修饰胡须与眉毛；自己的行为失去大道之理的约束，就无法分辨对错。西门豹生性急躁，所以他常常系着柔韧的皮带，以此提醒自己遇事沉稳；董安于心性迟缓，常常佩带弓弦，以此策励自己遇事敏捷。

因此以多余补不足，用长处来弥补短处的就称得上是英明的君主。

寓意：虽言人贵有自知之明，但人的认知总是受制于自我认知的局限。所以人若能够像借助镜子来修饰面部一样，以大道之理权衡是非利弊，进而修正自身的行为举止，这是一个人能够不断提升自我的关键所在。

Urgency vs. Slackness

Since ancient times, humans have been unable to see their own faces with their own eyes, and they must rely on mirrors to see the dirt on their faces clearly; given that it is difficult to understand things beyond their own cognitive limitations, they must weigh the right and wrong with the principles of the great way to correct their own behavior. Therefore, a mirror doesn't need to bear the blame for showing dirt, and the principles of the great way should not be complained about for revealing people's faults.

One cannot trim his beard or eyebrows if he cannot see his reflection in the mirror. One cannot distinguish right and wrong if his behavior is not constrained by the principles of the great way. Xi Men Bao was born with a hasty temperament, so he always wore a flexible belt to remind himself to be calm and composed when faced with situations. Dong Anyu, on the other hand, was slow in temperament, so he wore a bowstring to urge himself to act more quickly when necessary.

Therefore, those who compensate for their deficiencies with their surplus and make up for their shortcomings with their strengths can be called wise monarchs.

Meaning: Although it is said that it is important for a person to have a self-awareness, human cognition is always limited by self-cognition. So if a person can weigh up the pros and cons according to the principles of the great way like using a mirror to decorate his face，and then correct his behavior and conduct, it is the key for a person to constantly improve himself.

人之本性《韩非子·安危》

使天下皆极智能于仪表，尽力于权衡，以动则胜，以静则安。治世使人乐生于为是，爱身于为非，小人少，而君子多。故，社稷常立，国家久安。奔车之上无仲尼，覆舟之下无伯夷。

故（因此），号令者，国之舟车也，安则，智廉生；危则，争鄙起。故（所以），安国之法，若饥而食，寒而衣，不令而自然也。先王寄理于竹帛（文书），其道顺，故（故然）后世服。

今使人去饥寒，虽贲（即：孟贲）、育（即：夏育）不能行；废自然，虽顺道而不立。强勇之所不能行，则上不能安。上以无厌责已尽，则下对"无有"；无有，则轻法。法所以为国也，而轻之，则功不立，名不成。

译文：使天下百姓在法律许可之下，尽情发挥每个国民的天赋，并且通过自己的努力赢得社会尊重。拥有这样国民的国家，抗击入侵的敌军则能取胜，和平时期则国内安定。治理国家要让百姓在法律许可之下快乐地生活，爱惜自己的生命，不做违背法律的事情。在如此治国理念的实施之下，违法的恶人少，守法的君子多。因此，社稷常存，国家久安。逃亡的车子上没有像孔子那样的智士；倾覆的舟船下没有像伯夷那样的廉士。

因此，法令就像国家的舟车。国家安定，智士廉士才能产生；国家危乱，贪吝诈伪便会涌现。所以，安定国家的根本，宛如：饥饿时要吃饭，寒冷时会加衣，无需发号施令，民众也会为了自己的生存而努力争取丰衣足食，这是人性使然。中华先祖将"民以食为天"的大道理，书写在竹简与白绢上，告知后来者：民众口中有食，身上有衣，社会才能安定。这是人类的天性。

假如：让天下百姓在风雪里不顾饥寒大干苦干，即使象孟贲、夏育这样的大力士也难做到。违背自然之道，君令难从。强迫连勇士都做不到的事情，那么君主的位置则不能久安。上级以无限的贪欲搜刮民膏，民众会说："我已经一无所有。"民众一无所有，就会轻视法律。法律是立国之本，民众轻视法律则国不立，名不成。

寓意：人生之途，先有生存，后有理想。生无所乐，死有何惧？

The Nature of Human Beings

Let all people under the legal permission, give full play to the talents of each citizen, and win social respect through their own efforts. A country with such citizens can defeat the invading enemy in war and maintain domestic stability in peacetime. Governing the country should allow the people to live happily under the legal permission, cherish their own lives, and not do anything against the law. Under the implementation of such governance concepts, there will be fewer bad people who violate the law and more gentlemen who abide by the law. Therefore, the country will exist forever and be safe for a long time. Thus, there will be no wise men like Confucius on the runaway cart; there will be no honest men like Boyi on the overturned boat.

Therefore, the laws and regulations are like the boats and carriages of the country. When the country is stable, wise and honest people will emerge; when the country is in danger and chaos, greed, deceit, and fraud will emerge. Therefore, the foundation of a stable country is like hunger for food and cold for clothing. Without issuing orders, the people will strive for their own survival and strive for ample food and clothing, which is human nature. The ancestors of China wrote the great truth of "Food is the paramount necessity of the people" on bamboo slips and white silk, informing the later generations that only when the people have food in their mouths and clothes on their bodies can society be stable. This is the nature of human beings.

Suppose: asking all people to work hard and tirelessly in the snow and cold, regardless of hunger and cold, is something even great warriors like Meng Ben and Xia Yu would find difficult to accomplish. It goes against the laws of nature, and the orders of the monarch become difficult to obey. Forcing people to do something even brave warriors cannot achieve will not allow the monarch's throne to remain secure for long. When the superiors endlessly extort the people's wealth with greed, the people will say, "I have nothing left." When the people have nothing, they will disregard the law. The law is the foundation of a nation. If the people disregard the law, the nation cannot stand, and its reputation will be tarnished.

Meaning: The journey of life is first about survival, and then about ideals. If there is no joy in life, what is the fear of death?

法规之重《韩非子·用人》

释法术而心治，尧不能正一国；去规矩而妄意度（揣测），奚仲（夏代车正）不能成一轮；废尺寸而差短长，王尔（巧匠）不能半中。使中主守法术，拙匠守规矩尺寸，则万不失矣。

君人者，能去贤巧之所不能，守中拙之，所万不失，则人力尽，而功名立。

译文：放弃法律而凭着君主的主观意识治理国家，即使唐尧在世也难匡正一国；舍弃规矩胡乱揣度，奚仲连一个车轮也做不出来；废弃尺度，仅凭目测估计尺寸，王尔做不出一半符合标准的产品。让中等才能的君主谨守法律，笨拙的工匠遵守尺度，则可达到万无一失。

为君者，放弃连圣贤巧匠都难以做到的事情，谨守中庸之道，便可使天下百姓人尽其才、物尽其用，而达到功成名立的效果。

寓意：所谓无规矩不成方圆，设立可使万众遵循的规矩与法度，在此基础上发挥个人之才干，是举国上下得以有效运作之本。

The Importance of Laws and Regulations

Abandoning laws and governing the country with the monarch's subjective consciousness, even Tang Yao *(the legendary emperor)* can't correct the country; giving up the rules and guessing randomly, Xi Zhong *(the legendary inventor of carts)* can't make even a wheel; abandoning the scale and estimating the size only by eyes, Wang Er *(a skilled artisan)* can't make half of the products that meet the standard. Let the moderate monarch abide by the laws and the clumsy craftsman abide by the scale, then the result would be infallible.

As a monarch, by giving up things that are difficult even for wise men and skilled craftsmen to achieve, and adhering to the golden mean, he can enable all the people in the world to make the best use of their talents and resources and achieve fame and success.

Meaning: As the saying goes, "Without rules, there is no square or circle." Establishing rules and regulations that can be followed by all is the foundation for effective operation of the entire country. On this basis, individuals can give full play to their talents.

梦 灶 《韩非子·内储说上》

卫灵公之时，弥子瑕有宠，专于卫国。

侏儒有见公者，曰："臣之梦践矣。"

公曰："何梦？"

对曰："梦见灶，为见公也。"

公怒曰："吾闻，见人主者梦见日，奚为见寡人而梦见灶？"

对曰："夫，日兼烛天下，一物不能当也；人君兼烛一国人，一人不能拥也。故（因此），将见人主者，梦见日。夫灶，一人炀（yáng 借指：烤火），则后人无从见矣。今，或者一人有炀君者乎？则臣虽梦见灶，不亦可乎！"

译文：卫灵公在卫国执政时期，弥子瑕是他的宠臣，在朝独揽大权。

有位体形矮小的官吏见到卫灵公说："臣的梦应验了。"

卫灵公问他，说："你做的是什么梦？"

矮小的官吏说："我梦见灶火，预示着您要召见我。"

卫灵公生气地说："我听说，将要见到君主的人，就会梦见太阳，为什么你梦见灶火就是预示君主召见？"

矮小的官吏说："太阳的光辉普照大地，任何一物都无法遮挡太阳的光芒；一国之君的光辉，也是普照举国上下，任何一人无法遮挡君主的光辉。所以要见到一国之君时，就会梦见太阳。至于梦见灶火，好似一人在灶前取暖，身后人见不到火光。今者，好似一人在君的面前遮蔽了君主的光辉。所以，微臣梦见灶火，预示君主召见，不是也可以吗？"

寓意：为君者，本应像太阳一样以恩惠普照天下万民，若偏听偏信宠臣一人之言，正如灶火前有人挡住了光芒，使得其他有才华的忠臣良士难以施展才干。

A Dream Come True

When Duke Ling was ruling over the state of Wei, Mi Zixia, the duke's favourite minister, wielded absolute power in the state.

A dwarf came to see the duke.

"My lord," said the dwarf, "my dream has come true."

"What dream did you have?" asked the duke.

"In my dream I saw a kitchen stove, which means I will see my lord," replied the dwarf.

The duke was enraged. "I have heard that those who get to see their sovereign will dream of the sun. Why do you say that dreaming of a kitchen stove meant you will get to see me?"

"The sun," the dwarf replied, "shines over all the earth and no single object can block its light. The sovereign of a state sees all that goes on in his country and no single man can block his view. That is why seeing the sun in a dream means one gets to see the sovereign. As for a kitchen stove, when one person stands in front of it warming himself, no one behind him gets to see the light. Now perhaps there is someone who is doing just that to you, my lord. Then is it not understandable that I dreamed of a kitchen stove?"

Meaning: A king should be like the sun, showering his benevolence upon all the people of the nation. If he listens to and trusts only one favorite minister, it is like someone blocking the light in front of the kitchen fire, making it difficult for other talented loyal ministers and wise men to display their abilities.

王亡其半者《韩非子•内储说上》

张仪欲以秦、韩与魏之势伐齐、荆（楚），而惠施欲以齐、荆偃兵。二人争之。群臣左右者皆为张子言，而以攻齐、荆为利，而莫为惠子言。

王，果听张子，而以惠子言为不可。攻齐，荆事已定，惠子入见。

王言曰："先生毋言矣。攻齐、荆之事果利矣。一国尽以为然。"

惠子因说："不可不察也。夫，齐、荆之事也诚利，一国尽以为利，是何智者之众也？攻齐，荆之事诚不可利，一国尽以为利，何愚者之众也？凡谋者，疑也。疑也者，诚疑：以为可者，半；以为不可者，半。今一国尽以为可，是王亡半也。劫主者，固亡其半者也。"

译文：张仪想利用秦国、韩国和魏国友好的时机，攻伐齐国与楚国。然而，惠施却希望与齐国、楚国休兵息战。二人在大堂上争论不休。群臣都为张仪帮腔附和，也都认为攻伐齐国与楚国有利可图，不为惠施进言。

魏惠王果真听从张仪之言，认为惠施所言不是。攻伐齐国与楚国的国策已定，惠施入后宫觐见。

魏惠王说："先生不必多言，攻伐齐国与楚国之事果然有利，举国上下都是这样认为的。"

惠施因此提出不同看法："起兵讨伐，这是国之大事，不可不慎察。如果讨伐齐国与楚国诚然有利，一国尽认为有利，为何智者如此之多？如果讨伐齐国与楚国无利可图，一国尽认为有利，为何愚者如此之多？凡是谋略国之大事，必有可疑之处。有可疑，诚然有疑；有一半人认为可行，就会有一半人认为不可行。认可者与不认可者，必有争论，有争论才会越辩越明。然而，当下举国上下都认为这件事可行，这说明君主失去了一半国人的智慧。挟持君主意念的人，正是以失去一半国人真实想法为代价。

寓意：争议朝堂，明辨是非，称为：大道之行。反之：一言堂。

Speaks with One Voice

Zhang Yi wanted to take advantage of the friendly relationship between Qin, Han, and Wei to attack Qi and Chu. However, Hui Shi advocated for a truce with Qi and Chu. The two argued forcefully in the hall. All the ministers sided with Zhang Yi and agreed that attacking Qi and Chu was profitable, refusing to speak in favor of Hui Shi.

King Hui of the state of Wei truly followed Zhang Yi's advice and dismissed Hui Shi's opinions as incorrect. The national policy of attacking Qi and Chu had already been decided. Hui Shi entered the palace to meet with the king.

King Hui said, "Mr. Hui, there's no need for further arguments. The matter of attacking Qi and Chu is indeed profitable, and this is the consensus throughout the country."

Hui Shi then put forward a different perspective: "Launching a military campaign is a major national decision that cannot be taken lightly. If attacking Qi and Chu is truly beneficial, why are there so many wise men in the country who do agree? And if attacking Qi and Chu is not profitable, why are there so many foolish men who believe it is profitable? Whenever there's a plan for a major national decision, there's bound to be doubt. Doubt exists because there are doubts; if half the people think it's feasible, there will be half who think it's not.

There will always be disputes between those who agree and those who disagree, and disputes can lead to clearer understanding through debate. However, if the entire country agrees that something is feasible, it means that the monarch has lost the wisdom of half of his people. The people who influence the Monarch's decisions do so by sacrificing the true voices of half of the country.

Meaning: Controversy in the court, clarification of right and wrong, is known as "the way of the great path." Conversely, it is referred to as "dictatorship of one voice."

宠信之祸《韩非子·内储说上》

叔孙（叔孙豹。鲁国执政的三大贵族之一）相鲁，贵而主断。其所爱者曰竖牛，亦擅用叔孙之令。

叔孙有子曰壬（即：仲壬。次子），竖牛妒，而欲杀之，因与壬，游于鲁君所。鲁君赐之玉环，壬拜受之，而不敢佩，使竖牛请之叔孙。竖牛欺之曰："吾已为尔请之矣，使尔佩之。"壬因佩之。

竖牛因谓叔孙："何不见壬于君乎？"

叔孙曰："孺子何足见也。"

竖牛曰："壬固已数见于君矣。君赐之玉环，壬已佩之矣。"

叔孙召壬见之，而果佩之，叔孙怒而杀壬。

壬兄曰丙（孟丙），竖牛又妒而欲杀之。

叔孙为丙铸钟。钟成，丙不敢击，使竖牛请之叔孙。竖牛不为请，又欺之曰："吾已为尔请之矣，使尔击之。"丙因击之。

叔孙闻之曰："丙不请而擅击钟。"怒而逐之。

丙出走齐。居一年，竖牛为谢叔孙，叔孙使竖牛召之，又不召而报之曰："吾已召之矣，丙怒甚，不肯来。"

叔孙大怒，使人杀之。

二子已死，叔孙有病，竖牛因独养之，而去左右，不内人，曰："叔孙不欲闻人声。"不食而饿而。叔孙已死，竖牛因不发丧也，徙其府库重宝空之，而奔齐。夫，听所信之言，而子父为人僇，此，不参之患也。

译文：叔孙豹身居鲁国国相时，地位尊贵而专权独断。他宠信的小臣名叫"竖牛"。竖牛常常盗用他的名誉干些坏事。

叔孙豹的次子名叫仲壬。竖牛嫉妒他，想要杀仲壬。因此，竖牛唆使仲壬到君主那里游玩。君主看见仲壬，便赐予他玉环。仲壬拜谢君主接受了玉环却不敢佩戴。于是,特意恳求竖牛替他请示父亲。过了几日竖牛欺骗他说:"我已经向你父亲请示过了,许可你佩戴上玉环。"所以仲壬才敢佩戴玉环。

不几时,竖牛对叔孙豹说:"您为什么不让仲壬去拜见君主呢?"

叔孙豹说:"小小孩儿,如何拜见君主?"

竖牛说:"仲壬早已经多次拜见过君主了,君主还赐予他玉环,仲壬早已佩戴在身上了。"

叔孙豹立刻召见仲壬,果然看到仲壬佩戴着玉环,叔孙豹因此怒而杀了仲壬。

仲壬的兄长名叫孟丙。竖牛也嫉妒他,想杀了孟丙。

叔孙豹为长子孟丙铸了一口大钟。钟铸成之后,孟丙不敢首先敲响,于是恳求竖牛请示父亲。竖牛也是不予请示,而欺骗他说:"我已经替你请示过了,你父亲让你先敲。"孟丙因此击响了大钟。

叔孙豹听到钟声大怒说:"孟丙不来请示就敢敲钟。"一怒之下把孟丙赶出家门。

孟丙流落到齐国。过了一年,竖牛借口替孟丙向父亲谢罪,叔孙豹一时心动,指派竖牛召回孟丙。竖牛又是不召回,反而禀报说:"我已经派人前去召唤孟丙,没想到孟丙大怒,不肯回来。"

叔孙豹怒火中烧,特意派人前去杀了孟丙。

孟丙与仲壬已经死了,叔孙豹患了病,竖牛因此独自赡养。他退去左右近侍,不许其他人入内,并且说:"叔孙豹不愿意听到有人的声音。"由此,竖牛不给叔孙豹喂食,将其活活饿死在后宫。叔孙豹已经死去,竖牛不发丧,只为窃取叔孙豹库中的财物。随即竖牛携带贮物逃奔齐国。因此,只听信宠臣的话语,其结果是父子都被他人所害,这都是因为不参照事实而造成的祸患。

寓意:宠信奸佞之臣到了怀疑亲生儿子的地步,不辨是非地处置贤子,最终招致覆灭的祸端。可见,用人乃一门智慧的学问。

The Calamity of Favoritism

Shu Sunbao, when he was the prime minister of the State of Lu, held a prestigious position and exercised arbitrary power. His trusted servant was named Shu Niu. Shu Niu often abused Shu Sunbao's reputation to commit bad deeds.

Shu Sunbao's second son was named Zhong Ren. Shu Niu envied him and wanted to kill him. Therefore, Shu Niu encouraged Zhong Ren to visit the king. When the king saw Zhong Ren, he gave him a jade ring as a gift. Zhong Ren thanked the king and accepted the ring, but he was afraid to wear it. So he specially begged Shu Niu to ask his father for permission. After a few days, Shu Niu deceived him and said, "I have already asked your father for permission, and he allowed you to wear the jade ring." So Zhong Ren dared to wear the ring.

After a short while, Shu Niu said to Shu Sunbao, "Why don't you let Zhong Ren go to visit the king?"

Shu Sunbao replied, "He's just a child, how can he visit the king?"

Shu Niu said, " Zhong Ren has already visited the king many times before, and the king even gave him a jade ring, which Zhong Ren has been wearing for a long time."

Shu Sunbao immediately summoned Zhong Ren and indeed saw that he was wearing the jade ring. Angry about this, Shu Sunbao killed Zhong Ren.

Zhong Ren's elder brother was named Meng Bing. Shu Niu also envied him and wanted to kill him.

Shu Sunbao cast a big bell for his eldest son Meng Bing. After the bell was cast, Meng Bing was afraid to ring it first, so he begged Shu Niu to ask his father. Shu Niu, however, did not ask and deceived him, saying, "I have already asked your father for you. He said you can ring it first." So Meng Bing rang the bell.

Upon hearing the sound of the bell, Shu Sunbao was furious and said, "Meng Bing dared to ring the bell without asking for permission first." In his anger, he banished Meng Bing from the house.

Meng Bing fled to the state of Qi. After a year, Shu Niu used the excuse of apologizing to his father for Meng Bing, and Shu Sunbao was momentarily moved. He instructed Shu Niu to summon Meng Bing back. Shu Niu, however, did not summon Meng Bing, but instead reported, "I have sent someone to summon Meng Bing, but unexpectedly, he was so angry that he refused to come back."

Shu Sunbao was furious and sent someone to kill Meng Bing.

After Meng Bing and Zhong Ren had died, Shu Sunbao fell ill, and Shu Niu took care of him alone. He dismissed his attendants and did not allow anyone else to enter, saying, "Shu Sunbao doesn't want to hear anyone's voice." Using this opportunity, Shu Niu did not feed Shu Sunbao and starved him to death in the palace.

Shu Sunbao had already passed away, but Shu Niu did not announce the death and instead stole the treasures from his vault. He then fled to the state of Qi with the stolen goods. Therefore, by only listening to the words of his favorite minister, both he and his sons ended up being harmed by others. This was all caused by not consulting the facts.

Meaning: The emperor trusted treacherous ministers to the extent of doubting his own son, failing to distinguish between right and wrong when dealing with his virtuous children, and ultimately leading to the downfall of the family. It is evident that selecting and appointing individuals is a profound wisdom that requires careful consideration.

董阏于之治《韩鹏子·内储说上》

董阏（yān）于为赵上地守。行石邑山中，涧深，峭如墙，深百仞，因问其旁乡左右曰："人尝有入此者乎？"

对曰："无有。"

曰："婴儿、痴聋、狂悖（bèi 精神失常）之人尝有入此者乎？"

对曰："无有。"

"牛马犬彘尝有入此者乎？"

对曰："无有。"

董阏于喟然太息曰："吾能治矣。使吾治之无赦，犹入涧之必死也，则人莫之敢犯也，何为不治？"

译文：董阏于担任赵氏的上党郡守。一天他巡视到石色山中，山涧很深。陡峭的山崖像墙一样垂直，深有数百尺，他问居住在山涧边的人说："曾经有人掉入山涧吗？"

回答："没有。"

又问："婴儿、白痴、聋子、精神失常的人士，可曾掉入过吗？"

回答："没有。"

又问："牛马狗猪，可曾掉入吗？"

回答："没有。"

董阏于长叹一声说："我可以把上党郡治理好了。假如严厉惩治犯罪的人不予宽容，罪人如同掉入深涧必死一样，就没人敢冒犯法律，岂能治理不好此地吗？"

寓意：法必明，令必行，禁必止，行必果，岂能不治？

Good Governance

Dong Yanyu was the governor of Shangdang prefecture under the Zhao family. One day, he inspected the Shi Se Mountain where the mountain streams were deep. The steep cliffs were as straight as walls, reaching hundreds of feet deep. He asked the people living near the mountain stream, "Has anyone ever fallen into the mountain stream before?"

They answered, "No."

Again, "Have babies, idiots, deaf people, or mentally ill individuals ever fallen into it?"

"No," they replied.

Lastly, "Have cows, horses, dogs, pigs ever fallen into it?"

"No," they answered.

Dong Yanyu sighed deeply and said, "I can govern Shangdang prefecture well. If we severely punish those who commit crimes without leniency, just like how those who fall into the deep gorge are bound to die, no one will dare to violate the law. How can we not govern this place well?"

Meaning: If the law is strictly enforced, orders are executed, prohibitions are not violated, and actions always lead to consequences, how can there not be good governance?

魏惠王之慈 《韩非子·内储说上》

魏惠王谓卜皮曰："子闻，寡人之声闻亦何如焉？"

对曰："臣闻王之慈惠也。"

王欣然喜曰："然则，功且安至？"

对曰："王之功，至于亡。"

王曰："慈惠，行善也。行之而亡，何也？"

卜皮对曰："夫，慈者不忍，而惠者好与也。不忍，则不诛有过；好予，则不待有功而赏。有过不罪，无功受赏，虽亡，不亦可乎？"

译文：魏惠王对卜皮说："你听到的有关我的名声，是如何评论的？"

回答说:"我听到的都是赞誉君主仁爱的言辞。"魏惠王高兴地说:"既然如此,我的功绩达到何种程度?"

回答说:"君主的功绩快要达到亡国的地步。"

魏惠王不解地问,说:"以仁爱治理国事,是行善。积德行善反而亡国,这是为什么?"

卜皮回答说:"仁慈的君主,不忍心对犯有过错的臣子用刑,然而对于有恩的人又好施舍。不忍心,就不会对有罪的臣子实施刑罚。好施舍,即使臣子没有再立新功,也可得到赏赐。有罪的没有受到惩罚,无新功的也能得到赏赐。长期下去,国力衰亡不也是应该的吗?"

寓意:赏罚分明,乃立国之本。

The Kindness of King Hui of Wei

King Hui of the state of Wei said to Bu Pi, "What have you heard about my reputation? What are the comments?"

The response was, "I have only heard words praising your benevolence, my king." King Hui was pleased and said, "If that's the case, how far have I achieved in my deeds?"

The reply was, "Your deeds, my king, are nearing the brink of causing the downfall of the nation."

King Wei Hui expressed his confusion and asked, "Governing the state with benevolence is considered virtuous. Yet, how can accumulating virtue and kindness lead to the downfall of a nation? Why is this so?"

Bu Pi replied, "A benevolent king is reluctant to punish his ministers for their mistakes, yet he is generous with his rewards for those who have shown favor. When mercy prevents the punishment of guilty ministers, and generosity grants rewards even to those who have not earned them through new achievements, then it is inevitable that the nation's strength will decline over time. Isn't it natural for the country to perish in such circumstances?"

Meaning: Clearly distinguishing rewards and punishments is the foundation of a country.

滥竽充数 《韩非子·内储说上》

齐宣王使人吹竽(yú 古代吹奏乐器,像笙,有三十六簧),必三百人。南郭处士请为王吹竽,宣王说(悦)之,廪食(lǐn shí 公家供给口粮)以数百人。

宣王死，湣王立，好一一听之，处士逃。

译文：齐宣王指派乐手吹竽，必须足足三百人一同吹奏。南郭处士请求给君主吹竽，宣王很高兴。由官方供养的吹奏者就有数百人之多。

齐宣王死后，齐湣王登上王位，湣王喜欢听一个又一个的独奏，南郭处士即刻逃走了。

寓意：审查不严苛，容易使滥竽充数的臣子混入朝中。

Safety in Numbers

Whenever King Xuan of the state of Qi ordered musicians to play the yu, an ancient wind instrument consisting of reed pipes, he insisted on three hundred musicians playing together. Nanguo, an educated man in retirement, asked permission to play the yu for the king. The king graciously gave his consent and Nanguo received the same salary as the other several hundred musicians.

After the death of King Xuan, King Min became the ruler of Qi. He liked to listen to the musicians one by one. Nanguo fled.

Meaning: If the vetting process is not rigorous, it can easily allow incompetent ministers to infiltrate the imperial court.

吏 势《韩非子·内储说下》

靖郭君（即：田婴）相齐（出任齐国相十一年），与故人久语，则故人富；怀左右尉（慰藉），则左右重。久语怀尉，小资也，犹以成富，况于吏势乎？

译文：靖郭君在齐国任国相时，他与往日的老友多聊几句话，他的老友就会因此富裕起来；他慰藉左右侍从，左右侍从就会因此被众人器重。

身居宰相之位的靖郭君，与故友多说了一会儿话或慰藉几句，就能使地位低下的人被他人看重，甚至使其达到生活富足的境地，更何况他本人所掌握的权势呢？

寓意：官吏的轻微举动和言行就可以达到改变他人命运的结果，那么可见此官吏自身权势之大。需要警醒的是权势本应有所约束，因为权势可能会影响到法度、规则和改变社会习气。

Power

When Jingguo Jun served as the prime minister of the State of Qi, his conversations with his old friends would often lead to their prosperity. His words of comfort to his attendants would cause them to be respected by the people.

As the prime minister, Jingguo Jun's mere conversation or words of comfort with his old friends can elevate their status and even lead to their prosperity. How much more so with the power he himself possesses?

Meaning: The slightest actions and words of an official can lead to changes in the fate of others, indicating the vast influence he has. It is important to remember that power should be restrained, as it has the potential to influence laws, regulations, and social norms.

夫妻祷者《韩非子·内储说下》

卫人有夫妻祷（祈祷）者，而祝曰："使我无故得百束布（布：古代的一种钱币）。

其夫曰："何少也？"

对曰："益（多）是子将以买妾。"

译文：卫国有夫妻二人一同祈祷，妻子祈愿说："愿神灵无缘无故赐予我百串钱币！"

她丈夫连忙说："为何祈求这么少呢？"

她回答，说："祈求多了你就会拿去买妾。"

（韩非子以此言说："君臣之利异，故人臣莫忠，故臣利立，而王利灭。"）

寓意：此寓言以夫妻祈祷的内容各异来警示：君臣之间若因利益的不同，不能同心协力管理国家以求强盛，心怀各异则会阻碍国家的发展。

Earnest Prayers

In the state of Wei a couple was praying to the gods.

"Please, let me have one hundred strings of cash without having to work for it," prayed the wife.

"Why so little?" asked her husband.

"If we have more," came her reply," you'd go and get a concubine."

(Han Feizi said, "If the interests of the king and his ministers are different, so ministers are not loyal. When the Ministers' interests are served, the king's interests are destroyed.")

Meaning: This fable warns that if the monarch and the minister cannot work together to manage the country for prosperity due to different interests, their divergent intentions will hinder the development of the country.

买椟还珠《韩非子·外储说左上》

楚人有卖其珠于郑者，为木兰（又名：杜兰、林兰、木莲。木质优美）之椟（dú 匣子），薰以桂椒（泛指高等香料），缀以珠玉，饰以玫瑰（红色的玉），辑（集）以羽翠（翡翠：绿色的玉）。

郑人买其椟，而还其珠。此可谓善卖椟矣，未可谓善鬻（yù 卖）珠也。

译文：楚国有一位人士要去郑国卖珍珠，他用木质优美的木兰做成盛放珍珠的包装匣子，并且使用高等香料的肉桂与山椒枝熏制盒体，又在盒体四周点缀上红绿双色美玉。

郑国人买下他的包装匣子，还给他珍珠。这样的行为可以称作他善于卖珍珠的包装匣子，不善于卖珍珠。

寓意：卖珠者将盛放珍珠的匣子装饰地比珍珠还要光彩夺目，此举可谓喧宾夺主。买者却只看到匣子外表的华丽，而忽略了匣子内真正可贵的物品，可谓只看其表，忽略其里。

The Casket and the Pearl

A man from the state of Chu wanted to sell a precious pearl in the state of Zheng. He made a casket for the pearl out of the wood from a magnolia tree, which he fumigated with fragrant osmanthus and spices. He studded the casket with pearls and jade, ornamented it with red gems and decorated it with kingfisher feathers. A man of the state of Zheng bought the casket and gave him back the pearl.

This man from Chu certainly knew how to sell a casket but he was no good at selling his pearl.

Meaning: The seller of pearls decorated the casket containing the pearls more brilliantly than the pearls themselves, which can be described as stealing the show. The buyer only saw the gorgeous exterior of the casket and ignored the truly valuable thing inside, which can be described as only looking at the surface and ignoring the inside.

燕王学道《韩非子·外储说左上》

客有教燕王为不死之道者，王使人学之，所使学者未及学，而客死。

王大怒，诛之。

王不知客之欺己，而诛学者之晚也。夫信不然之物，而诛无罪之臣，不察之患也。且（况且），人所急，无如其身，不能自使其无死，安能使王长生哉？

译文：游客中有人想要传授燕王长生不老法术，燕王信认为真，便派人跟他学。派去的人还没有来得及学成，那位游客却死了。

燕王大怒，杀了派去学法术的人。

燕王没有领悟到游客是在欺骗他，反而以延误之罪杀了去学习的人。因此，相信不存在的事物而诛杀无辜的人，这是不明察的危害。况且人所看重的莫过于自己的生命，那位游客不能使自己长生，岂能使君主长生不老呢？"

寓意：君王遇事若不加思辨而滥杀无辜，使得伪诈得以横行，良善无所立身，此为不察之害。

King Yan Learns the Way

Amidst the crowd of visitors, someone claimed to possess the secret of everlasting life and convinced King Yan of its authenticity. As a result, King Yan sent a man to learn this secret from the visitor. Before the man could even begin to master the art, however, the visitor died unexpectedly.

Enraged, King Yan ordered the execution of the man he had sent to learn the secret.

King Yan failed to realize that the visitor was deceiving him, and instead killed the man he sent to learn the secret on charges of delay. Thus, to believe in non-existent things and kill innocent people is the danger of not exercising discernment. Moreover, what people value most is their own lives. The visitor lost his own life, how could he possibly taught the king not to lose his?

Meaning: If a king does not exercise discernment and indiscriminately kills innocent people when confronted with situations, it allows deceit and fraud to flourish and leaves no room for goodness and virtue. This is the danger of not exercising discernment.

说 画 《韩非子·外储说左上》

客有为齐王画者，齐王问曰："画孰最难者？"

曰："犬马难。"

"孰易者？"

曰："鬼魅最易。"

夫犬马，人所知也，旦暮罄（qìng 引申为尽）于前，不可类之，故难。鬼魅，无形者，不罄于前，故易之也。

译文：有位游客为齐王绘画，齐王问他，说："画什么最难？"

游客回答说："画狗和马最难。"

齐王又问："画什么最容易？"

游客回答说："画鬼怪最容易。"

狗和马，是人人熟知的动物，早晚都在人们的眼前窜动，人们熟悉它们的形态，难以画出它们的神色。鬼怪没有固定形态，人们都没有看过它们，所以画起来容易。

寓意：绘画真实的物体，难以画出它的神色。现实生活中，说真话容易，说假话难，因为假话容易露陷。

Ghost Drawing

The king of the state of Qi asked his guest who was drawing a picture for him," What is most difficult to draw?"

"Dogs and horses are the most difficult."

"What is the easiest?"

"Ghosts are the easiest. Dogs and horses are familiar sights that we behold from morning till evening and it is not easy to capture the likeness. That is why they are so difficult to draw. As for ghosts, they have no shape and they do not appear before us. That is why it's so easy to draw them."

Meaning: It is difficult to capture the essence of a real object when painting it. In real life, it is easy to speak the truth but difficult to tell a lie, because lies are easy to be exposed.

尘饭涂羹 《韩非子·外储说左上》

夫婴儿相与戏也，以尘为饭，以涂为羹，以木为胾（zì 切成大块的肉），然，至日晚必归饷（xiǎng）者，尘饭涂羹可以戏，而不可食也。

夫称上古之传颂，辩而不悫（què 实），道先王仁义而不能正国者，此亦可以戏，而不可以为治也。

译文：儿童在一起相互游玩，用尘土当饭、用稀泥作汤、用木块当作肉，然而到了傍晚，必定要回到各自的家中吃饭。这是因为尘土做成的饭、稀泥做成的汤，只能当作游戏，而不能当作食物。

当下，称赞上古圣贤的传颂，虽然动听却不现实；宣扬先王仁义之道，却不能使国家步入正轨。此事可以戏说，而不能用此治理国家。

寓意：不切实际地颂扬之词，难以利国只会误国。

Dusty Rice and Mud Soup

Children play with each other, using dust for rice, mud for soup, and wooden blocks for meat. However, by evening, they must return to their respective homes for dinner. This is because dust-made rice and mud-made soup can only be used for games, not for food.

Nowadays, praising the legends of ancient saints and wise men may sound pleasant but is not realistic; promoting the moral principles of the former kings cannot put the country on the right track. This is just something that can be talked about and cannot be used to govern the country.

Meaning: Words of praise that are not grounded in reality can only mislead the country and not benefit it.

病疽者 《韩非子·外储说左上》

吴起为魏将，而攻中山。军人有病疽（jū 中医指一种毒疮）者，吴起跪而自吮（shǔn 吮吸）其脓。

伤者之母立泣。

人问曰："将军于若子如是，尚何为而泣？"

对曰："吴起吮其父之创，而父死，今是子又将死也，今吾是以泣。"

译文：吴起任魏国将军时，领军攻伐中山国。军中有士兵患了毒疮，吴起跪下亲自吮吸士兵毒疮里的脓液。

这位士兵的母亲得知此事，立刻痛哭起来。

有人不解地问她："将军对待你的孩子如同自己的儿子一般，你为何还要伤心地痛哭呢？"

母亲回答说："吴起为我儿子的父亲吮吸伤口，儿子的父亲就战死沙场。现在，我的儿子就要战死沙场了，我正是为此而哭泣。"

寓意：报达善意的代价，竟是以死明谢。

Dilemma

When Wu Qi was a general in the State of Wei, he led his troops to attack the State of Zhongshan. There was a soldier in the army who had a poisoned sore, and Wu Qi knelt down to suck the pus out of the soldier's sore.

When the soldier's mother learned about this, she burst into tears immediately.

Someone who didn't understand asked her, "General Wu treats your son as if he were his own, so why are you crying so sadly?"

The mother replied, "Wu Qi sucked the wound for my son's father, and my son's father died on the battlefield. Now, my son is going to die on the battlefield, and that's why I'm crying."

Meaning: Ironically, the cost of returning kindness is to give thanks with one's death.

郢书燕说《韩非子·外储说左上》

郢（yǐng 楚国都城）人有遗燕相国书者。夜书，火（灯）不明，因谓持烛者曰："举烛。"云而过书"举烛"。举烛，非书意也。

燕相受书而说（悦）之，曰："举烛者，尚明也；尚明也者，举贤而任之。"

燕相白王，王大说（悦），国以治。

治则治矣，非书意也。今世举学者多似此类。

译文：楚国郢都有位给燕国宰相写信的人，他在黑夜写信，由于烛光不明亮，因此他对待从说："举烛。"说话间，无意识地将"举烛"也写进了书信里。其实，举烛，并非书信的本意。

燕国宰相收到来信，看罢很喜悦，说："举烛，是崇尚光明；崇尚光明，则是推举光明磊落的圣贤人士委以重任。"

宰相把举烛的意义向君主表明，君主也很乐意，准许宰相实施此方法，燕国因此治理的很好。

燕国固然治理的很好，却不是信中的本意。如今的学者，大都是类似这样的作法。

寓意：学者若凭误打误撞写出治世之作，不过是偶然。治理国家的理念、政策不可依赖偶然性。因此筛选出真正有才、忠贞之士为国效力，而不是任用凭借一时偶然凸显才干的伪学者来治理国家，方为正道。

Chance Events

There was a man in Yingdu, Chu State, who wrote a letter to the prime minister of Yan State. He wrote the letter in the dark, and because the candlelight was dim, he said to his attendant, "Hold up the candle." Unconsciously, he wrote "hold up the candle" into the letter. In fact, "hold up the candle" was not the original intention of the letter.

When the prime minister of Yan State received the letter, he was very pleased and said, "Holding up the candle means advocating for brightness and enlightenment. Advocating for brightness and enlightenment is to promote upright and honest wise men to be entrusted with important tasks."

The prime minister explained the meaning of "hold up the candle" to the king, and the king was also pleased to allow the prime minister to implement this method. Therefore, Yan State was well-governed. Although Yan State was well-governed, it was not the original intention of the letter. Nowadays, most scholars are similar to this approach.

Meaning: If scholars happen to stumble upon a work that can govern the country, it is merely a coincidence. The philosophy and policies of governing a country cannot rely on coincidences. Therefore, it is the right way to identify and cultivate truly talented and loyal individuals who can make valuable contributions to the country, rather than appointing pseudo-scholars who only demonstrate their talents occasionally due to coincidences to govern the country.

农夫惰于田 《韩非子·外储说左上》

赵主父使李疵（cī）视中山可攻不（否）也。还报曰："中山可伐也。君不亟（jí 急切）伐，将后齐、燕。"

主父曰："何故可攻？"

李疵对曰：其君，见好（讨好）岩穴之士，所倾盖与车以见穷闾陋巷之士以十数，伉礼（平等礼节）下布衣之士以百数矣。"

君曰："以子言论，是贤君也，安可攻？"

疵曰："不然。夫，好显岩穴之士而朝之，则战士怠于行阵；上尊学者，下士居朝，则农夫惰于田。战士怠于行陈者，则兵弱也；农夫惰于田者，则国贫也。兵弱于敌，国贫于内，而不亡者，未之有也。伐之不亦可乎？"

主父曰："善。"举兵而伐中山，遂灭也。

译文：赵武灵王指派李疵前去察看中山国是否可以攻伐。李疵察看后回报说："中山国可以攻伐，如果君主不早日攻伐，将会落后于齐国与燕国。"

赵武灵王连忙问："是什么原因可以攻伐？"

李疵回禀说："中山国的君主很喜欢隐居在山野里的人士，并且亲自驱车访问穷巷陋室里的读书人就有十余次，以平等礼节对待布衣书生达百次之多。"

赵武灵王不解地问："依照你所讲的，这是一位贤君，怎能冒然攻伐？"

李疵说："不是这样。如果君主喜好隐居人士而请他们入朝，那么士兵就会懒于行列布阵；尊宠学者，下士入朝，就会造成农夫懒于田间劳作。士兵懒于行列布阵的练习，则兵力弱；农夫懒于田间劳作，则国贫。兵弱于敌国，国贫于内，这样的国家不灭亡，还从未有过。攻伐这样的国家岂不是很容易吗？"

赵武灵王听罢说："很好。"于是出兵攻伐中山国，很顺利地灭了它。

寓意：凡事都有度，过度太甚，则会造成适得其反的后果。

Laziness in Farming

King Wuling of the state of Zhao sent Li Ci to inspect whether Zhongshan State could be attacked. After inspection, Li Ci reported back, "Zhongshan State can be attacked. If our king does not attack Zhongshan early, we may fall behind Qi and Yan States."

King Wuling asked quickly, "Why can it be attacked?"

Li Ci replied, "The king of Zhongshan State has a great fondness for hermits who live in the mountains and personally visits scholars in impoverished neighborhoods more than ten times, treating scholars from humble backgrounds with equal respect and courtesy on hundreds of occasions."

King Wuling was puzzled and asked, "According to what you've said, this is a benevolent king. How can we attack him so rashly?"

Li Ci replied, "It's not like that. If a king likes to invite hermits to the imperial court, soldiers will become lazy in formation training; if scholars are respected and inferior officers are invited to the court, farmers will become lazy in their fieldwork. When soldiers are lazy in formation training, the military strength will weaken; when farmers are lazy in their fieldwork, the country will become poor. If a country's military strength is weaker than its enemy's and the country is internally poor, such a country has never survived. Isn't it easy to attack such a country?"

After hearing this, King Wuling of Zhao said, "That's excellent." So he sent troops to attack Zhongshan Kingdom and successfully conquered it.

Meaning: Everything has a limit. If one overdoes it, it will lead to counterproductive consequences.

裹十日粮《韩非子·外储说左上》

晋文公攻原，裹十日粮，遂与大夫期十日。至原，十日而原不下，击金而退，罢兵而去。

士有从原中出者，曰："原三日即下矣。"

群臣左右谏曰："夫，原之食竭力尽矣，君姑（姑且）待之。"

公曰："吾与士，期十日，不去，是亡吾信也。得原失信，吾不为也。"遂罢兵而去。

原人闻曰："有君如彼其信也，可无归乎？"乃降公。

卫人闻曰："有君如彼其信也，可无从乎？"乃降公。

孔子闻，而记之曰："攻原得卫者，信也。"

译文：晋文公准备攻伐原国，命令军队携带十日军粮。并且与士大夫约定期限为十日。到了原国，十天没有攻下，于是击响锣声，收兵而还。

从前线退下来的将士说："原国再有三日便可攻下。"

群臣左右也劝谏说："原国已经到了断粮力尽的关键时刻，君主姑且再坚持几日。"

晋文公说："我与士大夫约定期限为十天，到期不退兵，是我丧失信誉。为了得到原国，而失去我的信誉，我不愿做违背诺言的事情。"于是，罢兵回国。

原国人听说了此事，说："有这样讲诚信的君主，怎能不归顺呢？"遂即向晋文公投降。

卫国人听说了此事，说："有这样讲诚信的君主，岂能不顺从？"于是，卫国也向晋文公投降。

孔子听说此事，用文书记载下，说："本来攻伐原国，不但赢得原国屈服称臣，也得到卫国屈服称臣，这都是因为晋文公守诚信的缘故。"

寓意：诚实守信的行为，赢得意想之外的收获。

Honest Monarch

Duke Wen of Jin prepared to attack Yuan State, ordering the army to carry provisions for ten days. He also made a pact with the officials that the operation would last for ten days. When they arrived at Yuan State, they were unable to capture it within the ten-day period. Therefore, they sounded the *gong* and retreated.

The officers returning from the front line said, "Yuan State could be conquered in another three days."

The ministers and attendants around him also advised, "Yuan State is at a critical point of exhaustion with limited food supplies. The monarch should persist for a few more days."

Duke Wen of Jin said, "I made a pact with the courtiers to withdraw within ten days. If I fail to do so, it means I have lost my credibility. I am unwilling to compromise my promise for the sake of capturing Yuan State." Therefore, he ordered the troops to withdraw and return to their country.

Upon hearing this news, the people of Yuan State said, "How can we not submit to such a trustworthy monarch?" They then surrendered to Duke Wen of Jin.

Upon hearing this news, the people of Wei State said, "How can we not submit to such a trustworthy monarch?" Therefore, Wei State also surrendered to Duke Wen of Jin.

Confucius heard about this incident and recorded it in writing, saying, "The original plan of Jin was to attack Yuan State, but not only did it submit to Jin, but Wei State also surrendered. This was all because Duke Wen of Jin upheld his credibility."

Meaning: Honest and trustworthy behavior can bring unexpected rewards.

曾子杀彘《韩非子·外储说左上》

曾子（即：曾参。孔子弟子）之妻之市，其子随之而泣。其母曰："女（汝）还，顾反为女杀彘。"适市来，曾子欲捕彘杀之。

妻止之曰："特与婴儿戏耳。"

曾子曰："婴儿非与戏也。婴儿非有知也，待父母而学者也，听父母之教。今，子欺之，是教子欺也。母欺子，子而不信其母，非以成教也。"

遂烹彘也。

译文：曾参的妻子要去集市，她的儿子哭着也要跟着走，其母对孩子说："你回去，等我回家后给你杀猪吃。"

她从集市返回家，曾参听说了此事，就去抓猪要杀。

妻于连忙制止说："我只是给孩子说了一句戏言，何必当真？"

曾参说："小孩不是父母开玩笑的对象。孩子没有判断和认知的能力，都是依照父母的言行学习，听从父母教诲。现在你欺骗他，等于教导孩子学会欺骗。再者，身为母亲欺骗孩子，孩子从此不再相信父亲的说教，这样的作法，不是正确教育孩子的方法。"

于是，曾参为此杀猪煮给孩子吃。

寓意：诚实守信的品德，是从少年培养的结果。

An Example to Follow

As Zengzi's wife set off for the market, her little son followed her, crying.

"Go home," she said to the boy," when I come back, I'll kill the pig for you to eat."

When she got back from the market Zengzi wanted to catch the pig and kill it.

His wife stopped him." I was just humouring the child."

"Children cannot be humoured in this way," he replied. "They have little understanding. They learn from their parents and listen to what their parents teach them. By deceiving him now you are teaching him to deceive. If a mother deceives her son, her son would not believe his mother any more. This is not the way to teach a child." So he killed the pig and cooked it.

Meaning: The character of being honest and trustworthy is the result of cultivation from childhood.

私仇不入公门《韩非子·外储说左下》

中牟（县邑名）无令。晋平公问赵武曰："中牟，吾国之股肱（股：大腿。肱：胳膊。意指：首都重要城邑），邯郸之肩髀（意指：国之要冲）。寡人欲得其良令也，谁使而可？"

武曰："邢伯子可。"

公曰："非子之仇也？"

曰："私仇不入公门。"

公又问曰："中府之令，谁使而可？"

曰："臣子可。"

故曰："外举不避仇，内举不避子。"

赵武所荐四十六人，及武死，各就宾位，其无私德若此也。

译文：中牟县还没有县令。晋平公问执政的卿相赵武，说："中牟县城，是我国守卫都城的重要城池，又是国之要冲区域。我希望有一位良臣在此担任县令，派遣谁最合适？"

赵武说："邢伯子可以。"

晋平公不解地问："他不是你的仇人吗？"

赵武说："私怨不可带入朝中公事。"

晋平公又问："中府还缺府令，谁最合适？"

赵武说："我儿子可以胜任。"

所以说："对外举荐人才不避开仇人，对内举荐人才不避开自己的儿子。"

赵武推举的四十六名官吏，等到赵武死后出殡时，都坐在吊唁席上表达对他的敬仰。这正是赵武执政时不施行私德的缘故。

寓意：手握重权，还能以公德对待众生，必定会赢得众生敬仰。

Recruiting Talents Without Bias

There is no county magistrate in Zhongmou County yet. King Ping of Jin asked Zhao Wu, the chief minister in charge of governance, saying, "Zhongmou County is an important city for our country to guard the capital, and it is also a strategic location. I hope to have a good minister serve as the county magistrate there. Who is the most suitable person to be sent there?"

Zhao Wu replied, "Xing Bozi can do it."

King Ping of Jin asked in confusion, "Isn't he your enemy?"

Zhao Wu said, "Personal grudges should not be brought into official business."

King Ping of Jin asked again, "The Middle Office is also lacking a director. Who is the most suitable candidate?"

Zhao Wu replied, "My son is capable of the position."

Hence it is said, "When recommending talents externally, one should not avoid enemies; when recommending talents internally, one should not avoid one's own son."

The forty-six officials recommended by Zhao Wu all sat in the condolence seats to express their respect for him when he died and was buried. This was precisely because Zhao Wu had not practiced favoritism during his term in office.

Meaning: Holding great power and treating all beings with virtue will undoubtedly earn the respect of all beings.

赵简主说税 《韩非子·外储说右下》

赵简主（原名赵鞅。世称赵简子）出税者，吏请轻重。简主曰："勿轻勿重。重，则利入于上；若轻，则利归于民。吏无私利而正矣。"

薄疑谓赵简主曰："君之国中饱。"

简主欣然而喜曰："何如焉？"

对曰："府库空虚于上，百姓贫饿于下，然而，奸吏富矣。"

译文：赵简主派遣官吏征税，官吏请示征税标准。赵简主说："不要太轻也不要过重。过重，民众的收益都归于君主；如果太轻，则利归于民。只要收税的官吏不存私心，就是征税标准。"

薄疑对赵简主说："君主的国中富裕。"

赵简主欣然而喜，说："是何缘由？"

薄疑回答说："君主国库空虚，天下百姓贫饥。然而，奸吏借征税之机中饱私囊富得流油。"

寓意：国策制定本应有规矩、有法度，税收也依照标准执行。可若将税收的权重给予一国收税之官吏，却忘了如何管理税收官的行为，无异于放纵贪墨，使国家陷入不利之境。

Talking about Taxes

King Jian of Zhao sent officials to collect taxes, and the officials asked about the tax rate. Zhao Jianzhu said, "Don't make it too light or too heavy. If it's too heavy, the profits of the people will go to the lord; if it's too light, the benefits will go to the people. As long as the tax collectors don't have ulterior motives, that's the tax rate."

Bo Yi said to King Jian of Zhao, "Your country is prosperous."

King Jian of Zhao felt pleased and asked, "Why is that?"

Bo Yi replied, "The nation's treasury is empty, and the people of the land are poor and hungry. However, corrupt officials take advantage of the tax collection to enrich themselves at the expense of the public."

Meaning: The formulation of national policies should follow rules and regulations, and taxes should be collected according to standards. However, if the power of taxation is given to tax collectors in a country without proper supervision and management, it is tantamount to indulging corruption and putting the country in a disadvantageous position.

矛 与 盾 《韩非子·难一》

楚人有鬻（卖）盾与矛者，誉之曰："吾盾之坚，物莫能陷也。"又誉其矛曰："吾矛之利，于物无不陷也。"

或曰："以子之矛，陷子之盾，何如？"其人弗能应也。

夫，不可陷之盾与无不陷之矛，不可同世而立。

译文：楚国有个卖盾与矛的商贩，他夸口说："我的盾非常坚固，任何器物不能刺透。"转身又自夸其矛说："我的矛非常锋利，能够刺穿任何器物。"

有人说："用你的矛，刺你的盾，如何？"此人无言以对。

因此，不可刺穿的盾与无不刺穿的矛，不能同时存在。

寓意：说话、做事不可不假思索、相互矛盾，否则贻笑大方。

His Spear Against His Shield

A man of the state of Chu had a spear and a shield for sale. He was loud in praises of his shield.

"My shield is so strong that nothing can pierce it through."

He also sang praises of his spear.

"My spear is so strong that it can pierce through anything."

"What would happen," he was asked," if your spear is used to pierce your shield?"

He was unable to give an answer.

It is impossible for an impenetrable shield to coexist with a spear that finds nothing impenetrable.

Meaning: Speaking and doing things should not be thoughtless or contradictory, otherwise it will become a laughingstock.

守株待兔《韩非子·五蠹》

宋人有耕者，田中有株（树桩），兔走触株，折颈而死。因释其耒（lěi 未耜。古农具）而守株，冀复得兔。兔不可复得，而身为宋国笑。

译文：宋国有位农夫正在耕田，田当中有一个大树桩，一只兔子飞奔而来撞到树桩上，撞断了脖颈倒地而死。这位农夫便放下犁杖，守在那棵树桩前，希望再次得到兔子。

兔子不可能再次得到，然而，他的行为却成了笑话在宋国传开了。

寓意：错把偶然当必然，惹得世人笑开颜。

The Vigil by the Tree Stump

In the state of Song there was a farmer in whose fields stood a tree stump. A hare which was running very fast dashed against the stump and died, having broken its neck. So the farmer abandoned his plough and waited by the tree stump, hoping to get another hare. He did not get his hare but became a laughingstock in the state of Song.

Meaning: Treating chance as necessity will make people laugh.

姜太公钓鱼 Jiang Taigong Fishing

《姜子牙》：

姜子牙，名尚，字，子牙，号：飞熊。亦称：吕望、吕尚。他是商末周初时期著名政治家、军事家、韬略家，兵学奠基人。西伯侯姬昌拜他为"太师"，尊称他为：太公望。周武王即位后，尊他为"师尚父"。

司马迁《史记·周本纪》："武王即位，太公望为师，周公旦为辅，召公，毕公之徒左右手，师修文王绪业（遗业）。"周武王灭商纣，建立周朝。"于是，封功臣谋士，而师尚父（姜子牙）为首封。封尚父于营丘（今，山东淄博），曰齐。封弟（武王弟）周公旦于曲阜，曰鲁。"

《诗经·大雅·大明》："牧野洋洋，檀车煌煌，驷騵彭彭。维师尚父，时维鹰扬。凉彼武王，肆伐大商，会朝清明。"

Jiang Ziya:

Jiang Ziya, also known as Shang, courtesy name Ziya, and literary name Feixiong, was also referred to as Lü Wang and Lü Shang. He was a renowned statesman, military strategist, and strategist during the late Shang and early Zhou dynasties, and the founder of military science. Duke Ji Chang of the Western Bo State appointed him as "Tai Shi," respectfully addressing him as "Tai Gong Wang." After King Wu of Zhou ascended the throne, he honored him as "Shi Shangfu.".

太公望封于齐《韩非子·外储说右上》

太公望（约生于公元前？——公元前 1015 年卒）东封于齐。

齐东海上有居士曰狂矞（yù）、华士昆弟（兄弟）二人者立议曰："吾不臣天子，不友诸侯，耕作而食之，掘井而饮之，吾无求于人也。无上之名，无君之禄，不事仕而事力。"

太公望至于营丘，使吏执杀之，以为首诛。

周公旦从鲁闻之，发急传而问之曰："夫二子，贤者也。今日飨（xiǎng 同：享）国而杀贤者，何也？"

太公望曰："是昆弟二人立议曰：'吾不臣天子，不友诸侯，耕作而食之，掘井而饮之，吾无求于人也。无上之名，无君之禄，不事仕而事力。'彼，不臣天子者，是望不得而臣也；不友诸侯者，是望不得而使也；耕作而食之，掘井而饮之，无求于人者，是望不得以赏罚劝禁也。且（况且），无上名，虽知（智），不为望用；不仰君禄，虽贤，不为望功（建功）。不仕，则不治；不任，则不忠。且（尚且），先王之所以使其臣民者，非爵禄则刑罚也。今，四者不足以使之，则望当谁为君乎？不服兵革而显，不亲耕耨（gēng nòu 耕种）而名，又非所以教于国也。今，有马于此，如骥（jì 良马）之状者，天下之至良也。然而，驱之不前，却之不止，左之不左，右之不右，则臧获（zāng huò 古称奴婢）虽贱，不托其足。臧获之所愿托其足于骥者，以骥之可以追利辟害也。今，不为人用，臧获虽贱，不托其足焉。已自谓以为世之贤士，而不为主用，行极贤而不用于君，此非明主之所臣也，亦骥之不可左右矣，是以诛之。"

译文：姜太公受封东方齐国。

齐国东部渤海之滨有隐士，名为狂矞、华士兄弟二人。他们得知姜太公将要在此出任诸侯，便立下誓约说："我们不臣服当今的天子，也不友善诸侯。吃自己种的粮食，喝自家掘出的井水，我们万事不求人。无需天子赐予名分，也无需诸侯赐于爵禄，不求仕途加官进爵，只求自食其力的生活。"

姜太公一到营丘，立即派遣使臣杀了他二人。

周公旦在鲁国得知此事，急切发函询问，说："狂矞、华士二人是贤士。现在您刚享有封国就杀了贤士，这是为什么？"

姜太公回复说："兄弟二人立下誓约说：'我们不臣服当今的天子，也不友善诸侯。吃自己种的粮食，喝自家的井水，我们万事不求人。无需天子赐予名分，也无需诸侯赐予爵禄。不求仕途加官进爵，只求自食其力的生活。'如此不臣服于天子者，是我难以使他们臣服；不善待诸侯，我就无法驱使他们。吃自己种植的粮食，喝自己掘出的井水，自以为万事不求人，我怎么实施赏罚劝禁约束他们？况且，目无天子、诸侯，虽然有智，不为我用；不仰慕君主的爵禄，虽有贤能，不为我建功立业。不愿意做官，则不受治理；不接受任用，则不会为国尽忠。尚且，古代先君驱使天下臣民的法则：不是爵禄便是刑罚。现在，爵禄刑罚都不能驱使他们，那么我将做谁的君主？不参军打仗却要显露尊贵，不亲身耕耨劳作却要扬名天下，我何以教化天下众生？当下好比：有良马在此，宛如良骥之形，良马之优。然而驱使它向前，它不向前；驱使它退却，它不向后退却；驱使它向左，它不向左转；驱使它向右，它不向右行。即使卑微的奴婢也不会用它当坐骑。奴婢愿意的是骑上良马便可以追利避害。当下，再好的良马不为人用，奴婢也不会使用它。自认为是当今世上的贤士，不为君主所用，再好的贤能不为君主效力，这样的臣子不是明君能够驱使的。犹如良骥不听从驱使一样，尤其是他们傲慢不逊的气势盖过天子、诸侯的威严，败坏社会风气，所以必须杀一儆百。"

（此处无下文，可以臆想，周公旦看罢姜太公略回复，定是：哑口无言。）

寓意：国与家是不可分割的共同体。《孟子·离娄上》："人有恒言，皆曰天下国家，天下之本在国，国之本在家，家之本在身。"

To Set an Example

Jiang Taigong *(also known as Jiang Ziya)* was awarded the Eastern State of Qi.

Near the coast of the Bohai Sea in the east of Qi, there were two recluses named Kuang Yu and Hua Shi. They learned that Jiang Taigong would be appointed as the feudal lord of Qi, so they made a vow: "We will not submit to the current emperor, nor will we be friendly with feudal lords. We will eat the grain we grow and drink the water from our own wells. We will not ask for help from anyone. We do not need the emperor to give us titles, nor do we need feudal lords to grant us ranks and salaries. We do not seek advancement in officialdom, but only a life of self-sufficiency."

Upon arriving at Yingqiu, Jiang Taigong immediately dispatched messengers to execute the two brothers.

When Zhou Gongdan learned of this in the State of Lu, he urgently wrote a letter inquiring, saying, "Kuang Yu and Hua Shi are wise men. Now that you have just inherited your fiefdom, why did you execute the wise men?"

Jiang Taigong replied, "The two brothers have made a vow, 'We will not submit to the current emperor, nor will we be friendly with feudal lords. We will eat the grain we grow and drink the water from our own wells. We will not ask for help from anyone. We do not need the emperor to grant us titles, nor do we need feudal lords to bestow ranks and salaries. We seek no advancement in officialdom, only a life of self-sufficiency.' Such people who do not submit to the emperor are difficult for me to make them obey; If they are not friendly with the feudal lords, I cannot compel them. And those who eat their own crops and drink water from their own wells, believing that they do not need anyone else, how can I implement rewards, punishments, persuasions, and constraints on them? Moreover, those who have no respect for the emperor and the feudal lords, even if they are intelligent, they will not serve me. Those who do not admire the rank and rewards of the lord, even if they are talented, they will not establish achievements for me. If they are unwilling to serve as officials, they will not be subject to governance; if they do not accept appointment, they will not be loyal to the country.

Furthermore, the ancient kings governed the people with the rule of either through ranks, rewards or through punishment. Nowadays, neither rank and rewards nor punishment can attract them. Then, who am I the lord of? Those who do not participate in military operations but want to show their dignity, and those who do not cultivate but want to be famous throughout the world, how can I educate all beings in the world? It's like this: There is a fine horse here, which looks like a good steed and has the advantages of a fine horse. However, when driven forward, it doesn't move forward; when driven backward, it doesn't move backward; when driven to the left, it doesn't turn left; when driven to the right, it doesn't turn right. Even humble servants won't use it as a mount. Servants want to ride a fine horse so that they can pursue benefits and avoid harm. Certainly, even the finest horses, if they are not used by people, it also would not be ridden by servants. Similarly, those who consider themselves wise and talented in today's world, but they are not recognized and employed by the king, cannot be effectively commanded by a wise lord. Such people, despite their excellent abilities, would not serve the king faithfully. Just like fine horses that do not obey commands, especially when their arrogant demeanor overshadows the dignity of the king and feudal lords, corrupting social mores, they must be punished to serve as an example to others."

Meaning: The foundation of the world lies in the nation, the foundation of the nation lies in the family, and the foundation of the family lies in the individual.

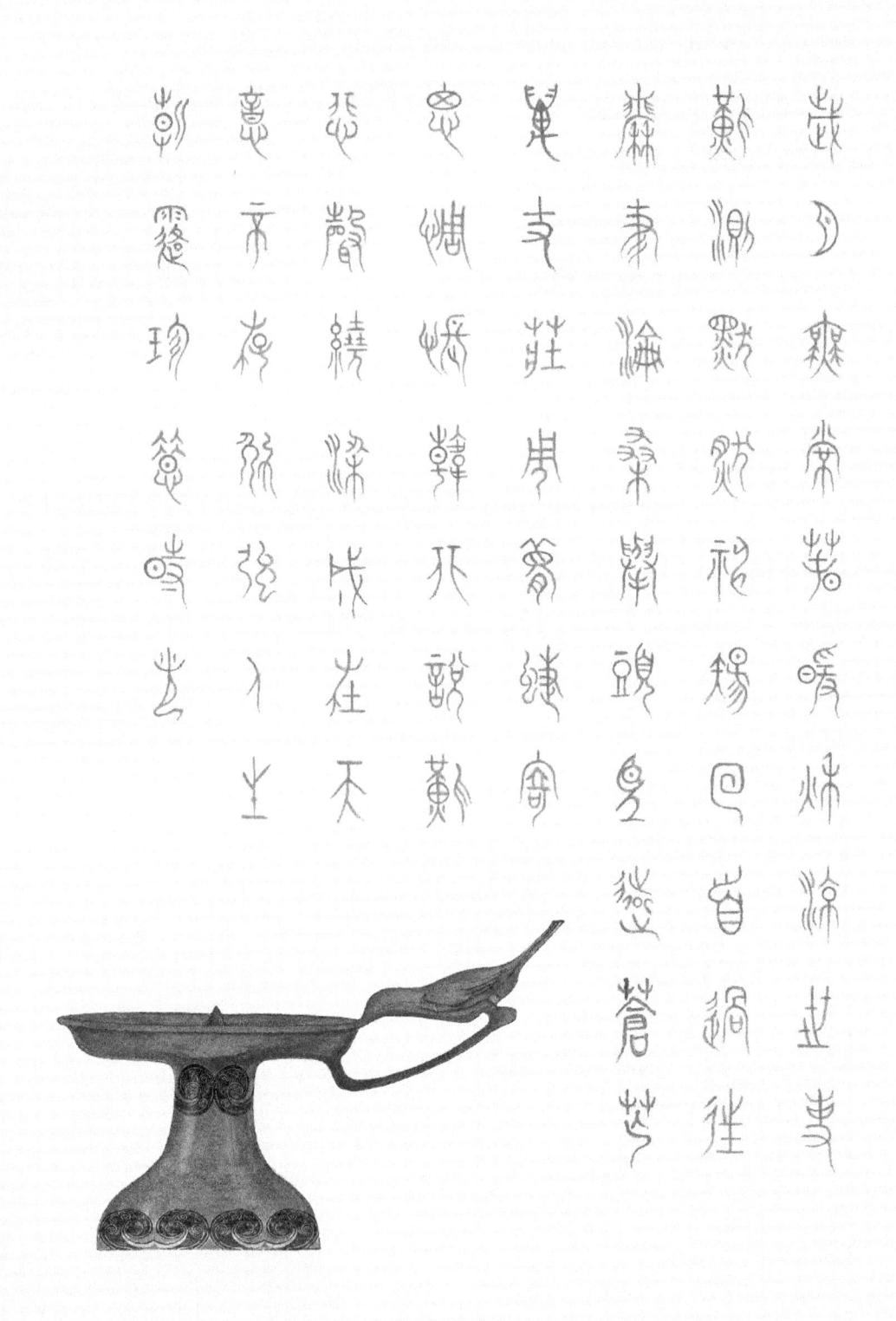

铭文注解 Annotation of the Inscriptions

岁月无常　春暖秋凉
世事难测　黯然神伤
回首过往　历尽沧桑
举头望远　苍茫万丈
庄周梦蝶　寄思惆怅
韩非说难　悲声绕梁
成在天意　不存勉强
人生朝露　珍惜时光

Time changes, warm spring and cool autumn.
Life is full of surprises and things are always changing.
Raise your head and look into the vast distance.
Zhuang Zhou Dreams of Butterflies, talking of Sorrow.
Han Fei's voice of grief echoes around the beam.
Profound philosophy is always enlightening and awakening.
Try your best, and leave the rest to destiny.
The life of is like the morning dew, cherish time.

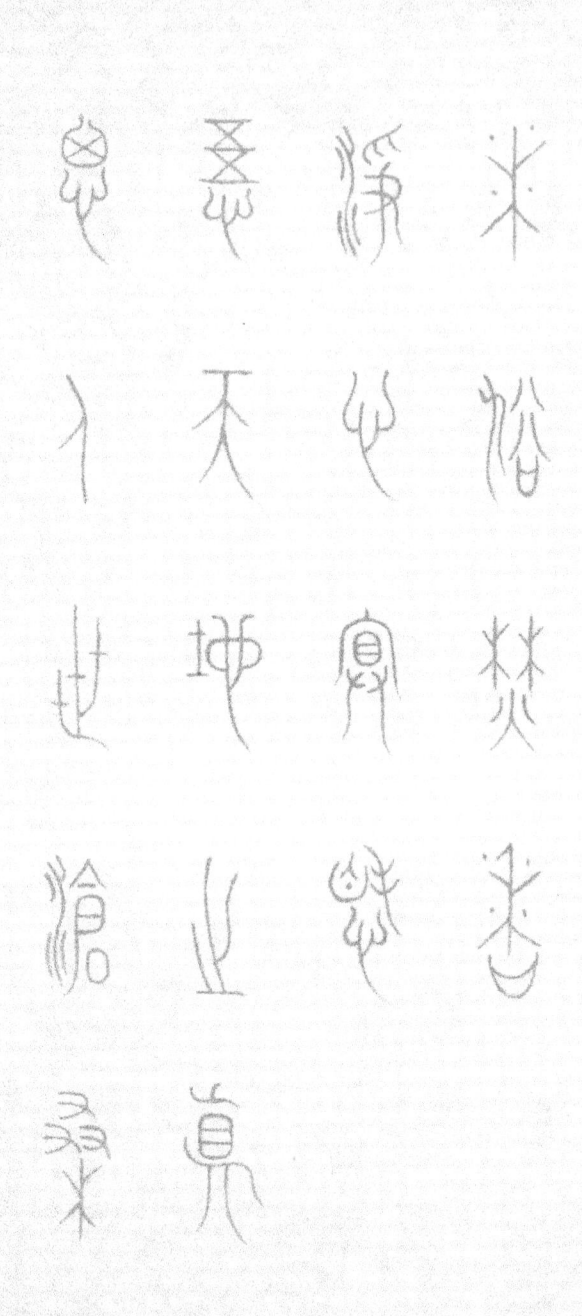

铭文注解 Annotation of the Inscriptions

沐浴焚香　净心冥想
悟天地之真　思人世沧桑

Bathing and burning incense, purifying the mind and meditating.
Realizing the truth of the universe and reflecting on the vicissitudes of life.

Milton Keynes UK
Ingram Content Group UK Ltd.
UKHW031141081224
452079UK00011B/66